THE NATURE OF HUMAN SOCIETY

SAINTS OF THE ATLAS

THE NATURE OF HUMAN SOCIETY SERIES

Editors: Julian Pitt-Rivers and Ernest Gellner

SAINTS OF THE ATLAS

Ernest Gellner

Professor in the Department of Sociology
at the London School of Economics

THE UNIVERSITY OF CHICAGO PRESS

Standard Book Number: 226-28699-1
Library of Congress Catalog Card Number: 78-89515

THE UNIVERSITY OF CHICAGO PRESS, CHICAGO 60637
WEIDENFELD & NICOLSON LTD., LONDON W1

Published 1969

Printed in Great Britain

To Susan

CONTENTS

vii

CONTENTS

CONTENTS

LIST OF ILLUSTRATIONS

(Between pages 136 *and* 137*)*

ACKNOWLEDGEMENTS

An anthropologist's first debt is to the people who allowed him to study them, and I here wish to put on record my deep gratitude to them.

My informants were too numerous to list. But some were particularly helpful: Sidi Ahmad son of Caid Sidi Mha, attached to the Amhadar family; the late head of the Bel Lahcen family; U Ben Ali; and Fatma n'Zida, all of Zawiya Ahansal. Among the Ait Abdi, the head of the Ait Tus family was particularly informative.

The second debt is financial. My first trip was possible thanks mainly to my father, and in this respect at any rate this study belongs to the nineteenth-century tradition of middle-class scholarship. Subsequent trips belong more to the twentieth century, and I am much indebted to the Central Research Fund of the University of London, and the Anthropological and Geographical Research Division at the LSE, and the Committee for Mediterranean Studies, for support. The final preparation of the MS for publication was only made possible by a scholarship at the Institute of International Studies at the University of California at Berkeley, and to secretarial help at that Institute.

At the LSE, I am very much indebted for secretarial assistance to Mrs E. Llewellyn, Mrs H. Frankiss, Miss Kathleen Phillips and Miss Helen Wheeler.

I am indebted to my colleagues at the LSE for moral and intellectual support, but I should cite specifically Paul Stirling, who supervised the research admirably, and Raymond Firth, who gave his support at a time when the enterprise must have seemed a doubtful one indeed.

Various drafts of the book were read in whole or part by the following: Eric Alport, Lorraine Baric, Ken Brown, Eric de Dampierre, Jeanne Favret, Raymond Firth, Maurice Freedman, Clifford and Hildred Geertz, John Hartley, Elie Kedourie, Clem

Moore, Emrys Peters, Julian Pitt-Rivers, Paul Stirling and Nicolas Thompson. I have profited enormously from their comments, though of course neither they nor anyone else can be held responsible for my views or errors.

Over the years, I have had very many instructive conversations on Moroccan topics with people well qualified in the field and also received much practical help from them, and I cannot list them all. But I should at least mention some. In addition to those already listed above, I have learnt much from Jamil Abun Nasr, André Adam (to whom I am particularly indebted for help at the very start of the inquiry), Douglas Ashford, Nevill Barbour, Mehdi Ben Barka, Humphrey Beckett, Patrice Blacque-Belair, Denis Bogros, Pierre Bourdieu, G.-H. Bousquet, Terry Burke, Audrey Butt, Jim Bynon, Sybil Crowe, Ross Dunn, Maurice Flory, Lionel Galand, Ahmed Handor, the late Damien Helie-Lucas, Marie-Aimée Helie-Lucas, David Hicks, J.-A. Ithier, Roger and Terri Joseph, A. Khatibi, R. Lapham, Grigori Lazarev, Remy Leveau, Bill Lewis, Elizabeth Monroe, Vincent Monteil, Pierre Rondot, Larry Rosen, Mohamed Saadani, Stuart Schaar, Bill Schorger, Wilfrid Thesiger, John Waterbury, and Bill Zartman.

In this connection, David Hart deserves a very special mention and gratitude. Since 1959, he has himself worked intermittently in the central High Atlas, and he has been amazingly generous in making his own valuable material available to me.

In the field, I owe much to the assistance of Mouhseine Mbarek, now an engineer in Rabat, himself an Ahansal on his mother's side, who worked with me during the summer of 1956. During the Christmas vacation of 1957–8, I should have never reached the field through the heavy snows without the help of Amzil Baouch, of Tillouguit n'ait Isha. But my greatest debt in this respect is to Youssef Hazmaoui, now of Marrakesh, himself a native of Amzrai. He began working for us as a boy, and has since become a professional assistant to scientific expeditions, and has reached a very high level of skill in eliciting, collecting and comparing information. He must by now be considered one of the most expert of Moroccan ethnographers.

I worked under a variety of opposed administrations, a veritable Vicar of Bray: a French military one, a Moroccan Leftist one, a Moroccan military one, and finally, a Moroccan royalist civilian one again. To many administrators, I am indebted for invaluable aid; to others, for not obstructing me; to others still, for not obstructing me effectively.

It is customary to express one's debt to one's wife. But I can say truthfully not merely that this study owes its existence to my wife, but also that I owe my wife to this research. Also, during the crucial field trips which she joined, she did invaluable work as research assistant, secretary, nurse, cook, psychotherapist and PRO: in the words of my application for research funds, she performed services which, if purchased locally, might have been more expensive and less satisfactory. Contrary to convention, however, she neither typed the MS nor read the proofs nor compiled the index. The photographs are hers and mine.

The cover photograph shows the Ait Tighanimin at prayer in a maize field.

'The inhabitants of these mountains . . . are agile, robust and brave in war. . . . They employ stones which they throw with great skill and force. They are continuously at war with the population of the Tadla plain, so that traders cannot pass the mountain without a safe-conduct and the payment of high duty.

Dades is also a high and cold mountain where there is much forest. . . . The habitations are appalling and infested by the smell of the goats kept there. Neither castle nor walled town is to be found in these mountains. The people are grouped in villages of houses of dry stone. . . . The rest of the population lives in caves. I have never seen so many fleas as in those hills.

The men are treacherous, thieves and assassins. They will kill a man for an onion. Violent disputes break out amongst them for nothing. They have neither judges nor priests nor anyone possessing a competence with respect to anything whatever. Traders do not come to this land, where laziness prevails, where there is no industry and where travellers are robbed. When traders equipped with safe-conducts from some local chiefs transport their wares, which are of no interest to the mountaineers, they make them pay one quarter of its value for the right of passage.

The women are as ugly as the devil and even worse dressed than the men. Their condition is worse than that of the asses since they carry on their backs the water they draw at the wells and the wood they collect in the forest, without ever an hour of rest.

To conclude, I do not regret visiting any part of Africa except this. I had to pass this mountain to go from Marrakesh to Sijilmassa, being obliged to do so by an order. That was in 918 AH (1512/13 AD)'

Observations on the central High Atlas by Leo Africanus in *Description of Africa*.

DRAMATIS PERSONAE

The dramatis personae of this story are not individuals, but communities. They are all introduced and described in the course of the account. Nevertheless, the reader may wish to be able to refer to one place in which the principal characters are listed and where their most important relationships to each other are briefly indicated.

The characters fall into two groups: settlements of saints, of *igurramen* possessors of *baraka* (sanctity, holiness, manifested also in prosperity and magical powers); these settlements, if the sanctity of their inhabitants is recognised and powerful, are referred to as a *zawiya*, a term which is rendered in English as a 'lodge'. The other group of 'characters' are ordinary, lay tribes.

Principal settlements of saints:

Zawiya Ahansal. Also referred to as 'main lodge'. Its inhabitants are also referred to locally as Ait Aggudim.

Amzrai, Taria, Tighanimin. This group of settlements are all physically close to the main lodge. The ancestry of the people of Tighanimin is contested.

Temga, Asker, Sidi Aziz, Sidi Ali u Hussein. This group of settlements, though not physically very close to each other, forms a group which is, jointly, in rivalry with the main lodge (though ultimately sharing the same ancestry with it). The first three in this group are the main settlements, but the last houses the most important specific shrine of this group.

Bernat. A settlement which, as a separate centre of saintly influence, only hived-off from the main lodge in the 1920s, as a result of conditions arising from the French advance.

Tidrit. A small but active centre of sanctity, which hived-off,

xvii

according to local belief, from the people of Tighanimin (of the contested ancestry) some four or five generations ago; but is now more influential than its village of origin, with which, however, it maintains close and friendly ties. This is the only settlement in the list which is located on the Sahara side of the main Sahara/Atlantic watershed of the Atlas.

Principal lay tribes :

Ait Atta. A large tribe, whose clans stretch astride the Atlas, from the Sahara to the edge of the Atlantic plain. Most of its strength lies on the Sahara side. Many of its members, however, come each summer to the high pastures on the Atlantic side of the watershed. According to legend, its ancestor and founder was a friend and ally of the ancestor of the saints. One of the clans permanently settled on the Atlantic side of the watershed, close to the main lodge, is located at Talmest. (These are the *Ait Bu Iknifen* of Talmest.) The Ait Atta are proud to claim a Berber (*Berraber*) origin.

Ait Sochman. A large tribe, located between the Atlas watershed and the Atlantic plain. Its clan closest to the main lodge is the *Ait Abdi* of the *Koucer* plateau. Its clans particularly associated with the Temga group of lodges are the *Ait Daud u Ali* and the *Ait Said u Ali*.

The Ait Sochman claim an oriental origin, though not a very prestigious one – that of being descended from a freed slave of the great Muslim saint Mulay Abd el Kader.

Ait Messat. A large group of tribes, not very clearly defined or with a definite myth of common origin, on the Atlantic side of the water-shed and to the west of the Ait Sochman. Some segments claim partially Christian ancestry. The most important tribe in this group, associated with both sets of lodges, is the *Ait Isha*.

Ait Yafelman. An important group of tribes, deriving its unity from an association rather than belief in common ancestor, located astride the watershed and to the east of the two preceding groups. The tribes in this group most connected with this set of saints are the *Ait Haddidu* and the *Ait Merghad*.

These are the four big groupings of the central High Atlas. Their frontiers meet near the main lodge of the saints, which helps to explain its importance.

In addition two other tribal groupings should be mentioned.

Ait Mhand.[1] Apparently a fairly 'new' tribe, whose area was a cockpit in the struggles resulting from the push of Ait Atta pastoralists towards northern pastures, and which was particularly tied to and dependent on the saints, first of the main lodge, and since the 1920s, on those of Bernat. This tribe is sometimes classed with the Ait Messat.

Ait Bu Gmez. A rich agricultural tribe, in whose life pastoralism is less important than it is for the other tribes mentioned, inhabiting a rich alluvial valley close to the main watershed. With no myth of common origin but a clearly defined territory, this tribe identifies itself territorially.

[1]Sometimes referred to Ait Mehamed on maps.

CHRONOLOGY

Dates refer to Christian era unless stated otherwise

1397–8 (AH *800*) According to legend, Sidi Said Ahansal, ancestor of all Ihansalen, arrives in the region to found his zawiya. Seven years later, is aided by Dadda Atta, ancestor of the Ait Atta tribe.

1598 (AH *1006, month of Shawal*) His great-grandson, Sidi Lahcen u Othman, signs land deed which finally transfers to him the lands previously owned by the proto-inhabitants, and now inhabited by the saints of the main lodge and the three adjoining saintly villages, and by the Ait Atta of Talmest.

Late seventeenth and early eighteenth centuries. According to legends collected independently and outside the region, Said ben Yussif el Hansali, of the lineage of Sidi Said Ahansal, founds a religious order, the Hansalia, which survived in eastern Algeria well into this century and may still exist. He dies in 1702 (AH 1114). His son and successor disappears under suspicious circumstances – political murder is suspected – during the troubles following the death of Sultan Mulay Ismail (1727).

1883–4 Father de Foucauld passes through the region of Ahansal influence and reports on it.

1905 Marquis de Segonzac visits the area of the Northern Lodges and reports the visit.

1912 French Protectorate declared in Morocco, though the French do not complete conquest of Berber tribal lands in the Atlas till 1933.

1916 Ahansal saints lead resistance to first French advance into the region.

xxi

1922 Saint-led tribesmen of the region defeat numerically much superior, French-aided troops of the Glawi, Pasha of Marrakesh, in the vicinity of the valley of the Ait Bu Gmez. This battle decides the political future of the region until the Independence of Morocco: it escapes incorporation in the Glawa empire-within-an-empire.

1923 The most important Ahansal saint of the time makes his submission to the French and is named caid (government-appointed chief) for the tribes which follow him into submission. Other Ahansal saints continue to lead tribes which remain dissident. Some (those of the Temga group) do so wholeheartedly; others (those of the main lodge) cooperate covertly with the saint-caid who is established in French-occupied territory at Bernat.

1933 The French conquer the remainder of central High Atlas, including the two main groups of lodges. Indirect rule set up by the French, and administered by military personnel. Some further saints become caids or khalifas (deputy-caids) under this system. Tribal customary law remains in force.

1956 Morocco obtains Independence, and after a brief interregnum a new Moroccan administration takes over the region. The term 'caid' comes to be applied to its officials, and not to chiefs drawn from within the tribes. Tribal customary law is officially replaced by a unified national legal system. No local chieftaincies are continued above the level of headman for villages or small groups of villages. Political parties organise and recruit in the region, and saints are prominent among their officeholders.

1960 Small tribal rising of the Ait Abdi of the Koucer plateau, triggered off by a political murder in the provincial capital, Beni Mellal. The murderer, a member of the Left party, flees to the Ait Abdi, who give him help. The rebels fail in a bid to seize arms. The Royal Army moves in, and the rebel chiefs first hide and then surrender, after pressure had been applied on their people by quartering soldiers on them. In consequence of the rising, the administration becomes military again, though now, of course, the officers are Moroccan.

Early 1960s The saints do well in various new-style local elections that are instituted.

Late 1960s The political climate changes and the political parties cease to operate visibly in the region. The administration becomes civilian again.

CHAPTER ONE

THE BACKGROUND

The Static Frontier

Power, belief, wealth: the questions about human society are clustered around these notions. They concern the manner in which a society controls its members; the manner in which it forms their thought, and in which their thinking sustains it; and the manner in which it keeps alive and uses its resources.

The study is concerned mainly with power and belief, and less specifically with wealth. It is concerned with the politics and religion of a tribal people, who are mixed pastoralists and agriculturalists. Their ecology does affect the understanding of local religion and local power, but it enters into this account only to the extent necessary for the understanding of politics and faith.

The Berbers of the central High Atlas of Morocco are, or were, an ungoverned people. Until 1933, no effective or outside government exercised authority over the region. Its tribesmen lived in the state of *siba*. This term, in local as well as in general use in Morocco, is best translated as 'institutionalised dissidence'. Moroccan and French writers sometimes translate it as 'anarchy', but this is too strong a term.

Siba was a political condition, and a condition of which people were explicitly aware: local tribesmen themselves employ this concept.

There is perhaps an interesting difference between tribes without rulers for whom this is the only known condition, and tribes whose internal structure is otherwise similar, but who are conscious of an alternative. Such tribesmen know the possibility, indeed the most ambivalently regarded obligation, of being incorporated in a

I

more centralised state, sanctioned by their own religion; indeed they may have deliberately rejected and violently resisted this alternative. The tribes of the central High Atlas are of this kind. Until the advent of the modern state, they were dissident, and self-consciously so.

Thus if their traditional condition were to be described as 'anarchy', then it was an anarchy opposed to something, contrasted with the central Moroccan Government, or, to give it its usual and surviving name, the *Makhzen*. The history of Morocco until the nineteen-thirties is written largely in terms of the relations between the land of *makhzen*, the pale, and the land of siba, beyond the pale. Each of these constituted a permanent menace to the other.

It is common to think of tribal societies, prior to their incorporation in the modern world, as self-contained, politically, economically and culturally as islands unto themselves. There is still a half-conscious tendency to see such 'island' tribalism as the condition which has generally preceded the emergence of more complex, centralised and effective government.

But siba or dissident tribalism is not of this kind. Tribes of siba-land are, indeed, politically independent. But they are not culturally independent. They are in this case embedded in the wider civilisation of Islam. In large measure they share the religion, concepts, symbols of the whole of the Muslim world.

Thus, their tribalism and political autonomy is not a tribalism 'prior to government', but a political and partial rejection of a particular government, combined with some acceptance of a wider culture and its ethic. Perhaps one should distinguish between 'primitive' and 'marginal' tribalisms: 'primitive' tribalism would cover a tribal group which is a closed political unit, recognising no obligations outside itself, and which is also a kind of ultimate cultural unit, lacking conceptual or symbolic bridges to the outside world. A tribe which did not share its language with neighbouring groups and had only wholly unregulated hostile relations with them would be an example of this.

'Marginal' tribalism, on the other hand, would cover the type of tribal society which exists at the edge of non-tribal societies. It arises from the fact that the inconveniences of submission make it attractive to withdraw from political authority, and the balance of power, the nature of mountainous or desert terrain, make it feasible. Such tribalism is politically marginal. It knows what it rejects.

For some purposes of social anthropology, the distinction between 'primitive' and 'marginal' tribalism may be of little significance: the internal mechanics of, say, an unilineal segmentary society may be much the same whether or not the society is a dissident from a wider and politically more centralised civilisation. For other purposes the distinction may be essential. Muslim tribes are, almost by definition, marginal rather than primitive. Generally they exist on the margins of larger political units with urban capitals, with whom they are liable to be on partly hostile and partly symbiotic relationship. They may be a danger for the central society, but they can also be its shield. Muslim tribes, even if not located physically on the border of non-tribal political units, must moreover be 'marginal' in the sense of recognising the wider community of Islam.

It seems to be a striking feature of the history of Muslim countries that they frequently, indeed generally, have such penumbra of marginal tribalism. In European mountain areas, excluding the Balkans which in any case were the penumbra of a Muslim power, the phenomenon occurs but is much rarer.

Before European penetration in the nineteenth and twentieth centuries, Morocco and North Africa generally remained tribal within as well as without the governed pale. The rural population within the land of makhzen, like that of siba, remained clustered in tribal groupings. It was only the superimposition of a European administration which led to the atrophy of the larger units of tribal organisation. In Algeria, this erosion of the larger units has taken place (though kin groupings at village level have in some areas retained, or perhaps even increased their vitality). In Morocco, the French conquest came only in this century, and it is still possible to draw a tribal map for the whole of Morocco and to identify larger tribal groupings.

Morocco prior to the twentieth century sounds like a parable on the human condition in general. The country could be seen as composed of three concentric circles: the Inner Circle of tribes who extracted taxes, the Middle Circle of tribes who had taxes extracted from them, and the Outer Circle of tribes who did not allow taxes to be extracted from them. In other words, there were the sheep-dogs, the sheep, and the wolves.

The Outer Circle is, of course, the land of siba. The inner circle of privileged tax-extracting, dynasty-supporting tribes were known as *guish*.[1] The history of Morocco can be written as the story of the struggle of successive dynasties to maintain their power and authority. The two main problems facing them were the recruitment of the guish and the holding or expanding of the land of government against the land of siba. The history of America is sometimes written in terms of its receding Frontier. The history of Morocco can be seen in terms of this stable or oscillating one.

No definitive solution was ever found for either of these problems. Successive Moroccan dynasties used a number of different principles of recruiting their military support: their tribes of origin; foreign (e.g., Christian) mercenaries; imported Arab tribes that had been defeated in expeditions abroad; trained Negro slave armies; or a combination of privileged tribes and standing army. This failure to solve the Platonic problem of finding watchdogs effective against the wolves but gentle with the sheep is not the subject of this book, which is concerned with the wolves beyond the pale, rather than with the sheep-dogs. Particularly it is concerned with the political and religious organisation of certain wolves.

The existence of the wolves outside the wall, of a permanent external proletariat to use Toynbee's term, has of course profound implications for the society which has to keep them out. At the worst, they present a permanent threat to the existing dynasty: a permanent reservoir of potential new conquerors and new dynasties. At best, they are still raiders and robbers, a moral scandal and a political offence, instances of unpunished sins against *les bonnes moeurs* as well as against public safety, a standing example of the defiance of central authority.

In fact, successive Moroccan ruling houses have historically emerged from this outer realm, which is thus also a kind of political womb. If one thing mitigates this danger from the outer margin of tribes, it is their own inner divisions. The internal organisation of the outer tribes is such that they do not easily unite. Indeed, the new dynasties generally emerged only thanks to a kind of relatively rare crystallisation of authority by religious charisma, which enabled them to fuse tribal support into a unified force.

If siba meant, for the ruling dynasty, an ever-present danger

[1]An account of the inner workings of the *guish* system, with its grants of land in return for military service, can be found in Dr William Schorger's *The Evolution of Political Forms in a North Moroccan Village*, to be published.

and source of raiders or rivals, then the central authority in turn, or its nearest representative,[1] also meant for the inhabitants of siba an ever-present danger and source of possible aggression and oppression.

The curious consequence of the existence of such an internal frontier is that the inhabitants of the state of nature, of siba, were faced with a rather Hobbesian choice between accepting or rejecting the Social Contract: they could submit to the inconveniences of power and escape the inconveniences of anarchy, or vice versa. Not all of them, clearly, chose the alternative commended by Hobbes as rational. Indeed it was more often a matter of struggle rather than of choice and it is important to stress that the line between the 'state of nature' and Leviathan was neither stable, nor sharp or unambiguous. Urban life in Morocco was, of course, concentrated in the area of the Inner and the Middle Circle. There were no towns in siba-land.

Doctor and Saint

The traditional Muslim state in North Africa was both turbulent and in a left-handed sense stable. Tribal violence made it turbulent, but the turbulence affected only the personnel, not the structure itself. The movement within it was explored and schematised by the fourteenth-century Arab sociologist Ibn Khaldun. In substance, his schema remained valid, especially for Morocco, until the intrusion of the modern world in the form of a colonial invasion.

His account could be summed up as a theory of a tribal circulation of élites. In this model there is a kind of social mobility which works for whole tribal units rather than individuals, and which, however violent, does not transform the basic pattern itself. His philosophy of history holds out no promise of permanence and stability to any one group; a cyclical change of fortune awaits all. Yet at the same time it holds out no hope of radical transformation

[1]With the coming of Moroccan Independence in 1956, it was, in the then atmosphere of patriotic fervour centred on the ruling house, somewhat embarrassing for the inhabitants of erstwhile siba lands, and for any Moroccan intellectual given to reflection, about his country's past, to remember the traditions of dissidence. The characteristic reaction to this was to say that dissidence was not against the Sultan as such, but against his oppressive local representatives. There is an element of truth in this: reverence and some kind of religious acceptance of the sherifian dynasty on the throne may in certain cases have been combined with resistance to his political representatives.

5

or fundamental progress either. The basic social form remains unchanged.

His premise is that there is a tragic antithesis between civilisation and social cohesion. Only cities have civilisation; only tribes have social cohesion. Thus only tribes can provide the basis for the political order, which cities and civilisation need but do not engender. But as they provide it, the tribes destroy themselves.

This is the driving force for the tribal circulation of élites: every so often, every three generations in Ibn Khaldun's schematised version, a new set of wolves throw up a new dynasty from their own number, replacing the exhausted sheepdogs, and have their turn until the time comes for them to be displaced.

A pattern of this kind continued to hold for Morocco until this century, if not in quite so neat and regular a form. A minor modification occurred: the mediaeval dynasties which inspired Ibn Khaldun's analysis were founded by religious movements, whereas the later ones sprang from the ranks of *shurfa,* religious personnel credited with descent from the Prophet. This change does not really affect the principle of the rotating movement. In either case, it was religious prestige, external to the tribal structure proper, which enables a set of wolves to co-operate sufficiently to move the political wheel.

The last time the wolves came seriously under the walls of the city in the old style to threaten it was in 1912. That time, however, they did not cause the wheel to rotate in the old manner. The threatened dynasty inside the walls appealed to foreign help, and provided the excuse for foreign intervention and the establishment of a colonial 'protectorate'.

This type of society, with a monarchy based on towns which are centres of trade and religious learning, supported by privileged tribes but facing dissident tribes beyond the pale, resembles neither feudalism, nor that other recently popular stereotype of the pre-industrial state, 'oriental society' with its bureaucracy supervising the establishment and maintenance of an irrigation system. The characteristic Muslim state, with its town-based and religiously legitimated monarchy, its concentric circles of privileged, autonomous and dissident tribes, its administration based on either a peripatetic court and army, or recognition of local power-holders, rather than on bureaucratic nominees, is a distinct and characteristic type of its own.

What kind of religious life is favoured by such conditions? The society has one faith, a scriptural faith in *the* Book, which can only be in the keeping of the literate inhabitants of the towns and which legitimates the ruler based on the town; yet this faith is also accepted by the tribesmen, some of whom defy the ruler and threaten the towns. The manner in which this one religion is experienced and rooted in life in the various segments of the society cannot but vary. It is worth quoting a summary[1] of Max Weber's view of the nature of urban religion:

This religiosity of bourgeois strata seems to originate in urban life. In the city a religious experience of the individual tends to lose the character of an ecstatic trance or dream and to assume the paler forms of contemplative mysticism or a low-keyed, everyday piety. For the craftsman, steady work with customers can suggest the development of concepts like 'duty' and 'recompense' as basic orientations towards life.

The town provides the conditions for a form of religion which is restrained in manner, learned, scholastic, sustained by a class which can divide its energies and its personnel between sacred knowledge and trade.

In general terms, such urban religion will tend to exhibit characteristics of a syndrome which one could, arbitrarily, call type *p*. The features of the syndrome are:

Stress on Scripture and hence on literacy.

Puritanism, absence of graven images.

Strict monotheism.

Egalitarianism as between believers; minimisation of hierarchy.

Absence of mediation, abstention from ritual excesses.

Correspondingly, a tendency towards moderation and sobriety.

A stress on the observance of rules rather than on emotional states.

These features have an affinity with urban life and with each other. Towns make literacy possible and valuable. Literacy makes possible direct access to revelation and hence makes easier the dispensing with intermediaries, whether in this or another world, whether priest or spirit, and hence with hierarchy or cult of personality. It makes possible insistence on rules and their elaboration and abstention from ritual excess, hence a general puritanism.

[1] R. Bendix, *Max Weber, an intellectual portrait*, 1960, p. 114.

7

By contrast, the religious life of the tribe may be quite different. Illiteracy makes the audio-visual aids of religion, a richer and more ecstatic ritual life, desirable or essential. Having no access to the Book, the tribesman needs a personalised religion. He also needs revered and special religious personnel, not only to mediate with God, but also to help with inter- and intra-tribal political mediation. All these tend to produce a religious life with characteristics drawn from quite a different syndrome, which one may, for contrast, call c. It contains the following traits:

Personalisation of religion, tendency to anthropolatry.

Ritual indulgence, and absence of puritanism.

Proliferation of the sacred, concrete images of it.

Religious pluralism in this and the other world and local incarnation of the sacred.

Hierarchy and mediation.

These various traits, once again, have an obvious inner affinity with each other.

Thus the town constitutes a society which needs and produces the doctor, whilst the tribe needs, and produces, the saint. But this is not the whole story. It is not as simple as that. The towns have not merely their learned *ulama*, but also their Sufi mystics. In the towns, mysticism is an alternative to formal Islam. In the tribe it is a surrogate for it. The moderate, literate, rational religion may satisfy the well-established bourgeoisie, it may in fact minister admirably to its tastes: but the lower classes may often have more emotional needs, and turn to religion not as a form of scholarship and contemplation, but as an alleviation of suffering, as a more drastic alternative to ordinary life. They need religion, not to ratify a style of life, but to escape from it. This need is met by the more extreme religious 'fraternities', with their sometimes wild mystical techniques.

The holy men of tribe and town, holy lineages in the tribe and leaders of religious Orders in the town may and often do employ the same terminology, and may well belong to the same 'order', the same system of lodges: yet the social reality they represent is quite distinct. A *zawiya* (lodge) in a tribe, is a kin group like any surrounding tribal segment, recruited by birth, and merely somewhat differentiated in role from other tribal settlements. An urban zawiya on the other hand may possibly have a kin-defined nucleus, but essentially it will be a religious club, recruited by enthusiasm or

8

religious interest, and defined not by kinship but by specialised ritual practices.

Religious life among the tribes will also not be quite exhausted by its indulgent, socially acclimatised, illiterate, arbitration-oriented holy lineages. The very fact that these holy lineages in or among the tribes are so numerous, in a way devalues them and makes them unsuitable for really exceptional tasks. They have charisma, but it is fairly routinised. They officiate at annual festivals and pilgrimages, and other holy lineages do so in the next valleys, and both are just a bit commonplace.

This may not matter under normal conditions, but it makes the humdrum tribal holy man less than ideal for some truly exceptional task. Opportunities for truly exceptional performances do very occasionally arise, or are on occasion created. After all the wolf tribes do from time to time fuse into a larger unit: leadership for such exceptional political crystallisations cannot easily be provided by the humdrum holy men. They neutralise each other in their parochial jealousies, much as their client tribes and clans normally neutralise each other. The exceptional, large-scale leader needs some special differentiating mark. This can be obtained in various ways – sheer success is liable to snowball, however initiated – but one obvious way is revivalism, the preaching of a purer religion. This pure religion has little place in the day to day life of the tribe, but it does serve as a legitimation of the rare, exceptional leader, when the day to day life is transcended and the tribes combine to form a larger and more effective movement. The puritanism and unitarianism may help to identify and ratify such an exceptional leader, for after all, the tribesmen, however dissident, are parts of a wider society which accepts a scriptural faith, and in which the urban clerics have set the tone and diffused the idea, however ambivalently received, that *the* Book sets the norm, and that real adherence to its teachings and precepts as elaborated by learned townsmen is the truly binding norm. The ultimate norms of the wider society legitimate the monist and puritan, and thus provide an ideological lever for the really exceptional occasion. The ultimate standard, normally sinned against but known and accorded a tacit recognition, provides an excellent legitimation for political revolution, a justification for a new wave of wolves entering the city. In their daily life, the tribesmen use an anthropolatrous, questionably orthodox religion; but when they arrive in the town as the new conquerors, they come under the banner of a puritan unitarianism.

Thus over time, the picture is complex. The towns and the tribes each have both doctors and saints. But in normal stable times, the tribes have the saints only, whilst in the towns, though both species co-exist, it is the doctors who set the tone. The religious polarity is thus an essential part of the dynamics of the society, of the collective circulation of élites. The unitarian puritan preacher, normally part of the urban establishment, on occasion provides the leadership, that rather special legitimation, which on very propitious occasions unites the tribes and turns the political wheel. There will thus be a certain tendency in the society as a whole to oscillate between the two poles. Often, the tension between the two forms may remain latent, and the two forms may interpenetrate and accept each other without much friction. This largely happened in Morocco in the period preceding the impact of modernism. In the twentieth century, however, the tension re-emerged.

Within this wider society, there are also other, minor, less dramatic cyclical changes. Those big turns of the wheel may be initiated, characteristically, by an urban learned and pious man who is revolted by the moral and religious decline of the dynasty and goes to preach a revival and found a new one. But more commonly the man of piety will make a less striking career. He may go out among the tribes as a missionary bringing them purer Islam, be received, and end not as a new ruler, but simply – in his own lifetime or in his progeny – as one further holy man and lineage, living as arbitrator between tribes and intermediary between man and the divine, situated humbly in the interstices of the tribal structure. Imperceptibly, the missionary of the purer faith ends as a pillar of the impure.

A different kind of development is as common: an exceptionally gifted or successful holy man from the tribes may acquire a reputation beyond the limits of the habitual arbitration area of his line, and his charisma will enable him to become a leader of a genuine religious order, with lodges in the towns, recruited by conversion and not by birth. The histories of the various religious orders must contain countless developments of both kinds, forward and back.

This pattern inspires various reflections. One: it has curiously seldom been noticed how North African Islam holds up a mirror-image to Western Europe. In Europe, one is habituated to a situation in which religious life of syndrome c – organised, hierarchical, ritually rich, given to mediation, constitutes the central tradition, continuous over space and time and majoritarian, whilst religious movements exhibiting traits of syndrome p are minoritarian, fragmented and discontinuous. In North Africa, it is the central tradition which has the 'Protestant' traits, and the fragmented cults of the primitives and tribes which exemplify the 'Catholic' features. The contrast is striking. The general model of North African society helps us in some measure to understand why the two religious traditions should be so diametrically opposed.

Islamic towns were generally close to the political centre of the state, closely identified with it and dependent on its protection. They were not independent growths in a rurally based feudal order, with the opportunities and incentives for developing an independent ideology. In Islam, it is the towns and religion of the 'Protestant' kind which is conservative and politically conformist.

A sociology of religion inspired primarily by Christianity has led to a typology of church, denomination and sect: it is the church, identified with the society as a whole, which makes the greatest concessions to social requirements, whilst the marginal sect, recruited from people who opt out from this world and society, is the most demanding and uncompromising in its scriptural requirements. All this is inverted in Islam. It is the fragmented saint-cult of the tribes which is most enmeshed in a social order, has given most in the way of hostages to society and makes the greatest concessions to it, which comes closest to simply being 'social': it is the unitarian and united central tradition which is more severe and demanding.

The other reflection concerns the now popular triad derived from Max Weber, of the three types of authority, traditional, bureaucratic and charismatic. This typology in its present popular form is unfortunate in as far as one element in it, 'traditional' authority is a pseudo-category. Nothing is explained about the manner in which a society conducts its affairs by calling it 'traditional': even tribesmen are not in the vice of some powerful social force called 'tradition'. Moreover, the type of opposition which exists between those genuinely most illuminating notions, 'charisma' and 'bureaucracy', also exists within tribal, 'traditional' society. Of course, in general tribes do not have a bureaucracy:

the opposition arises between charisma and kinship. Kinship is to the tribe what bureaucracy is to a modern organisation – the set of terms and techniques for allocating people to their social positions. The proper working of this principle is as opposed to charisma in the tribal context, as bureaucratic orderliness is opposed to it in the modern world. Yet, of course, charismatic claims and their recognition is known in tribal society. (Thus one really requires a quadruple division at least, with 'traditional' authority falling apart into two species, 'kin' and 'charismatic'.)

The 'saints' of the Atlas are, I suppose, charismatic leaders: they are identified and legitimated by the possession of *baraka*, a concept used by them, which is about as close to the sociologist's notion of 'charisma' as one could hope to find. But theirs is a charisma heavily routinised by kinship, and making its contribution to stability rather than acting as an explosive force. In the tribe as much as anywhere else, charisma does become routinised, but in the tribe it is routinised by kinship.

Thus from the viewpoint of the typology of authority, the study of the saints is a study of tribally routinised charisma. From the viewpoint of the model of the wider society, it is a study of how tribal requirements push an inherently 'protestant' religion – scriptural, literate, egalitarian, theoretically lacking in clergy – towards the other pole of the spectrum of religious life.

Arab and Berber

Traditional Morocco was a predominantly Muslim country, with a small but important Jewish minority, and no significant Christian minority. All the Muslims are Sunni, of the Maliki rite. The sheer fact that there is no contrast to the Sunni faith makes adherence to it something of which the average Moroccan is hardly aware. The Shiite heresy is hardly present to his mind. Since the European penetration early in this century, there is also a Christian minority, of European (predominantly French and Spanish) origin.

Morocco has only two indigenous languages, Arabic and Berber. Berber dialects vary from tribe to tribe and even from village to village. Diversified though they are, they fall into three major regional groups: Tarifit in the Rif in the North, Tamazight in the centre, and Tashlehait in the South. Dialects within each of these three groups are mutually intelligible without much difficulty. The transition from one group to another takes a native Berber speaker some time, but it is not a major obstacle either. With the certain rare exceptions of the use of Arabic script for Berber texts, Berber is not a written language. No one Berber dialect is dominant.

Ethnically, traditional Morocco also has a Negro minority. Many of these Negroes lived as individual slaves in non-Negro communities, but some constituted whole communities of oasis cultivators in southern Morocco, in a collective rather than individual relationship of political dependence on Berber or Arab tribes. They spoke Berber or Arabic.

Thus the linguistic distinction cuts across both the religious and ethnic lines: there are (or were until the recent exodus) Berber-speaking Jewish communities, and there are Berber-speaking Negro communities (*haratin*).

But for all practical purposes, a 'Berber' is a native Berber speaker who is both Muslim and white. Jewish and Negro Berber-speaking minorities are sociologically distinct.

Berbers make up something less than half of Morocco's population: how much less, is difficult to estimate. The distribution of Berbers in Morocco, and indeed in North Africa as a whole, follows a certain pattern. This pattern resembles that of Celtic-speaking territory in Britain: a set of discontinuous pockets, some large, some small, in the main occupying mountainous territory. (There is one obvious difference: Berbers are sometimes found not merely in mountains, but also in the desert.) The reason for this discontinuity and occupancy of backwoods terrain is the same in both cases. Berbers are the 'survivors' of the earlier inhabitants of North Africa, displaced in the richer plains and the towns by the later comers, and surviving in the less accessible regions.

This 'survival' is to be interpreted in a linguistic and cultural sense. In a genetic sense, it is probable that many of the Arabic-speaking regions of North Africa also have populations composed in large part of arabised Berbers. Similarly, it is unlikely that the Berber-speaking regions are of 'pure' ancestry.

Morocco has a very marked personality, historically and geographically. It is the only part directly or indirectly, of the Ottoman empire. Geographically it consists of the Muslim Mediterranean world which was never part of 'inner Morocco', the Atlantic plain open towards the ocean but separated from the Mediterranean by the Rif range and from the Sahara by the various Atlas ranges.

'Outer Morocco' consists mainly of the valleys, plateaux and oases between these various ranges, and between them and the Sahara. Roughly again, Berber tribes occupy the high grounds and outer Morocco. There are exceptions: the western extension of the Rif range, the Ghomara and Jebala region, is Arabic-speaking, and the oases and semi-desert on the Sahara edge are inhabited by a patchwork of both Arabic and Berber speaking tribes.

Despite the many minor complications and exceptions, there is a rough tie-up between high ground, Berber speech and political dissidence (in the traditional setting). The situation has a certain similarity to that of pre-1745 Scotland, and justifies Arnold Toynbee's reference to a 'Highland line' in Morocco. The Highlands provide the new dynasties, but the lowlands have the cities, and the sophisticated and literate civilisation, tied by language to a much wider, indeed an 'universal' civilisation. Those who wish to pursue the analogy further may note that Fes is the Edinburgh of Morocco, a town of lawyers and theologians, whilst Marrakesh is its Glasgow – a rougher town on the edge of the highlands, populated by detribalised highlanders.

What is a Berber?

From the outside, one can only define a Berber by his speech. Even then, one must exclude the Jewish, Negroid, and Ibadi Berber-speakers, (the last found in Algeria and Tunisia) whom other Berbers would not class with themselves, not because they are 'not Berbers', but because, respectively, they are not Muslim, not white, or not orthodox. This, however, leaves the overwhelming majority of Berber-speakers. How do they see themelves.

They are, without serious exceptions, either tribesmen, or men who are but recently tribalised. Berber speech survives in rural areas where the old kin-based groupings have also maintained themselves. Naturally, a Kabyle worker in France, a migrant labourer in Morocco, a tribesman settled in a town, or modern intellectual educated at what used to be called the College Berbère of Azrou in French days, has also kept his Berber speech: but unless he retains his niche in the village, he is unlikely to transmit his language to subsequent generations. This is of course tied up with the absence of Berber writing, and of any one dominant dialect.

Hence, basically the Berber-speaker is a tribesman. This provides the crucial clue to his own vision of himself, the concepts available to him for identification with wider groups. He is, of course, a member of the nested series of kin units which constitute his tribe (or what has remained of it in modern conditions), and of territorial units which may sometimes cut across the kin-defined ones. But beyond this? He is, firmly and in a manner pregnant with consequences for his life, a Muslim – irrespective of whether he is specially pious or well-informed in matters of religion. But are there intermediate classifications, concepts bestowing an identity and generating a loyalty, between the ceiling of tribal notions and the general idea of Islam?

There is the difficult question of the extent to which modern North African states have succeeded in establishing the notion of territorial states with claims on the ultimate loyalty and deep identification of their citizens. This question is hard to answer. These states have not repudiated Islam; they profess, mutual quarrels notwithstanding, a certain acceptance of either a pan-Arab or a pan-Maghrib (North Africa) loyalty, and thus they do not quite claim to be ultimate; and the 'native' on whose behalf the anti-colonial struggle was fought was, for all practical purposes, the Muslim. As it is not quite clear yet what the modern loyalties are intended to be, it is difficult even to guess to what extent they have replaced the old ones.

In terms of the traditional situation, one may say that the notions intermediate between tribal and Islamic were hazy and of doubtful social significance. The tribesman, for instance, may have had some sense of the legitimacy of the Moroccan state: but this would be because it was, within his social horizon, the Islamic state par excellence, and not because of some sense of territorial belonging. Did his notions include that of being 'a Berber'? Certainly not in any pan-Berber sense, involving an awareness of linguistic and cultural affinity of islands dispersed from modern Egypt to the Atlantic, and possibly including those only unambiguous linguistic cousins of the Berbers, the Tuareg. Where a notion of being Berber did exist, it was roughly co-extensive with the regional linguistic block. Historians have dug up signs of Berber consciousness, a mediaeval heresy with a Koran in Berber, or a religious movement of the seventeenth century, opposed to all 'who did not speak Berber'. But on the whole, the striking thing about these signs is not their occurrence, but their rarity.

The regions no doubt vary in their degree of self-consciousness. (The Rif, for instance, probably has a well developed sense of itself at present, not merely thanks to the memory of Abd el Krim's Republic, but also because most of it was governed by Spain: Independence meant unification, in which southern Morocco was the dominant partner, generating resentments perhaps similar to those of southern Italy towards the North after the unification of that country). Of the various regions, it is central Morocco which actually uses the term *Berraber* to describe its own people.

One may sum up this situation by saying that there is no sense of universal Berberhood, as there now is, whether politically effective or not, a sense of belonging to an all-embracing Arab nation; and there is a nebulous feeling of regional belonging, but its importance is doubtful. There are no institutions, no recognised forms of leadership, to activate this sentiment. Such leadership as on occasion emerges – whether religious in the traditional order, or political in the modern context – may perhaps exploit this latent sentiment now and then, but it does not take it seriously enough to delimit its own ambitions regionally or ethnically. In other words, such loyalties as have from time to time crystallised in the middle area between the tribal ceiling on one hand, and the universalist claims of Islam on the other, were ephemeral, and were not firmly articulated in either ethnic or territorial terms.

Ibn Khaldun divided Berbers into three great ethnic subdivisions, the Zenata, Masmuda and Sanhajja. Scholars have sometimes taken over this classification, and an assumption that it correlates with modes of life, with nomadism and sedentarisation, and in consequence some tribal studies deem it their duty to begin by speculating which of these three labels is to be attached to the tribe in question. There are even attempts to interpret North African history as a whole in these terms, seeing the dynastic and religious conflicts as a series of return matches in a permanent struggle between these alleged groupings, rather in the way in which one could see periods of European history as, say, a succession of Franco–German conflicts.[1] One may wonder what sanctions and motivations could possibly have given social reality to these very far-flung classifications in the minds of mediaeval tribesmen: what motives could have made this kind of abstract

[1] Cf. G. H. Bousquet, *Les Berbères*, P U F., 1957, pp. 55 and 56. See also C. S. Coon, *Caravan*, Revised Edition, N.Y., 1965, p. 42.

'belonging' more powerful and urgent than the more normal, concrete, observable strivings for land and pasture, for power or booty, or the loyalties of closer kin or of religious adherence. It is however quite clear that this classification corresponds to nothing whatever at present. The tribesmen know nothing of these categories, and there is nothing in their tribal organisation either to communicate their existence or to underwrite loyalty to them. The allocation of Berber tribes to these three classes is at best a harmless, but pointless exercise. The employment of this trichotomy by French scholarship seems to be a case when the alleged genealogical predilection of the Arabs infected the Gallic mind.

Morocco's Recent History

Morocco remained remarkably unaffected by the outside world and its development until the twentieth century, much less so than the Middle East. This insulation, comparable perhaps to that which persisted in the Yemen until recent years, is all the more remarkable if one considers Morocco's geographical proximity to Europe, and that on its eastern border there was French controlled Algeria, and above all, that this insulated society was not only a tribal one, but also contained large and flourishing cities and an urban civilisation. The reasons for this imperviousness to outside influence would no doubt repay investigation: it would be interesting to know why Morocco was comparatively so short of 'young Turks' and similar stirrings. Such influences as did reach it came from the Muslim world, notably the puritanical Islamic 'Reform Movement' from Egypt and the rest of the Maghrib (North Africa).[1] The political and military factors aiding the preservation of isolation are easier to discern. The great powers neutralised each other, and indeed it was not until some horse-dealing took place between them early in this century that the way was open to western military penetration.

This penetration began seriously in the first decade of this century. Serious French landings began in 1907. The Moroccan Government was caught between the external enemy and its own dissident subjects. A certain circle manifested itself: the government was unable to cope with the latter without foreign assistance, but

[1]Cf. Jamil Abun-Nasr, *The Tijaniyya. A Sufi Order in the Modern World*, OUP, 1965, p. 3

the acceptance of such aid only exacerbated the xenophobia of its own subjects and increased the number of its own internal enemies. A Sultan might be deposed for being insufficiently firm with the foreigner, but his successor, carried to the throne on a wave of xenophobia, would soon be forced to pursue a similar policy. This process culminated in the establishment of the French protectorate in 1912. With Berber tribesmen under the walls of Fez, the Sultan, who had himself supplanted his predecessor in the name of hostility to alien penetration, was forced to seek foreign aid and come to terms with the French.

The French occupation of most of what had been the old governmental pale was completed by the beginning of the First World War. A new wave of xenophobic pretenders was defeated. The traditionally dissident areas, however, were only conquered slowly and painfully after the world war, in a series of campaigns only terminated in 1933 and 1934.

Only in the Rif did these campaigns face a united enemy. In other areas, including the one we are concerned with, it was a piecemeal matter of coping with small tribal units, almost one by one. This 'pacification' was as much a political as a military affair. It was the ambition of those who engaged in it to achieve as much of it by political means as possible, and the view was expressed that ethnographic reconnaissance and exploration was the best preliminary to successful pacification.[1] The consequence was a sociological orientation and curiosity from the very start, a tradition which persisted in the administration – much of which remained military – even after pacification had been achieved.

Apart from the pacification and its conclusion, the most significant political event of the period was the promulgation in 1930 of the famous *Dahir Berbère* (the Berber decree). This decree was to regulate the legal status of the pacified Berber tribal territories. Its essence was to offer these areas the option of remaining separate from the national Moroccan Muslim legal system, and to continue to be ruled by tribal customary law under supervision of the new French administration. The promulgation of this decree triggered off modern Moroccan nationalism. It offended traditional Muslim sentiment by appearing to underwrite heterodox non-Muslim practices, and indeed to encourage them: moreover, at the time it aroused the suspicion that this was merely the first step in the

[1]Cf. V.Monteil, *Les Officers*, 1958, p. 130.

18

attempt to convert the Berbers from Islam. It equally offended emergent modern nationalist feeling by exemplifying a policy of divide and rule, and attempting to alienate the Berbers from the rest of Morocco. Its two aspects were thus well designed to antagonise both the first and the second generation of Moroccan nationalists: both those who were Muslim reformers first and nationalists in consequence, and those who were at heart modern nationalists and secular modernisers. The merit of the traditional situation had been a certain ambiguity. The tribes practised their own custom but also honoured and revered holy lineages which were descended, so they believed, from the Prophet. Thus the deviance between custom and faith was only half articulated, and was very decently obscured. When the French formally and publicly underwrote tribal custom, thereby underscoring and publicising its idiosyncrasy, they so to speak turned a mere sin into a heresy.

Some aspects of this decree were subsequently abrogated, but a very large proportion of the Berber tribes did continue to maintain their customary law until the end of the protectorate in 1956. (Some did not, notably the ones in the Rif where it had been abrogated by Abd el Krim; and those in the areas dominated by the great chieftains such as the Glawi, who found customary tribal law inconvenient, not so much for its content, but owing to the fact that it required for its administration the survival of independent tribal assemblies. The *content* often survived in such areas, without this form.)

From the sociologists' view point, the consequence of the *Dahir Berbère* was the placing of tribal custom and institutions into a kind of ice box, between the time of 'pacification' of the tribes and 1956. This ice box did not, of course, preserve that custom exactly in the form in which it existed originally. For instance, things incompatible with a modern administration or repugnant to its more fundamental moral convictions, such as blood feuds or slavery, were abolished. (But blood money in case of murder was not.) For another thing, the sheer fact that some practice or rule was operating in the context of a superimposed colonial administration gave it a different social significance from that which it had in the context of tribal anarchy. Again, the administration of tribal customary law was reformed and stylised: the competence and hierarchical ordering of various tribal tribunals was settled with greater order and less inherent ambiguity, than they had possessed in their original form.

Nevertheless, the preservation even of a distorted and stylised traditional Berber tribal society did greatly facilitate the reconstruction of the earlier situation for the observer. The function of an institution might change, but its nominal continuities provide valuable clues to the previous working of it. Moreover, throughout the period of the French protectorate many of the Berber areas were comparatively isolated from the rest of Morocco where change was more rapid. Before the Second World War, extensive areas were still classed as 'zones of insecurity' and movement from and into them was restricted. This situation reappeared when the Franco–Moroccan political crisis developed not so very long after the second war, except that now it was the new urban areas which were now politically 'insecure' rather than the old tribal ones: the townsmen were more dissident, and the tribesmen were to be protected from contagion. Still, the insulating effect was the same.

The conflict between Moroccan nationalism and the French authorities gathered momentum after the Anglo–American landings in North Africa during the war. The leadership of the Moroccan nationalists had roughly speaking two kinds of members: an elder generation of people with a primarily Muslim traditionalist orientation, formed by the ideas of the Muslim Reform Movement, and a younger generation of mainly French trained intellectuals whose ultimate ideological inspiration was modern European rather than Islamic. In the struggle for independence, the opposition between these two tendencies on the whole remained latent. Such splits as occurred did not at that early stage follow this fundamental line of fission. This only came into the open after independence.

The nationalists succeeded in obtaining the support of the new urban proletariat, notably in Casablanca, and in some measure, limited by caution, that of the monarchy. The French attempted to use traditional elements against them, such as the religious fraternities and the 'bled'. 'Bled' literally means 'country' and became an adapted French word, meaning the countryside and rural society, and in effect meant the authorities in rural society. Of these, the most formidable were the powerful Berber chieftains, notably the Glawi.

The crucial event in the struggle was the exile of the late Sultan by the French in 1953. He was exiled in response to a questionably spontaneous movement against him organised by various rural chieftains under the leadership of the Glawi, together with the leaders of certain religious orders, and supported more or less overtly by both official and unofficial French groups. This gave the Nationalists their chance, and they made use of it with very great effectiveness. The symbol of the exiled king over the water, in 'Madam Cascar' (Madagascar) as the tribesmen called it, enabled them to rouse opposition to the French not merely from the intelligentsia and the new proletariat, but in due course from the countryside as well. When, in the end, this opposition threatened to spread even into the recesses of the mountains, this in conjunction with the outbreak of the Algerian war decided the issue, and the French gave in. Morocco became independent in 1956.

The acute period of the crisis from '53 to the end of '55 meant increased isolation for the mountain areas, but also an increased awareness of the outside conflict into which the tribesmen were beginning to be drawn. Nevertheless, in the deeper recesses of the mountains, the Nationalists had not yet succeeded in forming effective cells, though individual tribesmen were in contact with cells in the market towns on the edge of the plain. When the French surrender and Moroccan independence came, it took the tribesmen, and perhaps others, somewhat by surprise.

In the tribal areas with which we are concerned, independence meant not the abrogation of a superimposed centralised administration, but after an interregnum, simply its continuation with the French personnel replaced by Moroccans. Secondly, it meant, after a little delay, abrogation of the hitherto preserved customary law, and its replacement by a centralised legal system which does not differentiate between Berber and Arab, nor between one tribe and the next. Thirdly, it meant the end of the official use of tribal notables as intermediaries between larger groupings and the administration. (In brief, tribes as such ceased to be parts of the administrative system.) Finally, it meant easy movement between the villages and the towns, and the emergence of a new institution, the rural cells of political parties, and participation in national elections.

The Struggle for Morocco's Past

It is natural that a tribesman's social and political life should be of interest to the anthropologist and, no doubt, to other tribesmen. But it is surprising that it should also turn out to be of concern, even of passionate concern, to people who are neither tribesmen nor anthropologists. Berber tribes have on occasion aroused such interest. There are, it so happens, features of Berber tribal life which arouse wider political passions.

Three related questions about Berbers are politically septic:

1. Are they heretics?
2. Are they rebels?
3. Are they democrats?

All these three related issues were activated in modern times by contemporary political struggles, though the first one has a longer history.

1. Ibn Khaldun narrates that the Berbers were guilty of repeated apostasy after the initial Islamisation. Whether or not his sources were accurate about events which happened nearly seven centuries before his own time, his account is significant as evidence for the kind of image Berbers already possessed in his time for urban learned men. No doubt the image was kept alive by the antagonistic relationship between the city of Fes, the centre and paradigm of learned Islam in Morocco, and the Berber tribes to the South, who were ever seen by the townsmen as heterodox, immoral and violent.[1]

In modern times, the question was given a new and acute topicality by the French relationship to the tribes. As the French conquered them, they allowed them to retain, if they chose, their tribal custom, divergent though it was from holy Koranic law. This enraged both Muslim and emergent nationalist sentiment, and in effect opposition to this either anti-Islamic or 'divide and rule' measure constitutes the transition from the old anti-infidel to the modern anti-colonial sentiment. (See above, p. 20).

Robert Montagne summarised the position as follows:

[1]The manner in which tribal law differed from Koranic law was sometimes curious. In the area with which we are concerned, the rule governing pologamy in that a man may have four white wives and the fifth must be a negress. Then he can go on and marry a further four wives over, but the tenth must again be black, and so on, in a kind of modulo five pattern. The tribesmen mistakenly believed this rule to be Koranic. The rule has little if any application, as few men have more than one wife, or very few have more than two.

22

... l'opposition naturelle qui existe entre le gouvernement despotique du Makhzen, soutenu par le principes de la loi divine, et l'anarchie organisée des tribus. Cette dernière prend sa force ... dans la vigeur d'un droit coutumier ... l'opposition subsiste dans les ésprits. C'est ce qui nous permet de comprendre l'importance que jouera dans l'histoire du nationalisme marocain, depuis 1930, la lutte contre la coutume berbère.[1]

Since those lines were written, the situation has changed somewhat: as in the Yemen, Jordan, or for that matter Stuart Scotland, tribes whose independence had troubled the monarchy under the old order, became, at least in part, its support against the forces of modernism in a changing world. Nevertheless, the passage quoted conveys the situation as it was in the earlier days. Today, this is no longer a major issue: when independent Morocco abolished tribal custom, it did so more in the name of the unification of a national state, than in the name of religious orthodoxy. The issue of heresy has been submerged by the others.

2. The second issue is that of the historic role of Berber dissidence. This is an issue which, initially, arose between Moroccan nationalism and the French. When a colonial power in Africa contested the claims of nationalists, its argument generally ran: prior to us, no unified society, no real state, was to be found here. *We* created it. In Morocco, this argument could not be used. Morocco (unlike neighbouring Algeria) has a very marked historic reality and continuity. But another argument was invoked instead: the insistence on the fact of siba, on the permanent, conscious, institutionalised dissidence of so many tribes. By this token, the French, though they had not created Morocco, had been the first to unify it.

The manner in which this issue relates to the question of heresy is obvious: the heretics in law and custom were also rebels against government. In the modern world, religious heresy generally matters less than political rebellion, though in Morocco, heresy still does matter: post-Independence Morocco must be one of the few modern states in which the sentence of death has been passed (though not carried out) for religious apostasy.

The French view of Moroccan history has often been formulated. It would be quite wrong to suppose either that it was motivated only by divide-and-rule considerations, or that there

[1] *Révolution en Maroc,* 1953, p. 110.

was one unique and consistent French view on these matters. For one thing, there was a genuine element of romanticism in it, a concern with the preservation of tribal institutions. It is quite fallacious to suppose that a romantic infatuation with Muslim tribal peoples is a monopoly of Anglo-Saxons reared in ball-playing boarding schools: French officers were also susceptible to it. There was also an ambivalence in the romanticism, concerning whether it was directed to the tribes or to the more central Muslim institutions. It is well recorded in the following reminiscent passage:

> L'auteur de ces lignes se rapelle notamment la première visite du maréchal Lyautey à Taza, venant d'être occupé par nos troupes ... Il fut signalé au maréchal Lyautey le particularisme de ces chefs berbères régionaux, celui des tribus, celui des confréries religieuses locales, qui déclaraient accepter l'autorité française mais répugnaient à leur soumission au Maghzen. L'un des officiers présents ne craignit pas de dire: 'C'est le moment d'établir à Taza une république berbère qui sera loyaliste envers nous ...' ... le maréchal ... répliqua: 'Vous êtes certainement dans le vrai, mais ... je suis au Maroc pour restaurer l'autorité du Sultan dans tout le pays, et je ne puis faire autrement!'[1]

Thus the main theme in the French interpretation of Moroccan history is the stress on siba, the fact of dissidence, the failure of the historic Moroccan state, not to come into being at all, but to become effectively centralised. No Richelieu, Mazarin or Louis XIV had arisen to do unto the tribes what the French monarchy had done to the nobles. And so it was. The most interesting, indeed fascinating, Moroccan reply to the French case, can be found in a book which appeared in 1958, and which received an endorsement in the form of a preface from Mehdi Ben Barka, who was, until his kidnapping and presumed murder, the most important leader and thinker of the Moroccan left.[2]

The interesting thing about this book is that it does not, like more simple-minded efforts at rebuttal of the French, consist of an attempt simply to deny this feature of Moroccan history. Instead, it reinterprets its significance.

Lahbabi's argument seems at first to be an attack on the French

[1] General P. J. André, *Confréries Religieuses Musulmanes*, Alger, 1956, p. 346.
[2] Mohamed Lahbabi, *Le Gouvernement Marocain a l'Aube de XXe Siècle*, Editions Techniques Nord-Africaines, Rabat, 1958, Preface de M. Mehdi Ben Barka, President de l'Assemblée nationale consultative.

view of the Moroccan constitution and the theory of the French Protectorate (which, by the time this book appeared, had been dismantled for two years). Lahbabi's account of the French position makes it hinge on the assumption that Morocco is an absolute monarchy, and on the Islamic theory of delegation, as elaborated by the classical jurist Mawardi. The French view was, according to Lahbabi, that this theory allowed the absolute monarch to delegate what he chose to whom he chose: he could, if it so pleased him, hand over irksome tasks, such as for instance the running of his country, to anyone he chose, such as, let us say, the designated representative of the French republic.

The interest of this negative, destructive part of Lahbabi's thesis is limited. The Protectorate, allegedly rationalised by this theory, no longer existed, and one may doubt whether its legalistic justification mattered much, one way or the other. There is in any case little to suggest that Lyautey carried a copy of Mawardi in his knapsack.[1]

What is fascinating is Lahbabi's *positive* theory. He does not deny the fact of dissidence, though he comments on its use by the French: 'On connaît l'insistance, maladroite par sa persistance, sur la prétendue division du Maroc en Bled Mahkzen et Bled Siba. On a vu ce qu'il en était effectivement.'[2] What *was* it really like?

Lahbabi gives his own account earlier: '. . . bled makhzen . . . le territoire où la population *a consenti* à la délégation des pouvoirs d'administration supérieure au Sultan; . . . bled siba . . . territoires qui *ne veulent* pas déléguer au Sultan les droits de propre administration, territoires où les populations n'ont pas adhéré à la *beia*'.[3] In brief, Lahbabi used the historic fact of a distinction between government-accepting and government-rejecting tribes, to establish a democratic, Consent theory of government. He strengthens his case by appealing to the existence of a ritual act (*beia*) used for recognising the authority of a ruler. Lahbabi does not deny (p. 65) that the beia may not always be quite voluntary, but invokes the fact that it is solicited and desired by the ruler, to establish a

[1] In his unsycophantic preface, Mehdi Ben Barka makes the following criticism (p. 5): 'Le second reproche me semble découler de l'importance excessive accordée à la théorie de Mawerdi . . . le Traité de Mawerdi ne fait qu' idéaliser outre mêsure un état de fait particulier, dû à l'affaiblissement des califes abbassides . . .'

[2] Mohamed Lahbabi, op. cit., p. 200.

[3] *Ibid.*, p. 41 (Italics mine).

Consent theory of government, the proposition (p. 66) that '. . . la communauté marocaine . . . est la source des pouvoirs . . .'.

The student of modern Moroccan politics will be interested primarily in the way in which a manifestly anti-French thesis is latently, and more significantly, a critique of absolutist pretentions of the monarchy. Lahbabi's view is endorsed by Ben Barka in the preface (p. 4) '. . . nos appels à la démocratie ne sont pas . . . des simples emprunts extérieurs . . . Au contraire, ils sont l'expression de notre vocation nationale profonde . . . Le Sultan tenait son pouvoir par délégation de la communauté; son investiture était une sorte de contrat.' This thesis is not the one conventionally held: for instance, *A Survey of North West Africa (The Maghrib)*, says 'Morocco cannot be called a democracy, since all power is legally concentrated in the hand of the King'.[1] But the student of Berber society, or of ideology in general, will be interested in the way in which the very same facts which were invoked to justify foreign intervention can equally be invoked not only to condemn it, but also to establish a democratic, contractual constitutional theory.

3. The question concerning the role of tribes (largely Berber tribes) in Moroccan history, and their contribution towards the democratic or other interpretation of the customs of the Moroccan constitution, leads us on by a natural transition to the question of the internal organisation of the tribes – their 'democratic' or other character. This matter has also become ideologically pregnant in modern times.

The best starting point for understanding the practical relevance of this question is that most brilliant study of Berber political sociology, the work of Robert Montagne. Montagne put forward two principal theses: one concerned the role of moieties in Berber society. (See below, p. 65.) The second and related thesis, which is relevant here, is that Berber society oscillates between two rival and opposed social forms, between on the one hand democratic or oligarchic tribal republics ruled by assemblies or hierarchies of assemblies, and on the other hand ephemeral tribal tyrannies, exemplified in modern time by the 'great caids' of the South.[2]

---

[1] Edited by Nevill Barbour, Royal Institute of International Affairs, 1959, p. 109.

[2] A *caid* is a governmentally nominated chief, as opposed to the tribally elected *anghar*. The post-independence Moroccan government employed the term *caid* for what was, in reality, the successor of the colonial district officer – a nominated administrator *not* drawn from the administered tribe or tribes.

This idea is a reflection, an echo, of the dilemma faced by French policy in rural Morocco, of the tension between two rather contradictory policies adopted by the French Protectorate towards the tribes. On the one hand, there was the use of and support of the tribal tyrants of the South, and on the other, the underwriting of tribal customary law, notably in central Morocco, and hence indirectly of tribal assemblies which applied it and which are presupposed by much of that custom.[1] The fact that Montagne's thesis reflects a political dilemma does not in any way invalidate it, (though it does throw interesting light on its origin). In some respects, it is an interesting anticipation of a similar idea, elaborated later by Dr Edmund Leach for the tribes of Highland Burma.[2]

Reading Montagne, it is impossible not to be sensitive to the regret he communicates concerning the decline of tribal institutions. Would it not be possible to make a direct transition from tribal democracy to modern democratic local government? This hope led to the plan of establishing 'rural communes', which was only implemented after Independence. It also made a natural appeal to the left. In practice, the realities of power led the post-Independence political parties to struggle for the control of the administrative machinery, rather than work for its dismantling and replacement by rural self-government. The rural councils, though they exist, are not powerful. The local chieftancies, the squierarchies established or fortified by the French, were however abolished.

It would perhaps be wisest, in Morocco or anywhere else, not to make one's commitment to democratic or liberal values contingent on historical or anthropological interpretations. So one may look at this question of Berber 'democratic' traditions for its

---

[1] In practice, the alternatives were not quite so clear-cut. Even in the regions in which tribal custom was maintained, the predilections of a colonial administration could not fail to create chiefs more permanent and powerful than custom would have tolerated. In the case of the southern tyrants, who nominally abolished custom and replaced it by Koranic law, the situation also was not so simple. The 'great caids' cared little about the content of law, one way or the other: as long as it was administered by their appointed *kadis* and not by assemblies, and did not create rival centres of power, they had no objection to the retention of customary rules. For instance, an English expedition visiting the very heart of the country controlled by the famous Glawi, in the last summer of his rule (1955) came across and took part in the traditional custom of punishing transgressors by imposing a fine which is given to, and divided by, the village collectively. See Bryan Clarke, *Berber Village*, Longman, 1959, p. 96.

[2] E. R. Leach, *Political Systems of Highland Burma*, London, 1954, 1964.

intrinsic interest, rather than as a means of legitimating or explaining specific political developments. (For instance, during the Algerian war, some people explained the remarkable abstention of the FLN from the use of a single charismatic leader, in terms of the democratic traditions of the Algerian Berbers.)

It is better perhaps to speak of Berber tribes in the categories of anthropology, as segmentary societies with, indeed, an unusual diffusion of power and tendency towards egalitarianism, with important assemblies and elective leadership. The notion of 'segmentation' seems more useful than that of 'democracy' for laying bare the actual mechanics of the society. Nevertheless, if one insists on characterising this society as 'democratic', how much truth is there in such a contention?

Berber tribal life can be described as democratic only with the following qualifications:

a. This is a structural, rather than an ideological democracy. It is not based on a theory, on a set of principles or norms. In the words of Pierre Bourdieu,[1] it is a *démocratie vécue*. It does not preach or practice any inalienable right of political participation. On the contrary, the poor and weak are not merely excluded informally from political decision, but are even formally excluded from important aspects of legal life. A man who has no property to risk cannot take part in the crucial institution of collective oath.[2] Tribal practice is also fully compatible with the exclusion from tribal citizenship of people on grounds of profession, religion or pigmentation. (Jewish cobblers or Negro blacksmiths are not members of the tribe.)

[1] *Sociologie de l'Algérie*, PUF, 1958, p. 27, et seq.

[2] See below, p. 104. One should add, however, that a man who is too poor is also not a full member of the community: his poverty is a consequence, rather than a cause, of his exclusion. Just as tribal groups practice confiscation of goods and their distribution as punishment for transgressors, they also practice a kind of village scale welfare state, in the form of setting up a man economically, by contributions from other villagers, if he is impoverished and it is desired to retain him. (Hence if a man remains impoverished, his exclusion from the collective oath is logical enough: if his agnates or co-villagers do not value him highly enough to set him up, they should not use his voice at the oath.)

This institution is now in decline. The villagers say: if he is poor, let him seek work elsewhere, or enlist. The real reason is, of course, not the fact that these alternatives, which may be less than realistic, are held to exist, but that, under conditions of pacification, there is little motive for trying to retain a man, even if he is valued in terms of his personal characteristics. I do not believe that the stories about the past functioning of this institution, for which an appropriate ritual exists, are simply a case of idealising the past.

Tribal democracy does, it is true, possess one so to speak negative ideological trait: it sees its own customs as emanating from the practices of ancestors and as alterable by consent, and not as holy and God-given. The only recent deliberate changes in custom I came across concerned, admittedly, points of detail,[1] but still, this would seem to establish the principle.

b. Historically, when more-than-tribal political units crystallised among Berbers, they were no longer democratic but monarchic.

c. Berber democracy and egalitarianism is complemented by the anthropolatry of the holy lineages. The reverence shown to hereditary saints is neither absolute nor free from irony; but it exists. Above all, it is not a concession, a deviation from, the normal principles of tribal life: it is, on the contrary, essential and complementary to it. The egalitarian traits of tribal life, the symmetrical diffusion of power, the elective nature of leadership – these are only made possible by the unsymmetrical, inegalitarian saints.

The Central High Atlas

There are mountain ranges which rise so gently, with so many graded foothills, that arriving in their midst is a bit of a disappointment: the preparation was too gradual. Not so the central High Atlas. It rises dramatically like an enormous wall out of the flat Tadla plain (itself part of the Atlantic plain of Morocco), in the vicinity of what is now the provincial capital of Beni Mellal.

[1]One reform was concerned with a change in the number of couples allowed to combine their marriage feast; the other concerned the number of men whom a husband, divorcing a wife at her request, could single out as *in*eligible to be her future spouses.

In the central High Atlas, bride-price is insignificant. The real expense of a marriage to a previously unmarried woman is in the cost of the marriage feast. 'Collective' weddings are a form of economy, and not, of course, survivals of some kind of group marriage. A tribe reduced the maximum number who could share in a feast, as a compromise between the view that the sharing was shameful, and the impracticability of forbidding it altogether.

The case of the prohibited spouse should delight the ethical relativist. In our society, people who in principle dislike divorce, condone it in some measure if at least it makes possible another and happier union. Berber reasoning is the opposite: they give their woman some freedom to seek divorce, but are concerned lest this should encourage those who covet another's wife for their own, to lead on that wife to demand a divorce. To discourage this, a husband, complying with his wife's request of a divorce, may single out a certain number of men as ineligible for purposes of re-marrying her. (Thus a man coveting another's wife is well-advised to use decoys.) The tribe in question decided to reduce the number of men who could be so listed by the divorcing husbands.

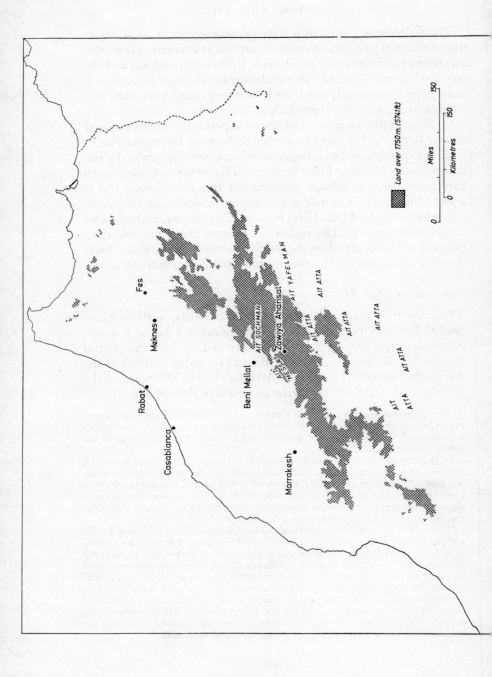

Land over 1750 m. (5741 ft)

Fes

Meknes

Rabat

Casablanca

Beni Mellal

AIT SOCHMAN

MESGITA

Ait Ali

Zawiya Ahansal

AIT ATTA

AIT YAFELMAN

AIT ATTA

AIT ATTA

AIT ATTA

AIT ATTA

AIT ATTA

AIT ATTA

Marrakesh

Miles

Kilometres

0   150

0   150

Here and there, there are sharp, narrow, dark gaps in the wall: gorges through which the waters of the mountains make their way out to the plain. Here, it is perfectly clear why the geographical boundary between plain and mountain was also, for so long, a political boundary between the 'land of government' and the 'land of dissidence'. Prior to modern times, there is no record of an army of the central state successfully penetrating these gorges, though some did try.

If one does ascend that wall, one finds that it does not fall away as much or as steeply on the other side. One enters a world of high pastures and forests, occasionally cut by a deep gorge, sometimes opening into broader valleys, some even rich in alluvial soil.

After traversing the world of the tribes of the north-facing slopes, one finally reaches the main watershed. The southern Sahara-ward slopes are bare and without forest. But even they are covered with snow in winter, offer pasture in spring, and the valleys which collect the rivers lend themselves to irrigation agriculture. The waters of these rivers do not reach the sea: but before these waters fade out in the Sahara, they create long, thin oases, miniature Nile valleys, with intensive agriculture.

Beyond the Atlas, there is another range, less high – the Jebel Saghro – before the desert proper is reached.

This southern region, between the High Atlas and the Sahara, was inhabited by a patchwork of tribes, Berber-speaking and Arabic-speaking; mixed pastoralists and agriculturalists, living in a complex symbiosis, which has never been fully explored, with Negroid oasis-dwellers, Jewish artisans, and holy lineages of both Berber and Arabic speech. But in this southern world, the largest and dominant group were the Berber Ait Atta tribe, in whose life pastoralism is of very great importance.

Throughout both the central High Atlas, which is purely Berber, and the area to the south of it, climatic and ecological conditions vary enormously, according to altitude and other factors. The main form of adaptation has been transhumancy, the seasonal migration of flocks and people, intended to exploit diverse areas at various periods of time. This movement takes a number of forms: in some tribes the shepherds merely move up and down the

Map of Morocco, showing location of Zawiya Ahansal and the four principal tribal groupings which use it for arbitration.

slopes of the same valley, from the main farm by the fields to the high pastures or the forest.

But at the other extreme, there are the long-distance annual migrations of the southern shepherds, with their camels, sheep and goats, and tents.

An enormous migration of this kind is virtually dictated by nature. The highest pastures in the mountains are almost uninhabitable in winter, being without trees and covered in deep snow. But when the snows melt in spring, the pastures are excellent by North African standards, and the hollows in the uplands retain moisture and good grass late into the season. These pastures are a standing and irresistible invitation to the tribes of the south, whose homelands are scorched in the summer. The permanent population of the north-facing valleys and gorges is not large enough to use up those pastures, nor strong enough to prohibit entry to the southerners. Thus Cain and Abel – very relatively speaking – confront each other each spring. (Relatively speaking, for the southerners also practice agriculture, and the northerners also have flocks. It is merely a matter of stress.)

The two parties confront each other each spring, but for most of history, there was no higher authority to keep the peace between them. (Since 1933, there has been such a government; but neither the French nor the independent Moroccan administration have succeeded in making this confrontation quite peaceful.) Yet at the same time, the effective use of the high pastures does require orderly procedures. The pastures which dry up first must be used first; those which last longest must be reserved till the end. Also, the whole balance of power in the region shifts drastically with the presence or absence of the annual 'invaders'. At the same time, balance of tribes and tribal segments was the main principle available to this society. How can such balance be maintained, if ecology dictates constant and massive movements?

Near the point at which the pastures are at their highest and most extensive, there is a deep gorge, plentifully provided with water and forest, and to some extent provided with irrigable land. From the viewpoint of tribal geopolitics, this gorge is a bit of an anomaly. If it were inhabited by a segment of the northern tribes, this segment would be in a terribly precarious condition in late spring and in summer, when the high pastures all around pullulate with the southern shepherds. In summer, you can hardly move on the high pastures without coming across a black tent and being harried by its dogs. But suppose the southern tribes were to leave a segment in occupation of this deep gorge, which sticks like a thin finger into the highest uplands: this segment in turn would find itself in a precarious and isolated position in winter, when deep snows on this watershed all but cut it off from the south. They would be at the mercy of the other permanent inhabitants of the much larger valleys of the Atlantic-ward side.

The problem of how to maintain order between the annual visitors and the permanent inhabitants, and the problem of what to do with this most isolated of gorges, have one and the same solution. The valley is inhabited by professional neutrals, by hereditary saints whose lineage connects them to the founder of the religion shared by both sides, and excludes them from identification with either.

From the viewpoint of the external, sociologically minded observer, it looks as if the saints had to be invented, and appropriately located, had they not existed. From the viewpoint of the tribesmen, it is the other way round: the founder of the saints invited, by magical telepathic means, the founding ancestor of the southerners to come and help establish the status quo now found in the region. The saint's holiness, rooted in the generally shared religion and confirmed by magical powers, legitimated the arrangement; but the military strength of the southerners is acknowledged to have helped to bring it into being. At the same time, they must not push too far: the lay northern tribes provide the balancing arch, and the saints are the cornerstone.

Thus the southerners come to their Promised Pastures by sacred invitation. The story differs from the biblical one, with which it has parallels, in some interesting ways. The main invasion is annual and not permanent (though some segments of the southerners are now permanently installed north of the watershed). The 'invaders' come for pasture rather than agricultural land. Above all, they come by invitation of the local Baalim and not against them. Their arrival is legitimated not by an exclusive deity of the desert, jealous of rivals and local manifestations: it is, on the contrary, legitimated by forms of the holy with a very much local anchorage – the shrines and holy men of the northern valleys. It is a form which is not at all jealous or exclusive – except on its home ground – for it belongs to a form of the holy which clearly acknowledges the legitimacy of other, similar and equal, incarnations.

Muslim saints, whether they are heads of lineages or of brother-hoods, admit pluralism and the right of rivals to exist: they compete with them for priority, locality and marginal advantages, but make no exclusive claims. That is reserved for the shared embracing religion of which they all claim to be a manifestation.

We shall probably never know whether the southerners really came by invitation from a previously established local holy lineage, or whether they just came and brought their 'local' invitation with them. The former alternative is by no means inconceivable, and they are what the local legends claim to be the truth. The founding saint was first settled with some northern tribes, but it was his disagreements with them which made him call in the southerners.

But whilst we shall probably never know for certain what had happened historically, it is easy to see how the general ecological situation, and the absence of central government which is itself a consequence of that situation, creates certain problems: and how an eminently plausible and elegant solution is the one which is actually found, and which consists of locating a centre of professionally neutral, obligatorily pacific, saints-arbitrators in the narrow gorge closest to the point of maximum friction, of the greatest movement of transhumants, and near the meeting point of the four largest tribal groups of the central High Atlas.

CHAPTER TWO

THE PROBLEM

The Problem Stated

The problem concerns, essentially, the working of a hagiarchy, 'government' – if this is not too strong a term – by hereditary saints in a near anarchic tribal environment.

The area surrounding Ahansal displays a number of interesting features: a strong religious influence in political matters, and apparently a *stable* one. On the other hand, it does not manifest those regular moieties which have been claimed to be the characteristic features of Berber political life.

To what extent may one speak of a 'maraboutic state',[1] a dynasty, an hagiarchy? Or, to put it the other way, how is an anarchic State of Nature mitigated by hereditary saints?

In brief – how did the Rule of Saints, or Anarchy Mitigated by Holiness, maintain itself and function?

Segmentation and Ancestors

The Berbers of the Central High Atlas, like all other Moroccan and indeed Maghrebin tribes, are a segmentary patrilineal people.

---

[1]The term 'marabout' has become an adopted French word. (The local Berber word is *agurram*.) For instance: 'Ainsi associés aux républiques indépendantes les marabouts participent souvent de leur étonnante stabilité et de la force qu'y conservent les traditions. Certaines dynasties réligieuses – celles des Ahansal, que les traditions locales font remonter au XIIIe siécle . . . parviennent ainsi à conserver le pouvoir plus longtemps que les chorfa maîtres de l'Empire'.

R. Montagne, *Les Berbères et le Makhzen dans le Sud du Maroc,* Paris, 1930, p. 411.

It should be noted that this passage appeared in a book published three years before the final conquest of the dissident two thirds of the 'dynasty' of Ahansal, and of Zawiya Ahansal itself, and of the major part of Ahansal-land.

The general nature and functioning of segmentary societies is a familiar and well explored theme in social anthropology. To some extent, accounts applicable to similar societies elsewhere are valid here. Hence one must restate the general features of segmentation for the sake of the completeness of the account, familiar though those features are to anthropologists.

The affiliation of a Berber to a social group is generally expressed in terms of his alleged patrilineal descent. Most of the rights and duties allocated him are such in virtue of his male ancestors in the male line. Social groups in Berber society generally have the name Ait X. X is usually, but not always, the name of a person, such as Brahim or Mhand. In principle, a man is a member of a group Ait X in virtue of being a descendant of X. 'Ait' can however also be combined with a place name, to designate the inhabitants of the place: for instance, Ait Talmest, the people of Talmest.

A man's name generally consists of three linked parts: first, his own proper name, second, his father's name, and third a name indicating the immediately larger group which will often also be the name of a recent ancestor, possibly his grandfather. The name of the woman has a similar structure and does not change on marriage: apart from her personal name, it will include her father's name and his immediate group. In daily life, the names are of course often abbreviated by omitting the last or the last two constituents.

One should perhaps stress the general point that the notion of 'a man's name' is ambiguous. We tend to forget this: passports and other identity documents and legal conventions of our society unconsciously turn us into Platonists of a kind, wedded to the supposition that there is some one sound or group of sounds which 'is' a man's real name. In fact of course this is not so, and names like other things depend on context. If we define his 'name' as the term by means of which he is identified or to which he will respond if called, the 'name' will vary according to the situation, and the crucial thing in the context will be the implied contrast. In the context of his immediate family, his first name will be sufficient. In the village, his first name conjoined with his father's name will be adequate. In the context of a wider tribal assembly or a market, a fuller name which refers also to his clan may be required. If his clan in the narrower sense is a prominent and well-known one, then the 'narrower' clan name may be used. If on the other hand his immediate clan is obscure, and the use of the wider clan name does not lead to ambiguity, then the wider term may be invoked. Identity cards and their implication of a unique name for all contexts only came in to the Atlas during the French Protectorate. Although the possession of an identity card was essential for purposes of travel, it did not effect the way in which tribesmen saw their names. The habit of inventing family names in the European style is almost unknown, and occurs only in the cases of permanent migration to a town or in the very rare cases of the possession of a modern education.

Nevertheless, allowing for the context-bound nature of the traditional names, one might say that roughly speaking a man's name consists of three parts, and that the relationship of these three parts is governed by certain loose principles.

For instance, a man's name might be *Daud u Said n'ait Yussif,* David son of Said of the people of Yussif. Ideally, Yussif would be the name of his grandfather, and the Ait Yussif, the people Yussif, would cover all other families descended from the same grandfather. In fact, various adjustments may take place: Yussif may have had no sons other than Said, the Ait Yussif thus being coextensive with the Ait Said, and there is little point in dwelling on the grandfather's name; but there may be some point in stressing the little-clan affiliation inside the village, Daud's clan being (say one of the three in the village) the Ait Ahmad. He may then describe himself as Daud u Said n'ait Ahmad. Other adjustments of such kinds occur.

In daily intercourse, a man may be called by his own name, or that in conjunction with his father's or it in conjunction with the clan's name, or by his father's name alone (prefixed by 'u'), or by an accepted nickname.

Daud's sister Tuda would describe herself as Tuda Said n'ait Yussif (or n'ait Ahmad), or might in imitation of Arab ways describe herself as Tuda bint Said etc. Her name does not change on marriage.

Feminine names seldom appear 'higher up' in the name, so to speak, though occasionally they do. A slave, particularly a female one, may be identified by her mother rather than her father, e.g., Fatma n'Zida, Fatma of Zida's; or parallel clans, claiming descent from the same ancestor, may name themselves not after the sons of the shared ancestor, but after his respective wives, who are alleged to have given birth to the sons fathering the segments, as for instance Ait Sfia, Ait Ash'sha in Zawiya Ahansal.

The basic feature of the local law of inheritance is that brothers inherit equally. The whole system is symmetrical as between brothers.

Social groups are strongly endogamous. The preferred form of marriage is to the patri-lateral parallel cousin, to the father's brother's daughter. This preference is expressed negatively, as the right of all male parallel cousins, including more distant ones, to object to and prevent a marriage of a girl to someone outside the agnatic group. The suitor from outside the group has to obtain the consent of the male patri-lateral cousins of his would-be-bride before he can marry her. The concept of father's brother (*ami*) is used in a semi-classificatory way, as is son-of-father's-brother (*yus n'ami*): on examination, it often turns out that the 'uncle' or 'cousin', in this sense, is further 'away' than the narrowest interpretation of the terms would suggest.

In order to conceptualise and express the segmentary patrilineal organisation of their society, Berbers do not generally draw diagrams. The situation is expressed and described genealogically. The most standard kind of Berber genealogy is as it were Occamist: Ancestors are not multiplied beyond necessity. The individual knows the name of his father and of his grandfather: after that, he will name or know of only those ancestors who perform the useful task of defining an effective social group. Ancestors who do not earn their keep by performing this task are not worth the wear of remembering (or inventing).

It is a commonplace of the treatment of such genealogies that they cannot be taken at their face value. For one thing, and the most obvious one, the remembered ancestors are simply too few: if one believed these genealogies, one would have to assume a most phenomenal growth of population over the recent centuries, and imagine the Atlas, not so very many years ago, inhabited by a very small number of extremely virile old men, ancestors of virtually the whole of the present population. But genealogies of this kind are inaccurate not merely through their omissions, through the 'forgetting' of all socially redundant ancestors. It would be equally rash to assume that the remembered ancestors are survivors from genuinely real lines of descent, islands of true memory sticking out of a sea of oblivion. The islands themselves may be spurious. To realise this, one needs only reflect that the existing social groups generally need an ancestor as a kind of conceptual apex: an ancestor, however real, does not need a social group. He is indeed past needing anything, and not in a position of bringing it into being if he wished. The presently existing social group on the other hand is in a position to satisfy its need for a concept which it requires to express its very existence (leaving aside the need, suggested by anthropological theory, of reinforcing its solidarity).

The most typical Berber genealogy, the Occamist one or an approximation thereof, with a remembered father and grandfather, and thereafter only ancestors who in fact define existing groupings, is however but one form a genealogy may take, though the most common and basic type. Two factors above all may lead to a modification to this type of genealogy: extreme sedentarisation and sanctity.

Very sedentarised tribes, i.e., those in whose lives agriculture (with irrigated and hence immobile fields) plays a far larger part than pastoralism, may dispense with genealogical definitions of the larger, higher level social groupings. In their case, the wider and more general groups may be defined geographically. There may be, at the top, levels of segmentation where the word Ait is followed

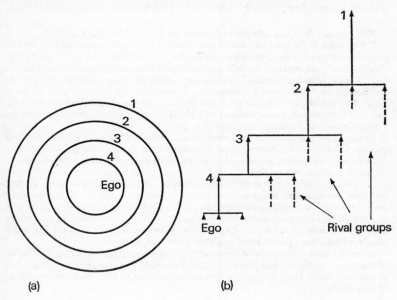

(a)   (b)

not by a personal name but by a place name. The genealogical conceptualisation of groups only comes in at the lower levels. Within the region I am concerned with, there is one tribe where this has unambiguously happened. It is worth noting that the situation seems similar in the western High Atlas, where most or all tribes are very sedentarised.[1] All this however, does not disturb the tree-like neatness of the segmentary system, though it does conflict with some widely accepted theories about Berber mentality.[2]

The manner in which sanctity affects genealogies is far more important for our purposes. Saints do not have Occamist genealogies. On the contrary, they have Veblenesque ones, indulging in a kind of conspicuous display of genealogical wealth. The more ancestors the merrier, and certainly the better. A typical successful saint will possess a genealogy which contains a long string of names of whom only a few have the role of defining existing corporate groups, by standing at the apex of their genealogy; and indeed only few have any kind of image or personality attached to their name. (In the case of the Occamist ancestors of lay tribes' segments, an image may also be lacking – but such a faceless ancestor defines a group instead.) Such ancestors, faceless and groupless, simply add to the richness of the ancestral line.

---

[1]Cf. Jacques Berque, *Structures Sociales du Haut-Atlas*, 1955, p. 63.

[2]'A ce sujet, le lecteur, peu familiarisé avec les façons de penser arabes, doit se pénétrer fortement de cette idée, qu'Arabes et Berbères ont une conception "biologique", non territoriale de la patrie; ils ne ditent pas: "Je suis de tel village", mai "J'appartiens à telle tribu". (Récemment, nous avions en main un livre sur la préhistoire en Angleterre; il s'intitulait: *The earliest Englishman*; qu'il ait pu y avoir des Anglais, en Angleterre, avant de l'arrivée des Angles, est un point de vue qui échapperait à nos indigènes!') (G.H. Bousquet, *Les Berbères*, Presses Universitaires de France, Paris, 1957), p. 52.

In general this is true, but exceptions exist, notably amongst well-sedentarised groups. Consider the following quotations from Prof. Jacques Berque's *Structures Sociales du Haut Atlas*, (Presses Universitaires de France, Paris, 1955), p. 63.

'Montagnards, Sédentaires.

. . . Or le premier résultat de l'analyse c'est qu'ils sont des immigrants, et que, fait plus instructif, ils n'ont aucune gêne à avouer une origine étrangère. Ils y mettent même . . . quelque coquetterie . . . On sent que leur snobisme n'est pas de revendiquer une ascendance arabe ou chérifienne. Il est de subsister ensemble, alors qu'on vient de si loin . . . On ne pose pas au beau fils venu d'Orient, mais plutôt à l'astucieux petit bâtard qui s'encastre à sa juste place.'

A similar description would apply to the important highly sedentarised tribe of Bu Gmez in the central High Atlas, and possibly to some others, though not to the four really large groupings who make up most of the clients of the saints of this study.

A schematic representation, (page 39), of a simplified segmentary society. Diagram A displays its appearance from the viewpoint of any one individual; Diagram B displays its structure from the viewpoint of the group as a whole. If (a) only one sex is allowed to be significant in ancestry, and (b) only shared ancestry is allowed to define groups, and (c) the whole group ('tribe') shares one ultimate ancestor, it follows that the individual is a member only of a series of 'nested' groups, the largest defined by the most distant ancestor (and so on downwards), with no groups of which he is member cutting across each other. From the viewpoint of the total group, what follows is that, at each level of size, there are groups opposing, 'balancing' each other. (For the sake of completeness of argument, I am spelling out points which are trivial to anthropologists. The main argument will be concerned not with such a neat scheme, but the complications introduced in it by the saintly system.)

Divide That Ye Need Not Be Ruled. (*The Concept of Segmentation*)

Berbers of the Atlas are segmentary and patrilineal. There are important differences between the segmentation of holy and of lay groups, and minor differences within each of the two general classes.

The notion of segmentation, as developed by modern social anthropology, above all by Professor E.E.Evans-Pritchard, is simple, applies in various degrees to very many tribal societies, and is extremely illuminating. It deserves to be more widely known outside the anthropological community. It throws a very great deal of light on the problem of how order is maintained in societies – both in societies in which the segmentary principle is the most important factor in maintaining order, and for societies in which it is merely subsidiary.

The notion of a segmentary society comprises several connected elements:

(1) It contains a theory of social cohesion, a theory which describes an improvement on the maxim 'divide and rule'. The Roman maxim recommends a technique for facilitating government. Segmentary societies employ the same technique for doing without government altogether: divide that ye need not be ruled.

The idea underlying the theory is that the functions of maintaining cohesion, social control, some degree of 'law and order', which otherwise depend largely on specialised agencies with sanctions at their disposal, can be performed with tolerable efficiency, simply by the 'balancing' and 'opposition' of constituent groups. Cohesion is maintained not by agencies of coercion at home, but by a threat from outside; and hence at every level of size for which there *is* an 'at home', there must be a corresponding 'outside'. There is of course nothing at all remarkable about the employment of this principle: it is well known in all contexts that cohesion and co-operation can often best be secured through a threat from a common enemy. It is easy to observe the operation of this principle in our own society, which is by no means segmentary. *What defines a segmentary society is not that this does occur, but that this is very nearly all that occurs.*

The possibility of achieving so much by so simple a device depends on other features of segmentary society:

(2) A 'tree-like' structure: groups to which a person can belong are arranged in a system such that, starting from the largest group, there is within it a set of mutually exclusive sub-groups, and each of these similarly has a set of sub-subgroups, and so on, until one arrives at the ultimate atoms, be they individuals or families.

Again, what defines a segmentary society is not that a system of groups satisfying these conditions can be found within it, but that *only* such a system (or very nearly) can be found within it.

The consequences of this are obvious and striking: from the viewpoint of any group, its composition can be specified without ambiguity, and without any danger of using criteria of membership which might cut across each other.

A group is sub-divided into sub-groups: they in turn sub-divide, and so forth. This principle of division and sub-division generates *all* the groupings which are to be found in the society. In other words, there are no cross-cutting groups and criteria. In a non-segmentary society, clubs, sects, associations, guilds, age-sets, secret societies and so forth may cut across the clan divisions and sub-divisions. The cross cutting of ties itself constitutes an interesting principle of the maintenance of social order – but this is another and not a segmentary principle. A segmentary society is defined by the absence, or by the approximation of absence, of such other ties. In an ideally pure segmentary society, they would be totally absent. In the actual societies known as segmentary, these cross-cutting ties are at least relatively unimportant, and the neat divisions and sub-divisions on the one 'tree' are very important.

The social universe in such a segmentary society consists of groups always definable in the logically simplest and neatest way, by genus and differentia, by specifying the next higher-level group (genus) and the principle separating the sub-group-to-be-defined from the others within it (differentia). Where the segmentation is genealogical, one ancestor provides the genus, another one, often his alleged son, the differentia. Such a social world is of course very different from those numerous other universes, social or other, in which principles of sub-division untidily cut across each other, leaving open or ambiguous borderlines, conflicting criteria, and so on.

From the viewpoint of any individual, the consequence is that he finds himself at the centre of a series of concentric 'nested' circles, a series of larger and larger groups to which he belongs, whose boundaries can never cut across each other.

The innermost circle will consist of the independent household; the next circle, the group of households sharing a real or supposed common ancestor, and defining a 'little clan'; the next circle, a bigger clan unit, or a whole village; and so forth. A member of a segmentary society can perhaps experience a conflict of priorities (should he attend to a feud between sub-groups before attending to a war between groups?), but he can hardly experience an outright conflict of loyalties, groups being at least in principle so arranged that there are no overlaps.

Segmentation is a kind of model of abstraction at its neatest. Distant ancestors are like abstract concepts, denoting more (people alive now) and connoting less; close ancestors are more concrete, 'denoting' fewer descendants and 'connoting' more intense relationships.

It is a formal property of 'trees' in the mathematical sense that there is only one route from any point to any other point. Segmentary systems, as expressed for instances in the genealogies[1] of persons involved in them, are indeed also 'trees' in just this sense. On the genealogical tree, one way only leads from any one man to any other. Hence, in as far as obligations and loyalties are defined agnatically, there can be no ambiguity in the relationship between two men located on the same 'tree', nor in the moral claims and expectations generated by that relationship. The formal property of uniqueness of connection between any two points on a 'tree' has

[1]Berbers use the Arabic word for 'tree' to describe genealogies.

this important social correlate – the social relation between any two individuals is (again, at least ideally) unambiguous and unique.

A tree-like structure of the kind described is essential if the first and critical feature, namely reliance on opposition to generate cohesion, is really to characterise the society. The tree-like structure ensures that for *any* conflict that may arise, there are some groups that can be activated and which will 'balance' each other. A balance of power does not need to be devised, pressure-groups and counter-pressure-groups do not need to be invented and recruited: they are ever-ready, they exist potentially all along the line, available 'in all sizes', and their rivalry, even if latent, ensures the activation of the relevant groups when a conflict does crop up.

Such series of groups of all sizes are required, if the segmentary principle is to do its work. This is important, and perhaps not immediately obvious. Conflict may arise anywhere. Two brothers may quarrel over the use of a tool, two cousins may quarrel over a field, two clans in a village about the upkeep of an irrigation channel, two villages may quarrel about a pasture, two tribes may come into conflict at a large market. In an anarchic, rulerless society, whenever a conflict arises, whether it be between two individuals who are closely related or who are extremely distant, or whether it be between whole groups of people, it is no use appealing to the police, or the government to protect you and to settle the matter, for the simple reason that there is no police and no government. You can only hope that your own group will be activated into loyalty and cohesion by the threat of the other group, either because the interests of the other members of the group are directly threatened, or because they need your help in familiar cases, and also because they can suppose that tolerated aggression in one case will only encourage repetition. But before such a threat can activate 'your' group, there must in some latent sense be such a group, there must be a set of people who can identify themselves as belonging to the group. Because, as indicated, one cannot tell in advance at which level of size, or at which distance in relationship, the conflict will arise, a segmentary society can only work if groups are indeed available in all sizes.

The point that a segmentary society provides cohesion-precipitating hostile groups 'all along the line', in all sizes, is liable to require two qualifications, one concerning the top, the other the bottom, of the scale of social units. The scale must come to an end

44

somewhere, at both ends, and at these ends (by definition: what makes it the end is that there is no further wider or smaller group) there is no-one to be activated into opposition, no one available to right a wrong. Concretely: at the bottom, if one of two brothers kills the other, who is there to right the wrong? From the viewpoint of other groups of brothers, he – or rather the fraternal pair which has now weakened itself – has merely spited his own face: he hasn't harmed them. Similarly, at the top, once we reach the largest available group which can even conceive of itself as a group, we again enter the realm of political and moral anarchy. There is no entity which could apply sanctions, which could be activated into action, at that level either.

This conclusion – no one is available to resist or penalise aggression at either the ultimate molecular, or the final top-size levels – follows from the model of a 'pure' segmentary society. A pure segmentary society is one in which there is no agency which could resist or punish transgressions of rules in the abstract, but one which only has groups and sub-groups so arranged that groups are always available to resist the transgressions when directed at them.[1]

To what extent does this conclusion, deduced from the abstract and simplified model, apply to the concrete society under consideration? The answer is that it applies in part: the society does approximate to the pure model in some degree, but it does not conform to it completely.

First, consider the respects in which it does conform to the model. At the top level of scale, there are no regional or other concepts in terms of which groups can even name or conceive themselves, once one gets past the top rung of names on the segmentary ladder (such as Ait Atta, Ait Sochman, Ait Yafelman, Ait

[1]Note that this does not mean that segmentary tribalism knows no 'universal' moral rules. A stereotype of the tribesman, popular among laymen, notably philosophers, is of a man totally enslaved to the rules within his in-group, and totally amoral outside it. This is doubly wrong. Segmentary societies are very common. Tribesmen within them cannot be enslaved to rules within them, for there is no absolute 'within': what is an in-group for one purpose, is an out-group for another. Secondly, it is not the case that universal, open, impersonally formulated rules of morality are not present: they are, on the contrary, quite clearly present. Their enforcement will vary according to the strength and determination of the group which has suffered from their violation; but that determination will depend in part on the merits of the case. The mechanism of this is discussed in detail below, in connection with the 'collective oath', p. 104.

Messat). And in fact, on the last occasion on which something occurred which might have activated cohesion of the Atlas as a whole, during the French conquest, no such total group was indeed stimulated into existence. The conquest consequently could be and was a piecemeal affair.

At the molecular level, tribesmen of the central Atlas recognise the concept of 'good' fratricide, which is no concern of anyone outside the group of brothers among whom it concerned, and which consequently fully confirms to what one should expect from the abstract consideration. Cases of such fratricide are remembered.

On the other hand, there are ways in which the society diverges from the pure segmentary model. At the top, there is the concept of being a Muslim which can on occasion, and historically has, united or rather created groups of any size, well above the ceiling set by the existing stock of nested tribal names and groups. To engender such groups is not easy, and of course it helps if the opposition to such a group consists of infidels or heretics. The leaders who, throughout Moroccan history, succeeded in bringing about such supra-segmentary cohesion, were either religious reformers (during the mediaeval period) or persons possessing special Islamic holiness through descent from the Prophet (during the subsequent centuries).

At the molecular level, a non-segmentary principle can also be seen in operation in the concept of 'bad' fratricide, in the case of which the killing of the brother is held to be unjustifiable, and the larger group (village, clan) exacts compensation to itself from the 'bad' fratricide. What makes this unsegmentary is that the total group takes action against a part of itself for the maintenance of moral order: in the segmentary case, it is always one group which takes action against another, to defend itself against an infringement of the moral order directed at it.

'Good' fratricide, of a brother held to be a scoundrel, is of course liable to be not merely permissible, but laudatory and even obligatory. Take a brother whose misdeeds are not only a direct nuisance to his own brethren, but which are also liable to activate outside aggression against them by other groups, who will of course in this context only be able to revenge themselves on the brothers as a whole, not on the individual culprit. In such circumstances, killing a member of one's own kin-group may be the only way (one step more drastic than letting him down at the collective oath) of maintaining external peace. The occasions on which fratricide is *not* held to be an offence fit admirably into the segmentary pattern.

But a group can be activated by an offender within it and not merely by an opposed group outside, and it can take corporate action, qua groups, against a part of itself. This is un-segmentary behaviour. This can happen in the cases of offences other than fratricide. For instance, adultery may be expiated by a donation towards the group to which both adulterer and cuckold belong, and not just to the offended sub-group. The adulterer expiates by providing a feast for the group as a whole. Here a group is demanding and obtaining restitution for the violation of its moral order, rather than that a sub-group is obtaining restitution from another for a wrong suffered. Defence of the moral order as such, as opposed to defence of the group, is un-segmentary behaviour.

At the top, this society does possess devices for activating groups irrespective of whether a pre-existing notion of such a group (territorially or in terms of kinship) is available. One such device is the possibility of affiliation, which of course also operates at lower levels where pre-existing groups are available, and which is quite essential in facilitating re-alignments, the threat of which in turn is a necessary sanction of cohesion inside groups (e.g., when facing the ordeal of collective oath). But more important for our purposes is the leadership provided by the saints and the common sentiment of allegiance of Islam, which finds its expression in respect for the saints as descendants of the Prophet, and for their arbitration as (supposedly) *Shra'a* or divine law. (The general illiteracy has, until very recent years, obviated the danger of checking their pronouncements against documentary evidence of the divine law, i.e., the Koran.) Saintly leadership makes it possible, given the need and favourable circumstances, to weld together groups, particularly large-scale groups, which do not correspond to any of the groups latent in the segmentary system, or even groups which cut across them.

The saints themselves are also segmentary: but just as their services modify and indeed facilitate the pure operation of the segmentary principle amongst the lay tribes, so also its working is modified, in quite a different way which is to be described, amongst the saints themselves.

(3) Unilineal descent. The connection between this and the

notion of a segmentary system is not always wholly clear. In *Tribes without Rulers*,[1] a general and comparative account of this type of society, John Middleton and David Tait write:

... the essential features (of being segmentary) are the 'nesting' attribute of segmentary series and the characteristic of being in a state of continual segmentation and complementary opposition. The series may be one of lineages ... or it may be one of territorial groups ...

This seems to imply (rightly) that segmentation cannot be defined in terms of unilineal kinship, for the segmentation may be simply in territorial terms. Nevertheless I doubt whether the two – segmentation and unilineal kinship – can be wholly separated. The crucial defining characteristic of segmentary societies is not merely the presence of segmentation, but also the absence (or very nearly) of anything else. Hence it follows that kinship would either have to be unimportant, in the sense of not generating any significant social groups, or, if present and defining social groups, it must do so on lines parallel with the general principles of segmentation of the society. But it can only do this if it is tree-like in pattern, in other words if it is unilineal. It follows that, although a segmentary society need not be organised in lineages at all, it can be, at most, unilineal. Any more complicated kinship system would generate conflicting ties.

(4) Monadism: I use this term for one very interesting feature of segmentary societies: namely that groups of all the various sizes resemble or mirror each other's structure. The smaller group is an embryo tribe, the tribe is the smaller group writ large.[2]

I suspect that the presence of this characteristic is sometimes

[1] London, Routledge and Kegan Paul, 1958, p. 7.
[2] Professor E. E. Evans-Pritchard, in *African Political Systems* (edited by M. Fortes and E. E. Evans-Pritchard), p. 283:
'A tribal section has most of the attributes of a tribe: name, sense of patriotism, a dominant lineage, territorial distinction, economic resources, and so forth. Each is a tribe in miniature, and they differ from tribes only in size, in degree of integration, and in that they unite for war and acknowledge a common principle of justice.'
With Berbers the recognition of common principles of justice has no neat upper social ceiling. It is not quite clear from this passage how far down the scale of segmentation Professor Evans-Pritchard intends his assertion of similarity to extend: but granting a kind of formal similarity, and the importance of the fact that units of different sizes look similar and are conceptualised similarly by their members, it seems also important to stress the differences in function of groups of different sizes.

exaggerated, or alternatively that this may be a case of taking too literally a mode of conceptualisation which is indeed found within segmentary societies. For it is indeed true that the relationship between two large clans may, by the clansmen, be conceived as the relationship between two brothers, in virtue of the supposed descent of the two clans from two men who were brothers to each other. But in reality, the operations and functions of various sizes, at different levels of the segmentary system, is inevitably very different. The lowest groups are concerned with daily life, the next group with balance of power within the village, the village with preservation of its territory and fields, the wider clans with collective pastures, and wider groups still with the defence of the region as a whole: the types of concern which activate the groups at various points of the segmentary 'nested' scale are very different and call for different types of relationships and activities.[1] This fact emerges most clearly if one examines the consequences of the superimposition of a modern administration on a segmentary society: the higher-level groupings tend to wither away, whilst those at the lower end of the scale continue to function vigorously. All the same it is true that in a segmentary society, large and small groups resemble each other far more closely than they do in non-segmentary societies. In complex societies, the state or the city are quite unlike the family. In a segmentary tribe, there is a resemblance between the tribe or clan on the one hand and the family on the other, not merely in terminology, but also in reality.

Density of Segmentation

An intriguing area for comparative research is this: what determines the number of steps in a segmentary system, the number of nested units? Or in other words, given an Occamist genealogy in which ancestors are not multiplied beyond necessity, what determines the number of necessary ancestors? Various possibilities arise:

(a) That the number of steps in the system depends on the

---

[1] For instance: disputes between small groups tend to be focused on some one personality, and co-jurors in collective oaths are selected by agnatic proximity to that personality. Disputes between large groups are different: they tend not to have a person as their focus, and co-jurors are in effect selected representatives rather than co-responsible agnates. Interestingly, these representatives are liable to be selected by the opposing group rather than by the group they represent.

number of common interests-bonds, each step corresponding to a shared interest. The lowest group is a set of people who are liable to inherit from each other and have priority over each others' daughters, for instance: the next group might be one sharing a continuous stretch of irrigated land and hence sharing a joint stake in the defence of it and its water-rights, the next group might be one corresponding to the joint use of an extended pasture, and so on.

(b) Shared interests, by generating a group, may also generate segmentation downwards: if, for instance, a group X is generated by shared rights in a pasture, then the self-administration of X, given that it is a segmentary society, also requires that there be sub-groups of X which should balance each other in the internal running of X, irrespective of whether these sub-groups themselves also correspond to some natural shared interest in the local ecology.

(c) Possibly the steps or nestings are determined simply by the need of a certain density of them: a ladder is not a ladder unless the rungs are reasonably close to each other. This could be simply a matter of definition: a 'segmentary' society (in other respects) with only very few nested steps might simply fail to be classified as such.

But perhaps there is more to it than that: it is difficult to see how a society with very few nestings – say a large tribe with only one step between the total tribe and the extended family – could possibly function as a segmentary society, that is to say maintain some degree of order by means of the balancing of groups. There would only be a large number of small sub-groups belonging to a large one, but not organised in any intermediate groups. Hence, if any conflict arose involving more than two of the minute groups, but less than the total groups, there would be no pre-arranged alignments to keep the peace through 'balance'. The number of possible alignments would be too great and too unpredictable. Either such a society would not function at all and be genuinely anarchic, or some principle other than segmentary fusion and fission would be involved. So one may argue that just as, for instance, a physical inverted pyramid of acrobats requires that the 'expansion' from the solitary man at the apex on the ground to the n men at the top, should be by gradual steps leading from *one* to n, so a segmentary system can only work if the multiplication of segments at any one level is not too great. (This argument is in a way a generalisation of argument (b).)

This point can be put in another way: The question of the density of nesting is connected with the important feature of segmentary societies: in such a society, one does not simply belong to a group, one has a definite position in it, a niche. (And this does not mean, of course, what it would mean in our context: it does not mean that the society is stratified and one belongs to some stratum nor does it mean occupational specialisation. Indeed, segmentary societies are often fairly unstratified and without much occupational specialisation.) These niches are located vertically, as it were, and not horizontally, and in a social rather than a geographical space (though the two have a certain limited correspondence, the nature of which varies a great deal). A Berber's niche is located by inquiring after the identity of his co-jurors, who are those who will be called to account for his acts, and vice versa, and with whom he shares inheritance expectations (unless he is an accepted stranger) and rights over brides. When as an exile or for some other reasons he has to settle in a new location, the first thing to do – they point out and stress – is to find co-jurors. A procedure exists for placing a shame-compulsion on a group to admit a member in this way.

It is a feature, perhaps a defining one, of segmentary society that it pre-arranges (but does not fully pre-determine) what in fact are alliances (and thus in principle products of human volition), in terms of real or putative facts about kinship, or sometimes in terms of territorial allocation.

The game differs from some international free-for-all in that there are 'natural allies' and that the rules are biased in favour of honouring these natural alliances. At the same time, the game also presupposes that they will not always be honoured, that the option of re-alignment exists and that it is sometimes advantageous to take it.

The need for 'density' of nested segments arises from the need for pre-arranged alliance. Suppose nesting not to be dense, so that from a large group one descends immediately to, say, thirty-two sub-groups. If conflict arises within the larger group, and no pre-arranged alliances, expressed in terms of special joint rights and in terms of kinship myths exist, the possibility of manœuvre in seeking alliances is so great as to make the situation excessively unstable. Hence, if stability-without-government is to obtain – and this I take to be a central characteristic of segmentary societies – it is essential that there be some further step or steps between the *one* and the *thirty-two*.

Of course, there are tribes, in other ways segmentary, where there is such a great jump from one to thirty-two do occur.[1] But then they have, and needs must have, a permanent reasonably strong leadership, a politically specialised and elevated sub-group, and to this extent they then are not purely segmentary, in that the relationship of this sub-group to the rest cannot be simply explained in terms of 'balance'. Central Atlas Berbers are more purely segmentary in this sense, and manage to avoid the use of specialised permanent power-holders within tribes, in a way to be described. Correspondingly, nesting is dense. There are no big leaps between rungs on this ladder.

(d) The precise extent and density of segmentation may in part genuinely depend on historical factors. There are amongst Berbers, for instance, phenomena which strongly suggest this: the survival of small groups or even mere families who 'structurally', in terms of the genealogy, have the position of clans and ideally should balance a whole populous clan, as its ancestor was a brother of the ancestor of that populous clan, thus making the two groups co-ordinate on the genealogy. But in reality, demographic inequality forces the small group to act as a sub-part of the larger one with which, genealogically, it could claim parity. Demography and genealogy may diverge, and the former will generally prevail: and the genealogy is not always 'manipulated' so as to make the situation neat and symmetrical. There is indeed often a good motive for clinging to positions in genealogical systems which have effectively lapsed; such retained positions imply claims which it may be impolitic or impracticable to assert at the time, or even for the foreseeable future, but which one day it may be opportune to re-activate. Perhaps Berbers are not unique in clinging to more or less dormant claims, ready for re-assertion should the time come (like the alleged custom of some Fez families of retaining the keys of their houses in Granada, ready for the day when the expulsion of Muslims is reversed). A step in the segmentary ladder, a nested group, may be kept in being not by a present shared interest, but by a past one, coupled with the possibility that it may one day become an effective one again.

---

[1] I have two examples in mind, one from Iran and the other from Arabia, and I am indebted to Dr Fredrik Barth and to Mr Al Faour of the Fadl tribe for this information.

Self-maintaining Order and Disorder

There are some other crucial questions about segmentary society in general. One is, how efficient is in fact this balancing mechanism? A sceptic might well object that the idea of a beautiful natural equilibrium looks too good to be true: what prevents it toppling over? The answer is that in fact it does frequently topple over. The segmentary mechanism has some efficacy, but in part its 'functioning' is a kind of optical illusion: when it fails, when it does topple over, the subsequent arrangement comes once again to exemplify the same pattern as obtained before the break-down: what other pattern is available? The participants may lack the concepts or customs required for anything more elaborate (whilst those of segmentary organisation are easily available to them), and in any case, a segmentary organisation is a kind of minimum of what can be re-established: anything more would require not merely the break-down of the previous equilibrium but positive inventiveness and great effort. If the surrounding area is segmentary, the pattern has an obvious tendency to spread, by a kind of imperative emulation: either combine like us or join us! (Or both!) The result is the same. So, in all but the name of the groups, and possibly even in name, the old order is re-established.

So as to work at all, the system also must not work too well. (The same will be seen to hold in connection with a specialised application of the system, the legal procedure of collective oath.) The driving force behind the cohesion of the groups is fear, fear of aggression by others in an anarchic environment. If the balancing system really worked perfectly, producing a kind of perpetual peaceful balance of power at all levels, the society would cease to be anarchic, and fear would cease to be a powerful spring of action. (It would be too much to expect people to be motivated by a distant memory or awareness of the theoretical possibility of anarchy.) In this, most unlikely, contingency, we might perhaps find ourselves with a perfect anarchist (but not 'anarchic') society without constraint or violence, in which both violence and government were absent – but not with a segmentary society. The persistence of a segmentary society requires, paradoxically, that its mechanisms should be sufficiently inefficient to keep fear in being as the sanction of the system.

Equality

A further and crucial question is, to what extent are segmentary systems, by definition, egalitarian?[1] To what extent must it be equal segments that balance? In fact, societies which in some ways may plausibly be described as segmentary are not always egalitarian and unstratified.[2]

Nevertheless, it seems to me desirable to regain egalitarianism in the definition of segmentary society, or at any rate of a pure segmentary society, for the following reason: in as far as inegalitarian and/or unsymmetrical relationships exist and are sustained in a society, it can hardly be the segmentary principle alone which is responsible for sustaining them, for keeping them in being. Indeed, these unsymmetrically related groups may have a tree-like structure internally, and they may even be incorporated in a wider 'tree'; and, moreover, the opposition of segments at each level may be a factor, amongst others, in maintaining the tree. Nevertheless, the asymmetries themselves cannot be explained in this way, at least not without qualification. 'Segmentary' explanations always cut both ways: asymmetrical relationships are those which do *not* cut both ways.[3] Hence asymmetrical, inegalitarian relationships cannot be explained by segmentation alone!

However, segmentary systems are seldom if ever pure. The

[1]Middleton and Tait (p. 8) observe that Durkheim's use of the term 'segmentary' is different from the one relevant here. But there does seem to me to be an essential connection between the two uses (though perhaps Middleton and Tait do not wish to deny this), through the notion of non-specialisation and repetition contained in Durkheim's concept. These entail, the egalitarianism which is also essential for the mechanics of a 'segmentary' society in the current sense. If specialisation of groups – politically or economically or ritually – occurs, they cannot simply 'balance' each other, but their complementarity gives rise to a new factor of cohesion; conversely, if they do simply balance each other, they cannot be specialised.

[2]Cf. E.E. Leach: *Political Systems of Highland Burma*. 1954, p. 288.

[3]Professor E.E.Evans-Pritchard makes a similar point, in connection with the Bedouin of Cyrenaica who, unlike the Berbers, do have permanent heads of segments (*The Sanusi of Cyrenaica*, Oxford, 1949, p. 59): 'The tribal system, typical of segmentary structures everywhere, is a system of balanced opposition ... and there cannot therefore be any single authority in a tribe. Authority is distributed at every point of the tribal structure and political leadership is limited to situations in which a tribe or segment acts corporately ... There cannot, obviously, be any absolute authority vested in a single Shaikh of a tribe when the fundamental principle of tribal structure is opposition between its segments ...'

'pure' ideal type is useful primarily in highlighting the kinks and unevennesses of real segmentary societies. Some of these may require extraneous factors for their emergence, others may be precipitated, as it were, out of the even, undifferentiated texture through its own needs without an initial asymmetry. This is the case with the 'saints', who are a kind of uneven excrescence in a segmentary society.

What accounts for the asymmetries? One must distinguish between the explanation of why they are there at all, what mechanisms sustain them and what needs they satisfy, and the explanation of why they arise at the particular points of the society at which in fact they are found. The latter type of explanation might be thought particularly difficult, in as far as a segmentary society is, by definition, symmetrical. What reasons could be found within a symmetrical society for an asymmetry? If all clans are like, why should just this or that segment turn itself into (say) a holy one, unlike the others?

This problem is not as serious as it may sound when formulated in the abstract. The main thing is to answer the first question – why the society needs this or that asymmetry at all, what needs and mechanisms will sustain this or that asymmetrical institution. Such an explanation would not necessarily require an account of the first appearance and origin of the institution; but when (as in this case) the account of the functioning of it also includes an account of how the institutions ensures its own diffusion, then the explanations of origins (at least of individual instances, if not of the very idea of the institution as such), and the explanation of how it is sustained, are one. The normal functioning of the institution includes its own reproduction and diffusion.

When this question is answered (when we know why the society has saints at all), the second question, of the form – why just *here* and not *there*? – would not be so important. Societies are not like Buridan's ass, paralysed by a totally symmetrical situation which excludes the possibility of a reason for this rather than that (for in the case of that unhappy animal, every reason favouring the left bundle of hay was paralleled, ex hypothesi, by a similarly strong reason for the right bundle). In fact, as will emerge, it is possible in this case to give reasons not merely why saints should flourish at all, but why they should flourish in the very locations in which they are found.

Disposition and Process

Segmentation denotes both a process or episode on the one hand, and a condition or disposition on the other. When a previously joint family one day splits up into separate units based on each of the hitherto 'undivided' brothers, or if a large tribe acquires a new piece of territory distant from its previous habitat, and a part of it goes off to settle there, these are definite, concrete, dateable events. This is an episode or process. On the other hand, two segments of a tribe, or two related families, can also live in a permanent state of 'segmentation': that is, they simultaneously keep each other in check by mutual hostility, and yet also ward off outside aggression by being ever ready to combine in defence against it. This is a permanent condition: it is not necessarily manifest in any one dateable action. Its manifestations are manifold, and may even remain latent rather than visible.

Men in general have a difficulty in conceptualising such latent, discontinuous, dispositional states, and tend to think of them as somehow permanent and substantial. One way of doing this is to invent some mystic quality which is conceived as permanently present, thus conferring permanence and substantiality on a disposition which, at the phenomenal level of events, is discontinuous or even erratic. Segmentary societies do not necessarily take this path: they do so if they are also 'totemic', and explain the relationship of various clans to each other in terms of a permanent mystic relationship between clan members and totemic animals. Berber tribes are of course not totemic.[1] They employ the other method available for conceptualising a social relationship: they conceive it as hinging on a specific and concrete past event. The fact that two large groups are in a friendly, 'fraternal' relationship to each other, is conceived to be the consequence of their being the descendants of two men who were brothers. A supposed past concrete event – cohabitation and subsequent separation of two brothers and their families – symbolises a present dispositional, permanent relationship of two large groups.

At this point, it is essential to note an asymmetry between large

---

[1]Some slight traces of totemism can be found. There is a Panther segment of the Ihansalen settled among the Ait Bu Iknifen of Talmest. There is also a Jackal clan. But the use of an animal name does not in these cases lead to any totemic practices.

and small groups. In the case of small groups, the concrete episodic symbol and the discontinuous dispositional reality are congruent. The symbolism tends to be veridical. Two related families have 'fraternal' ties, and often, in reality, two now deceased grandfathers were in fact brothers and really did once have a joint household which subsequently divided in a peaceful manner. In other words, the belief not merely ratifies a present set of relationships, but also (in many typical cases) is literally true.

In the case of large groups, the matter is more complex. If a tribe divides through the acquisition of new territory and its settlement by some of its members, it is unlikely (supposing the tribe to have two sub-clans, *A* and *B*) that all members of one clan will go to the new territory, and all members of the other will stay behind in the old. It is far more likely that some from each clan will go, some will stay. Thus the actual process of large-group fission does not correspond to the neat parting-of-brothers image. The real process (the parting of large numbers of people, drawn from both clans, now) does not correspond to the symbolic process (two brothers-ancestors parting long ago), which is invoked to explain dispositional reality, and the non-correspondence is more than merely a matter of the symbolic event, high up the genealogy, being simplified, and of reducing the number of dramatic personae. Stories about brothers can and do correctly, though selectively, account for what really happened to small groups, but they are very likely to distort more fundamentally the true story of what happens to large ones. At both levels, they can correctly 'symbolise' the *disposition*: brothers oppose each other but combine against outsiders, and this is indeed true, both of fraternal families and of fraternal clans or tribes. But only at one level (that of small-scale groups), does the story about brothers also correctly represent what actually happened at the historical point of fission. Two fraternal families are in fact generally descended from two brothers who one day decided to separate their households: but two parts of a tribe, settled in two distinct areas, say two valleys, are not in fact descended from two brothers who, as single households, went to each of the two valleys in question. And, more important, it is not even the case that the territorial division between the two valleys corresponds to the division of the tribe into two clans prior to the occupation of the second valley (if, in fact, such expansion did occur historically). For if a tribe conquers new territory, it is generally not the case that all members of one clan occupy it, whilst all members of the other stay at home: more plausibly, the spoils are shared, and some members of each clan go to the newly acquired lands. With time, this may, but need not, be obscured by the formation of two new top-level clans, corresponding to the new territorial division but supposing themselves to date back to some original pair of brothers.

The memory of what 'really happened' (i.e., what I believe truly happened) is moreover perpetuated in many of the larger tribal groups by current genealogical belief. A large tribe (e.g., the Ait Atta, or the Ait Daud u Ali of the Ait Sochman) will possess a number of sub-clans, say *A*, *B*, *C*, *D* and *E*. The total tribe possesses territory in two or more areas. Each of the sub-clans will possess lands and pasture rights in both areas (as is the case with the Ait Daud u Ali) or in *all* the numerous areas (as is the case with the Ait Atta). Why so? It seems to me that an explanation can be offered both in terms of 'true history' and in terms of the continued and contemporary usefulness of the associated beliefs and institutions. Historically, when a tribe acquires new lands, it can only do so by a joint effort in which a number of clans co-operate, and when the new land is acquired, each of the participant clans claims its share of the territorial booty, and none is willing to give up its original lands. Hence fission takes place cutting across each of the old clans: henceforth, territorial division cuts across the old clan lines (as indeed is conspicuously the case with the two tribes cited).

But a functional explanation in terms of the current usefulness of the division, is also available. Once the arrangement exists, a motive exists for the tribe as a whole to perpetuate it, and moreover, sanctions also exist causing each sub-group to toe the line. Suppose a tribe to possess two or more distinct frontiers (i.e., frontiers with diverse other tribes and potential enemies), as it virtually always does: if each clan is represented on each frontier, this increases sanctions making for cohesion of the tribe as a whole. If conflict breaks out at a frontier distant from a given tribesman or face-to-face group, a conflict which does not constitute an immediate threat to the individual or group in question, then not merely the abstract and high-level obligation of tribal loyalty, but also the more concrete and lower-level obligation of clan-loyalty calls them to action. And what is to sustain even this more concrete clan-loyalty? Not, indeed, unaided sentiment. The call of the blood is sustained, roughly, by pasture rights, inheritance expectations, and rights to brides.

Pasture rights are possibly the most important of these factors, or at least constitute a consideration which, in the ecological conditions prevailing in the Atlas, even in principle (unlike inheritance and preferential bride-right, the other factors) is not liable to erosion by time and the passage of generations. It hinges on ecological differentiation. In the case of both the tribes mentioned, tribal lands range over areas suitable as pasture at quite different seasons or under different conditions. The land of the Ait Atta is particularly striking in this respect, ranging from the scorched Sahara edge to the highest regularly snow-covered plateau grasslands on the north side of the Atlas watershed. A tribesman knows that he may need the distant pastures in which he has a stake and which are guarded by his clan brethren, when, in due course, snow or drought, as the case may be, will render his nearby pasture useless. Such conditions may render him particularly sensitive to the call of the blood, when he hears that his geographically distant brethren are being threatened (notwithstanding the fact that, blood or not, he patently wishes his cousins to the devil when they in turn come to share his own pastures, when their flocks trespass on his fields, and particularly when, under modern political conditions, he no longer needs their aid to guard his frontier). The Ait Atta are a tribe occupying particularly extensive and diversified territory, and their legends bear testimony to the danger of failure of cohesion between distant territorial groups, unless each clan (in terms of whom pasture rights are defined) is represented at each frontier. Each clan is also represented at the territorial centre. The Ait Atta segmentation and chieftaincy system is double: clan and territorial considerations are, as it were, shot through. A chief-of-the-land (amghar n'tamazirt) is elected by each territorial group, by rotation-and-complementarity (see below, p. 81) amongst the locally represented clans; but if a threat to the total tribe activates the institution of chieftaincy for the Ait Atta as a whole, the upper chief is elected by rotation and complementarity in terms not of the territorial sub-divisions, but of clan-subdivisions.

Not all the tribes within the Ahansal sanctity catchment area exhibit variants of this type of pattern. Other tribal types can be found. Those tribes inhabiting fairly compact territory, especially if it is a distant valley or valley-system, may not need territorially discontinuous clans. For instance, the Ait Bu Gmez do not even possess a genealogical theory to account for their larger units, and hence could not have a cross-cutting system even if they wished: at the level of the larger units, they only possess territorial groups anyway. Also the Ait Bu Gmez are agriculturalists above all, and diversified pasture rights would not in their case constitute such an important social cement. The Ait Messat possess a fairly compact valley system, though not an alluvial one like that of Bu Gmez; but their territory is not ecologically diversified, and their clans are territorially compact. The Ait Mhand possess territory not clearly delimited by natural features, and not rich agriculturally; but they seem to be a fairly 'new' and ad hoc tribe, without belief in a common origin, and the clans they possess could hardly afford to be discontinuous – each needs contiguity to establish such cohesion as it can muster.

Fission and Fusion

A father may have two sons, but no son can have two fathers. It follows that a segmentary and patrilineal society, which mostly conceives of relationships between its own sub-groups in genealogical terms, borrowed from paternity alone, possesses notions through which it can express fission, but none for fusion. This, of course, creates no difficulty with respect to segmentation as a condition. The condition is timeless. When it needs to symbolise the union of the group, it goes back to the shared and distant granddad, and when it wishes to highlight internal dis-unity, it looks to the plurality of brothers or grandsons in the subsequent generations. It is not time which is a moving image of eternity: it is timeless genealogy which is a static image of social movement. But there would seem to be no concepts which would characterise fusion as a definite, dateable process.

Yet fusion plainly does occur. On the rough assumption of a stability of population and unchanging density of segmentation, at any one level of size, the number of fissions, minus the number of extinctions of lines, must equal the number of fusions. We have no means of establishing the truth of the assumption of stability of population or segmentary density, but something roughly of that kind must presumably have held for at least some periods during the traditional order. Moreover, there is also plenty of direct evidence of the occurrence of fusions. To assume that they did not occur would lead us to postulate an absurd and phenomenal rate of population growth in recent centuries, as implicit in the tribal genealogies (were these taken at face value). How is fusion conceptualised?

One can assert as a general principle about Berber society that whenever one finds a relationship, it will be based either on a belief about kinship, or on a prestation, or both. Either a kin link or a 'sacrifice to' a person or group is the ratification of obligation. A person or group wishing to re-allocate itself on the tree of alignments will make a sacrifice of an animal to the desired new group, thereby placing it under an obligation to receive it. It is asserted that such an act places the recipient under an obligation, and that the receiving group cannot refuse the request. I certainly have not heard of such a request being refused, notwithstanding the undisputed fact that certain quarrelsome and litigious people, who frequently re-allocate themselves by this method in the intra-village structure of co-juring and hence co-responsible groups, are a well-known nuisance. Re-allocation, it should be added, can, but need not, involve physical transplantation: an individual can re-align himself in a village, or a whole clan can re-align itself with another tribe (as one of the clans of the Ait Isha aligned itself with the Ait Mhand), without any physical movement being involved. On the other hand, if an individual or family seek a new niche in a new tribe, obviously they must migrate.

It is not quite clear why nuisance re-alignments within a village should be tolerated by the receiving group. In fact they are, and locally it is explained simply in terms of moral obligation, of shame-compulsion. Possibly part of the answer is that the time to let down the unwelcome new ally – if such he is – is at the next conflict and collective oath, and that this helps to explain why the procedure of collective oath is not always pre-determined in favour of the testifying party (see below, p. 104). In the case of re-alignment of large groups, or the migration of small ones or single individuals, the answer is more obvious: one is receiving a new ally, a free reinforcement. Note that in the central High Atlas, (unlike possibly the Western High Atlas or parts of the Anti-Atlas), population pressure had not reached the point of saturation:

there was still more land, notably forest, which could be tilled, and by and large the property of a group was not so much what they owned but what they could cultivate and what they could defend. (Individual settlements might well reach saturation. For instance, the main lodge of the Ihansalen tended to find new homes for refugees from feuds who sought its sanctuary, rather than absorb them itself.)

The main motive for individual migration was, of course, homicide and the feud, a flight from the avengers. As one travels around the villages of the areas, one comes not infrequently across individuals who either underwent such a transplantation in their youth, or are offsprings of such immigrants. It is said that if you flee from a feud within group *A*, whose member you are, the best place to flee *to* is the general enemies of *A*. Far from taking their own vengeance on the refugee, they will apparently welcome a recruit who now can be relied on to be loyal, for his way home is barred. In effect, it is possible to 'choose freedom' by fleeing to the enemy, even though in this society the enemy is not differentiated ideologically. In the days of the French, such migratory flights ceased to be customary. Larger groups were not allowed to indulge in collective violence, and individual murderers, if caught, found involuntary sanctuary in prison. (The institution of blood money continued, tribal customary law continuing to be valid, and the tribesmen assimilated imprisonment to the exile which had previously been imposed on the murderer, unless the victim's family agreed to forego it.) On the other hand, the game of intra-village re-alignment, involving no physical transplantation, went on.

Given this possibility of, as it were, 'naturalisation' in a new group, independently of kinship belief and contrary to systems of alliances, one might ask whether the whole idea of a segmentary structure is not a myth, whether in fact the society is not much more fluid than the neat tree-like patterns of group genealogy and alignment would suggest. Such a conclusion would be quite mistaken. Berber society of the central High Atlas may not be totally rigid – birth and kinship do not hold the individual in an iron vice – but it is certainly not very fluid. This is emphatically not one of the societies in which a floating population settles in variable patterns around a framework defined in 'segmentary' terms. In any one village, the proportion of male immigrants will be under ten per cent, usually well under this ratio. People do not re-allocate themselves to the point of migration unless they must (usually because of homicide). Berber society really is agnatic throughout: it is not a case of cognatic clusters around an agnatic skeleton. The odd uxorilocal family does turn up, but it is fairly rare, and the practice is held to be dishonourable.[1] The immigrants, 'people of the sacrifice' (u tighsi), do gain new co-jurors, but they are significantly located at the bottom of the line of jurors. In general, inheritance expectations at home and the disadvantages of immigrant status in the new community, are sufficient to discourage any easy and frequent mobility between geographically distinct groups.

Leaving aside individual migrations, how weighty is the segmentary structure in the life of the society at large? Some indication can be obtained by looking either at the way in which tribal groups come to pay homage to the saints, or at the way in which they resisted or submitted to the French or, for that matter, at their comportment in post-Independence party politics or during the one rising in the region since Independence.

We find that policy decisions do not necessarily follow the cleavages of the segmentary structure. Nothing would be more erroneous than to see the tribesmen enslaved in thought and deed to their clans, unable to weigh consequences or to act independently. But it would be equally wrong to disregard the ordered hierarchy of tribal groups as some kind of decorative elaboration, without weight when the moment of political decision comes. The segmentary organisation displays a set of alignments, ratified not merely by custom, sentiment and ritual, but more weightily by shared interests which provides the baseline for alliances and enmities, for aid and hostility, when conflict arises. Calculation, feeling, new interests, diplomatic ingenuity, may at times cause the final alignments to depart at some points: but the initial and fairly strong presumption is that allegiances of tribe and clan will be honoured, and that other inducements must have been operative if they were not honoured.

---

[1]Some Middle Atlas tribes institutionalise a special status, which conflates that of uxorilocal husband and client-labourer (of his wife's patrilineage). Cf. Cmmdt. R.Aspinion, *Contribution à Él'tude du Droit Coutumier Berbère Morocain,* 2nd Edition, A. Moynier, Casablanca and Fes, 1946, p. 153.

The Relevance of Segmentation

The organisation of the Berber tribes of Central Morocco is of a theoretical interest for a number of reasons. Roughly speaking, there are two scholarly traditions to which their study is relevant: previous studies of North African societies, and the tradition of 'structural' analyses in social anthropology. In the past, these two traditions were sometimes insulated from each other. This is no longer true.

From the viewpoint of structural social anthropology, the interest of Berber society is that it provides an exceptionally good specimen of the segmentary principle, of the maintenance of political order over extensive areas, large populations and diversified and complementary ecologies, without much in the way of a concentration of power, a centralised state. In many ways, the segmentary principle operates among them with remarkable purity: Berbers are not stratified into aristocrats and commoners, clans do not possess permanently dominant sheikhly families, the pattern of preferred (parallel patrilateral) marriage merely reinforces the patrilineal structure and does not create any cross-cutting links, the elective and rotated nature of leadership prevents it from congealing into a stratification of wealth or power, the genealogies tend to be Occamist and serve the segmentary structure and no more, the steps of segmentation are dense enough to avoid the need of other principles. From this viewpoint, my main argument is that this relative segmentary purity of the lay tribes is made possible by the saints: these inegalitarian, stratified, pacific, 'artificial' outsiders perform functions which enable the egalitarian, feud-addicted tribesmen to work their remarkably pure segmentary system. Here, a separation of powers is not merely a check on tyranny, as intended in classical political theory, but also a check on inequality. The inegalitarian potential of the society is as it were drained by the saints. Here, at least, equality and liberty go together.

In relation to previous studies of North African societies, the present argument can be seen from a different angle. In modern times, the truly outstanding analysis of Berber politics is to be found, as stated, in the studies of Robert Montagne.[1] If his work,

[1] *Les Berbères et le Makhzen au Sud du Maroc*, 1930. *La Vie sociale et la Vie politique des Berbères*, 1931.

rich in ideas and documentation, can be summed up briefly at all, it would be as follows. First, the main order-maintaining institution amongst anarchic Berbers is a special kind of society, of internal bifurcation – the *leff*. Secondly, Berber society tends to oscillate between two social forms – egalitarian tribal republics, governed by assemblies (or hierarchies of assemblies) and using the leff system, and ephemeral personal tyrannies, exemplified in our time by the great caids of the South. The inherent instability of the republics and the leffs leads from time to time to the crystallisation of personal power: this, however, does not produce anything like a stable 'feudal' system (the suggestive appearance of the castles of the great robber chiefs notwithstanding), but on the contrary, in due course collapses again, and returns to the previous condition. Thus Montagne put forward a remarkable structural analysis not of a stable system, but of a permanently oscillating one, rather reminiscent in some of its general features of the theory put forward later by Dr Edmund Leach for the political systems of Highland Burma.[1]

Robert Montagne was fully aware of a certain significant exception to his theory of political oscillation: the 'maraboutic states', the hagiarchies, such as that of the Ihansalen. His remarks en passant about these quasistates are perceptive and accurate. His observations about Zawiya Ahansal are all the more remarkable in as far as Ahansal-land proper was unconquered at the time he did his study, and no European had visited Zawiya Ahansal itself. In one way, the present study simply fills in the details concerning this exception, the general characteristics of which he fully understood. The maraboutic state provides an exception, above all, by its stability: there was no oscillation, and the general political system of the tribes of the central High Atlas enabled them to escape the temporary personal tyrannies. It is curious to reflect that this hagiarchy inverts Max Weber's famous definition of the state: here we have a state, if we are to class it as such, *in which it is the subjects who have the monopoly of legitimate violence, and the rulers were ex officio excluded from employing force.*

I have no particular comments on Montagne's oscillation theory. I believe it to be true; but study of a recognised exception to it does not specially qualify one to discuss it. His remarks about this exception, which is the subject of this study, seem to me

[1]*Political Systems of Highland Burma*, London, 1954, 1964.

admirable. But I do have reservations concerning this theory of the leffs. These doubts about the leffs are both empirical and theoretical. The former are less interesting, but still worth mentioning.

By leffs, Montagne meant systems of alliance which were territorially discontinuous in a chess-board-like manner, and which were what I should call 'transitive': if tribal group A was of the same leff alliance as B, and B as C, then A and C belonged to the same leff. Montagne believed he could trace these chequerboard patterns in the Western High Atlas and elsewhere. It may, however, be significant that the one intensive study carried out in that very region since his day led its author to conclude that the tribe studied, the Seksawa, did not fit into the leff system.[1]

Whatever may be the case elsewhere, no leff system in Montagne's sense existed in the central High Atlas. The tribesmen do indeed know and use the word: but it means simply 'alliance'. (By a characteristic quirk, the same root also means the opposite – division and divorce, and the same root also does service for marital divorce. This ambivalence of meaning is, of course, perfectly logical, especially in a segmentary setting: what is an alliance, a union, at one level, is from the viewpoint of the next higher level a division, a separation.) But alliances are not transitive, nor permanent, and they certainly do not form any chessboard pattern. If such a system existed, it would have to complement and cut across the segmentary structure: but it does not exist. Alliances do take place and links are established in addition to the segmentary alignment, but these additions form no system. Moreover, it is not possible to interpret the segmentary division itself as a leff system in that sense: the number *two* has no pre-eminence. Sometimes, indeed, tribal groups, large or small, divide into two segments; but just as characteristically, they may subdivide differently, into (say) three or five sub-clans.[2]

So much for the empirical disagreement. The theoretical one is more important. Suppose that the leff system does exist, and is of crucial importance in maintaining order, through the balance of power between the two *ilfuf* (plural of leff). The two moieties can

---

[1] J. Berque: *Structures Sociales du Haut-Atlas,* (PUF, Paris, 1955).

[2] It is only fair to put on record a disagreement on this point. Cf. Georges Drague: *Esquisse d'Histoire Religieuse du Maroc*, p. 174. General Spillman (who used 'Drague' as a pen-name) in conversation with me confirmed his position on this point.

only maintain order with respect to conflicts *at the level of segmentation* at which the discontinuous, chequerboard alliance happens to be found. Suppose that the units composing the leff are villages: then, indeed, the leff may keep peace when inter-village strife arises, for each of two quarrelsome villages may invoke its own leff, and the balance of power between the two may make for peace, or indeed, cause the conflict to spread.[1] But suppose there is conflict *inside* a village, between two sub-clans; or suppose that a pasture-sharing *group* of villages need to defend an adjoining pasture. (If the leff is articulated in terms of villages and is discontinuous, the adjoining villages cannot be of the same moiety. If the leff system is articulated in terms of larger units, the same argument applies to those units.) In brief, unlike the notion of segmentation, the notion of one-level moiety simply isn't strong enough to account for the relative maintenance of order in an ungoverned society. (It can only control conflicts arising at the one level of segmentation, in terms of which it is itself articulated.) It can only be made to appear to do more, by a surreptitious and unconscious assumption that something like centralised or specialised agencies (chiefs or assemblies, presumably) operate and maintain order at levels other than that of the moiety. In fact, however, though chiefs and assemblies do exist, and indeed conspicuously exist at more than one level of size (this is shared ground), the mechanism of order-maintenance is not all that different at the various levels. If conflicts are contained at the levels other than those at which the leff is drawn up, then the leff is not essential at the one level where it does exist.

All this does not exclude the possibility of permanent chequerboard alliances in some regions: in highly sedentarised ones such as the Western High Atlas, it is not implausible. (In the central High Atlas, the migratory traditions and opportunities of the tribes make such a system less likely.) But it shows that, even if and where it exists, it is not the crux of the matter: it is only relevant to one level of segmentation, and it is only one further, albeit intriguing, kink and variant in the segmentary structure, which is itself the crucial order-maintaining institution.

[1]Cf. André Adam, *La Maison et le Village dans quelques Tribus de l'Anti-Atlas*, Paris, 1951, p. 41, 'C'est la vieille querelle autour des alliances: empêchent-elles la guerre ou la rendent-elles fatale? On en disante encore ... La mission des leffs semble plutôt avoir été d'interdire l'écrasement ou l'anéantissement d'une *taqbilt* par une autre. Dans l'ensemble, ils l'ont parfaitement remplie'.

Thus the interest of the saints is manifold. From one viewpoint, they are the clue to the maintenance of a remarkably pure, symmetrical and egalitarian segmentary system. From another, they are a clue to a certain political stability within anarchy, to the absence of the periodic lapse into tyranny which Montagne saw elsewhere. From another viewpoint still, they show how complex ecological interdependence of largish populations can function without any centralised administration endowed with means of enforcement. From another viewpoint still, they show how mountain tribesmen can embrace a scriptural religion without being able to read, and can yet opt out from a centralised state which is legitimated by that religion, without appearing to be heretics.

The Problem Restated

Initially, the problem was stated as concerning the existence and the nature of a hagiarchy, or rule by hereditary saints. Was there, in the central High Atlas, something describable as a state, based on the religious prestige of *baraka*-possessing holy lineages?

This formulation is perfectly legitimate. A visitor to the central High Atlas would be assured, and in the past could have observed, the *igurramen*, possessors of *baraka*, are held worthy of reverence and with it of obedience; he would have noticed that baraka is highly concentrated, more so than its explanation in terms of descent would warrant, but in a way conducive to the effective concentration of influence; he would be assured by the igurramen that they appoint the annual secular chieftains (though he might notice that this is a misleading exaggeration), that they are the supreme court of the region, and that they communicate the unique *Shra'a*, Koranic legislation (though again the visitor might have his doubts about the accuracy of this claim). He would, in turn, be puzzled by some features of this 'state', such as the lack of clear boundaries, the fact that it has more than one capital and centre of power, that its citizens may have multiple allegiances within and without its boundaries, sometimes depending on the season, and so forth.

But the visitor might approach the region not with the categories of political theory in mind, but simply with an interest in kinship and segmentary organisation. A different set of phenomena would then strike him, notably that two different types of organisation are to be found, though both are patrilineal and segmentary. He would find holy and lay villages and lineages, and a tendency towards the following correlations:

Lay groups tend to be symmetrical and egalitarian; larger tribal groups tend to occupy continuous territory, they revere shrines of saints who are not their own ancestors, their own genealogies are roughly Occamist, and their segmentation is dense enough to satisfy the requirements as discussed above, but no more; there is a fairly strong tendency to endogamy, but the tribesmen make no claims to asymmetrical rights (e.g., to import but not to export brides).

Holy groups, on the other hand, display an inegalitarian organisation, with uneven and sometimes very sharp concentrations of wealth and prestige (particularly the latter), an unsymmetrical kinship system, with some groups (the prestigious ones) appearing to have more ancestors than their other kinsmen (or lay tribesmen), thus providing a kind of genealogically rich spinal column with poorer, shorter branches sprouting off it. As their genealogies are richer, the nesting is sometimes denser and goes beyond what the internal balancing of segments would require; their settlements are highly discontinuous in geographical space, and it is only rarely that there are adjoining villages of the same general kinship groups. They claim unreciprocated rights to wed other tribes' daughters, their settlements are centred on shrines housing their own ancestors, and so forth.

The problem concerning this striking differentiation within one territory, and the problem of the nature of the saintly state, are in fact the same. They have the same solution.

CHAPTER THREE

DISTINCTIONS

Sacred and Profane

The Berbers of the region we are concerned with can be divided into ordinary, 'lay' folk, who do not need to be characterised further – they simply exemplify the natural condition of human kind as locally conceived – and *igurramen* (singular: *agurram*), latent and actual, or *shurfa* (singular: *sherif*). Igurramen are, shall we say, hereditary saints. They are people endowed with special status and the capacity to mediate between humanity and the Deity, a status they owe, ideally, to their birth.

In fact, three conceptually distinct, but not always socially distinguishable, notions are involved:

(1) Igurramen
(2) Shurfa
(3) Ihansalen

Ihansalen are all descendants (in the male line) of Sidi Said Ahansal, a saint locally believed descended from the Prophet Mohamed through King Idris of the first Muslim dynasty in Morocco, and to have arrived in the region in 800 AH (1397–8 AD) and to have founded Zawiya Ahansal and fathered the lineages associated with it.

Shurfa, a term in general use in Morocco, designates the descendants (again, in the male line) of Prophet Mohamed. In Morocco, a very sizeable proportion of the population is believed to be of this descent, and shurfa are distributed in towns (where they form a kind of corporation) and country (where they form lineages), amongst Berbers as well as Arabs. When they occur amongst Berbers, it is nowadays assumed, by those who take the claim of sherifian origin seriously (and this includes, in my experience, most or even all those with a 'modern' education who come to Berber regions as part of the administration), to have become Berberised despite their Arabic origins. It is my strong impression that the question of how this Berberisation came to pass is not one which would have occurred to people prior to the modern period. The historical fact that Berbers, and the Berber language, are in Morocco older than Arabic, is not locally reflected in the folk mind.

Being an *agurram* is to fulfil a certain role and/or to be in a certain state, and the definition of this state or condition would include transcendental elements. An agurram can only properly be defined in terms of what an agurram does and what is done unto him, and this will be described in a following section.

Logically, Ihansalen are clearly a sub-class, indeed, a segment, of shurfa, whilst the notion of an agurram cuts across the notion of an Ahansal, and seems (locally) to be a sub-class of shurfa. Igurramen appear to be a sub-class of shurfa, in so far as all igurramen in the Ahansal heartland also claim to be shurfa, and the same is also true of most igurramen visible on the social horizon. Moreover, being a sherif is somehow a ground of agurram-like qualities and the explanation of their possession. Nevertheless the notions are separable, even in local terms, and functions similar to those of igurramen are sometimes performed elsewhere by people not claiming sherifian descent.

Whilst logically, and in national and pan-Islamic terms, Ihansalen are but a sub-class, and proportionately an extremely small one, of shurfa, nevertheless in local terms sherif and Ahansal are almost – but again not quite – co-extensive. In the heartland of Ahansal – that is, say, within a day's march in any direction from Zawiya Ahansal – there are almost no permanent inhabitants claiming to be shurfa other than the Ihansalen themselves. Such permanent ones as may exist are of no particular importance for the local social structure; and the impermanent, wandering shurfa who come as visitors are of some significance,[1] but not very much. Given this near-equivalence, locally, of Ahansal and sherif, the terms may in some local contexts be used interchangeably.

The matter is of course further complicated by the fact that, as in all social situations, it is not the case that someone simply 'is an *X*', but is an *X* in the eyes of *Y* speaking to *Z* in situation *S*.

[1] See below, p. 279.

Contextual considerations do affect these particular classifications in some measure. For instance, although sherif is defined genealogically, in practice it tends to be applied only to those (genealogically qualified) who claim the rights of and live in a manner befitting a sherif. Even the notion of an Ahansal may be narrowed down within the descendants of Sidi Said Ahansal.[1] For instance, the inhabitants of Amzrai, whose descent from SSA is acknowledged by all and denied by none, nevertheless are liable to refer to the inhabitants of the near-by Zawiya Ahansal itself as Ihansalen, as distinguished from themselves, the Ait Amzrai. Roughly speaking, where Ihansalen are scarce, any Ahansal is an Ahansal; but where they are two a penny, some are more so than others.

The notion of an *agurram* is of course more context-bound than the others, in as far as it does not have a formal definition in terms of descent, though one becomes an agurram in virtue of Ahansal descent plus other qualifications, and in adjoining regions also in virtue of sherifian but possibly non-Ahansal descent.[2] It is however quite clear that *agurram*hood is a status, and not a membership of any actual or potential corporate or kin group.

Not all Ihansalen are effective igurramen. Yet all Ihansalen are, as it were, *latent* igurramen. The main and first explanation given locally for why someone is an agurram is that he is descended from SSA – though this ancestry can be claimed by all Ihansalen, including those not normally, or in most contexts, described as igurramen. This matter, the conflict, so to speak, between the connotation (*any* descendant of SSA) and the denotation (*some* descendants of SSA) of agurram, will be discussed in some detail. The conflict is not accidental or due to some logical sloppiness. It is an essential part of the workings both of the concept and of the society.

Finally, members of ordinary Berber tribes, who make up the great majority of the population, are of course neither sherifian nor Ihansalen nor igurramen.

[1]Henceforth, I shall sometimes use the abbreviation SSA for him, or also the locally used expression Dadda (ancestor) Said.

[2]There is no formal delimitation of zones of influence. *Agurram*hood, the possession of *baraka*, is in God's hands. If social processes underlie the manifestations of divine will, they are not explicitly regularised or consciously recognised by the tribesmen.

Group and Status

Arab and *Berber* are not corporate groups; they are simply linguistic classifications.

Agurram is a role and a condition, but one tied fairly closely to being a sherif and, locally, to being an Ahansal sherif.

Shurfa in general are not a corporate group – though their being such is conceivable (for locals if not for the administration, e.g., for taxation purposes) – but they are or can be such in local contexts in many localities.

Ihansalen are a kinship group with a segmentary structure and thus, very theoretically, a potential corporate group. Nevertheless, in fact they never act as one body, partly because of their dispersion; but even over a more limited area where dispersion would not be an absolute obstacle, they do not do so, for sociologically interesting reasons which will be described, and which are essentially connected with the status of some of them as igurramen.

There is no local term which would isolate the region (i.e., the area of the influence of Ahansal igurramen). People outside the region may sometimes use the name of one of the larger tribes within it to describe the region as a whole. Which tribal name they use will tend to depend on the geographical direction from which they view the region. For instance, people living to the west of it may sometimes use the term Ait Messat, meaning not that tribe alone but the whole group of tribes under Ahansal leadership.

Despite this namelessness, the region is capable of acting as a corporate group, in virtue of Ahansal agurram leadership. It should be noted that some important tribal groupings are partly in and partly outside the region; others are wholly inside it; and some groupings are in and out of it seasonally.

Are there non-Ahansal igurramen in the region? The basic answer is that there are almost none, in the heartland of Ahansal influence, but there are more near the rim, and there are many on the horizon. Annually, for instance, the descendants of Sidi Bu Mohamed Salah visit the region[1] and are revered as sherifs: are they igurramen? The question does not arise, but if pressed, locals might, or might not, say yes. They are called 'shurfa' or Ait Sidi Bu Mohamed Salah. Again, a village, even a 'latent' Ahansal one, may invite a 'foreign' sherif to settle amongst them –

[1] See below, p. 279.

D 73

I know of such a case – and treat him with respect.[1] But to my knowledge, there is no important case of this kind.

Igurramen

Definition (1).

Ideally, an *agurram* is one who is descended from the Prophet, (in our region: through Sidi Said Ahansal), and is thus a *sherif*,

is visibly a recipient of divine blessing, *baraka*,

mediates between men and God and arbitrates between men and men, dispenses blessing,

possesses magical powers

is a good and pious man,

observes Koranic precepts (or any held to be such) is uncalculatingly generous and hospitable and rich,

does not fight or engage in feuds (nor, by extension, in litigation), hence turns the other cheek.

Definition (2).

An alternative outsider's definition must be offered: An agurram is simply he who is held to be one. One attains agurramhood by being held to possess it. Agurramhood is in the eye of the beholder.

But that still isn't quite right: agurramhood is in the ey*es* of the beholders – all of them in a sense squint to see what is in the eyes of other beholders, and if they see it there, then they see it also. Collectively, this characteristic is an ascription, but for any one man, it is an objective fact, an inherent characteristic: for if all others see it in a man, then, for any single beholder, that man truly has it.

It would be impossible to say just which of the characteristics in the first list are the essential minimum for being an agurram. Let us say, as a first approximation, that in order to qualify for agurramhood one must have at least some of them. But this objective

---

[1]It is worth noting that *Sherif*, like *Hajj*, (pilgrim, to Mecca) is used and favoured by Ahansal families as a family name i.e., occurring in the second or third place of the fully expanded name (see above, p. 37). The ancestor who actually earned the appellation Hajj by an actual pilgrimage may be nebulously distant. But in the construction of the name of his descendants, his earned name or nickname replaces his personal name proper. This can occur with other appellations also.

qualification, the passing-of-the-test, as it were, has to be seen in the light of the second definition, which seems potentially to conflict with it and which says, in effect, that this status is simply ascribed, that the qualities follow the ascription.

Yet it would also be wrong to say that it is simply ascribed. For a number of complications arise. It is held that it can only be justly ascribed to someone who satisfies at least some of the listed characteristics. But here we come upon a crucial circularity: these characteristics tend only to be acquired in consequence of (a previous state of) being an agurram, a state which they are also invoked to explain.

These circles, the manner in which possessing some of these characteristics is a consequence of being held to be an agurram and vice versa vary in kind and in length:

Genealogy: a man who is recognised to be an agurram will be believed when claiming and citing a holy genealogy.[1]

Possession of baraka: this, again, will automatically be predicted of igurramen. He is an agurram because he has baraka, and he has baraka because he is an agurram. This circle is very brief. It can however become longer. Stories of magical powers, of greater or less complexity, will be told and believed of igurramen. Causal connection between objective blessings or disasters (good or bad harvests, cures or illnesses), and the acts, blessings and curses, of igurramen will be postulated and believed.

Generosity and wealth: an agurram will receive donations from people seeking blessing, which will enable him to be generous and hospitable. Thus his agurramhood helps to procure the wealth which also marks him out as an agurram. This is a very crucial circle.

Pacifism: an agurram will be revered and not be an object of aggression, and so will be able to survive without defending himself – and be expected to do so, and allowed to do so without, in general, earning contempt. Being pacific, he will be able to carry out the tasks of an agurram. Agurramhood enables him to be pacific, and the pacifism demonstrates his agurram status.

One can approach the meaning of being an agurram in two ways: by asking Berbers what an 'agurram' is, and by observing, as

---

[1] It should not be supposed that, in villages where everyone knows each other from birth, it is normally easy or even possible for an individual suddenly to invent a new ancestry.

far as we can, the social processes by which people come to be igurramen. But neither method by itself will give us the essence of agurramhood – which lies in the ambiguities and inconsistencies and interplay between the two. This again is crucial.

If we request definition, two difficulties arise. First, the definition offered may not correspond to the characteristics which igurramen in fact possess, or possess distinctively. Berbers, like anyone else, may be bad at defining. In fact, of course, I have often requested, or obtained unasked, accounts of what it is to be an agurram. The various characteristics listed were variously brought up. One might be tempted to say that divine mediation (possession of baraka) was the essence of agurramhood, that sherifian descent was the (quasi) causal explanation, and the other characteristics the signs and the consequences of it.[1]

If we consult the actual social reality, it may again be difficult to sort out what are merely the causal conditions of achieving agurramhood (e.g., igurramen are schemers who accumulate wealth and influence), from the activities carried out in virtue of being igurramen.

The answer is, of course, that there is no 'correct' account. We understand agurramhood when we see the interrelation between the image, the rationale, and the realities of the situation. It would be preposterous to expect these to be consistent. Indeed, in this case they cannot be.

The circles involved are some of them 'logical' and some causal. It inheres in the notion of agurram, in its 'logic', that if a man is held to be so by all or many others, then he is one: for an agurram is one chosen by God, and God reveals His will in the hearts of men, and if other men recognise him as an agurram, that is the best sign of his being one. But corresponding to this tacit reasoning, there is of course a social reality: an agurram is he who has enough authority to be able to arbitrate and have his verdicts respected, and if a man is held to have enough authority to do this, then indeed, ipso facto, he is one.

But apart from this logical interdependence of recognition and reality, there are also the causal circles. A very important sign of agurramhood is riches and the willingness and ability to entertain all comers. But only a successful agurram, one effectively recog-

---

[1]The concept of *baraka* itself is very fully explored by E. Westermarck, *Ritual and Belief in Morocco*, London 1926, chapters II and III.

nised to be such, will in consequence receive the donations sufficient to enable him to live and entertain as an agurram should. (There are of course subsidiary circles of various kinds: only an effective agurram will attract the clients, refugees and so on to enable him to have the entourage necessary for a proper agurram.)

These circles, of course, also sometimes involve contradictions between the ascribed image or definition, and the necessary steps in keeping the circles in motion. Ideally, an agurram must be spontaneously, uncalculatingly, indeed impulsively, generous: concerned with others, and also secure in possession of baraka and the knowledge that God will provide, he does not count his reserves when the needy or the visitor come to the lodge. He appears to act on the 'consider the lilies' principle. An agurram who really did entertain in this fashion would soon dissipate his resources and, unable to fulfil the expectations one has from one endowed with baraka, lose his status.

Igurramen are jealous and irritated with each other in this connection. The chief possessor of baraka in one lodge assured me regularly enough that his rivals sit by their windows and watch whether a visitor comes with gifts or not: if well laden, they went out to bring him to their houses, but if empty-handed, they hid. The rivals of this baraka-possessor said as much about him, of course.

Thus the characteristic agurram values include two which look very Christian to European eyes: pacifism, and the requirement of a 'consider the lilies' attitude. It would be quite mistaken to see in this some element of cultural diffusion of the Sermon on the Mount. There are indeed in the Atlas occasional signs and hints in tribal legends of the presence locally of Christianity prior to Islam. But the ideal values of the igurramen should not be counted amongst these signs. It is far too easy and fitting to explain them structurally. The pacifism, for instance, ceases to be even an ideal requirement, immediately it ceases to be structurally fitting: even people of Ahansal descent, if not in the running as potential arbitrators for the feuding tribes, (let alone others without such aspirations) do not recognise pacifism as a value. This pacifism, though it is extreme – it requires the possessor to refrain from repaying violence with violence – is clearly tied to a very specific role, and not to any general beliefs about the moral worth of violence, or of abstention from it.

Agurram is as agurram does, and only he can do who is suitably done by.

The Actual Role of Igurramen

The services performed by igurramen are:

The supervision of the election of chiefs (imgharen, sing: amghar) amongst the lay tribes.

Mediation between groups in conflict.

Acting as a court of appeal in the settling of disputes.

Providing the machinery and the witnesses for the main legal decision procedure, namely trial by collective oath.

Providing a sanctuary.

Acting as a bureau de placement, as it were, for those who are forced to seek a new place within the tribal structure. (I prefer the French term to 'labour exchange', for what is at issue is placing a person in a social niche, rather than just finding him work.)

Providing continuity: (ordinary lay tribal offices have impermanent occupants).

Providing leadership if large units need to combine, e.g., against outside aggression.

Providing a rationale for the existing inter-tribal status quo, and indeed, if necessary, for changes in it: notably in connection with the complex spatio-temporal territorial boundaries which arise from transhumancy. (Rights of pasture are limited in time as well as space – for instance, a tribe may only enter a given pasture after a certain date.)

Providing a rationale for the religious establishment, so to speak, of the area.

The protection of travellers, of inter-tribal trade and of inter-tribal religious festivals and other activities. One of the main traditional passes over the Atlas, much used by caravans in the past, is close to the lodge.

Being centres of information.

The establishing and guranteeing of such inter-tribal links as exist, notably arranging the pairing-off of families in distinct tribes, for purposes of exchanging hospitality in connection with trade (see discussion of trade, below, p. 137).

Working divine blessing, performing miracles etc.

This list comprises both services which are clearly seen for what they are by those who benefit from them (e.g., mediation between tribes), others which are perhaps not seen or at any rate not spoken about explicitly or clearly conceptualised (e.g., continuity), and some which are seen subjectively in a different way from what they 'really' are, i.e., for the sociologist (e.g., acting as guarantors of collective oaths).

The power to invoke divine blessings in the form of prosperity, cures, and so forth and, indeed, the accompanying power to cause harm by transcendental means, I have deliberately left at the end of the list. In any account based on superficial impressions of the role of igurramen, or on the Berbers' own account of what igurramen are, they might figure near the head of it. They would be stressed as their primary distinction and the one which accounts for all the others – possibly in conjunction with their sherifian ancestry. In fact, this aspect of sanctity, central though it is to the image of an agurram, seems to me epiphenomenal. To be sure, an agurram should have tales about magical powers, performances and achievements circulated and believed about himself. In a sense, someone must have invented them, on the questionable principle that everything must have a beginning: though I rather doubt whether any conscious disingenuousness is necessarily or frequently involved.[1] To be an agurram, one must be a person who has the skill or luck, or more likely to be a person in the position which evokes, the circulation of such beliefs. But the point is that igurramen are in a position which makes the attribution of such powers a necessary consequence, as a kind of rationale, accompaniment or manner of conceiving of that position itself.

Berber beliefs in the transcendental powers of igurramen, shrines, and holy places, have two relevant characteristics: Berbers have a low or negligible insistence on the falsifiability of such beliefs, and readily invoke the ultimate dependence of everything, including magical powers, on the will of the Deity, as an ever ready ad hoc hypothesis which also accounts for individual failure without refuting the initial belief. Secondly, the beliefs about igurramen vary from inherently incredible attributions (e.g., direct and extremely speedy flights to Mecca unaided by any mechanical

---

[1]My experience with a previously published study of the interaction of an ideology, a set of practices and of social relations, makes me chary of even seeming to impute disingenuousness.

contrivance) to perfectly plausible attributions which really only testify to intelligence, cunning or common sense on the part of the possessor (e.g., the ability to surmise that a man, sent to fetch some butter from an upland shelter, will have consumed a little of it on the way down).

CHAPTER FOUR

HOLY AND LAY

Elections

Igurramen and ordinary tribesmen are complementary: the various services performed by igurramen can only be properly understood in the context of the organisation of the lay tribes. The role of igurramen in supervising elections presupposes the context of the nature of traditional chieftaincy amongst Berbers of the central High Atlas, and the mode of electing chiefs.

Chiefs are, in principle, annual: as a rule immediate re-election is excluded (though it may occasionally occur by consent of all the interested parties). The principles governing election are rotation and complementarity. Suppose a tribe to consist of three sub-clans, A, B and C. If this year it is the turn of A to provide the chief for the tribe as a whole, then the electors will be the men of B and C. Next year, the chief will be chosen from B, and it will be A and C who provide the electors; and so on. You can be part of the pool of candidates, or have the vote, but not both. This is complementarity.

The consequence of this mode of election are obvious enough. It prevents the emergence of real and permanent concentration of power in anyone's hands. The effect of the rules of complementarity and rotation may be, and frequently is, reinforced further by the existence of more than one chief, i.e., by the independent election of further chiefs with special responsibilities (for instance, the supervision of the market, or of the restricted pasture, or of the collective storehouse-forts). Nevertheless, there is the chief-of-the-year, *amghar-n-asgwas*, the man responsible in the first instance for the maintenance of order. (But the others are annual too, or even merely ad hoc.)

It may sometimes be supposed that even segmentary groups need some sort of a focus and symbol of their latent unity, in the form of reasonably permanent leadership, a dominant lineage or something of the kind. Central Atlas tribal groupings manage without dominant lineages, and not merely is leadership elective rather than inherited, but the mode of election is such as could hardly be bettered if one wishes to prevent the emergence of permanently dominant individuals or sub-groups.[1] If one considers that, by all accounts[2] the main danger to most other Moroccan Berber societies, outside the central Atlas, was the periodic if ephemeral emergence of petty tyrannies, one cannot but admire the elegance and effectiveness of the check-and-balance constitutions of the central High Atlas Berbers.

But this lack of any permanent internal office-bearers, symbols or providers of continuity, is made easier, or perhaps is only made possible, by the existence of permanent external ones: the saints.

The transient nature of chieftaincy turns all lay chiefs into lame ducks. The conduct of the chief is not that of a ruler guided by the concern with the long-term stability and possibly increase of his power. It is the conduct of a citizen temporarily enjoying power, responsibility and prestige, or having them thrust upon him, or accepting them lest they fall into worse hands, but who, in accepting them, knows that whatever he does will be counted in his favour or against him when, in a very short time, he once again, becomes, so to speak, a private citizen. Within the rules of the game, he cannot aspire to becoming a tyrant, to usurping permanent and real power; moreover, the general situation, the relative strength of forces and their lay-out, reinforce the formal rules and make any such aspiration, any hope of breaking the rules, vain, or at any rate unlikely of fulfilment. The current chief has been elected by the members of clans other than his own, by rival clans in effect, who are the last people to wish for the concentration of

---

[1]To say this is not to deny, of course, that some families are 'bigger', in both size and prestige, or richer or more influential than others. But there are limits to the degree of such differentiation, limits very narrow by comparison with other societies, and which exclude both the emergence of a special privileged social category – here rich and poor exemplify unambiguously the same *kind of human being,* in the view of all participants – and also exclude the *congealing* of power, as it were.

[2]Cf. R.Montagne: *La Vie Sociale et la Vie Politique des Berbères*, Paris, 1931.

power in his clan, and who can be expected to bear this in mind when making their choice.

One should not conclude from this last consideration, important though it is, that the electors from *B* and *C* clans will actually choose the feeblest and most ineffectual member of *A* to be the annual amghar. It is to their interest that he should not be wholly ineffective: one does not wish every feminine row at the well, or every dispute about the location of tents, or a mix-up of flocks, to end in violence. The chief should be a forceful personality; that much is to everyone's interest. The formal qualifications given me by the chief of the Ait Bu Iknifen in 1959, as the general recognised tests of fitness for amgharhood, were very close to the classical Islamic criteria of the Khalifate, as cited in M. Lahbabi's *Le Gouvernement Marocain a l'Aube du XXe Siècle*:[1] they include, apart from moral characteristics, the requirements of sound sight, hearing, speech and limbs. (Lahbabi suggests that these criteria spring, on the part of the classical lawyer cited, from an attachment to the social forms of seventh-century Arabia.) It seems that this is a case of diffusion of genuine Islamic learning amongst the illiterate tribesmen, for although the need to exclude the physically infirm may spring from the conditions of the central High Atlas as much as from those of Arabia, the stressed and explicit formulation of the criteria does not. For how many blind, deaf or dumb men were likely to present themselves for election for chieftaincy? The problem is a much more plausible one for the Arab societies which, unlike central Atlas Berbers, are liable to acquire their political leaders by accident of birth rather than by election.

Thus the tribesmen will not elect a man they hold dangerous. They clearly will not elect someone whom they have cause to suspect of undue ambition. His own clansmen, the natural profit-sharers of any usurpation by the chief, are without franchise at the very moment when one of their own number is eligible for election. Of course, an apparently innocuous personage might reveal unsuspected, Caesarean aspirations after election: still, a single solitary year is not much good to him. It is not a very long time, even for a skilled manipulator, to graduate from an elected and limited functionary into a permanent tyrant. Most dictators, generally operating in a much more favourable natural and social environment than this one, required more time than that.

[1] Rabat, 1958, p. 28.

The system, in brief, constitutes a very effective check and balance against excessive, indeed against any serious, political ambition. Its weakness lies in the opposite direction: the discontinuity and feebleness of leadership. The chiefs are so weak that, in effect, they only govern by consent: hence elections must end in unanimity. There is indeed no rule specifying the proportion, such as simple majority, or two thirds of electors who would constitute a majority sufficient for election. In the end, there has to be unanimity. Hence no rule exists specifying that a successful candidate must gain more than half the votes, or some other proportion.

For after all, the chief after election hardly possesses much greater means of enforcing his decision other than such physical and moral force than he possessed anyway, as an ordinary tribesman, as head of household or influential member of his clan. He is allocated no levy, no resources, no personnel of any kind, only representatives (*idbaben-n'imur*: elders-of-parts) in sub-clans, whose position in this respect, however, is no different from his own. Hence, if he is reduced to having to enforce a decision, he is, not quite but very nearly, in no better position to do this than if he were enforcing a private decision on his own with the sanction of violence.

His moral force is indeed much augmented by his being chief: he who defies him is also defying the public opinion which had elected the chief. But this kind of moral strength is precarious and volatile. Public opinion, in taking up a position in a conflict, will be partly swayed by the fact that he is chief and that his authority must be reinforced, right or wrong; but it will also, inevitably and in proportion to the importance of the issue to them, be swayed by substantive considerations of the rights of the case and indeed by the might of the parties and their alignments. Suspiciously, Berbers are liable to protest too much about how much obedience and respect is due to the chief.

A chief whose election were not, at the end of the process of election, recognised by some part of his constituents, would be in a weak or hopeless position vis-à-vis that part from the very start: who would, at best, be in the position of a leader of those who do accept him against those who do not. But the point of having a common chief is to be a political unit with internal peace, and this central purpose would be defeated from the start, and the whole process of electing a chief lose its point, if it were merely a prelude to fission and strife. So the annual chief must be, inescapably, one who is accepted unanimously. And if you accept him, you might as well acclaim and elect him: there is no point in accepting him and yet at the same time antagonising him by openly ending as one who had voted against him. So, Berber elections end in unanimity or, shall we say, at least the external appearance of unanimity. Elections end in a snowball. A resolutely unappeasable opposition could only mean secession by the recusant sub-group. This is the one alternative: fission. Sometimes fission does occur. But normally the snowball effect takes place, and in the end everyone accepts the successful candidate for the year.

Perhaps one should not call this a snowball-effect or band-waggon-jumping: for the 'election' is not strictly comparable with what we call 'elections' in other contexts. These elections really comprise, in a fused form, two elements which in non-segmentary societies are distinct: election proper (i.e., choice from amongst candidates) and acceptance and recognition of his authority (which in non-segmentary societies can be taken for granted, or if not, may follow on a separate occasion). Even here, the two are partly distinguishable: the actual ritual of election is only the acceptance and recognition, whilst the process of decision takes place before, during the preceding negotiations and palavers.

In these negotiations, mediation, persuasion and pressure by the saints plays an essential role (as it does in the settling of inter-group disputes and in legal cases). This part is so great that when the saints describe the procedures of elections in lay tribes, they frequently claim that they, the saints, appoint the lay tribesmen's chieftains for them. This is not simply a boastful exaggeration of their own role: from their viewpoint, when the tribesmen in their opposed groups and with rival candidates turn up, it may really look like being requested to make an appointment.

The actual mode of election is that whilst the electors assemble in one place, accompanied by some of the igurramen, the men eligible for election sit in a circle in some other place or outside. When the decision is reached, the electors walk around the inward circle of potential chiefs and after circling it three times, place a tuft of green grass, so that the year be 'green', prosperous, on the clean, newly washed turban of the new chosen chief. The person actually performing this 'crowning' may be, but need not be, an agurram. The discussions and negotiations constituting the election or its preliminaries may of course have gone on for days: the elections take place during the period when the tribe, or other large representative part of it, assembles at the zawiya, the village of the igurramen, sometimes for as long as eight days.

Thus the necessity for igurramen is manifest: it is they who, as benevolent hosts and outsiders to the fissions of the tribe, smooth over the election and persuade reluctant electors to accept the emergent trend. They also provide a kind of continuity from one election to the next.

But if they are essential at elections, they are equally invaluable during the period between elections. The precarious annual chief may succeed in dealing on the spot with minor issues. It is in his interest, and that of the disputants or litigants, and everybody, that disputes should be settled rapidly if possible: for one thing, everyone involved in a dispute as an arbitrator or adjudicator will require a recompense, and there is also a loss of time and effort. But important or bitter disputes will not be settled rapidly, and the igurramen are there as the court of appeal when settlement fails at the level of the chief or arbitrarily elders chosen to arbitrate. Moreover, if it comes to trial by collective oath, all important matters, those requiring ten or more co-jurors, automatically go up to be sworn at the shrine of the igurramen. (Smaller matters may be settled by an oath at a local mosque or shrine, or holy place.) Furthermore, there are also issues between groups larger than those which currently have an elected chief at all: such disputes, of course, need a mediator for any negotiations.

Despite the striking general polarity of holy-permanent-agurram-by-the-will-of-God contrasted with the lay-annually-rotated-amghar-by-the-will-of-the-complementary-segments, it should not be supposed that even chieftaincy was seen in an altogether secular manner. A good chief meant that the harvest would be good and the flocks prosper; if these things occurred, it showed that the chief was good. Where kinks occur in the neatness of the complementarity-rotation system, e.g., when certain segments are excluded from eligibility for election,[1] such exclusions are again

---

[1] The only kink which I have properly explored is of course the crucial one of the saints. A saint could not, of course, be an amghar, though ineffective (latent) saints could be and were elective imgharen within their own saintly communities, for purposes of their internal administration, though under the much stronger

expressed or justified in terms of transcendentally mediated negative effects, i.e., if they were elected, the harvest would be bad. In the one case of this kind about which I know a little (in the Ait Isha chieftaincy election rotation system) the excluded segment are also credited with much wisdom and held to be very suitable people to consult on such issues as may arise. It is of course tempting to connect these two attributes of theirs by an argument similar to that connecting the exclusion and pacifism of the saints themselves with their influence, and to conclude that we have here something like the saintly system in embryo, and a potential and in some measure even actual rival of it. (Every consultation of the excluded lay segment means one consultation less, and one donation less, for the saints.) But I do not know enough of this case to come to any definite conclusion, having heard of the excluded segment from other Ait Isha but not from the members of it themselves.

The supervision of lay tribal elections, the assistance in reaching a concensus of chieftains, the provision of a neutral locale for the occasion (and one which is safe as a holy sanctuary), the provision of a transcendental sanction and ratification for this process and its conclusion, these are, of course, only part of the services performed by the saints for the surrounding lay tribes. It is, however, one which, apart from its intrinsic importance, deserves to be listed first, for it brings out most clearly the differences and the complementarity of saints and lay tribesmen: the permanence of sanctity and the transient nature of lay chieftaincy; the pacific saints and the feuding, 'balancing' (i.e., reciprocally frightening) lay tribes; the rotation and consequent equality and secular status amongst the tribes, and the uneven concentration of baraka and influence amongst some few of the igurramen (who in any case, even without this further but equally essential concentration, are already much less numerous than the lay tribes).

---

authority of non-elective effective igurramen, who act primarily vis-à-vis the lay tribes, and are not directly concerned with the daily issues of the saintly village. (In *laicised* saintly villages, the internal amghar would of course not have local effective agurram above him.) By a distortion of the system under French indirect rule, during the period 1952–6, an effective saint was the elective amghar of the administrative unit 'Ihansalen' consisting of the four villages (Zawiya Ahansal, Taria, Amzrai and Tighanimin) – with that title, though politely he was called *caid*, which he aspired to be and would have become if/when he was made permanent (and not elective) by the French central authority, which however never occurred, Independence intervening.

Whilst the ritual accompanying the elections receives some mention in the literature,[1] the intriguing and important rules governing the actual content of the election have been neglected or wholly ignored, even for instance by the otherwise very detailed *fiche de tribu* established by the French district officer at Zawiya Ahansal. The probable reasons for this neglect are various: elections were not a part of that 'customary law' which was underwritten by the indirect rulers, for the choice of chieftains was one of the powers which in practice they reserved for themselves (though they sometimes chose to institute elections). Secondly, French ethnography in Morocco was, as indicated, over-fascinated by the notion of the moiety (leff), after the importance of it had come to Robert Montagne in a kind of flash of illumination,[2] a flash whose unfortunate long-term consequence was to blind some of Montagne's successors.[3] A third reason is interestingly connected with the very function of the elections itself: a continuity-providing institution such as that of the saints, even when it is deprived of its role and privileges, survives with its signs of distinct behaviour, wealth and so on. But the function of the rotation-complementarity elections was precisely to avoid any permanent differentiation, and it succeeded in this. Hence when the institution itself was abolished, it left few traces: that indeed was its task.

Segmentation and Elections

Thus the lay tribes' mode of electing and restricting the duration of their chiefs enabled these tribes, as groupings, to avoid crystal-

[1] For instance, in R. Montagne, *La Vie Sociale et la Vie Politique des Berbères*, Paris, 1931, p. 58, Rotation (though not, explicitly, complementarity) is reported for the Middle Atlas by Said Guennoun: *La Montagne Berbère*, Rabat, 1933, p. 164.

[2] R. Montagne, 'Les leff-s berbères au début du XVIIIe siècle chez les Masmouda', *Hesperis*, 1941, p. 93; cited in Jacques Berque: *Structures Sociales du Haut-Atlas*, Paris, 1955, p. 218.

[3] French ethnography was badly hampered by the lack of an explicit formulation of the notion of 'segmentary society'. This led to attempts to locate *the* crucial group along the segmentary ladder, then discounting others as 'survivals' or 'in decline', and it also led to a failure to see that the famous moieties, even in cases where they really did exist along one level of segmentation, could not be a sufficient explanation of the maintenance of some degree of order throughout at all levels. It also led to the seeing of moieties where they do not exist, a tendency aided by the fact that the word *leff* is used in some regions simply in the sense of 'alliance', or even just 'political co-operating' group, and can then be applied either to ad hoc allies, or to units at any level of segmentation, or both.

lisations of permanent and concentrated power in their own midst, it allowed them to dispense, surprisingly, with any permanent personal symbol of unity and permanent leadership: the personal symbols and agents of continuity were found outside, amongst the igurramen.

But we are dealing with a segmentary system, and hence all and any problems are liable to be duplicated at a number of levels, and solutions must likewise (though not necessarily in identical form) be found at a number of levels. (This point is something which was not present with sufficient clarity, as stated, in the minds of French investigators of the subject.) The corollary of this for the institution of annual elections by complementarity-and-rotation is that this must occur not at one but at a number of levels, that there must be a complex system of elective wheels within wheels. This is precisely what one does find. But the manner in which superimposed complementarily elected and rotated annual chieftains, and their choice, are related, is extremely complex and intriguing.

Much of the French literature on the political life of the Berbers may in one way overstress the role of the *jema'a,* the assembly (though rightly noting that there is a hierarchy of such). These accounts tend to be misleading in as far as they give the impression that these assemblies have a kind of corporate existence. But they have no existence independently of the social group, the segments, of which they are the assemblies. They simply are the natural form of discussing and settling issues for groups which are reasonably egalitarian and which have no other machinery available to them.[1] During French days of course, there were jema'as, both 'administrative' (composed of headmen of villages) and 'judicial' (composed of nominated or elected elders as a kind of permanent jury), which were small in number, had definite functions and a kind of continuity, which in other words were a kind of specialised and genuine institution. Some time after Independence I observed a 'natural' jema'a, so to speak, called into being by the need to cope with a crisis arising out of the disclosure of the corruption of a

---

[1]The one piece of evidence which seems to suggest that these assemblies did after all have a kind of sharply delimited nature is that in one of the few documents available in the region, the crucial land deed made out between Sidi Lahcen u Othman and the previous inhabitants, the signatories for the latter are described as signing 'for the *jema'a*' of the so-and-so. But this may equally be interpreted as simply being the way of representing the so-and-so.

number of headmen. The jema'a was largish, there was no formal election to it nor formal procedure, and quite young men were on it, especially from households where no older man was available.

To sum up, one can say that Berber jema'as have no sense of corporate identity distinct from that of the group of which they are the jema'a; they have no continuity other than that of that group; they have, of course, no kind of secretariat or records. On the other hand, they can, and generally do when larger groups are involved, consist of people who are delegates, who represent sub-groups. In dealing with the important matter of the mode of election of chiefs, we are, at the same time, describing the assemblies and hierarchies of assemblies in the fulfilment of their most characteristic and perhaps most important function.

In dealing with this matter, we are inescapably committed to attempting a reconstruction: the indigenous system of elections did not survive 1933, though of course many attitudes and assumptions which have found their expression in it did. In attempting such a reconstruction, it is a little difficult to sort out various kinds of contradiction: those inherent in the system itself, those arising from inconsistent accounts given by informants (in the sense that one informant may be accurate in his account whilst another, or the same one at a different time, may be simply wrong), and those arising merely out of an attempt to have a unitary picture when in fact there was regional and perhaps temporal diversification. I believe that the basic principles involved were identical throughout the region, though the details of their application varied, and that I have succeeded in eliciting them: but the fact remains that it *is* a reconstruction.

It is of the essence of a segmentary society that social units exist at various levels of size, the larger incorporating the smaller as subparts, and that no particular level is the crucial one. Some levels may be a bit more important than others, some may be used for this purpose and others for that, but no one is pre-eminent (as, for instance, in our society the national state is far more important and authoritative than social groupings of larger or smaller size). Hence it was a mistake for French ethnography in North Africa to be tempted by the search for *the* crucial group, and even to invent a name ('canton') for it.

It also follows that if one makes a statement about 'Berber tribes', the statement is quite inadequate unless one specifies which level of segmentation one has in mind: and if one has only one or some levels in mind, one must give reasons why those levels should be so singled out. Hence the contention that Berber tribes have annual elective chiefs, elected by the principle of complementarity and rotation, must be made unambiguous along these lines.

There is no privileged level at which chiefs and elections occur. They occur all along the line. The rotation takes place in large units, and at the same time in the small units composing them: there are as it were catherine wheels within catherine wheels. The only exceptions are at the very top and bottom levels, in the biggest and the smallest units, for different reasons.

Top Level

The top level of annual chieftaincy is only activated by the recognised need to have common leadership for very large units. When such a need is not felt, no chiefs are elected at this topmost level. The last occasion this need was felt, was during the period preceding the abolition of the system itself: the need arose from the requirements of joint resistance to the French advance. Thus the power which abolished the system, also began by reactivating its most extensive manifestation.

The 'total region' activated into co-operating by such a stimulus is larger than any unit definable in terms of either descent beliefs or even territorial units: it can only be described, not named, as the area of influence of the given saintly lineage under whose supervision the co-operation is ratified and the top chief elected. (Apart from being larger than any given unit in the local systems of segmentation, this area can also cut across some of them: the area of Ahansal influence, for instance, included some but not all Ait Haddidu, and some but not all Ait Bu Gmez.) The chief so elected is then known as 'chief-of-the-war', and is annual, and further elections for this position obey the rules of complementarity and rotation. The 'rotating' units are the large groups whose relation to each other, apart from the relationship created ad hoc by a 'sacrifice' and a joint meal, is simply that of fellow-venerators of the same shrine and holy lineage. The significance of the igurramen is manifest with particular clarity in this context, making possible large scale co-operation transcending the limits of supposed kinship or common habitation of a valley.

Grass Roots

The formal procedure of the lay tribes in electing their chiefs (or rather, in expressing their choice) is remembered as follows at Zawiya Ahansal, the main lodge:

All the 'eligibles' sit on a flat place, large enough to accommodate them all when seated in a circle. The remaining segments have each provided one or two men towards a group which, with grass in their hands, walk around the seated men. They go around them once, twice, and after the third turn they place the grass on the right side of the newly-elected chief's turban. Thereafter they pray, and a passage from the Koran is read.

Thereupon the newly elected Top Chief exclaims: 'Supply me with the Little Chiefs.' Then each of the segments-clans repeats the same performance as before, identically but for the fact that each of the groups involved is one unit 'lower down' on the segmentary ladder. This repeat performance on a lower level completed, the 'little chiefs' demand their 'elders-of-parts', that is, the minuscule headman of the segments on the lowest level. These are then supplied, by consultation between the little chiefs and the segments supplying their own heads, but this nomination in turn no longer involves the ceremony with circles and grass. These smallest units, for which it was worth having an 'elder of part' would have a total population something of the order of a hundred people or less. In case of a compact village, a 'part' in this sense would indeed be a part of a village. The Berber terms *taqbilt* (tribe) and *ighs* (clan) are indeed used in a proper 'segmentary' way, i.e., relative to context: the same unit will be described as either tribe or as clan according to whether a contrast is intended with a smaller or a larger group. But this relativity lapses at the top and at the bottom. No one would describe a part of a village as a tribe, or a total tribe (at the genealogical ceiling, so to speak) as a clan.

This account of the ceremony of election is based mainly on a description supplied by U Ben Ali, a respected elder (though not of 'top saintly' family) of the main lodge, old enough to have witnessed many such elections. This picture leads one to expect three levels of chieftaincy, and fits in admirably with the actual structure of such typical tribes as, for instance, the Ait Isha or the Ait Mhand, who regularly came to elect their chiefs at Zawiya Ahansal. Hence one must conclude that at times of its maximum development, i.e., when a topmost chieftaincy was activated into being, and a topmost chief was also elected to co-ordinate inter-tribal activities (e.g., resistance to the French), four levels of chieftaincy existed, of which the upper three were rotated. There is no doubt about there having been such a topmost inter-tribal chief, nor about the rotated elective nature of the office. This has been independently confirmed by many people at a great variety of places.

What is a little difficult to obtain is a simultaneous account of it and its relations to the lower levels. Informants, often one and the same informant, tend at any given time to stress either the elective nature of chieftaincy, or the arranged nomination from above which seems to apply only to the lowest level group when it is incorporated in wider ones; but they have difficulty in talking of the two at the same time and relating them. A coherent account fusing the diverse viewpoints is offered below.

Activation of Supra-tribal Co-operation

Without the saints, there are no means of obtaining inter-tribal co-operation at this high level. Thus, for instance, the main body of the important and large tribe of the Ait Haddidu (to the East of the Ahansal region) has a numerically small lodge of (non-Ahansal) shurfa-igurramen settled in their midst, whom they employed for mediation internally but not externally. (Their location made them ill-suited, of course, for external mediation. Certain segments of the Ait Haddidu also had relations with and regularly presented donations to the Ahansal saints at Temga, and others to those at the main lodge: this was, for the segments concerned, a matter of maintaining external contacts, having saintly protectors available for mediation with non-Haddidu groups.) These local saints 'internal' to the Haddidu, did indeed provide the leadership for the resistance of the Ait Haddidu who, with the tribesmen of Ahansal-land, share the honour of having resisted the Rumi (Roman, i.e., European) longest: but the Ait Haddidu did not combine in any supra-tribal coalition, and did not impede the French advance as it approached their own frontiers. On the contrary, on occasion they impeded other tribes who were then engaged in the struggle with the Rumi. The relevant moral of this is not the lack of sufficient pan-Islamic or even national sentiment – this is hardly surprising in a segmentary society – but that, in a segmentary society with impermanent, 'rotated' chieftains, common action is not to be expected from units larger than the range of influence of some one saintly centre.

The limits of this range are not rigidly fixed. Had the Ait Haddidu for some reason strongly wished to combine in a wider unit in opposition to the French, they could have joined the charmed circle of Ahansal influence, using those of their segments which were within it already by way of introduction.

On the other hand, there is a certain amount of inertia built into the system of allegiances-to-saints: to have joined the circle of Ahansal-following tribes would have meant going against the interests and hence no doubt the decisions of the local saints.[1] But

[1] It is interesting to note that this centre of sanctity, like the Ahansal one of Temga which similarly led the resistance almost to the bitter end, was 'without influence', as the French reports said, during the period of the French Protectorate. This seems to indicate that reverence for individual saints or lineages is not deeply and ineradicably 'internalised': this reverence does represent a most cogent motivation and social force, but its mechanics are connected with the social structure rather than the individual psyche. In simplest terms, one reveres and obeys because all others do – and this gives the saints' baraka a very real force – the force of all the other clients combined. Once broken and isolated, the charisma and reverence are gone too.

I visited this little centre of sanctity during the summer of 1956, when in this particular region the transfer of power completed elsewhere, was still in progress. A French captain and a rather depressed Caid, power-holder under the French, was initiating a detachment of the new Moroccan Royal Army – not quite happy in this most isolated of posts – in the intricacies of local administration.

The head of the little zawiya of local igurramen was busy trying to persuade the higher echelons of the new administration to confer upon him a post under the new dispensation, thus helping the local powers of agurramhood to emerge from twenty-three years of eclipse. As I have not been to the region since, I do not know whether he succeeded nor what the subsequent local political transformations were. The opportunities for intrigues and turning the wheel of fortune remained considerable: The Istiqlal party was established and provided, as elsewhere, a new channel of information and advancement. The then provincial governor, Addi u Bihi, subsequently rebelled against the central government, and further changes must have occurred during and after his suppression.

The Haddidu, who are noted for providing the poets and the wandering minstrels of the Atlas, at that time also composed new sets of couplets glorifying the exploits of the nationalists who had so suddenly and surprisingly brought a change of regime to these distant valleys. If only one possessed all the couplets, with their political and social commentary, invented and sung since the start of the century or earlier, one would have a most vivid account of the social history of the Atlas imaginable. After 1940, these couplets ironised the humility of the defeated French in German prison camps (Cf. V. Monteil, *Les Officiers*, p. 132); in 1960, in Bu Gmez, they ironised the instabilities and vacillations of the Moroccan administration by comparison with the French (information supplied by Wye College Expedition, 1960).

these after all were the agents of such local intra-Haddidu co-operation as already existed. So paradoxically would have to be ignored or contradicted in this new joint venture, when in fact it is they who normally make joint ventures of the tribe feasible. It is obvious that new crystallisations of a saintly range of influence are not an easy matter.

Where, on the other hand, there was a pre-existing range of influence of a saintly centre, transcending the apices of tribal segmentation, as it were, the consequence of the French advance was to activate wider co-operation and a top-level of chieftaincy. Two such political units are remembered in the general region in this period, between about 1915 and 1933, one each for each of the main centres of Ahansal sanctity, namely for the main lodge and for the Temga group. Tribesmen can recall the names of the individual annual chiefs-of-war. It is however very significant for our general analysis, that the saints under whose auspices these inter-tribal annual 'generals' were elected are remembered more clearly and admitted to be 'senior' and more influential than the annual chiefs-of-war, and this is confirmed by the fact that it is the saints, and not the elective generals associated with them, whose names figure in the French military literature concerning the 'pacification'. The figures who are noted in it, both as opponents and, in the end, as those with or through whom peace was to be concluded or whose submission and co-operation it was necessary to obtain, were Caid Sidi Mha and Sidi Mulay of the main lodge, and Sidi Hussein 'of Temga', as the French described him (though his actual home was the associated lodge of Asker, and to the Berbers he was known as 'of Asker'), then head of the Temga group.

The Intermediate and Ground Levels

At the 'ground level' of segmentation, that is to say, among the smallest groups rotation might be absent if it occurred at the next higher level. A chief elected by rotation and complementarity for a given group would name his representatives in the various sub-groups of the group of which he is chief. In naming them, he would consult with its members but not necessarily observe any principle of rotation: by the time we have reached this ground level, the groups involved might be so small, and co-extensive with the range of daily contact of its members and almost co-extensive with actual blood relationship, that the jealousy of opposed segments is, if not mitigated, at least much complicated by a variety of other immediate relationships and affinities. Hence in naming these representatives (idbaben-n'imur) of a higher-level chief, while note obviously had to be taken of local susceptibilities, there was no need or room for a formal regular rotation principle (which however could still be invoked if the little group found itself on its own and without a chief of a higher level). Nor was there, in the case of such a nomination from above, an occasion to invoke complementarity. The 'upper chief' (amghar n'afella) would consult all the notable members of the sub-group, including, naturally, the sub-sub-group from which he finally draws his representatives. There is no occasion for excluding some sub-group from voting and at the same time making it uniquely eligible for providing the office-holder: the sub-groups involved are too small.

It should be noted that, when an Outsider or a Superior is lacking, when there is neither an Upper Chief nor a Saint to mediate, the principle of complementarity is recognised not merely in 'natural' groups, i.e., reasonably permanent groups with some kind of stable identity, but equally by ad hoc groups which may be brought together temporarily by nothing more than a mutual dispute. For instance, if two groups come in conflict and no outsider is available (or none is invoked for some reason, e.g., economy, or the triviality of the issue) to mediate negotiations for a settlement, a master-of-ceremonies, so to speak, is elected 'internally', from among one of the two disputing groups, by the members of the *other*. Here of course there is complementarity but no rotation. The matter is not expected to come up again, the group is not a permanent one. (Conflicts which affect permanent groups tend, of course, to remain ever latent and to be re-opened when one side or another thinks the time propitious.) The identity of the electing and the eligible groups can be settled by lot; alternatively, as the situation of such conflict is obviously tending towards a solution by collective oath, a possibility which will certainly be invoked even if the crisis isn't allowed to go that far, the rules determining who is to testify (i.e., the accused party) may be applied to the choice of the mediator. These rules are, in theory if not in fact, unambiguous; the mediator will be from the non-testifying group.

To return to the theme of election of chiefs and representatives of chiefs in sub-groups: as described in the case of the final, ground-level sub-groups there generally (though not always) is a mediator in the form of an 'upper chief' of the next larger segment, and complementarity is not invoked any more than rotation. One has reached the lower limit, where political structure is co-extensive with a wide set of daily intimate relationships which complicate and overlay the simple segmentary principle.

In some ways, it is the intermediate levels between the highest and lowest which are the most bewildering. At first, interrogations tend to bring forth three kinds of mutually incompatible answers. (1) The minor chiefs (and indeed major and top ones) are nominated by the Saints – so the Saints are liable to claim. (2) They are nominated by the Upper Chiefs, whose representatives they are. (3) They are elected, as in the case of upper chiefs, by the tribe (*taqbilt*) whose chiefs they are to be.

From the viewpoint of the Saints, it may indeed look as if they 'appointed' chiefs, upper and little ones alike. The tribesmen arrive at the lodge for the election, many holding their counsel, others in disagreement, and it is the recognised task of the igurramen to aid in the achievement of consensus – after all, elections must end in agreement (or fission of group!) and there is no ballot, secret or other.

Yet the igurramen have no means of enforcing, at any rate directly and immediately, an unpopular appointment. They are numerically weak and ex officio pacific. What they generally can do is to assess the feeling and the prospects of the potential candidates and 'appoint' in the sense of ratifying what they guess to be the most acceptable choice anyway. Their ratification of him will make him more acceptable to such dissidents as may remain. Their prestige can only gain by their success as agents of harmony; and recourse to the ultima ratio of an agurram – magical curses or turning of other tribes on to the recusant group – is something which a Saint cannot use too frequently without excessive risk. It is not so much the danger that the curse would not work and divine punishment not be forthcoming (for sooner or later, something disagreeable always does happen, and it is recognised that this kind of punishment is liable to time-lag and to be shared by the innocent with the guilty – in fact, just this is its terror for the guilty, who fear the wrath of the innocent); what does matter is that if the curse lies on too many people, it loses the terror it owes to isolating some. A Saint can curse some of the people all the time, and all the people some of the time, but he cannot curse all the people all of the time.

So the Saints think and claim they appoint, when in fact they ratify and mediate. No doubt, occasions occur when a very well placed saint can indeed simply impose his will on a weakly placed group. He may sway the balance in an evenly matched struggle. And, most likely of all, the emergent concensus may be validated and made palatable to objectors, by being credited to him.

The same arguments apply in connection with the alleged nomination of Little chiefs by Upper ones: the nomination may, in fact, be simply a ratification of a tacit election. The extent to which it is the one or the other must vary from case to case according to context and the strength of parties involved.

One should add that Saints, and Upper chiefs, who claim to nominate lesser ones (as opposed to accepting and ratifying the verdict of an election) have less excuse for their exaggeration in as far as the public and conspicuous ritual act of election, as described in the previous section, sharply underlines the elective nature of chieftaincies, Upper and Little (but not minimal, as described). All the same, this objection to the claims of a boastful Upper chief or Saint is not absolutely conclusive: whilst the act of 'election', the march around the candidates by the other men of the tribe, the placing of green grass on his turban and so on, is solemn and conspicuous, its significance is not necessarily clear: is it the expression of a choice recently made, or the ratification of a choice made earlier? And if it is the latter, it is not crystal clear who made the real choice. My own view is that, in the case of non-Top chiefs, all the three interested parties – saints, Upper chiefs, assembly – in fact contribute to the decision: and in the case of Top chiefs, the same holds of the *two* parties concerned – the tribesmen and the Saints.

Complications

In the case of the 'representatives', of very small sub-groups, there is, as stated, no ritual with circle and green grass, and, superficially, the plausibility of interpreting the selection as a nomination from above are to that extent greater. Nevertheless, for reasons specified (connected with the intimacy of groups at this level) the matter is equally ambiguous or variable here.

There is, however, a strong probability of rotation being observed, if for some reason the group is acting in isolation and thus becomes, for the time being, a 'top group', a political ceiling, as well as a minimal one. Such isolation is quite liable to occur, and not merely as a result of a kind of diplomatic insulation, but simply because for some reason wider groups have not been activated that year. Then, rotation is to be expected, for such a group is of course in a position similar to an ad hoc one brought into being simply by some specific dispute. There being no outside mediator, it is only fair that if the arbitrator is chosen from sub-group A, it is the members of not-A who elect, and vice versa.

Groups which find themselves permanently, and voluntarily, in conditions of such 'diplomatic isolation' such that their own annual chief is the topmost one in his particular series, however small the range of his parish, are the laicised saintly villages. Their saintly origin, however latent and merely potential its actual saintly use, tends to be valuable enough to be safeguarded by avoiding permanent involvements or identification with surrounding groups that are lay in origin as well as in function; identifications such as would be entailed by regularly participating with them in a system of rotating and complementary annual elections. At the same time, the fact that such groups, though of saintly origin, are laicised, means that there are no outstanding sub-groups, families 'born to lead', to be found amongst them, so that the normal elective process takes place. Hence with these groups, the system operates but finds its 'ceiling' very rapidly, i.e., at village level.

The situation is more complicated in non-laicised, effectively saintly groups. Here leadership is, in the nature of things and by the will of God manifested in the flow of grace, vested in the leading families and the leading individuals within these families. At the same time, it would be somewhat below the dignity of an important saint to concern himself with the day to day minor issues of the saintly village: the commander-in-chief, so to speak, is not generally also the captain of HQ company. Thus within the effective saintly village there will be a rotating-complementary system for the internal annual chief, whose importance and authority will of course not be comparable with the local top saints, and whose concern will generally be only with internal and minor matters. In the internal elections of these local annual headman, top Saints would of course not participate either as candidates or as formal voters, though naturally their informal view might be decisive. In the main lodge, an internal system of this type existed, there being two 'rotating' halves of the village. The effective saints all came from one of these two segments, but this did not give that segment any political preponderance: the elections were really from among and by the residual majority of ineffective saints, whether close or distant relatives of the effective ones. This system in the main Lodge survived into the post-pacification period, though only intermittently: for during both a major part of the French period, and during the early years after independence, headmanships were not annual but made permanent, until revocation.

An Example : the Ait Abdi of Koucer

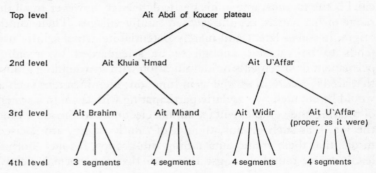

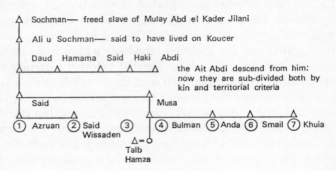

The general segmentation of the Ait Sochman

In 1967, the total population of the Ait Abdi of the Koucer plateau was, according to official statistics in possession of the headmen, a little over 1,800 people: The Ait Abdi, unlike the Ihansalen of the main lodge, seem to be taking part in the general and rapid demographic growth of Morocco. Hence it is reasonable to assume that in the days of tribal independence, which for the Ait Abdi only came to an end in 1933, the figure was much less, something not too far removed from the figure of one thousand.

This means that the segments on level 4 of the diagram, which now have the average population of 120, would then have consisted of about 70 people each. Within each of these segments, not surprisingly given their size, each family can trace its agnatic relationship to all others – at most with a little head-scratching and consultation of neighbours. These social units are not 'clans' in the sense that a man knows he is related to other members without knowing just how: they are 'lineages' in the sense that people know the actual genealogical steps by which they are related.

As described in the diagrams, each of these units, of course, fits into the wider series of nested units making up the Ait Sochman as a whole. Thus each individual can locate himself on a very extensive framework indeed.

The second diagram shows the position of the Ait Abdi in the general structure of the Ait Sochman. Their founder is two generations removed from the founder of the Ait Sochman, with his oriental but not particularly prestigious ancestry.

The diagram also shows the genesis of the seven segments of the important tribe of the Ait Daud u Ali. This tribe is territorially divided between the Taguelft and Anergui regions, a division which cuts across the seven segments. Important transhumancy arrangements exist between the two areas, articulated in terms of the segments. These movements are supervised by the saints of the Temga group from their key shrine of Sidi Ali u Hussein, which is well placed for this purpose; whilst their permanent habitations, as opposed to the apical shrine, guard frontiers between the Ait Daud u Ali and the Ait Said u Ali, and between the Ait Sochman as a whole and the Ait Messat.

The defining founders, as it were, of the seven segments are numbered on the diagram. (No significance attaches to the numerical order.) Note that one segment is Sochman by blood only through its 'mother', who was given in marriage to a *talb*, teacher, from a zawiya further East in the Atlas. One segment, the Ait Khuia, are known as 'children of an old man', being the fruit of a belated and questionable union between the old man Musa and the wife of one of his own sons, Anda. It is said that Musa was aided in this enterprise by Ismail but not by Bulman, who refused.

One of the odder kinks in the rotation-complementarity system of chieftaincy election is found amongst the Ait Abdi of the Koucer plateau, overhanging the Ahansal valley. These Abdi on their stony, high and inhospitable plateau, falling off in steep escarpments on a number of sides, are fairly isolated from their clan-brethren, the other Abdi, by geography, and rather more sharply isolated from most of their other neighbours by mutual hostility. In normal circumstances, they do not appear to have been a part of a wider system of common chieftaincy. But their internal system, restricted to the Abdi of the Koucer, is curious.

For purposes of chieftaincy election, four levels of segmentation must here be taken into account: first of all, there are the Ait Abdi of Koucer as a whole. This social group can only be defined geographically, as 'just those Abdi who live on the Koucer': for more than one clan of the Abdi live there, and neither of the clans who do live there are exhausted there, so to speak, but have members elsewhere too.

The next, second level are the two clans represented on the Koucer, the Ait U'Affar and the Ait Khuia 'Hmad.[1]

The third level: each of these is in turn bifurcated. The Ait Khuia 'Hmad are divided into the Ait Brahim and the Ait Mhand. The Ait U'Affar are divided into the Ait U'Affar proper, so to speak, and the affiliated Ait Widir.

Within the wider, general genealogical system of the Ait Abdi, the Ait Widir occur as a notion co-ordinate with the Ait U'Affar, and thus they should, logically, occur on the previous, second level. But on the Koucer plateau there aren't enough of them to form a group co-ordinate with the Ait Khuia 'Hmad, so they fuse here, socially, with the Ait U'Affar to form, at that level, one group. They happen to use the name of U'Affar at the upper level, though there are roughly as many Widir as there are U'Affar on the Koucer, and one might equally have done it the other way.

[1]See diagram, p. 100.

The fact that the name of the U'Affar rather than that of the Widir is used for the group consisting of both, does not give the U'Affar proper any privileged or special position within the wider group. In fact, the little sub-clan which during the period preceding the French conquest, during French rule, and during early period of independence until the abortive little rising of 1960, secured a pre-eminent position on the Koucer, the Ait Tus, came from the Ait Widir. (On their own account, the Ait Tus owed their dominant position to the fact that they were first to secure a modern, fast-loading rifle. Much has been written about the way in which the Glawi family owed their position to the possession of a Krupp cannon. The Ait Tus did the same at the microscopic level.)

Fourth level: each of the four groups on the previous level is divided into four (and in one case, three) sub-clans, which in turn are composed of individual cohabiting families.

The system of annual chieftaincy was as follows: Chiefs for levels numbers one and two were elected by rotation and complementarity. Top level chief had two rotating segments from which he was elected (these being on level two). Chiefs at level number two had seven or eight electing segments, respectively. (For him, the rotating sub-groups were drawn from level four.) The nominated 'elders-of-parts' were chosen as follows: at level three, by top chief; at level four, by chiefs at level two. Thus the top chief would work through four 'elders of parts', and the two second level chiefs through seven or eight each.

The striking thing about this is that we have here two overlapping systems of rotation and of authority. It is as if a military unit existed in which the colonel dealt with and through lieutenants, whilst captains dealt with and through sergeants (and colonels were elected from amongst captains, and captains from amongst sergeants).

Obviously the most interesting question about this intricate system is whether the two hierarchies, the first-and-third levels one and the second and fourth levels ones, operated simultaneously: the question whether elections and nominations with each of them occurred during the same year (as opposed to the possibility that either of the two systems was only activated, according to circumstances, in different years). Informants assert that the two systems did co-exist simultaneously. Some have asserted, most plausibly, that during years when there was no need of it, the top level system was not activated; others deny this, claiming that both systems were in operation all the time.

Even if this system is exceptionally complex, it constitutes only an elaboration of the characteristic local elements, and seems quite in the spirit of central High Atlas Berber society. In a non-segmentary society, an overlapping double hierarchy, with one chain of command as it were 'shot through' another, would be difficult to conceive,[1] and would presumably lead to an unmanageable confusion of authority. In a segmentary society, the system is conceivable and even plausible. After all, the conflicts which arise and call for arbitration, mediation or settlement by chiefs, arise at one or another of the levels, and involve groups of this or that size, so that the two levels of authority are perhaps unlikely to be invoked for the same occasions: hence confusion and conflict of authority is not likely to arise.

Collective Oath (All for One)

Collective oath has been described as the most characteristic feature of Berber customary law.[2] It is certainly the most interesting. It is of course not an institution unique to Berber society. It does however appear to have been present in all or most Berber societies, and is indeed characteristic of the type of social organisation which they exemplify. In recent times, advances either of full Islamisation or of modern type administrations have effected a decline of this institution, a decline culminating in the establishment of a national, non-tribal and non-variegated legal code in Morocco after Independence in 1956. In the central High Atlas, conditions had, however, favoured its survival until then. It was of course in full operation until the end of tribal independence in

---

[1] The 'parallel hierarchies' of revolutionary communist armies are, after all, parallel: the chains of officers and of political commissars do not 'leapfrog' each other (as they do here), and their functions are not identical, and indeed include mutual supervision.

[2] 'Selon Marcy, la pierre de touche du droit berbère est le serment collectif comme mode normal de preuve. C'est une institution extraordinairement archaïque qu'on retrouve en effet un peu partout, parfois à l'état de traces, de survivance, parfois en pleine vigueur; . . . On peut aussi ajouter le besoin pour de Berbères de ne pas arriver à une décision judiciaire proprement dite, mais bien à un arrangement amiable, à un stade plus ou moins avancé de la procédure'. G. H. Bousquet, *Les Berbères*, Paris, PUF, 1957, p. 113

1933, but it continued to operate, underwritten by the administration's recognition of tribal customary law throughout the period 1933–55.

Berber tribal law varies from tribe to tribe, and the four major and further minor groupings represented in the area of Ahansal influence differ in their respective customs, and indeed differences occur within each of them. Moreover, it would be a mistake to subscribe to a myth of a fully determinate, unambiguous custom, safe in the keeping of the memory of elders, which can be non-arbitrarily invoked at will and which subsists, unwritten but fully formed, in a kind of tribal Platonic heaven mediated by tribal assemblies. The determinacy and freedom from ambiguity which is not generally achieved by written law in the keeping of specialist lawyers, could hardly be achieved by an uncodified law in the keeping of, more or less, all members of the society it serves.

Qaida (this Arabic word for custom is locally understood) is conceived in contrast to *Shra'a* (Koranic law dispensed by those qualified by the appropriate learning or, supposedly, by the igurramen); but it would be wrong to conclude that the tribesmen have a clearly worked out theological notion of the distinction between custom and holy law, and necessarily or always conceive the former as opposed to the latter. This may be so at some times, particularly if there are motives for feeling hostile to Arabs; at other times, I have heard it asserted that there really is no difference between the two. In a certain sense this is true – in that the only 'Koranic law' locally available was dispensed by people ill-qualified in Koranic scholarship, to put it mildly, and did in fact not differ in any systematic way from local views on right and wrong and on proper procedures, which also find their expressions in the procedures, and verdicts of 'customary law'. In the traditional situation, the really significant difference between custom and what was locally believed to be *Shra'a* was not content, but the source of the pronouncement, the identity of the judge or arbitrator. In the traditional condition, if he was a fellow lay tribesman, it was custom, but if he was an agurram, it was deemed to be Koranic law. (When the French presented newly-subjugated tribes with the option of retaining tribal custom or accepting Koranic Law, the choice of course turned out to be quite a different one: between tribal custom adjudicated by tribal elders on the one hand, and on the other, Koranic Law applied by a more or less trained judge, imported from the plain by, and part of, the new administration.)

A further very significant point concerning the nature and conceptualisation of customary law is this: it was seen as something either produced by social convention, or at any rate alterable by it (though unanimity was required, at any rate in theory, to effect a change in tribal custom). In this sense at any rate, tribal custom was secular. What is more remarkable, and in conflict with certain widely held preconceptions of the nature of tribal society in general, is that this is seen and stated to be so by the tribesmen themselves. The existence of a contrastable Holy, written, and theoretically unchangeable Law may have assisted this interesting sophistication.

For a variety of general and specific reasons, it is not possible to include a full study of tribal law, or even its aspects relevant to collective oath, in the present study.[1]

But whilst a detailed account of tribal law and its tribe-to-tribe variations cannot be given, a general sketch of the essential features of collective oath is both possible and essential to the general argument.

Collective oath (*tagellit*) is a legal decision procedure. It is a method for determining the truth or falsity of an accusation, and thereby terminating (at any rate in theory) the dispute occasioned by that accusation. It is a method which invokes supernatural sanctions. It requires that a number of 'co-jurors' (*imgellen*) testify, according to a prescribed formula, in a fixed order, and in a holy place, that the accusation is false. If they do so, the accusation is held to be false. If they refuse to do so or fail to do so or make a slip when doing so, the accusation is held to be established, and the accused partly obliged to make to the injured party the reparation foreseen by customary law for the offence in question. (In theory, the 'fine' is predetermined, though in practice this too

[1]These reasons include: lack of legal competence; lack of space; lack of conclusiveness of evidence on many points of detail; the fact that legal cases in the days of the French were held in presence of a French officer, and I was not given permission to attend those which concerned the village in which I lived, whilst those cases I did attend concerned issues whose background I could not assess; that the notion of custom became politically septic after independence and always was so for the igurramen, who in terms of their own ideology should have had not custom but Holy Law – a belief they have found hard to sustain in modern conditions; the fact that collective oaths are generally held up till after the harvest, thus coinciding with a period when I had to be back in London.

is subject to negotiation and adjustment according to circumstance.)

The order of testifying of the co-jurors is the same as their proximity to the alleged culprit in terms of inheritance rights, by agnatic proximity, (with certain obvious exceptions: a man's son is the first claimant to his inheritance, but of course will not testify if he is under age). If the man's closer agnatic kin is insufficient to provide the required number of co-jurors, whilst a wider segment would provide too many, additional co-jurors can be provided by one of two methods: either one segment is selected from all the equally close segments within the wider one, by lot, to provide the jurors, or one or more is chosen from each of those segments to make up the number.

The connection between obligation to testify and rights on property is clearly understood by the participants: property rights and oath responsibilities follow the same kin lines. The co-jurors are of course also identical with those who must fear or exact vengeance in the case of feud. They are referred to as *Ait Ashra'a,* people of ten, though the number of ten need not be taken literally: a man may have more or less than ten people of ten. Indeed, for serious offences he needs more. The co-jurors are of course not witnesses:[1] it is not supposed that they necessarily or indeed generally have access to knowledge concerning whether the alleged culprit is or is not guilty. It is merely supposed that they know his general character, or are willing to vouch for his good conduct, and are prepared to share the penalties imposed by mundane or extra-mundane forces in punishment for their testimony, should it be false.

The number of co-jurors required varies according to a sliding scale with the gravity of the accusation. For instance, the theft of a single sheep may require two co-jurors, a rape four, a murder of a male forty, the murder of a women twenty.

There is also the kind of conflict in which two large groups (consisting say of several thousand people each) face each other, and the issue is something like the contested rights over a pasture.

---

[1]Professor G.H.Bousquet tells the story of French officers who had so completely misunderstood the institution of collective oath that they wished to penalise co-jurors for 'bearing false witness'. Though a misunderstanding indeed, its effect was that they blasphemously usurped a function of the deity. On this occasion, vengeance was not the Lord's but the District Officer's.

In this kind of case, in which the oath is also liable to be invoked (and was invoked though not used even after Independence, despite its non-recognition by the new national code), there is no culprit to act as focus, in terms of whose agnatic connections one could select the co-jurors. In such a case, the co-jurors are selected from the elders of the testifying side by agreement of both parties.

The time at which the oaths may take place are restricted. Some tribes lay aside certain days, a kind of sessions, at which oaths concerning disputes that have accumulated in the preceding period, are settled. An important rule, generally observed,[1] is that of a kind of 'closed season': no oaths are allowed from a certain date in spring, in April of the agricultural calendar, until one in the early autumn, in September, when the first and important harvest is in. The justification of this rule is that a perjuring party at an oath may bring divine punishment on a whole valley or region, in the form of drought or flood or pestilence. Who would be so foolish as to place his own harvest in jeopardy because some scoundrel has stolen some sheep, and his godless, irresponsible and mendacious kinsmen are ready to swear him out of his predicament? Much better wait until the harvest is in. And so it is. The effective consequence of the rule resembles its overt justification, in helping to safeguard the harvest: the rule prevents wastage of time on oaths, on the negotiations, manœuvres or possible hostilities associated with it, until after the harvest is in. (The matter was inconvenient only for the present observer, who by the time the harvest was safely in, was himself obliged to hurry back for the university term.) Oaths are generally banned during Ramadan, though an exception may be made at night.

The place of the oath varies according to the gravity of the issue, the identity of the parties in conflict, and within certain limits also depends on their agreement. The place may be a village mosque, a holy place, which is not a mosque or the shrine of a saint. The really important rule is this: minor issues are sworn at the nearest mosque or holy place, but major issues, defined as those requiring ten or more co-jurors, are taken to the shrine of the igurramen. This of course turns the igurramen into witnesses or informal masters of ceremonies at the settlement of major disputes,

---

[1] Though I know of minor violations of it, of oaths undertaken in smaller disputes and involving fairly few people.

(which they are in any case for disputes not culminating in oaths), in which their deceased saintly ancestor provides or mediates the transcendental sanctions of the veridicity, witting or unwitting, of co-jurors. This role can be seen in its full importance if it is observed that the demand and the offer of a collective oath are moves in prolonged and complex negotiations, in which there is much bluff on both sides, negotiations which are frequently settled 'out of court' (or perhaps one should say 'out of shrine') without actually reaching the point of oath – though the possibility of doing so or having to do so is one of the factors making for prior settlement. As in elections, the igurramen have ample opportunity for mediation and neutral persuasion in this pre-oath stage.

There are various other considerations affecting the choice of place for an oath. It is held that co-jurors should not be obliged to walk too far: various shrines or holy places tend to be strategically located so that each should serve its own catchment area of disputes. Disputes between members of tribes X and Y will customarily be settled at a shrine fairly easily accessible to both X and Y, whilst another shrine in a different place will be used for disputes between X and Z, and another shrine still for disputes internal to X. The shrine at which the X habitually swear in response to the accusation made by the Y, need not be identical with the shrine at which the Y deny charges brought against them by the X. For instance, the Ait Abdi swore at Timzgida n'Zagmusan when swearing 'against' the Ait Haddidu, whilst the Ait Haddidu, swearing 'against' the Ait Abdi, did so at Ait Tasiska near Imdghas. Or again, the Abdi swearing 'against' the Ait Amzrai did so at SSA, whilst the latter reciprocated at Sidi Bushaq.

But really major disputes will go to fully 'personalised' shrines, i.e., shrines of saints whose real or supposed descendants are extant and function as effective igurramen. Here again, there are very logical considerations governing the choice of the shrine. It goes without saying that, in kinship terms, the saint at whose shrine the oath takes place must not be close to the testifying party. It would be unthinkable, for instance, if one of the laicised (and hence feuding, litigating and oath-indulging) Ahansal group were involved in a dispute with a non-Ahansal one, to settle the conflict by an oath at a shrine of an Ahansal saint. It would of course be assumed and said, plausibly enough, that the deceased saint would be partial to his descendants or kinsmen, and that they could easily perjure themselves in the hope or expectation that, in consideration of the bonds and obligations of kin, the saint will refrain from punishing or invoking divine punishment on them. In the second example cited above, the Abdi are a lay group whilst the Amzrai are a thoroughly laicised village of Ihansalen, though their descent from SSA is in local eyes simply not in doubt and beyond challenge. It would plainly be absurd for the Ait Amzrai to swear at the shrine of SSA, for in consideration of natural ties and affection SSA could well be expected to be lenient to his own offspring and be tempted to overlook a little matter of an untruthful oath. A Berber agurram dead or alive, but especially when dead,[1] is not expected to behave like a Roman judge; he would scarcely be admired for doing so, and to put him in a situation where he might have to do so, borders on the irreverent.

Moreover, as one would expect, the habit of tribes X and Y to testify at the shrine of the (long-deceased) saint Z, correlates with the use by tribes X and Y of the descendants of Z (or rather, of his descendants in the effective saintly line) for such purposes of mediation and so forth as can only be performed by a living rather than a dead saint. One should add that the geopolitics of sanctity may be but need not be identical for the living and for the dead: the geographical-strategic location imposed by the situation on the dead and on the living are sometimes but not always the same. In the case of the main and original Ahansal lodge, it is identical: the shrine of SSA and the village housing his descendants in the most effective and, as it were, the 'straightest' line, are at the same location.

In the case of the next most important shrine, there is a divergence: the shrine of Sidi Ali U Hussein is deep in the middle of the territory of the Ait Daud u Ali of Anergui, a segment of the Sochman tribe. It is located at a place well suited to supervise internal Sochman transhumancy arrangements, notably those of the Daud u Ali tribe with its seven segments, in terms of whom its pasture rights are articulated. (For the internal structure of the Ait Daud u Ali, see diagram on page 100.) The three villages of his

---

[1] A live one might be sensitive to considerations other than kin links, he might even (this is only too likely) have scores to settle with rival kinsmen, and consequently he might even be expected to be less than fair to those close to him by blood.

effective descendants however are on the borders between Sochman and Messat tribes, and between the Daud u Ali and Said u Ali
segments of the Sochman. The guardianship of crucial frontiers,
and the supervision of transhumancy and its tensions, can not in
this case conveniently be done in the same place. So the dead
ancestor is located in one place, the living descendants in another;
and the live ones 'visit' the dead at times crucial for transhumance,
and suitable for receiving donations from the transhumants.

The theory of the oath is as follows: if the testifying group
testifies falsely, it will be punished by supernatural agency. To
swear is to challenge the possibility of supernatural punishment.
Stories are told of men paralysed or going mad or dying soon or
even immediately after taking part in a collective oath and swearing
falsely. There is a slight ambiguity in popular theology concerning
whether the punishment is arranged by the deceased enshrined
saint himself, directly, or whether he merely mediates, as it were
supplying the deity with information on the facts of the case, the
punishment then being meted out by God himself. (The same
ambiguity exists concerning whether grace or blessedness or
plenitude spring directly from the saint, or come from God and
are merely mediated by them.) There is a definite tendency for
locals to protest that only God can dispense baraka (or punishment), so that igurramen are merely the middlemen of Grace
rather than independent springs of it.[1]

It is socially very significant, of course, that the supernaturally
initiated punishment which follows false testimony often strikes
indiscriminately. If, as in the stories that are told, it takes the form
of sudden mysterious death or even of the appearance of a mons-
trous snake, it can of course, and does, wreak its vengeance only on
the culprit, who by his act and mendacity has led his fellows to

---

[1]When I first started working in the region, I was inclined to explain this
insistence on the deity as the prime mover, and others as mere secondary or
mediating causes, to a recent diffusion of more orthodox Islam at the expense of
local cults. I am now inclined to think, from the general tenor and distribution
of these kinds of remark, that this insistence on the deity has been there traditionally and is not something merely emerging in recent decades. The social
implications of this belief is *not* so much to make the position of individual
igurramen precarious, as to explain and justify a fairly low level of expectation
from saintly or magical interventions. One prays or makes a sacrifice, the saint
mediates the request, but it is God's inscrutable will if the prayer or sacrifice are
ineffective. In this respect, local tribesmen fully conform to the stereotype of
'Islamic fatalism'.

bear false witness. But if, as more frequently it does, the super-natural punishment works through natural forces such as floods or droughts, it strikes not the culprit alone but a whole valley or region. Hence indirectly, one who swears falsely and involves his agnates in false testimony, has not merely sinned against God, but equally, and perhaps more significantly, endangered his kin and his neighbours, in quite a wide sense: for they will have their share of the painful consequences and repute of his ill deeds. (And, of course, anyone responsible for involving his kin in an oath is liable to make himself open to accusations of responsibility when later a flood or drought comes, as sooner or later it will.)

The general rules for the operation of the oath as a decision procedure are as follows: if all the required co-jurors turn up, testify, and make no error, this, at any rate in theory, ends the matter: the accused man is vindicated, and the dispute settled in favour of the accused and his kin. (If they swore falsely, it is their look out and, alas, of anyone else unfortunate enough to be in the path of the flood, or similar disaster, when it comes.)

If, however, one or more of them fails to turn up or refuses to testify or makes an error in the course of his testimony, the case is settled in favour of the accusing party, and the accused must pay the compensation which custom foresees for the offence in question. The rules on this point are variable, ambiguous and adjustable, but I am schematically presenting the simplest case.

The procedure requires a master of ceremonies, an *anahkam*. He is not necessarily or generally an agurram: he is preferably a neutral outsider to the two groups in conflict. If the two groups already jointly have an *amghar,* or are parts of a wider group having one, the anahkam will be chosen by this chief. If not, he may be chosen by lot or by agreement, and if necessary may even be one of the two parties in conflict. (If so, the usual rule of comple-mentarity obtains: if chosen from one group, the other group does the choosing.)

The anahkam manages the proceedings, is empowered to allow and forbid participants to speak, and so forth. He tells the first of the co-jurors what it is that he is required to swear. He in turn is entitled to a certain number of 'rehearsals' for the benefit of the succeeding co-jurors, rehearsals during which a slip does not count. The number of such preliminary repetitions varies. (The figures given tend to be *six* and *three*.) After that, the real testimony begins.[1] The co-jurors are lined up, and each moves forward as his turns come, beckoned on by the first co-juror who has already dismissed the previous one, after his oath, saying 'Thou has spoken the truth'. A mistake counts as a failure to testify, but the anahkam is entitled to excuse a slip if he chooses.

The oath formulae (in Berber) tend to be as follows:

O Lord (three times)
I present myself before Sidi X (the saint before whose shrine the oath is taking place)
I have not killed your brother (for example).

Or again:

O Lord (three times)
All the way from here to Mecca,
The thing in this case I have not stolen nor seen.

Who pays the fine? The rules vary, but one rule frequently cited, and most characteristic and also most intriguing, is this: the minority within the set of agnates 'defeated' at the oath, if a defeat has occurred. If, for instance, the majority of the required agnates did testify, and a minority refused, thereby ensuring the defeat of their own whole party, then it is this recusant minority who is responsible for meeting the cost of the defeat which they have caused! If, on the other hand, the majority refuses to testify, it is the minority who did testify, and nevertheless lost, who bear the burden arising out of a suit in which the majority of their agnates had refused to participate.[2]

The striking thing about these rules is that they are clearly designed to reinforce, not the sense of obligation to truth, or the

---

[1]One minor rule of procedure is often cited, namely, that no-one must turn up with a stick. This rule is claimed to have its origin in an episode when a man came to testify, falsely, that he had repaid a debt. He turned up with a stick, and requested the accuser kindly to hold it for him whilst he, the accused, was testifying. Unknown to the accuser, the money owed was hidden inside the stick. So the culprit testified and of course escaped supernatural punishment, for whilst he was swearing, the money was indeed, in a sense, in the plaintiff's hands.

This rather popular and much recounted tale would seem to indicate that the agencies responsible for supernatural punishment are narrowly legalistic in its application. I do not think this is the implication of the story. Tales of cunning, successful or outwitted, are very characteristic of Berber oral literature.

[2]This rule is sometimes varied, and informants claim that the recusant majority will nevertheless make a contribution towards the cost, unless there is unanimity, everyone except the accused man refusing to testify, in which case he alone is responsible for meeting the cost as best he can.

fear of the supernatural, militating against perjury, but on the contrary, the sense of agnatic solidarity, conduct along the principle 'My clan, right or wrong!' The rules penalise the dissident, minoritarian non-conformist clansmen, whichever way things go: they place a premium on intra-clan conformity. That they do so could only lead one to suppose that internal clan cohesion is not always all it could be: and other evidence confirms that this precisely is indeed the case.[1] In as far as the system of trial by collective oath is precarious, it is so not in virtue of the excessive sense of clan loyalty – which is what the outsider would fear but for exactly the opposite reason! – namely, *lack* of agnatic cohesion: the rather surprising rules of 'liability' for fines bear eloquent testimony to this.[2] Berber society, at any rate, seems closer to the danger of Hobbesian anarchy than to that of a claustrophilic 'closed society' in which group-membership and loyalty overrides all else.

The popular belief that tribesmen, whilst opposed to each other, will always and automatically and wholeheartedly combine in their kin groups when in opposition to outside groups, seems a myth. Berber kin groups can sometimes be no more than, as it were, the diplomatic starting-position, the alignment which has geography, habit, inertia, inheritance and co-operation expectations, or information on its side, and which will not be altered by a diplomatic revolution without a positive incentive and some initiative – but which may well be broken if that incentive or initiative are present.

How could this system work? Let us begin with the theory held by the participants themselves, which is also the (in my view) naïve theory sometimes held by observers. This theory is, of course, the one which invokes the transcendental sanctions, or the belief in their operation, and explains the efficacy of collective

[1] During the French advance in the twenties and thirties social units resisted or made their peace with the Rumi in a way which sometimes cut across neat lines of kin solidarity. During the local political intrigues of the years following Independence, alignments by no means always followed kin lines.

[2] In the Isha tribe, it appears that during the French period, rules against unwilling co-jurors had to be *strengthened*, because 'people feared the power of the shrines so much that they were unwilling to take the risk of testifying'. In fact, there is no reason to suppose that the hold of transcendental beliefs over people increased during the Protectorate: but the need for kin support declined with security, and therefore also the willingness to take part in oaths.

oaths in terms of it. 'God or the Saint will in fact send punishment on perjurers; therefore co-jurors will not swear falsely; therefore collective oath is a good way of determining the truth of an accusation and ending a dispute.' This, indeed, is the official local belief. Or, in the third person, in the words of the beholder: 'The co-jurors believe that supernatural punishment will strike them if they testify to a falsehood; therefore they will not willingly do so; therefore, collective oath is a tolerable way of determining truth and ending disputes.'

The proposition asserted in the Third Person, as an explanation, seems to me false, redundant and insufficient. Empirically, the belief of Berbers in the transcendental sanctions is not so strong, or if strong not so compelling, as to prevent quite frequent occurrences of perjury. Perjury does occur. On general grounds, it is difficult to believe that some social arrangements could be sustained simply by a belief, though a belief may help: thus the theory is, on its own, insufficient. Moreover, it is redundant, for if the social mechanisms are considered, they turn out to be sufficient, without any additional assumption of a compelling superstition. (The unpredictability of the punishment for perjury, and the fact that it strikes the innocent with the guilty, both of which are clearly recognised by the locals, are relevant here.)

What is necessary is that the belief should be part of the social atmosphere: that everyone should be able to take it for granted, and notably that others seem to take it for granted, and hence that invocations of it should be possible without justification, indeed without any eyebrows raised. What else does belief mean? There are indeed circumstances and forms of life when it can mean a good deal more. But tribesmen, or even their village scribes, are not philosophers wrestling with faith and doubt. In this kind of context, believing, and acting as though one believed, are not to be distinguished sharply. And the type of conduct required is not that of a man fully confident of a material consequence and allowing for it in his calculations, but merely that of a man who, in the short run, allows for the fact that everyone else will pay reasonable deference to the belief. There is no good answer to the question whether the tribesmen 'really believe' the assumptions on which the oath is based. They say they do. The fact that they are willing to perjure themselves indicates that sometimes their faith is less compelling. Yet they are not sceptics either.

In order to work, a decision procedure must not be predetermined. A penny which always comes down heads, and is known to do so, is no use for a toss. A judge who always or never condemns is no judge. The first question which a theory of the functioning of collective oaths has to answer is – how does this procedure avoid being predetermined in favour of the testifying party, who can 'swear themselves out' of any accusation?[1] What would one think of a law court in our society in which the accused and the jury were identical, and in which nothing but a transcendental fear (of consequences well known to be capricious and unpredictable in their coming!) stood between the accused, and his acquittal of himself by himself in his capacity of juror? Yet collective oath really amounts to just this.

Collective oath is made possible by segmentary organisation. The two groups which face each other in conflict lack not merely an effective overwhelming power standing between them and enforcing law and order over them in the wider society of which they are both a part; but equally, they lack such effective and specialised enforcement agencies internally. This is the crucial fact. Conflicts are latent, and sometimes rampant, inside each of the groups as well as between them. The existence and nature of these internal conflicts is of course highlighted by the existence of the rules concerning the consequences of disunity amongst the co-jurors.

What sanction does a group possess against its own members (e.g., one whose acts cause trouble between it and other groups)? Ultimately, death. The tribesmen, as stated earlier, (p. 46), distinguish two kinds of fratricide, good and bad. Bad fratricide is such as is held to have been unjustified by the acts or character of the killed brother, and it calls for the payment of blood-money by the killers to the wider group of which both they and the killed man are members.[2] Good fratricide is the killing of a brother who

---

[1]This question must be answered, despite the fact, stressed above, that actually these clans are not as cohesive and loyal as they are sometimes held to be: which provides a further problem, but does not allow one to evade the first and crucial one.

[2]This possibility shows how this tribal society does not altogether conform to the ideal type of a pure segmentary society, in which groups existed only in opposition to other co-ordinate groups. It shows a group possessing a kind of corporate identity in opposition to its own erring members.

There are other, analogous respects in which Berber groups of about village

is recognised to be a nuisance to his kin and to others: and through being a nuisance to others, he automatically is a nuisance to his kin, for they will have to 'bail him out' by testifying, or by contributing to a fine, or by getting engaged in a feud. Informants remember cases of such 'good' fratricide: men taken off into the woods by their own kin and killed.

But things need not generally get so bad as to require killing, the ultima ratio of the kin group. There is also a penultimate sanction: let the culprit down at the oath! If there is a majority of those favouring and adopting this course, they do not even incur a formal liability (though if the group is to persist despite its division and defeat at the oath, the odds are that they will nevertheless contribute to the fine incurred by the defeat). But it may be unpredictable till the last moments what the internal 'voting' in the co-juring group will be, and reluctant co-jurors may take the risk, or may even prefer the certainty of incurring a liability of a fine, to facing the consequences, transcendental and social, of testimony in a bad case. Leaving out the transcendental fears, which however are significant in providing the reluctant co-juror with a good excuse, there are the social considerations. Of these, the most obvious is that a social group which habitually and persistently makes use of the collective oath to 'bail out' its own members, is inviting its various enemies to protect themselves jointly against it, and to form a defensive or indeed aggressive coalition. (The group itself may hope to form a counter-coalition and indeed such opposed groupings, in the state of latent or overt hostility, exist anyway: but to rely on this wider group, the least a group can do is not to overstrain its credit with it by asking its members too often

---

size (300 people or so) are not 'purely' segmentary but do have a corporate existence vis-à-vis individuals or sub-groups, (as opposed to the 'pure' segmentary situation in which groups are 'activated' into overt existence only by opposition to other co-ordinate groups at the same level). Thus bride-price paid to the bride's father is extremely small and nominal, whilst the real expense of marriage is the wedding-feast, paid for by the groom, which, however, profits the group as a whole and not the bride's family specifically. Or again, the traditional punishment for the adulterer is the provision of a feast for the *community*. Adultery-price, like bride-price or blood-money for 'bad' fratricide, is to 'society' rather than the wronged group. For a similar situation in the Aures mountains of Algeria, see Germaine Tillion, *Le Harem et Les Cousins*, Editions du Seuil, 1966, pp. 140 and 141.

to appear at collective oath.) The oath, particularly if it is one concerning a major issue and taking place at a saintly shrine, ensures publicity for the dispute and its context.

But equally, co-jurors, though reluctant to swear, may be reluctant to risk the open internal fission that may follow on a refusal to testify. There are thus generally two conflicts going on simultaneously: one between the accusing and the testifying parties, and the other inside the testifying party itself: a segmentary situation indeed. In fact, the putting of this strain or potential strain on the party of the accused is part of their ordeal or punishment.

Another consideration is this: the sanction of overt violence, of a feud, is in any case open to the injured group. They can embark on this course anyway, not giving the group of the offender the opportunity of an oath; or they may allow the oath to take place and when it has been (from the offenders' viewpoint) successfully accomplished, seize on some pretext (or, for that matter, without pretext) and re-open hostilities. So the accused party does not have such an overwhelming incentive to make use of the oath to 'clear' itself in all circumstances: when the opponent is too profoundly incensed, or very well placed to commence aggression, perjury is a doubtful way out.

It is noteworthy that the actual development of an oath-situation cannot be inferred simply from the formal rules (even if those rules when cited were always consistent, which is conspicuously not the case: on the contrary, it is contextual interpretation which alone seems to be able to make sense of these inconsistencies). For instance, it is claimed that the significance and the consequences of an oath 'broken' by a recusant co-juror depends on that co-juror's reputation and standing. If he is of low repute and his unwillingness is held to be just one further example of his moral turpitude and failing sense of loyalty, *he* is made financially responsible for the consequences of the lost oath, i.e., the fine. Recusant co-jurors are also not beyond the suspicion that they have been bribed by the opposite side. This possibility of corruption is easily invoked, and I was once given a list of corrupt recusant co-jurors by an eager informant in the evident hope that I should spread the news. If on the other hand he is a man of standing, with a reputation for responsible conduct, his failure to testify is held to indicate that the accusation was just, and the responsibility for compensation shifts to the culprit and those who would stand by him. Thus the oath (like elections) is not merely a matter of counting heads or following a rigid legal formula. It is a procedure which restores (perhaps only temporarily) the unanimity of the group, which invokes the future verdict of a supernatural authority on those who had imperilled it (a verdict which, however, is generally open to interpretation), and which in *two* conflicts – in the one between the two groups and the one within the testifying group – shifts responsibility for compensation and restoration of balance on to the weaker group, numerically or otherwise, on pain of remaining in the wider group at all. Conform, or pay, or find a new group! Another significant rule is that a man who is without buttermilk, i.e., a man too poor to have much to risk by false testimony or to be able to contribute to the consequences of a lost oath, is not allowed to swear.

One might well ask what sanctions can induce the defeated minority to pay up. Part of the answer is the official one – the pressure of public opinion requiring that right be done,[1] an opinion mediated by the amghar and sanctioned by the respect due to him.[2] This, and the desire to placate the kinsmen on the other side of (the minor of the major) fence in the case, do count for something.

But the real answer is that, in effect, there is no sanction. If the group is to continue as a co-juring group, co-responsible as objects or as pursuers of vengeance, the individual who does *not* swear with his group must either make up, or substantially help towards making up, of the resulting loss, or find himself another group. The correct way to look at the situation is to see that there is this alternative, rather than sanction.

And this alternative is actually formalised in the rules cited as governing the oath. A man who is unwilling to testify with his

---

[1] Berber saying: *Abrid abrid*! literally 'the way is the way', and uttered in semi-earnest, semi-ironic tones accompanying the English 'orders be orders'. It means, of course, that right must be done, though alas, it sometimes is not. It is perhaps characteristic of a non-segmentary society that *orders* are orders, and of a segmentary one, that the *way* is the way, for there is no authority to enforce orders.

[2] One who answers back to the amghar, they say, finds all his goods taken away by the incensed fellow-tribesmen. This picture, though it may have applied to given episodes, would in my opinion if taken too literally or generally give a quite false and exaggerated idea of the real power of the annual amghar.

co-jurors may do so by finding himself a similar number[1] of co-jurors to accompany him in his refusal. Having succeeded in doing so, the co-juror need not swear – in two senses: the rules say so and, more significantly, he has found a new co-juring group.[2] The initial question concerning the sanctions of the oath-procedure is perhaps misplaced. The oath is an opportunity not an obligation. (An opportunity for the accusing or testifying group to give in, and appear to give in to a supernatural authority, and not to a mundane rival.)

This rule is balanced by another, or rather by a valuation characteristically expressed: a man unwilling to testify by a kinsman should in all decency notify him in good time, so that his kinsman in trouble and facing the possibility of an oath should have time to find himself new co-jurors to fill the gap by the usual procedure of making a sacrifice 'to' a new juror or group. If it is improper not to swear with one's agnates, it is doubly improper not to do so without good notice.

Within Berber villages, there is in fact a good deal of jockeying for position and changing of oath-alliances, quite apart from the

[1] The rule has been given me in various forms, one requiring him to find the same number of co-jurors as those initially required, another requiring him to find double their number. I have no actual knowledge of such a case, and am not clear just what the second lot testify – whether merely their reluctance or the validity of the initial accusation. Nor is it clear whether the identity and order of the second lot is prescribed – e.g., to be drawn from further available agnates in order of proximity – or whether this is simply a case of finding a new group. Within village communities, this distinction would not be a sharp one. The first alternative is suggested by the fact that informants concede or even highlight the possibility of a regress, a chain-reaction of loyalty – that one of the second lot may again opt out and invoke further ones.

All this is probably just one of those cases of elaborate folk jurisprudence one frequently comes across here. But though of not too much significance when interpreted literally, it does highlight the reality of the oath-situation and the alternatives facing those involved: swear or find a new group with whom you will swear and who will swear with you!

[2] There is another recognised way of avoiding the oath. A co-juror may approach the plaintiff and request to be excused the oath, for a consideration or even without. If he does so overtly because he holds the accusation to be justified, this would of course 'break' the oath: but what he will characteristically do is to claim ignorance of the merits of the case, and simply profess fear of the transcendental commitment. The plaintiff may (but need not) accept the request, in which case the accused does not require to fill that particular gap in his list of co-jurors. The plaintiff may of course have motives for remaining on cordial terms with some of the agnates of the man whom he is accusing: if he insists, he might indeed drive them to loyal behaviour. If he lets them off, without thereby yet winning he may advance the isolation of the alleged culprit.

more important and permanent inter-village and inter-area re-allocations following serious feuds and violent conflicts. A self-re-allocation does not appear to be too difficult, even for notorious trouble-makers, and has on its side and belief that one should not, or even could not, refuse one who has 'sacrificed to one'. There is the cost of the sacrifice (one beast) to be considered. More impor-tant, a man who re-allocates himself in this manner does not acquire inheritance rights, or necessarily claims such as pasture rights where this is relevant (in the case of larger groups) in his new position. Nor does he lose his rights of this kind in his old position, though if distance is involved, he will do so in effect. It would be interesting to know whether the pull of inheritance rights causes these internal re-alignments to tend to come back to the initial position in the fullness of time. I lived mainly in a saints' village where internal politics are somewhat different in this respect and do not find expression in co-juring (top saints in principle don't swear), and hence cannot answer this question.

It is in the intermediate situations, when the rights and wrongs of the accusation are not all that crystal clear, or when the accusing party itself welcomes a justification for not starting a feud (always provided it does not lose too much face), that the oath is useful. The oath provides the injured party with a way of retreating for apparently objective reasons, and accepting a transcendentally under-written verdict, without appearing to confess weakness: if the accused are still guilty, it is now for the transcendental powers to punish them. It also provides an opportunity for the accused party to give in, for co-jurors to let down an agnate, without necessarily and finally destroying the cohesion of their own group of confessing fear of their opponents: for they can invoke their fear of the shrine, their moral concern with the wellbeing of their kinsmen and neighbours, not to mention abstention from perjury. The accused man would take a very poor view of an agnate and potential co-juror who refused from pure moral scruple, who claimed to be actuated in his refusal by a Kantian respect for the moral law as such: such pure-mindedness would be construed as sheer and unforgivable disloyalty. It is different if the reluctant co-juror can point to the dangers for the whole group – which is wider than the testifying subgroup – inherent in the oath and its perils.

Just as it would be wrong to suppose the oath always pre-determined in favour of the testifying party, so it would also be mistaken to see it simply as a cloak of right over mere might. It is true that the oath procedure favours a cohesive and determined group. Such a group, loyal towards its accused member, whom it does not consider a liability likely to involve them in endless oaths and feuds, and determined to help him out, will come out victorious from the ordeal by oath, quite irrespective of the 'objective' merits of the case. But just such a group could in any case only be constrained by force to make reparations for the wrong done, and there is, after all, none other than the injured group to apply the force. But it is precisely in such a case – when facing a cohesive and determined group – that it is least desirable to try and apply force. So one may welcome this opportunity for not having to do so. It is still open to the injured party to try and do so after all: not much is lost through the possibility of invoking the oath, and much is gained – the possibility of retreat without loss of face, and the exploration of the possibility that the opposing group may not be so cohesive, or so determined concerning the current issue, after all. The oath tests the cohesion and the feeling of the group. In brief, the oath is the continuation of the feud by other means.

It is a decision procedure whose verdicts are sensitive to a number of factors: the determination and loyalty of the testifying set of co-jurors, of their conviction concerning the merits of the case and in particular the character and likely future conduct of the accused man, of their assessment of the feeling and determination of their opponents. The feeling of 'public opinion' concerning the merits of the case is mediated and perhaps crystallised by the witnessing and information-diffusing saints and the strength of the parties, and the parties' assessment of the feelings of others. Thus one of the factors influencing the verdict is the feeling on both sides concerning the justice of the accusation, the merits of the case. This is only one consideration, but at least it is one. Thus justice does not fare as badly as it might.[1] In cases when all other factors

---

[1] If this account of the inner mechanics of the oath is valid, there are obvious and striking analogies between it and various other procedures for settling conflicts, procedures whose verdict is sensitive to the merits of the case and the strength and the cohesion and the determination of the parties. Strikes are one example. Others can be found in international relations, in the voting by 'blocks' at the United Nations where also the loyalty of one's block 'co-jurors' cannot be wholly relied on. Blocks at the United Nations are like clans, tending to vote together right-or-wrong, as clansmen testify together. Yet it would be a mistake to conclude that the voting procedure is a waste of time and the voting totally predetermined by the alliances. Conflicts occur within blocks as well as between

are poised against it, justice will be neglected – but in those cases, who could help it anyway? But in cases when those other factors are neutrally poised, or not quite determinate or unpredictable – and this is often the case, for who can really gauge the determination of the parties, of the accusers, or of the willing, and of the reluctant co-jurors? – in those cases, justice may as it were slip in between the other obscure factors.

A legal system sensitive only to justice and the merits of the case would be a positive nuisance in an anarchic society. As the weak are not always in the wrong, such a system would soon accumulate a mass of totally unenforceable verdicts which, remaining unobserved, would bring the whole system into disrepute – and in the end there would be no system at all. A system, on the other hand, such as that of collective oath, is subtly and all at once sensitive both to might and right: it probes the accused party both for conviction and cohesion and leaves it alone if either its conviction of the justice of its case, or its cohesion (irrespective of the merits of the case) is very strong. But it is just in those conditions that a verdict against the accused group would be unenforceable. Such a

---

them. One way in which intra-block discipline can be restored, short of violence, is by letting down an ally at the vote (equals oath, in the tribal situation). This will not be done lightly, but on occasion it may have to be done. The out-of-line clansman or clansmen may of course have been banking on clan cohesion prevailing when the crunch comes – and it may be that the only way to teach him or them a lesson is, for once, to let them down, carry the cost, and take the risk of irreparable damage to the alliance.

Just this of course happened in the Western alliance in 1956, during the Suez crisis. Out-of-line clansmen in the Western block were relying on not being let down by their allies when all had to stand and be counted, and were severely disciplined by being let down at the oath.

Analogies can of course also be found in modern society for the violent form of the oath, i.e., the feud. It is sometimes supposed that the feud, systematic revenge taken on the kin of the offender, presupposes a special kind of mentality, an undeveloped sense of individual responsibility. This is absurd. The feud makes sense when two groups face each other, without any third and strong party to keep the peace. In such conditions, each group can only police its own members, and each group will only restrain its own members if threatened, as a totality, by the other group. Without such a threat, it will be neither willing *nor able* to restrain its own members. When, for instance, the Israelis raid a neighbouring Arab state in retaliation for previous raids, this is not due to some kind of regression to an early and tribal stage of Hebrew history: it is part of the situation, not merely that no individually specific sanctions are available, but also that the rulers of the Arab state in question, even if they wished, because of the conflicts internal to the Arab side, could not restrain their own raiders unless *forced* to do so. Thus the feud depends on a structural situation, and not on something like a 'stage of mental development'.

system rescues some right from the wreckage in those cases (not so rare) where might, the balance of power, is unclear, generally owing to divisions within the accused party. The system is thus much better than none at all. It aids the attainment of at least temporary consensus, and places the responsibility for it on the supernatural.

The living igurramen as such do not necessarily have any connection with the oath: it is only their dead, enshrined ancestor who sanctions it, who through his prestige, his supposed powers or influence with the deity, provides it with its rationale. The living igurramen may but need not be the masters of ceremonies at the oath. But the fact that the oath does take place at their shrine has obvious consequences: not only does the prestige of the dead saint lend the proceedings solemnity (and the prestige of the dead saint has considerable correlation with the influence of his effective saintly descendants) but it also insures much publicity to the merits of the case and the comportment of the contesting parties. In a society which keeps few written records, this kind of publicity ensures a wide audience and remembrance for the act. Everyone is in touch with the saints. They are a centre of information. More-over, if parties turn to arbitration rather than decision by oath, it is to the igurramen they go as a neutral court of appeal.[1] But it is generally not clear till the last moment whether an oath really will take place or whether the parties will settle 'out of shrine'. So it is, naturally, convenient that the dead mediators and the living arbitrators should be located so close to each other.

---

[1] Bousquet remarks (*Les Berbères*, Paris 1957, p. 102) in connection with the systemisation of tribal legal procedure and organisation under the French, that '. . . on a créé de juridictions d'appel, supratribales, tout à fait contraires à l'esprit de la coutume'. It does not seem to me true that the notion of a court of appeal outside the tribe is contrary, let alone wholly contrary, to the spirit of Berber tribal law. This may be so in some places, but it is not so in the Central High Atlas. Traditionally, the tribes did employ extra-tribal appeals of at least two kinds: to the igurramen, and to neighbouring tribes with whom reciprocal arrangements existed for this purpose. It is true that generally, though not always, these reciprocal arrangements would be with a tribe to whom one was linked at possibly some high level of segmentary abstraction. Intra-tribal systems of appeal also existed, and were sometimes highly developed, e.g., with the Ait Atta, who had a final court of appeal at Igherm Amezdar.

It is true that in the earlier days of the French rules, going up to the second-world-war period, the grouping of tribes for purposes of appeal did not always follow affinities of custom, and did to this extent violate the spirit of it and lose some of its attractiveness to litigants, who were disinclined to make use of a court of appeal which might put them in the hands of men ignorant of their own circumstances. This was largely remedied during the later years of French rule.

After Independence, collective oath was abolished, and replaced by a modern oath on the Koran by accused or witness, but of course not by any agnatic collectivity. Tribesmen held this form of testimony as of little account, *kif walu*, as nothing. In terms of transcendental belief, one might suppose that the failure to use a shrine was what made the modern oath so feeble: but structurally, what mattered was the failure to commit and implicate, with the guarantee of maximum publicity, all the people on whom the accused is normally most dependent.

The Feud

I have concentrated on the oath in order to sketch in the type of relationship for which the igurramen, living and dead, provide mediation, appeal and sanction: but one might equally have taken the feud. Indeed, as stated, the two are correlative or alternatives: serious offences, supposed or real, are followed either by oath or by saintly mediation or by a feud, or indeed by combinations or successions of these. But the feud was abolished, and indeed suppressed with remarkable effectiveness, by the French during the period of their rule.[1] The oath was not: it continued to be the centre-piece of the (now somewhat stylised and systematised) customary law. Under the Protectorate, a man who committed murder went to prison *and* his kinsmen paid blood-money to the family of the victim. (This fitted in nicely with the traditional arrangements, when blood-money was paid and the murderer went into exile.)

It is very tempting to believe that the effectiveness of the suppression of the feud by the French was connected with the perpetuation of the oath. Of two possible reactions to a situation, which had always been in some measure complementary alternatives, one was suppressed but the other remained, providing an invaluable outlet. The intrigues and passion which clearly accom-

[1] The effectiveness of the suppression of the feud in Morocco is in marked contrast to the failure to do so in Berber parts of Algeria, notably Kabylia. The explanation lies partly in differences in administration: Kabylia was under-administered by lawyers; Berber areas of Morocco were administered by the army, by quite a well developed and fairly extensive system brought into being by the long years of the 'pacification'. Cf. G. H. Bousquet, 'Le Droit Coutumier des Ait Haddidou des Assif Melloul et Isselaten', in *Annales de l'Institut d'Etudes Orientales* (Faculté de Lettres de l'Universite d'Alger), Tome XIV, Année 1956, p. 206.

panied litigation under the French were striking features of Berber legal life: so were the cheapness, ease and frequency of litigation, which seemed to be the national sport. Sessions were frequent and prolonged, the cost minimal, involving little over and above the bribe of the members of the 'customary law tribunal' – now a permanent, formalised jema'a, with a small number of regular members – a bribe which was not very costly.

Effective igurramen (amongst whom I mostly lived) were required not to feud (nor, by extension, litigate): this part of their self-image is I think roughly true, (with qualifications), and indeed it follows from their central role. They claimed not to feud or litigate at all. A mediator who himself was involved in a network of hostilities and alliances would not be much use for mediation and sanctuary. The laicised igurramen who formed the immediate entourage of the effective ones, i.e., who lived in the same village (in the sanctuary), also did not feud (though these did litigate or appeal for arbitration). They lived in the shadow of the saintly peace. Of laicised Ihansalen who lived in separate villages, some did and some did not feud; some did so overtly, some claimed not to do so but in fact did, others did but only if very gravely provoked. Just this is one of the crucial features on the spectrum of effective-lay along which the tribesmen of saintly descent are strung out, and which will be explored more fully below.

Traditionally a murder, if it was not followed by simple overt hostility (feasible for larger or for more distant groups), was followed by the flight of the murderer and ten agnates, his *Ait Ashra'a,* people of ten. The flight would aim at safety by distance, or by flight to the tribe's traditional 'enemies', or to the sanctuary of the saints. Negotiations would then be opened through the saints, and after some days the group of the murdered man would allow the agnates, though not the killer himself, to return. Peace would be restored by the eventual agreement and payment of blood-money, and the exile of the murderer. The second condition might or might not, sooner or later, be withdrawn by the group whose member had been killed.

The rule cited as governing the payment and distribution of blood-money is as follows: the culprit pays one half and the rest of his Ait Ashra'a the remaining half, whilst the sons (or failing any, the brothers) of the murdered man receive one half, and the Ait Ashra'a share the other half.

Concerning the flight of 'the ten' I sometimes posed the following question: suppose there are nine agnatic relatives of a man of a given closeness, and at the tenth and eleventh place in order of proximity, there are two men, brothers, say, who are, of course, *equally* close in relationship to the murderer. Must they both flee, or may one of them procure immunity by claiming – *I am the Eleventh*?

The question of The Eleventh raised somewhat, if I may say so, my reputation for wit: it was received with much hilarity. The implication is, plainly, that it would be a most unwise Berber who placed his trust in such arithmetical considerations. In other words, the rules should not be interpreted too literally, despite the fact that numbers such as 'ten' occur in them. (Similarly, the fact that 'custom' is said to prescribe given fines for offences, or a specified blood-money, should not be allowed to obscure the fact that the precise sum was a subject for negotiation and no doubt varied with the strength of the offended party, the wealth of the offending one, and so forth.)

Amongst the Ait Atta of Talmest I was assured that the rules governing the murder of a woman by a woman were parallel to those governing male homicide, except that, as usual, the numbers involved were halved: only five women had to flee. It is to be assumed that they would have to be from her currently effective group (her husband's household, if married). I do not know whether cases of such feminine murders did really occur significantly: I am rather inclined to think that this particular rule is one further case of the folk jurisprudential elaboration in an l'art pour l'art spirit to which North Africans are often given. (All the same, feminine quarrels between women of different families are most plausible amongst pastoralists such as the Ait Atta: for it is the woman who generally go to the wells to fetch water and water the sheep and goats, and at the well they are naturally inclined to quarrels over precedence.)

Concerning the feud in general, there is an obvious difference between feuds according to the size and relationship of groups involved. Those involving small groups living in close vicinity of each other are settled, and needs must be, by blood-money and/or exile of the murderer or, if beyond settlement, by the exile of one of the two groups. Feuding of larger groups may be more permanent but still be occasionally in abeyance in the interests of a wider conflict, in which the two feuding parties find themselves on the same side. But such conflicts too may become so serious as to require a re-affiliation of one of the two groups, if not its migration. (Thus, for instance, the important segment Ait Hussein of the Ait Isha was involved so seriously and for so many years with other clans of the Isha, that it re-affiliated itself to the Ait Mhand, on whose borders it is situated.) The widest conflicts still, between very large tribal groupings, also do not generally manifest themselves as 'war' in the civilised sense: i.e., a permanent state of total hostility involving all sub-groups: but those hostilities, though sometimes latent, tend to be of long duration. The only wider shared loyalty mitigating them is a partial overlap in the range of saints to whom the two groups bring donations, and who can be invoked for mediation and settlement.

Finally, there may also be – contrary to ideology and principle, but nevertheless a reality one must shamefacedly confess – actual feuding as opposed to mere intrigue between saintly groups. At least two cases of this are remembered. To my knowledge, it has only occurred between saintly groups some distance, geographically, from each other. One striking instance was the prolonged and direct hostility between the main lodge and Zawiya Temga, occasioned by the theological issue of the Islamic propriety of dancing. (See below, p. 247). The other occurred within the Temga-Asker-Aziz group, despite the close links which still bind this set of lodges. In this case, violence only took place by proxy, two lodges in conflict each setting its clients at those of the other, thus exercising pressure on each other. The main lodge is also remembered as having at one stage set lay tribesmen at recalcitrant members of the village inhabited by its own cousins, Taria. These painful matters will be discussed in greater detail in connection with the saints.

Further Services

The services performed by igurramen for lay tribesmen were simply listed above (Chapter III, Section 4). The general features of the political life of the lay tribes, which provide the context in which the saints perform their services, were described, in connection with their key institutions, in the preceding sections of this chapter. It remains to describe in slightly fuller detail other services which in earlier passages were merely listed, or only seen from the viewpoint of the beneficiaries rather than the agents.

Their role in supervising elections and tending the shrine used for major collective oaths is already clear enough. Arbitration is a connected but separate function. Just as minor oaths go to the local mosque of the lay tribesmen's villages, and major oaths go to the shrine, so minor disputes destined by the parties for arbitration, go to the lay chief, whilst major ones go to the saints. The saints are, ultimately, arbitrators rather than judges: they cannot enforce their verdicts, but depend on the acceptance of that verdict by the tribesmen. It is illuminating to cite the rule given by members of the Ait Abdi tribe, in the close proximity of the main Ahansal lodge: if a dispute cannot be locally settled by appeal to the chief, it is taken to the saints to be arbitrated Koranically, according to the *Shra'a*. Three saintly centres are cited, and the two parties go from the first to the second if the verdict of the first is not acceptable, and then on to the third if the verdict of the second is not acceptable either. There is no fixed order for appealing to the various centres. Not all three are Ahansal centres. (Generally even tribes well enmeshed in the Ahansal set of lodges also have some contact with non-Ahansal ones outside the region.) The verdict of the saints appealed to in the third instance is binding on both parties, so the theory runs.

In a way of course the saints can be more than arbitrators in as far as defiance of their verdict is a serious matter, and their verdict is supported by considerable moral authority. To refuse an arbitration is to show disrespect to a saint, to risk antagonising him and hence, indirectly, his clients. (The more saintly he is, the greater the impiety: but also, the more numerous his clients, and the more dangerous the offence.) If one of the parties in conflict is willing to accept the saint's verdict, it is in a strong position. It can then challenge the reluctant party to an oath.

It is of some interest to note the internal inconsistency of the theory: the saints are appealed to so that they should adjudicate according to (theoretically unique) Koranic law. The fact that three saintly centres can be invoked in succession, entails the possibility, indeed the likelihood, that the various saintly verdicts – all Koranic – will not be identical. This contradiction, obvious enough to the observer, is not something which bothers or is present to the minds of the tribesmen. One might be tempted to say that there is for them no contradiction, as for them, Shra'a has come to mean simply That Which the Saints, the Prophet's Own Flesh, decree, rather than that which is contained in *the* Book.

But this again, would not be altogether correct. The 'proper' meaning of Shra'a is not completely ignored. The most striking feature of this is the – rudimentary, indeed – internal judicial organisation of the saintly lodges, and in particular of the main lodge. It contained one or more persons known as the *Kadi,* (Koranic judge), and it was his job to pass the (supposedly Koranic) verdict, under the general authority of the saint, the agurram. The Kadi was in fact a member of the saintly kin group, of the lineage of the lodge but a minor member, much inferior in authority and power to the igurramen of the dominant sub-lineages. As this institution has not survived the French conquest, one can only speculate about the precise details of the relationship of the Kadi and the Baraka-endowed saint. But there can be little doubt that the real decisions of importance rested with the agurram: the Kadi must have been, or rather acted the part of, a legal adviser, and also dealt directly with minor matters.

There are at present, in the main lodge, a number of (related) families called Ait LeKadi, who claim that their name derives from men who fulfilled this function two or three generations back. These Kadis are claimed to have possessed Koranic learning, acquired by long periods of study and legal practice, allegedly in Fez (the recognised centre of legal learning in Morocco) and Tafilelt (a trans-Atlas oasis of great importance, and centre of the shurfa from which the present Moroccan dynasty derives). Their period of study and legal practice in these foreign parts tend to be, somewhat suspiciously, multiples of seven years.

The post and function certainly existed, though one may have doubts about the genuineness of the Koranic knowledge and of the preparatory studies. To possess the services of a member so well qualified as to have served as a Kadi in Fez and Tafilelt is just the thing to raise the prestige of the lodge with the tribesmen. But tribesmen, even Ihansalen, from the region of Ahansal do not generally make careers in Fez or in Tafilelt, and men who do make good in those places are not generally willing to go – or go back – to backwoods such as Ahansal-land: and in as far as all this was probably at least as true in the Morocco of a few generations back as it is now, one can only view these stories with some suspicion.

But the significant fact is that claims of such Koranic learning were held to be necessary or useful.

There is at present in the main lodge another family (the Ait Troilest) whose head was frequently village headman (at any rate until implicated in a case of corruption in 1959), in which the brother of the head-of-house has been away for many years, and is claimed to be undergoing extensive and prolonged legal training. From time to time I was told that he was due back shortly, to collect a bride. What in fact he was doing, and where, I do not know, but legal training or practice in foreign parts is, I think, a favourite attributed occupation of absent kinsmen in a lodge.

Another minor family bears the name of U'Talb, sons of the scribe, and claim descent from one so qualified. One should remember that a scribe or cleric (*fquih* or *talb*) is generally anyone who can read (Arabic, of course, Berber not being written), and not very much at that, rather than a person who necessarily fulfils the functions of a Koranic teacher, though his literacy automatically makes him available for this role; and that indeed the notions of scribe and lawyer are hardly distinct, as the word fquih (derived from the word for 'law') indicates.

The role of lodge Kadi became extinct with the French conquest. By an irony of fate, the French presented the saintly villages, as they did other subjugated Berber tribes, with the alternative of choosing Koranic law and tribal custom. But a choice of Koranic law would have meant receiving not what had passed for such in the hills, but a relatively more genuine article administered by a real Kadi with possibly more genuine qualifications. So the saints opted for custom, which in theory did not have and would have had to invent. But this did mean the end of the title of Kadi in the lodge.[1]

The igurramen who held important administrative posts under the French did tend to have (as did other important chiefs) private secretaries-scribes, *foquaha,* in their service, and this may in some measure be seen as the institutional successor of the old lodge judges.

In connection with the possibility open to lay tribesmen to appeal to various (and rival) centres of sanctity, it should be stressed

---

[1] The Kadi-ship was not abolished in the lodge immediately after the French conquest of 1933, but only very shortly after. I was told that when first offered the choice by the French, the saints chose the Shra'a, but changed their minds soon after, being dissatisfied with the Kadi.

explicitly that of course there are no clear boundaries of the jurisdiction of various saints. The frontiers of the shepherds of flocks are laid down, but the frontiers of the shepherds of shepherds, of the saints, are not. Indeed they overlap. Each tribe has access to a number of saints – a significant limitation to the power of any of them – which it can use as alternatives or in succession as courts of appeal. Just as each saintly centre is surrounded by a number of lay tribes whose mutual opposition is the source of its strength, so every lay tribe is surrounded by a number of centres of sanctity whose mutual rivalry limits the power of each one of them.

There is, moreover, a kind of domino-like pattern. Tribe *A* has access to neighbouring zawiyas *X*, *Y* and *Z*. Its neighbour, tribe *B*, 'shares' in the use of the reverence displayed to *X* and *Y*, but is too far from *Z* to have relations with it, but does have relations with zawiya *T*, which is too far to have any effect on tribe *A*. There is of course no fixed numerical ratio between tribes and zawiyas, and indeed the segmentary nature of the tribes, and to some extent also the segmentary nature of the saints, would make any such ratio meaningless. At which level of size of the nested segmentary groups do you count?

But it is safe to say that every effective lodge has more than one client tribe. Large tribes tend to have more than one lodge with which they are associated: but here again, the tendency is to a one-many relationship, if only in virtue of the fact that a tribe has frontiers in a number of directions. But its relations with all but one lodge may be relatively tenuous. For instance, the Ait Mhand were very Ahansal-oriented. The Ait Mhand were a kind of cock-pit of the warfare of the pre-pacification days,[1] for good geo-political reasons: this was the high pasture land, between the heavily populated and well defended valleys of the Ait Bu Gmez and the Ait Isha, through which the pastoralists from the South were pushing towards more reliable pastures. Being open to multiple aggression, the Ait Mhand were particularly dependent on saintly protection. This is reflected in the fact that, unlike other tribes, they made two annual pilgrimages to the main lodge, and also in the amount of land on their territory owned by the saints. Yet even the Ait Mhand had another and non-Ahansal saintly

---

[1] Cf. G. Drague: *Esquisse d'Histoire Religieuse du Maroc*, p. 174.

lodge near another of their borders, in the vicinity of what is now the administrative centre of Azilal.

The consequence of this kind of series of overlaps is that one could move from one end of the Atlas to another without ever crossing an absolute frontier, so to speak, i.e., one not under the jurisdiction of any saintly centre whatever. The implication of this is that if one applied Professor Evans-Pritchard's definition of a tribe, one would get the paradoxical conclusion that there is but one tribe in the whole of the Atlas, or even the whole of Morocco. Evans-Pritchard defines the tribe in effect as a kind of moral ceiling – as that largest unit beyond which there is no longer any obligation to attempt to settle disagreements by mediation, but within which such an obligation is still recognised.[1] The saintly system ensures that, however high you go along the scale of nested units and however far in space, the means of mediation are still present, and the status of the potential mediators is such as to confer some degree of obligation on the use of their services.

There is a further limitation on the power of the saints: not only is no saint indispensable in virtue of the existence of rival saints (in his own lodge as well as in others), but also in virtue of the fact that lay tribes may and sometimes do use each other as courts of appeal. Tribes A and B may have an arrangement such that an internal dispute in A, which the local chief and influential elders have failed to settle, may be taken for arbitration to B, and vice versa. I am not clear about the precise mechanics of such appeals (i.e., just how the mediators from the other tribe were to be selected: presumably by agreement of the parties in conflict and with the aid of the local chief); nor is it clear how in such cases use of arbitration fitted in with use of the collective oath procedure. I have come across two such sets of tribes related by (the possibility of) such reciprocal arrangements, and no doubt other such sets existed. But this institution is not of an importance comparable with that of the saints.

Thus there is *a* sense in which the lay tribes as such are in opposition to the saints as such, a sense in which there is a tug of war, an exchange of advantages and an application of sanctions, between these two general (though hardly corporate) groups. (The

[1] ' . . . a tribe is the largest community which considers that disputes between its members should be settled by arbitration . . . ' *African Political Systems*, ed. by M. Fortes and E. E. Evans-Pritchard, OUP., 1941, p. 278.

lay tribes only become jointly corporate through the saints; the saints, never.) The lay tribes can on this or that occasion make use of so to speak institutional alternatives to the saints, who consequently must try to please their clients – though the existence of rival saints is, I believe, a far more important sanction.

Does this existence of institutional alternatives to the saints, undermine the suggestion that the saints are 'functionally' essential to the society? I think not. For one thing, the saints perform these functions much better. Two groups can choose an arbitrator by lot, or use each other as a court of appeal for disputes internal to each group: but it is better to have a permanent and reverence-endowed saint on the border, who at the same time guarantees that border, facilitates trade across it, and whose arbitration have the added authority bestowed upon it by the reverence he receives from other groups.

In other words, the saints can be dispensed with on this or that individual occasion, either because they are not easily available, or because the groups involved do not wish, for one reason or another, to use them. But if they were dispensed with systematically, this would lead either to an undesirable fragmentation, as it were, of services more effectively performed by one agent, services requiring moral authority and hence best concentrated in one agent or group, in whom they mutually reinforce each other; or, alternatively, if the services were still concentrated in one place and lineage, to the re-creation of the saints under another name.

This is highlighted by certain kinks in the structure of the lay tribes. One comes across, occasionally, segments of lay tribes credited with special wisdom, which causes them to be both consulted by other segments, and excluded from eligibility for election in the rotated election of chiefs. Is this not the saintly system in embryo? – this pattern exemplifies that characteristic division of labour, in which those credited with higher wisdom, more general leadership, are at the same time – and this is most significant – debarred from executive leadership. This also shows that the tribes are in a way ever-ready to grow new centres of sanctity, if for some reason deprived of the old. Thus the saints as an institution are essential, though no one centre of sanctity is indispensable, and the saints are not indispensable on any one occasion or even for any one of their functions in isolation.

These paragraphs mainly show and stress the existence of

alternatives in individual use of mediation or protection. The importance of these alternatives in specific situations should not be overestimated. Concrete circumstances generally dictate this or that condition: there will often, perhaps most often, be no real alternative. A village A is under aggressive pressure from its powerful neighbouring tribe B: it will generally be obvious that the only people with sufficient authority over B and at the same time accessible to A happen to be the saints of X. In such a situation, the theoretical possibility of also invoking the saints of Y or doing without saints altogether will be of no practical significance. Again, individual saints may and do become so influential, carrying the authority of their recognition by so many lay tribes and other nearby saints, that the parties to a dispute would hardly wish to offend so influential a baraka-holder by taking their troubles elsewhere.

In connection with the tribesmen's appeal to 'Koranic' arbitration from the saints, it is worth noting that the saints in reality constituted a brake rather than an aid to the full Islamisation of the tribesmen.[1] French studies of Berber customary law are inclined to say that this 'custom' tended with time to approximate more closely to Koranic law. This is probably true. The 'custom' certainly includes at least lip-service to Koranic principles such as feminine inheritance of one half of a son's share. It is difficult to assess these trends, except for the French period, when it seemed to hold. But this trend was hindered rather than aided by the Saints' practice of handing out custom and calling it 'Shra'a', thus aiding the survival of custom by giving it, locally, the cover of a respectable name. Ironically, the spread of true Islamisation reached the saints via the lay tribesmen, through a general diffusion unmediated by the saints, rather than vice versa.

But whilst not aiding the 'real' Islamisation of the area, (in the sense of the promotion of genuine conformity with what the Book really says), the saints do greatly assist the very significant 'nominal' Islamisation, i.e., the sense of identification, and above all the sense of enthusiastic and warranted identification with Islam. The tribesmen are not unaware of the fact that they are held in contempt as bad Muslims by Arab townsfolk. (Certain legends of, for instance,

---

[1] This is one of the ways in which these Berber zawiyas differ from the Sanusi ones described by Professor Evans-Pritchard.

the Ait Abdi bear eloquent testimony to this awareness.) This may or may not grieve them. But by giving donations to the Prophet's own flesh and blood, and accepting their arbitration and leadership, they make up for their ignorance of the inaccessible Book.

Apart from this rather general, undifferentiated service, the saints also underwrite the political and territorial status quo – and its changes. The complicated spatio-temporal boundaries connected with transhumance need witnesses with moral authority to achieve even such stability as they possess. For instance, the territorial settlement in the neighbourhood of Zawiya Ahansal is generally justified by a land-deed said to have been drawn up by Sidi Lahcen u Othman, the alleged great-grandson of SSA, which records the vesting of local land rights in him by the previous inhabitants. They were rewarded by new lands much further West, in which Sidi Lahcen found them new springs by magical means. The settlement of some Ait Atta around Talmest and the transhumance rights there of others is justified in terms of a reward for military services rendered to the saint (and to his great-grandfather, and presumably to the intervening saintly generations) by the Ait Atta. (It is understood that these military services were required to help persuade the previous inhabitants, saintly baraka and the magical provision of springs or wells having proved insufficient arguments.) Though the legend of the magical finding of springs for the dispossessed proto-population would suggest that the saints' legitimacy is connected with irrigation and agriculture, especially as SSA on his zawiya-founding wanderings is said to have come not merely with a cat and donkey, but also a sickle – it would be a mistake to suppose that the saintly state, if such it be, was based on irrigation. The real ecological basis of this system of political authority was transhumancy.

In connection with the oath and the feud, another service of importance provided by the saints is of course that of sanctuary. This serves in at least two ways: for one thing, it is useful to have a secure place in which rival tribes or groups in conflict can meet to negotiate without danger. Secondly, the lodges are useful for murderers fleeing vengeance, and for their kin during the early period following a murder, before blood-money is agreed and accepted. The murderers may spend prolonged periods of time in the lodges, before being either 'forgiven' and allowed to return

Zawiya Ahansal seen from the lower gully in the evening light

Zawiya Ahansal from the opposite hillside. The graveyard is located in the right-hand lower corner. The roofless shrine of Sidi Mohamed n'ut Baba is visible; so is the well-trodden path leading to the main shrine

The house of an agurram (effectively saintly) family

The houses of laicised
Ihansalen (main lodge)

The main shrine, in the
graveyard, and the life-
giving river with an island
field upstream

Detail of a saintly household with an agurram. This kind of white-washed building is not traditional locally but imitates urban Arab styles

A traditional leader in his home: the most *baraka*-saturated saint active at present in the main lodge

Saints of the main lodge re-enacting the kind of dispute they are usually asked to settle. They themselves neither fight nor litigate, in principle

Looking into the Ahansal valley at one of its broader points. The white summit near the middle of the skyline is the holy mountain of Azurki, a place of pilgrimage. The high pasture of Talmest nestles in the hills in the middle ground to the right of it.

The plateau of Koucer, which flanks the Ahansal valley on the side opposite to Talmest. The approaches to the crucial pass across the Atlas watershed

The high pasture of Talmest, supposedly a reward given to the Ait
Atta in return for their support of the founding saint. The capital of
the Ait Atta of Talmest is discernible at the base of the mountain
on the left

A closer view of the Forts of Talmest, the capital of the local Ait Atta.
The forts are collective and owned by clans. The small houses are
inhabited by craftsmen who are not full members of the tribe.

Two women of the Ait Atta.
(*above*). The beads are amber

A girl pilgrim on the summit
of Azurki (*above left*)

A woman of the main lodge,
photographed in December 1967,
she claimed to have a 'child
asleep' (*ygn*) in her womb.
This dormant pregnancy is
credited to her previous
husband, a rich man. Her
present husband was poor.
If the supposed dormant
pregnancy is ever re-activated,
the child can be credited to the
previous husband

Girls of the status-ambiguous village of Tighanimin

The dance has all the moral-emotive connotations which the theatre is said to have had for the seventeenth century puritans. Though acknowledged to be scandalous it is widely practised (Ait Isha)

A discussion concerning the animals destined for sacrifice. Some are eaten collectively, some are slaughtered and sold with the profit going to the collectivity (Ait Tighanimin)

Men of the main lodge at prayer on the roof of one of the outlying houses. The shrine of Sidi Said Ahansal is visible in the background

The sheep market in Bu Gmez

home, or resettled by the igurramen, or, if the lodge is under-staffed, as it were, swelling the lower, non-saintly ranks of its population.

The saintly services in connection with providing continuity, information and leadership for larger temporarily activated units have already been described.

There are also certain reciprocal services between pairs of lay tribes: these arrangements (*tada*) are said to have been initially organised, and can be sustained, by the saints. This relationship is such that the families of tribe A and tribe B are paired off, in a one-to-one relationship (and of course in some cases one-to-many, the sizes of the two tribes not being identical), after which the paired families are said to be in a tada relationship. This, roman-tically, involves them in the obligation of returning booty to each other if in the course of conflict between A and B, the family of one side finds itself, on the division of spoils, with some of the property of its own tada. (Perhaps steps are taken during such divisions to ensure that everyone gets the property of other people's tada. Or, there is the interesting possibility, which I cannot confirm, that the tada relationship is invoked when the return of booty is held desirable as a step towards making peace.) More significantly, tada aid each other on their respective territories, providing shelter and protection, and thus making possible travel for trade.

There is also the general problem of trade. Central High Atlas tribes are emphatically not islands unto themselves economically. They are not autarchic. In some cases this is very striking. Pastoral tribes often need to buy cereals; there is trade in salt and dates from the south; in more recent times (this century), trade from the plain in tea and sugar, the main local luxury, and more recently in more sophisticated goods. The saints provided guarantees, for both sides, enabling people to visit the weekly markets in the territory of other tribes. Thus, for instance, zawiya Temga is situated between the Ait Abdi and the Ait Isha. The Abdi, very short of cereals but famed for their wool, must export or die. They regularly visited the Isha markets, passing through Temga, where they left their arms and were accompanied by saints or their agents, who guaranteed both their safety and their good conduct. Moreover, the main lodge is astride the route to one of the best passes across the Atlas, connecting the Tadla plain of central Morocco with the Dades and Draa regions of the South. (No road has been built across this pass in modern times, so naturally it has declined in relative importance.)

Finally, of course, there are the more 'purely' religious or transcendental services offered by the saints. I have left this to the end not because it is unimportant, but because it is something not specific to the Atlas saints, not, as far as I can see, specifically connected with the local social structure. It is something which could perhaps be supplied by others, and therefore it cannot easily be invoked to explain such importance as the saints possessed. The saints do request divine assistance; good and black magic are rather liable to be confused, and some of them are credited with power over devils as well as with influence with the Deity and His angels. These services may be performed for collectivities or individuals: a tribe may wish its harvest to prosper, or a tribesman come to be cured, or a woman come to request supernatural assistance to become pregnant.

An interesting custom is that the tribes who brought grain for the saints as donations, received some seed grain in return, with the saints' blessings, thus aiding next year's harvest. Like European royalty or other functionaries, saints may lay the first stone of bridges, though they have had the sense to do so only for the magnificently placed bridge over the gorge at the capital of the Ait Isha tribe, which gives it its name (Bridge of the People of Isha). This bridge, unlike any other in the region, is so well placed, high above the torrent, that it is not periodically swept away like other bridges by the river when in spate. Its permanence is however credited to the Temga saints' assistance. Since after 1933, this bridge has been supplemented by another, close by, constructed by French engineers, and this unhallowed bridge has also, so far, survived.

This general function of providing opportunity of intercession, of requesting aid, of enabling men to feel they are 'doing something' about (though not controlling, for that is recognised to be impossible) important things which are out of control, the natural forces and events of life and death: all this is also provided primarily by the saints or their shrines, in addition to the 'structural' services described. In providing the minor services of this kind to individuals, they meet some competition from two classes of people: women, often from their own agurram ranks, and from the village scribes, whose indulgence in magic is aided by their partial literacy. (Koranic tags are known to be potent. When written in reverse, or recited whilst retreating, they constitute powerful black magic.) In recent years, no male saint in the main lodge was particularly active or reputed in this way, though some recently deceased saints were credited with such activities. During the fighting in the course of the French conquest, top igurramen were held to be magically invulnerable. Crack shots took aim at them, and found their bullets miraculously deflected.

CHAPTER FIVE

LIVES OF THE SAINTS

The Expanding Universe

The saints live in a Malthusian world. Saints multiply geometrically. Their predicament arises from the fact that the demand for their services does not even go up arithmetically. It does not really, in any one place, go up at all. There is too much baraka chasing too little saintly function.

The reasons for the proliferation, for the population growth of the saints can be divided into the objective and subjective ones. The latter are a kind of optical illusion.

The objective reasons first: thanks to the donations they receive, the saints are better off than the average lay tribesmen, and hence stand a better chance of having children and bringing them up to maturity during periods of shortage. Secondly, the pacifism which successful saints practice, (and more important, which they are able to practice without incurring disastrous consequences), must in some measure make a member of a saintly lineage a better life insurance risk than a lay tribesman. Thirdly, saints have a stronger position in the matter of obtaining brides than other people. Their beliefs prevent them from giving their daughters in marriage to outsiders. The beliefs do not however prevent them, in fact if not in theory – there is some ambivalence, and contradictory views on this – from accepting and getting brides from outside, lay lineages. (Also, the slave population in holy lodges contains womenfolk who are not without attraction for the saints. Indeed some are at any rate now liable to be married to minor members of a lodge. But I know of no important saintly lineage which has become coloured through such an alliance in the past.)

The 'optical illusion' reasons for saints having a relatively much higher reproduction rate, over a time, than lay tribes, are these:

belonging to the saintly lineage, even without knowing precisely by which genealogical steps, is a prestigious and almost always to some extent an advantageous matter. Hence members of this lineage, who in any case have a better chance of settling, on favourable terms, in the territory of other tribes than ordinary tribesmen do, continue to remember their origins during the generation which follow such a settlement. A lay tribesman who settles in another tribe in consequence of an unforgiven feud, for instance, will have offsprings who in all probability will forget their origins in a very small number of generations. Hence, the small-scale lay migrations which take place do not lead to genealogical pockmarks on the faces of the tribes amongst whom it takes place. Members of the saintly lineage, however, do 'remember' and thus continue to count as members of their original lineage, at least for nominal purposes.

Moreover, the saintly descent is not only seldom forgotten,[1] but it may be 'remembered' in instances where it had not been true in the first place. In other words, given a suitable opportunity, it will be invented. There are two social groups I know of (one consisting of about eight families, the other a whole village of somewhere about 300 members) who claim membership of a holy lineage, but whose claim is disputed. Other 'entrants' into the saintly lineage may have been more skilful, diplomatic or fortunate, and have brought off their entry without challenge.

Others, who have entered into some partial community of rights with a holy group (sharing a village) without yet being absorbed genealogically, are biding their time.

Thus the objective and the subjective factors between them lead to a greater rate of growth in the saintly lineages than among other kin groups.

The Saintly Diaspora

But whilst the saints proliferate, their saintly functions do not. On the contrary, it is of the essence of those functions that they should be very concentrated into one person or a small number of them, and that there should be a considerable degree of continuity in their

[1] There may however be a desire to forget it if a member of it settles so far away that he is right outside the region where that particular lineage is prestigious. In such a case, the advantages of being a full member of the local group may outweigh the advantages of this particular saintly genealogy. Ahansal families settled in the plain are liable to find membership of a backwoods holy lineage of little advantage.

performance. Sanctity is not, like chieftaincy, an annually ascribed office. It is a permanent state. Though God may cease to use some given saint as a channel of divine blessing, it is assumed that the deity is not very capricious or changeable in its choice of channels. The manner in which continuity enters into the concept of a saint is clearest if one thinks of the main explanation offered of the sanctity of any one man – namely, that his father and ancestors were also saints. The permanent and pacific saint complements the transient and non-pacific chiefs.

But he can only usefully complement them if he is not merely pacific, but also either unique or at least rare. Useful saints could hardly be in a one-to-one relationship to chiefs or lay clans.[1] They need to be in a one-many relationship to them. Their power and position depends on being a small minority and on being a kind of telephone exchange, a neutral central sanctuary which provides a common ground for many other tribes and clans. Their authority and usefulness for any one group, hinges on the respect given them by all the other groups.

So the deep contradiction of sanctity is that on the one hand saints multiply, on the other they must, of the very essence of their role, be rare. The contradiction also exists between the nature of sanctity, concentrated, and continuous over generations, and the local and Islamic rules of inheritance, which are egalitarian as between brothers and thus lead to diffusion, not concentration. These inheritance rules are recognised by the saints as they are by the lay tribes. Other goods do indeed get diffused: but sanctity and its fruits cannot be spread thin, of its very nature. The manner in which it remains concentrated, and is not inherited evenly, is a subtle matter, and indeed crucial to the understanding of this kind of sanctity.

The contradiction is resolved through the fact that only a very small proportion of the people entitled to be saints by their ancestry actually operate as saints: the others, whilst retaining the lineage-membership and the claim implicit in it, go lay. I shall refer to

---

[1] At the same time, I have to concede that elsewhere in the Muslim world, similar saints do stand in such one-to-one relationships to lay tribal groups. This is the situation, for instance (if I understand Dr E. Peters' material properly) amongst the bedouin of Cyrenaica, where the *marabtin bil baraka* appear to be attached as clients to lay tribes. At the same time, it may be just this which made it easy and desirable for the Sanusi to take over mediation and leadership functions amongst the tribes: they were not, or no longer, performed by the *marabtin*.

these others as latent or laicised saints. Needless to say, this kind of laicisation, which takes place in the traditional context, must not be confused with secularisation, with which it has little in common. Secularisation occurs as a result of the impact of the modern world, through the undermining of the social and ideological bases of the old institutions. The laicisation under discussion is not a consequence of any loss of faith, nor in any way connected, one way or the other, with fervour of conviction.

Members of the saintly lineage can go lay in various ways and to varying degrees. Sometimes, but rarely, the process can take place in the opposite direction: latent sanctity be reactivated. In the nature of the Malthusian situation, however, this is much rarer than the opposite process.

In the wider or latent sense, sanctity covers all those who claim the appropriate descent. In the narrowest and fullest sense, it covers only those who are highly, respectfully and widely acclaimed and above all *used* as saints by the lay tribes, and who exhibit or are held to exhibit all or most of the characteristics of sanctity on the list. Between these two extremes, there is a spectrum of more or less laicised saints, manifesting more than the minimum, and less than the full attributes.

The political life of the saints is totally different from that of the lay tribes. The lay tribes know the politics of a kind of fatalistic merry-go-round: *in* one year, and *out* for two or three or whatever it is, and little or no hope or perhaps even desire of individual or clan political advancement. Normally everything remains the same: only the personnel change, everyone gets his turn, if that, and no more than his turn. The system is egalitarian, and it is also fairly safe. It checks ambition with very considerable effectiveness. If it sins by not mitigating anarchy enough, it is correspondingly effective in obviating the danger of tyranny.

This is the politics of the merry-go-round. But the political fate of the saints is quite different. The rhythm, for one thing, is far slower. But also the principle is totally different. This is no fatalistic and regular merry-go-round. This is a game of musical chairs, played out slowly over generations. It is played not by removing chairs but by adding (through the natural and illusory increases) to the number of contestants. The number of chairs available for effective sainthood remains fairly constant, or only grows very slowly at any rate for any one region. (It can only be augmented by expanding into other areas where the market for sanctity is not saturated.) So, over time, or at any rate whenever there is a growth in the saintly population, some must go lay.

There is a variety of strategies open to a man or group who are on the verge of being pushed out into the cold, into the laity. He may struggle, he may settle for some intermediate status, he may give in. One of the most important of the alternatives, however, is emigration to a place distant enough not to be a rival of the original centre of sanctity and thus not to have its activities curtailed by the shadow cast by the original centre.

Such a leap into the dark is not necessarily easy: there are always perils and dangers facing him who wishes to set up a branch of a going concern in a new territory. Moreover, it requires a positive invitation, or at the very least a willingness, of the people amongst whom the settlement is to take place. But, it should be noted, such a willingness or invitation are most likely to be forthcoming in those very cases which also offer the best prospects for the future of a new holy settlement: namely, in the perilous territory between two major and potentially or actually hostile lay tribal groupings. It is there that the cultivation of land is difficult for either of the two lay parties, and it is there that the loss is least to them and the gain greatest, for at that point it will also be convenient to have an arbitrator, a sanctuary and a kind of holy guarantor of a frontier. One should also add that the invitation to form a new settlement is most likely (though not necessarily) to come to a group which hasn't yet declined very far, or at all, in the direction of laicisation. In local terms, they still have baraka. In practical terms, they have some experience of how to be an effective saint.

The simplest case of receptivity to such an invitation occurs when a very effective and influential saint has more than one son, and solves the problem of succession by helping some of them to form new settlements elsewhere. Legends about the foundation of lodges do characteristically have this form: tribes invite a saint to supply a son to found a new settlement.

For this kind of reason, the holy settlements are dispersed over a wide area in a discontinuous kind of way. Saints, like galaxies in some theories of the expanding universe, so to speak repel each other: if no other factors intervened they would diffuse over even larger areas, and never be too close to each other. If two saintly settlements are close, they can hardly both be effective centres of sanctity. There are of course other factors working in the opposite direction: an already laicised group of saintly origin may have little opportunity for new settlement, and profit from the protection of a nearby fully effective holy group. Or again, none of the sons of an effectively saintly father may be willing to move, each one hoping in due course to inherit the original central place.

It is, however, not only the top layer of fully effective saints which disperses although effective saints do so more than the laicised ones. Even the others, whilst in general not having the opportunity to reactivate their effective sanctity even my moving far off, may nevertheless have opportunities for settlement, and for surviving in the new place without changing their identity, better than those of ordinary lay tribes without any pretensions at all. In some cases – and there is at least one striking instance of this – moving far off may be an opportunity for positive reactivation of effective sanctity.

The Flow of Grace

The factors described earlier make for the concentration of holiness and influence amongst some of the totality of holy lineages and personnel. As described, the surplus of potential holiness is, from generation to generation, ever being pushed out into what is a mere lay condition, despite the possession of the qualifying, holiness-conferring ancestry.

But this process of elimination is not carried to its extreme conclusion. It is not like the football cup after the Final has been played and only one solitary team remains. It is rather like the football cup before the semi-finals have been played. At any given time, more than one serious competitor remains in the game. And, of course, new ones enter as some of the old ones are eliminated. If one were to draw a diagram of the dispersion, it would look something like this:

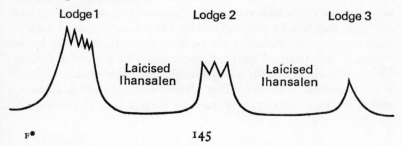

This diagram of course altogether ignores the lay tribes, who make up the overwhelming majority of the population. The lay or partially laicised Ihansalen in the troughs between the peaks of holiness live, as indeed do the effective saints, interspersed amongst the lay tribes: but where they form larger settlements, there is a tendency to be closer to the effective centres of sanctity. (These settlements, living in the shadow of their more successful cousins, tend of course to be correspondingly 'extinct' as saintly centres.)

The peaks of influence do not generally taper off to a sharp point but have at their summit a little plateau on which there is room for more than one family. For instance, in the main Zawiya, there were in the 1950s six or seven families of full saintly status, of which two were markedly more prominent than the others though most of the others were by no means knocked out of the race in the next generation. For one thing, the mere accident of distribution of male births might well put them into the running again. In as far as within each of these families, one individual will tend to be pre-eminent, the plateau itself may be seen as composed of little pinnacles, separated by lower points represented by those individuals in the families who are themselves of lesser importance.

Moreover, the general peak representing the principal Zawiya is not a solitary mountain rising from an un-differentiated plain. In the distance, but not very great distance, there are other peaks: the centres of holiness established by previous emigration, as described. Why do the peaks in most cases not taper to a sharp unique point, falling off precipitously into the plain of lay tribes and laicised saints?

When a holy father leaves more than one son, and their families finally undergo fission and separate (often they will not do so immediately after his death but only somewhat later), there is no immediate and rapid way in which the elimination match can be played and the succession decided. In a real state, where there is a real centre of government and the instruments of power can be seized, there could be a war of succession or at least a rapid palace intrigue. But this saintly quasi-state has no such central instruments, symbolic, bureaucratic or military, which could be so seized. Theoretically, I suppose, you could seize control of the key shrine. But this is morally inconceivable, and anyway such violence is incompatible with the saints' defining image, and a shrine – which is also sanctuary, and must be such if it is to perform its role – is a place to which everyone has free access. Saintly power depends entirely on habitual recognition by the lay tribes: in their use of the saints and their shrine for arbitration, elections and so forth. So, for a long time, perhaps for a very long time, the race may go on and the contestants be very evenly matched.

As stated, Berber law of inheritance, like Islamic law in this case, is egalitarian as between brothers. In practice, where there are indivisibles such as influence, or sanctity, there is a slight presumption in favour of primo-geniture, but by no means a decisive one. (In one of the two chief families in the main Zawiya in recent years, succession conspicuously did not go to the eldest surviving son. In the other, there was only one son.) Thus there is little in the order of births which would provide a sure basis for the decision. Again, it is hard for the closely related competing saints, brothers or close cousins, to kill each other off, much as they would like to. For one thing, ideologically their pacificism precludes this. If the Zawiya were a seething hot-bed of violent feuds (as opposed to being merely a centre of intrigue), this would diminish or destroy its usefulness as a neutral meeting-place and sanctuary for the surrounding tribes. Thus, if the competition between the remaining holy teams in the cup became physically violent, both sides would suffer, and not merely in the immediate literal, physical sense.

In fact, they do not go this far, and it would be disastrous for them if they did. They have other motives for mitigating their rivalry by co-operation: a good Zawiya should not be too small. When the lay tribes come to bring their donations and perform their elections, a great deal of entertaining has to be done. Indeed, the amount of this entertaining is such that it would be beyond the powers of any one family.[1] Donations are large enough to make their sharing less painful, whilst a sharp diminution in the size might reduce the influence of the Zawiya, and thus lead to a net loss even to the surviving family. It is true that they could, and would,

---

[1] The autumn of 1967 was particularly rich in pilgrims and donations. The harvest in surrounding areas had been good, and the government made it known that it favoured traditional religious festivals. (Partly it prefers the revival of the relationships connected with them to the networks set up by political parties, and partly this policy is connected with the national importance of the tourist trade – though of course Zawiya Ahansal is too inaccessible to profit from tourists.) The locals claimed that they received 800 beasts in donations that autumn. This of course is not a clear profit, for the visiting pilgrims must be suitably entertained. But a visitor to the lodge during this period found that all the households were *fully occupied* with looking after the pilgrims.

recruit clients who would aid them in providing services and claim less than kinsmen do. But there is no guarantee that they would be rapidly available.

In more than one way the situation is not unlike the economics of hotel-keeping in a summer resort. It would be rash to assume that the principal hotel would necessarily profit by the destruction of all its rivals. Though this would give the principal hotel a local monopoly, it might also reduce the size and reputation of the resort as a whole, and could thus lead to a loss even for the surviving hotel.

There are also rival centres of holiness in other Zawiyas in the distance, as a consequence of the opportunities of emigration and setting up new centres. The lay tribesmen may need a Zawiya at a place where two powerful lay tribes meet, where a guarantor of trade and free passage is required. The consequences of this simultaneous presence of a number of rival centres of holiness, both clustered within one lodge, and dispersed in a number of them, are important: as described, it provides the lay tribesmen with alternatives in their devotion to the saints. It thus provides a great check on the real power of the saints. Indeed it imposes a very great limit on it. An important and venerated saint may seem to have a good deal of power; he has, as it were, concentrated the respect of so many of the lay tribesmen on himself that he speaks with the authority of their respect. Facing any one group, let alone one individual, amongst the lay tribes, his power may indeed be overwhelming. If they defy him, he may be able to call in all the other lay tribesmen, who had remained loyal to him. (These may be all too delighted to have the holy sanction for a pillage, and without the authority of the saint they would probably be unable to unite amongst themselves.) Such things have happened and are remembered. But the situation is quite different if the saint wished to do something which a large proportion of his lay clients did not like. Faced with a widespread reluctance, he is quite powerless. And of course, he could not care to be in the position of asking for something which he would not be granted, so that a refusal would display his powerlessness and further diminish his influence.

Thus his power to impose unpopular policies or decisions is limited by the fact that close by, and also two valleys away, there are his near and his distant cousins only too willing to inherit his popularity and the respect and donations of the tribes. His cousin after all has the same ancestry and hence, in terms of the local ideology, as good a claim as he. All he needs in addition to the genealogy is perhaps a reputation for transcendental powers, but that can easily be made to follow on his recognition by the tribes.

The consequences of this situation are considerable for the kind of legal decisions which emanated from the saints. In theory, the saints' judgments are supposed to be those of Koranic law, and indeed they derive their prestige, or are said to do so, from this fact. As the saints are descended from the Prophet it is locally assumed (or was), that of the very nature of things they would not make any decision other than a properly Koranic one: they are, after all, the Prophet's flesh and blood. Koranic propriety emanates from their essence, as it were. Islam is what they do. They *are* Islam.

The reality of the situation is of course quite different. The legal custom of the local tribes diverges from the Koran in a variety of ways. The tribesmen would find it inconvenient to have their issues judged in accordance within what in effect is an alien, urban code. When they come to the saints for judgment, what they want, or are prepared to accept, is a verdict which, apart from being in accordance with the real power relations of the situation, also fits in with their own preconceptions. If a saint in fact behaved like a learned urban Kadi and imposed the proper code upon them, he would soon lose his popularity and hence, in due course, his effective saintly status. He really has no choice but to give the tribesmen the kind of verdict they want. And, indeed, he has no desire to give them anything else, nor indeed the ability. He lacks the learning, indeed the literacy, which would enable him to give the proper Koranic verdict if he wanted to. Descent is no substitute for book learning.

But the important point however is that even if he were willing and able (and he is neither) he would not be able to do so politically. The tribesmen would transfer their loyalty to a more complaisant cousin. In terms of the general conflict between tribal custom and proper Islam, the real function of the saints is to judge by custom, and call it Koranic law. The substance remains unchanged, but a new name and cloak of respectability is imposed on it by the saintly authority.

The functional utility of the alternative governments provided by the saintly cousins, can be seen not merely from the legal practices, but most clearly from the crucial decisions which faced the local tribes during the twenties of this century and the early thirties.

The tribesmen then faced the alternatives of either submitting to or resisting the French. One might suppose that they would be swayed in this matter by the decision of their saints, and indeed in some cases this was so. But on the whole tribesmen made their own decisions, dictated by various factors, amongst which the main was geographical position: those who were well placed geographically for resistance did resist, and those who were not did not. But – and this is the important point – whatever they did, an important saint was available to ratify their choice and provide them with leadership. If the saint's own geographical location did not fit in with the policy of his clients, well then, he changed his location. Various saints were the leaders both of submission and of resistance. In fact, three alternative strategies were pursued by three different branches of the saintly lineage: all-out resistance, open collaboration, and thirdly a double game of seeming to resist but in fact co-operating. The practitioners of the second and the third strategy were in concert. (When the final French victory came in 1933, the leaders of the second and the third group were rewarded with administrative posts, whilst naturally the practitioners of the first strategy were not.)

Thus in one sense the authority and leadership of the saints is a mere matter of appearance. They follow whilst appearing to lead, for the least they have to do if they are to survive as effective saints is to express and ratify popular will.

Vox Dei Vox Populi

How is this slow-moving elimination waltz decided? In local theory, by the flow of Grace, of baraka. God chooses those whom he wishes to use as his intermediates. There are no firm rules, such as primogeniture. There is only the elimination of all those who are unambiguously lay. God's love, the preference of the effective father-saint for one of his sons, the love of men, magical powers – these signs show where baraka is to be found.

The tribesmen do not, of course, have a written or an elaborate theology. But if one were to write it for them, I feel it should correctly be of a rather Calvinist kind, in the sense that the various signs of baraka are signs, rather than causes, of election. But there is perhaps no point in asking oneself what people would say in reply to questions of a type of logical sharpness which in fact is precluded by the kind of society they constitute.

What are the signs? They have already been listed in the account of what it is to be an agurram. Given the initial qualification of proper ancestry, the signs are wealth (one sense of 'baraka' is simply 'enough') provided of course it is accompanied by generosity, a 'consider-the-lilies' style of entertaining which appears to be indifferent to the cost and puts its trust in God; magical powers; influence with men as well as with God; pacific behaviour; upright and pious conduct, perhaps.

As described in the course of analysing the notion of 'agurram', the possession of these attributes is, through a set of logical and causal circles, the consequence of being credited with them in the first place. A man reputed to be an agurram will receive donations which will enable him to receive visitors in style. A man used to arbitrate will find that the wisdom required to give weight is ascribed to his verdicts. Stories of magical powers will be credited when told of him.

So the flow of Grace is really in the hands of the lay tribesmen: Vox Dei is, in the end, Vox Populi. Whilst the lay tribesmen overtly, consciously and formally elect their annual chieftains (under the guidance of the saints), they also tacitly and almost unwittingly decide the long-drawn-out competition for the possession of baraka. By attributing it to this or that saint, they indeed give it to him.

But it would never do to have this overtly conceptualised: if baraka were merely the consequence of the decisions of the lay tribesmen, it could not claim authority over them. What is in reality a choice – albeit not one made by an individual and not on any one occasion, but by many and over a long time – appears not as a choice but as the recognition of an objective and indeed trans-cendental fact. This 'objectivity' of the allegedly recognised characteristic has the social consequence of absolving him who 'recognises' it from the responsibility for it, which would attach to to such an act if it were seen to be a choice.

How does one compete for this recognition? Naturally, by per-forming the services of saints to the satisfaction of the lay tribes. The struggle is a very slow one; it is a struggle for recognition by an audience, and there are a number of even concentric circles into which the audience can be divided: there are kinsmen, there are the immediate fellow-inhabitants of the lodge, there are tribesmen of surrounding and of more distant villages. The near and the distant audiences have repercussions on each other: the tribesman who arrives at a lodge will be guided in his choice of person for reverence by the respect shown locally to this or that saint. But likewise, a saint's standing within his own lodge will reflect the reverence in which he is held by distant tribesmen, a reverence which pays off to the lodge as a whole in the form of donations. In brief, the First Law of Sociology (to him who hath shall be given) applies very fully. (The Second Law, which contradicts the First, i.e., 'The first shall be last' – does not generally apply to the saints.)

The struggle for recognition is subtle as well as prolonged, in that, as in other reputable professions, it is unseemly, but not unknown, for a saint to solicit. A successful saint will proudly point to the fact that he has no need to go wandering around the countryside like a beggar collecting donations: his clients come to him. Within the main lodge, one can guage the status distinction between the top effective saints and upper-middle semi-effective ones by the fact that the former wait passively in the lodge, the latter go out and solicit. One should add however that if a really effective saint chooses to go out and travel around, this breaking of the rules on his part is permissible and does not diminish his status, whilst if the marginal saint, who had to travel, gave up the practice, this will not by itself raise his prestige but only indicate that even when soliciting he cannot get much, and thus cause him to sink further still. (In French days, this matter was further complicated by the fact that the travel or non-travel habits of saints were affected, in the case of some, by the holding of office, and in the case of others, by being held to be 'politically unreliable', i.e., hostile to the administration. Either of these circumstances would greatly inhibit travel. The chief possessor of baraka in the main lodge did not travel to collect donations outside the area of the nearest district office in the period until 1956, but did undertake major donation-collecting trips in 1959. In the mean time, he had lost both an official position and some saintly prestige, and his change of habit can be attributed to either of these factors.)

The struggle is complex and interesting, as well as subtle. It is important to know which claims to make and which to fulfil, when

to make them and when to withdraw. It would not be possible
simply to make the maximum claims, hope for the best, see whether
they bear fruit, and if not retire to ordinary lay tribal life. There are
penalties attached to attempting and failing, and some may prefer
not to take the risk. A man who wanders about collecting donations
to that extent neglects his fields, and if he fails to obtain his donations may find himself falling between two stools. Also saintly life
is habit-forming, and it may be difficult to revert to ordinary modes
of livelihood.

The risks may occur in other ways. A community which claims
saintly status and boasts of its pacifism in evidence of it, may find
itself attracting aggression if, through insufficient recognition and
reverence for its claims, it cannot deter the aggressor by fear either
of its supernatural powers or of its lay clients. If saintliness fails to
protect, it may then be too late to seek ordinary allies.

If requested, igurramen assure one that there is no rule by which a
successor can be recognised, but maintain (implausibly) that it has
always in the past been obvious: God's favour was manifest. Nevertheless, the conflict is expressed even for the past in legends. For
instance, considerable numbers of segments in the main lodge trace
their separation from each other to the various wives of one and the
same effective saint: all the wives are said to have desired the succession for their respective sons, and to have given each one of them
the name[1] which according to prophecy would be the name of the
leader of the lodge. The actual selection of the successor was done
by a test imposed by the old man, a test which in fact was bound to
select the most uncalculatingly generous one of the competing sons.
The story is simple. The old man instructs his sons to accompany
him on a trip and to take along bread by way of provision. In the
evening, he orders them to take out the bread and prepare for
supper. All but one do so. The brothers sneer at the one who has no
bread for his folly, for they know that he foolishly gave it to a passing beggar. But soon, they are discomfited; the old man, seeing

---

[1] This name is said to have been Sidi Mha, indeed a characteristic name
amongst the Ihansalen. A Berber Nancy Mitford could point out that although
there are no inherently non-U names, there are inherently U ones – so designed
phonetically as to be very hard to use without the preceding 'Sidi'. *Mha* is
hardly usable unless you are confident of receiving enough reverence to be
addressed as Sidi. The igurramen also use *Mulay* as a personal name, which is
not done by the lay tribes or laicised Inhansalen.

what has happened, singles out the improvident son and says: he will be my successor!

The legend can convey the value of uncalculating generosity and indicate that it was crucial for selection, that it explains and validates the present inequality of status in the lodge; but this does not mean that the zawiya has a rule of succession. It would be impious to test, to examine someone for possession of baraka. The rule remains uncodified, the present remains fluid: the uncodified principle can only be invoked to explain or colour the past.

As for the present, the competition for leadership amongst the effectively saintly families is manifest, indeed blatant. It is characteristic of them to claim to receive the poor visitors to the lodge, who bring no gifts, whilst their rascally rivals hide when the poor arrive and rush out to welcome the rich who bring gifts. A saint who really lived up to these protestations would find himself impoverished and hence divested of his sanctity. Needless to say, during the period of 1933–55, the will of God made manifest its choice more through the voice of the Franks than that of the local people – although the Franks were not always unheedful of local sentiment, particularly when conjoined with other considerations – and this affected, during that period, the rules of inter-saintly competition.

Types of Holy Settlement

The reasons for the slow but persistent expansion of the saints into dispersed discontinuous settlements have been described. There is demographic pressure, appeal of the possibility of remaining an active saint rather than declining into a latent one (or even to re-activate latent sanctity) and, from time to time, the opportunity in the form of the willingness of lay tribes to tolerate or invite holy settlement. This is the 'expanding universe': holy settlements when they reach a crucial size as it were explode, albeit gently, and the exploded parts repel each other for they cannot both or all be saintly if they remain close, and if possible tend to move some distance from each other, and then, after further lapse of time, the process may be repeated. Apart from repelling each other, they need, if they are to flourish, to be located on an important frontier, between large lay groups. Such frontiers naturally cannot be close to each other.

Saintly settlements, if they are effectively saintly, are most likely to reach the critical size. They will attract clients to fill the lower ranks of the lodge, such as refugees from feuds. At the top, success itself, by bringing in wealth and brides, is likely to lead to multiplication. Growth through multiplication and assimilation of refugees will lead to expansion and finally hiving-off, in which there is a premium on distant resettlement. This retreat of holy galaxies from each other then goes on indefinitely, until some of them disappear beyond the horizon, or rather, until they get out of the area in which Ahansal descent has magic and carries prestige.

As described, the lay tribes and settlements are inherently stable in structure, if not in composition: whatever turbulent events may convulse them in this anarchic environment, when the turmoil subsides, the resulting pattern is the same as before in all but name, and often in name. Only the personnel may have undergone a turnover. Saintly settlements, on the other hand, in as far as they are effectively holy, are inherently unstable not only in composition, but in structure. Successful sanctity makes them grow and become more sharply stratified, with increasing competition at the top as the stakes grow. They may need to dispose of excess population at the bottom and excess unsatisfiable ambition at the top, exporting lay settlers from its lower stratum or saintly ones from among its élite.

In the region investigated, there are certainly well over 20 and perhaps as many as 30 Ahansal settlements. They differ in type, in size, influence, internal structure, ideology. Presumably, and according to their own belief, they also vary in age (in some cases demonstrably), in the length of time which has elapsed since their foundation and their hiving-off from some other more central Zawiya.

A kind of classification of types of lodges was already implicit in the earlier criteria of what it is to be an agurram. One can classify them by how many, and which, of the features of agurramhood are present. Some Ahansal settlements are as it were 'extinct' with regard to sanctity. Though they claim Ahansal descent, (and the claim is not challenged), they no longer have other attributes of effective sanctity. They feud, they receive no donations, they are not centres of pilgrimage, nor places of oath, they are not credited with magical powers.

There is the factor of size: the actively 'saintly' lodges tend to be large. Some extinct ones are large as well, and there is also one which is both small and effective, but it is plainly a product of very special circumstances in modern times.

Effective 'saintly' settlements are internally stratified. There is no exception to this rule. The reason for this is obvious: sanctity, as indicated, cannot usefully be diffused (though it needs assistants) but tends to be concentrated in individual personalities and families. There are subsidiary important factors making for internal stratification within Zawiyas: (a) there is the ideological factor that it is held proper for saints if possible not to work, and to employ slaves instead.[1] Consequently, successful lodges tend to have a bottom stratum of negro slaves who had been purchased. The existence of such slaves is not unknown in lay tribes but it is extremely rare. (b) An effective lodge will tend to accumulate around itself, it if has not reached the point of saturation, a number of permanently settled clients, people who for some reason or other have had to leave their original homes (because of a feud or poverty), and who form part of the village but do not share in the sanctity.

They may not share in full pasture rights and so forth, in virtue of their alien origin. It is possible that with the passage of time, they will 'forget' these origins and be allowed to forget them, and the descendants of the locally settled refugees will come to look like lay saints, that is to say will claim participation in descent from the founding saint.

---

[1] Muslim tribal people are sometimes supposed, in the image of the Arab bedouin, to value pastoral activities above agricultural ones. Perhaps this is so amongst the lay tribes around Ahansal, though I cannot say that I have experienced anything which would strongly give one this impression. One might, for instance, expect something of the kind from the Ait Atta, with their supposedly but recent sedentarisation: yet the Ait Atta of Talmest are most anxious and eager to plough up the pasture they are obliged to share as unploughed pasture with their clansmen from the South, and they display no sign of shame or conflict of values about this.

In any case, with the saints, this expected valuation is positively reversed. The general idea is that ideally, a saint should not work at all. But this ideal can seldom be attained. If work he must, it is much better that he should work in the fields, and that his slaves or clients should do shepherd's work on the high pasture. Saints 'must' have slaves so as to be spared this indignity although often it is not granted them, especially nowadays, to be so spared. Work in the fields is justified in terms of the saints' need to have bread to offer his guests. Amongst the big saintly families, it is the employed shepherd who has the lowest status.

There are other respects, apart from size and the existence of stratification, in which lodges or Ahansal settlements differ from each other. A variety of combinations is possible and occurs, with respect to such features as: pacifism, the possession of a shrine of one's own general ancestor (as opposed to having to visit the shrine of one's more distant ancestor at another lodge, thereby acknowledging its seniority), deep genealogies, the presence of a sharp 'peak' of authority as opposed to a 'plateau' of a set of more or less equal families at the top, the presence of alien clients (an unsuccessful lodge will have no such clients, but a very successful and old-established lodge may also have but few, because all the inhabitants have come to be genealogically incorporated), abstention from immorality such as dancing, participating in a lay alignments of the tribes, and so forth. The various combinations will be examined in connection with individual settlements.

The diversification of lodges over space, in conjunction with their own perception of their own past, gives us some insight into the way in which saintly settlements develop. A very young settlement is probably rather like Zawiya Tidrit: centred on the sanctity of one man or single lineage, his sanctity secured the possibility of settlement on a septic border, which sustains the lodge by providing it with a remunerated role, and which attracts client settlers. A more mature lodge will look rather like Zawiya Temga: bigger, with competing leadership, and a lower stratum of resident, second-class citizens, immigrant clients non-incorporated genealogically. A really mature lodge will look like the main lodge: stratified, with a top level of competing saints, a big middle class of genealogically incorporated but ineffective, 'latent' ones, (subtly stratified into dignified near-equal, economically independent supporters, sadly dependent ones, and independent yeomen), and a small slave stratum at the bottom. 'Extinct' settlements will be like Amzrai or Tabarocht, retaining a memory of once having been the seat of effective saints, but at present without pretentions to exercising the political arts of sanctity, and hence internally not stratified, but on the contrary evenly segmented like any lay tribal group. There will also be settlements of laicised saints whose village had never been a centre of effective sanctity (Taria), or villages which are in fact laicised and unstratified, but which strive to be effective saints (Tighanimin).

The line of development which is exemplified synchronically by

Tidrit-Temga-Aggudim(main lodge)-Amzrai, with sidelines leading towards the type of Taria and of Tighanimin, is only the simplest possible model of growth, decline and fall: the actual histories of lodges may well have contained more complex up-and-down vicissitudes.

Speculative history is (rightly) frowned on in anthropology. Yet I think the above schematic conclusions are justified, as a theory of saintly metamorphoses. A model which assumes stability over time is just as speculative as one which postulates change, and in this case less plausible. An account of the present working of the lodges shows that they are inherently unstable: success means growth, growth means transformation and competition and hence failure for some lines; failure also means transformation, in the direction of lay status. We see the lodges as they are at present, diverse in structure: they illustrate each other's possible future and past conditions. Occasionally, there is also genuine historical evidence: the last fission of the main lodge and the establishment of a rival centre at Bernat is well documented from French sources. Or again, adjoining the present site of Zawiya Temga, there are well-preserved ruins of the older lodge buildings which document Temga accounts of a smaller and more compact lodge in the past.[1]

I am no partisan of evolutionism in general. But lodges of the saints of the Atlas operate (or did operate until the impact of the modern world) against a stable background which was similar for all of them and which, though turbulent, was fairly stable in its general structure, so that variations in external factors were not large. The factors making for change within the lodges are clear

---

[1] Inter-tribal variations, which illustrate the past, are also sometimes found among the lay tribes. Thus, the Ait Isha at present have their centre at Tillouguit n'ait Isha, which is a large village. They say that there was a stage in the development of their tribe, when this place was their capital, but no one was allowed actually to settle there: only the collective storehouse-forts were located there, and anyone who lingered near them longer than the period held sufficient for a visit to his own particular cubicle-store, was liable to a fine, on the suspicion of contemplating theft. One's faith in the accuracy of this account is much enhanced by the fact that, except for the rule imposing fines on loiterers, the capital of the Ait Atta of Talmest is still of this type: it consists of the three collective store houses of the three clans (supplemented only, since the French conquest, by the house of the chief made permanent by the new regime), and a small group of half a dozen or so negroid artizans, attached to the tribe but not properly members of it. The full members of the tribe do not live at its capital, but merely have their fortified stores there. The cohesion of the three clans is enhanced by the fact that the three forts are very close to each other.

and isolable, and their effects are not swamped by outside variations. Hence we are in a position to reconstruct social change
in depth, to see society in time, at least in typical outline, by
examining in detail the variations as they are now found in space.

CHAPTER SIX

THE MAIN LODGE AND ITS LOCATION

The Village Itself

Zawiya Ahansal is the centre of the system of Ahansal lodges and villages. It is itself a village of about 300 inhabitants, and adjoining the shrine in which the body of Sidi Said Ahansal, and of some others, is said to be found. The village itself immediately adjoins its cemetery: on the other side of the cemetery, there is SSA's shrine, and those of some others. SSA's shrine also contains or is held to contain, the bodies of some other notable igurramen of recent generations, who are of course descended from Sidi Said Ahansal in the 'straightest' line, i.e., in the dominant lineage which is held to have been influential uninterruptedly and whose members have not migrated from their ancestor's home.

It is a curious testimony to the fame and influence of Zawiya Ahansal that it occurs, named simply Ahansal, on a map (plate 77) of *The Times Survey Atlas* of 1922. It is (with one exception much closer to the plain) the only inhabited place of the region to be so distinguished, and indeed there are no other places in the heart of the mountains which share the honour. Yet Zawiya Ahansal is no bigger than many Berber villages, and smaller than some, particularly if one counts some of the near-continuous settlements on the edges of alluvial valleys as one village, as well one might. The fame and significance of Zawiya Ahansal of course reflects its religious importance. It was a centre of agurramhood, of 'sanctity'. But of the many centres in the central High Atlas which possessed this, Zawiya Ahansal was perhaps the most noteworthy, and probably the one which had held it in the most stable manner. It was also a centre of a whole system of kin-related sanctity, unlike some other centres which were either isolated, or if parts of a system, were parts of a territorially more discontinuous one, whereas the Ahansal one was neat and fairly compact.

The inclusion of Zawiya Ahansal in *The Times Atlas* of 1922 is seen to be the eloquent testimony which it is, if one remembers not merely that the inclusion was wholly unwarranted in terms of its size, but also that at the time it had never been visited by a European, and that its occupation by the French in 1933 was still eleven years away.[1]

Zawiya Ahansal is located on the Ahansal river (Asif Ahansal) about two hours walk below its springs, which are themselves underneath the cliffs falling away from the main Atlantic–Sahara watershed in the central High Atlas. The village is on the right bank of the river. Like many agricultural Berber villages, in the central Atlas, it is placed on the rocky ground immediately above the irrigated, flat alluvial 'plain' on the side of the river, a plain which at this point only has the breadth of two or three small fields, and only achieves even this breadth through terracing. The point of this kind of characteristic location is of course that the buildings themselves do not waste any potentially valuable agricultural land, but are as close to the fields and the river as is compatible with not impinging on irrigable land.

The river is extremely fast flowing but fordable and bridged, and supplies villages along it with excellent water. From time to time, and especially in spring, it becomes a ferocious uncrossable torrent when in spate, and then it invariably carries away all local bridges (built of planks and stones), frequently changes its course somewhat, and carries away the lower fields and their crops. This is not an unmixed disaster, as the mud it brings down is, plausibly, said to be very fertile.

The central part of Zawiya Ahansal is built on the fairly steep slope between two normally dry gullies which descend towards the river. This central part is extremely compact. The walls of one house are frequently also the walls of the next. The compactness and the steepness of the slope have as a consequence a kind of three-dimensional quality: the flat roof of one house is sometimes

[1] The actual first entry of Europeans into Zawiya Ahansal preceded the conquest by a year or two, and consisted of a reconnaissance group led by Lieutenant Alexandre, as he then was, later the first local administrator, and subsequently an official at the town hall of Colmar. I am indebted for the confirmation of this story, to which my attention had first been drawn locally, to Monsieur Alexandre himself, whom I visited in Colmar in 1958.

also a part of the base or courtyard of the next house higher up. There is a network of narrow and winding 'streets' suggestive of streets of an urban slum rather than of open spaces between farm buildings.

Everyone of importance, and the majority of the inhabitants, live in the compact part of the village between the two gullies. A smaller number of houses, inhabited by people of no great prominence, are more dispersed on the outside of the two gullies. People in them are born on the wrong side of the gullies, one might say. The only important people on the wrong side of the gully are the dead: the cemetery is immediately adjoining the lower part of the East gully, and the shrines of the great are immediately beyond it.

Within the compact central part of the village, it is easy to distinguish the houses of the great from the houses of the ordinary. The houses of ordinary people are of a kind common to the central and Middle Atlas: unpretentious, square, with one or at most two stories, flat-roofed and not tapering. (This is different further South, where the common style is such that even ordinary people often have imposing houses. What otherwise is a regional difference in house styles, becomes a marked class difference within the main lodge.)

The houses of the great display the characteristic and most attractive 'castle-like' style of the south: tapering towers, flat-roofed but decorated with a kind of alcove in each corner which accentuate the fairy-tale-castle appearance. In Zawiya Ahansal, these towers never rise to more than three storeys.

One noble family (the Ait Sidi Yussif) have chosen to inhabit a house which is not of the castle (igherm) type, but exhibits rather solid bourgeois comfort and security without ostentation. Two-storeyed, well built and securely enclosed, it does in fact express the spirit of the family inhabiting it, a family which has chosen to pursue solid wealth and safety rather than fame, ostentation and influence. The Ait Sidi Yussif are one of the richest families in the village (perhaps *the* richest), and very well-born, close to the main current of Grace, but they neither play nor aspire to play any political role.

No non-noble family has a castle-like dwelling; but at least two noble families combine the possession of one with dire poverty, and fail to live up to their status and habitat.

In recent years, since the French conquest, the very beautiful tower-type houses with their designs in dried mud, have lost some of their prestige. They are associated with the past and with types of prestige which are known to be waning: they do not resemble urban dwellings of either Arabs or Europeans: the mud crumbles, the interiors tend to be dark, and they are unsuitable to types of entertainment which have come with the modern world. Hence conspicuous building assumes a new form: the building of more spacious and whitewashed rooms, with the use of boards rather than just branches, brushwood and mud for the roof. Both the two top families (but no-one else) in Zawiya Ahansal have acquired 'state-rooms' of this kind, which were valuable for the entertainment of French officers which was crucial in the political game of 1933–55. These state-rooms are normally kept unused and locked, and are opened for guests of note (including locals on special occasions). Traditional entertaining was less fastidious, and frequently took place out of doors. For the daily informal meetings and gossip, the area outside the mosque or outside the house of the top family adjoining the cemetery and shrine, is used.

One other innovation in style of house which is becoming fashionable in the region is not a consequence of new forms of political influence and prestige, but simply of the new tastes of returning soldiers. They tend to build houses more solid and with more light than the traditional unpretentious dwellings, but less decorative than the traditional conspicuous ones. A characteristic innovation in them is the use of chimneys. In traditional houses, smoke makes its exit as best it can, mostly through a hole in the roof.

The new style affects the dead as well as the living. Traditional shrines resemble Berber houses, except that they are smaller: they are square and generally flat-topped. When of stone rather than dried mud, they tended to be decorated by producing a zig-zag pattern, rather like an angular wavy line, at one or two levels by the positioning of the stones. In modern times, the shrines are altered to resemble those of the Moroccan plain: whitewashed, with sloping tiled roof and a knob on top. At Zawiya Ahansal, SSA's tomb has been decorated in this fashion. Other shrines of dignitaries retain their traditional appearance, and the shrine of Sidi Mohamed ut'Baba, the founder of the dominant lineage from which all the top saintly families are drawn, is in disrepair and roofless. It is claimed that supernatural powers pull down the roof during the night whenever one attempts to repair it during the day. On the face of it, it is simply claimed to be a fact that the roof of this shrine mysteriously collapses whenever one rebuilds it, and recently no attempts to defy these powers has been made.

There cannot be any doubt about the motives of these spiritual hooligans, nor of the human beings whom one may suspect of acting as their agents. Let us suppose that Sidi Mohamed n'ut Baba were allowed to have a shrine, thereby putting himself in the same class as SSA, and radically differentiating himself from all the other ordinary denizens of the graveyard with their customary nameless graves: it would immediately, visibly and conspicuously follow that his descendants are also radically distinct from those other Ihansalen who are also descended from SSA, but not through Sidi Mohamed n'ut Baba. Such people – the offspring of SSA minus the offspring of Sidi Mohamed n'ut Baba – make up the majority of the lodge.

Now it is indeed true and accepted that Sidi Mohamed n'ut Baba constitutes the most important parting of the ways on the Ahansal genealogy, at least as far as intra-main-lodge affairs are concerned. All effective saints in the lodge are descended from him (though not all men descended from him are effective saints). No one not descended from him, in the main lodge, pretends to possess effective agurram status, though some are much respected and two men at any rate seclude their wives, an important agurram trait. (Not one has presumed to have an agurram-like dwelling.)

Thus Sidi Mohamed n'ut Baba in fact defines, within the main lodge, effective sanctity, the non-extinct flow of grace. De facto recognition exists: the others refer to his offspring as the igurramen, in contrast to themselves. But the situation has not been ratified de jure, it has not been physically externalised by a donation-receiving shrine. Note that if such a shrine existed, non-descendants of the saint interred in it would have no claim to its proceeds, whereas at present, though the laicised Ihansalen have a proportionately smaller claim to the proceeds of SSA's shrine, they do as his children have *a* claim to them.

Thus a certain haze of obscurity surrounds the situation. The principal justification offered for receiving the wages of sanctity is descent from SSA, which however does not differentiate people within the lodge. Internal stratification can only be justified more nebulously, in terms of Sidi Mohamed n'ut Baba, the manifest signs of present grace, and the legend concerning the generous son. But no completed and effective shrine ratifies it.

Thus an incomplete building, a broken roof and some bared timbers, symbolise the ambiguity of the social situation, a differentiation which is recognised yet not altogether definitive. One should add that within the lineage of Sidi Mohamed n'ut Baba, some top families have succeeded in expressing their own very special status by having some recent notable figures interred in the shrine of SSA itself.[1]

Within the village there are four or five abandoned houses, which are attributed to the extinction of the families inhabiting them. In fact, there are reasons to suppose that Zawiya Ahansal is in demographic decline. Even without it, there would I think be a tendency to abandon very old houses: the 'mud concrete' style of building does not lead to structures which are too lasting, and it is sometimes easier to re-build on a new rather than the old site. A fair amount of building tends to go on between agricultural seasons, notably before the harvest. For ordinary habitations, the work will tend to be done by the family concerned aided by kinsmen or friends on a basis of reciprocity. In the case of the traditional tower-like buildings, more specialised masons will be employed, from the Southern side of the range (where this type of building is very common) or for instance from amongst the Ait Haddidu. No building of this style was erected at Zawiya Ahansal in recent years, but I watched one going up at Zawiya Asker in 1959, built for a local politically prominent personage by masons of the Ait Haddidu tribe. In brief, there is both the opportunity and the incentive for building. Labour is in easy supply during the slack agricultural season, as is the rocky land on the slopes above the valley bottom. At the same time, habitation – with carpets – is one of the few ways open to express status and accumulate durable property.

The really large families, with dependents of various kinds (the Ait Sidi Mulay, Ait Amhadar and the Ait Okdim) tend to have sprawling compounds, products of successive growth and building-on, which do not always manage to be continuous. The houses

[1]At Temga, the situation is somewhat different. The various rival top families all have their own shrines, of suitably equal distinction and size. The shrine they all share, which houses their shared ancestor, is not near their own lodge but at Anergui (cf. p. 242).

of the saints, including these three top families, tend to be along what might be termed the pilgrim's way through the village, i.e., the natural path taken by a visitor from down the valley making his way to SSA's shrine.

Such a visitor would, if he took the most natural route, begin by passing between the house of the Ait Okdim and the village mosque. He would then pass through a gateway built under one of the Ait Amhadar's houses, emerging on to a courtyard surrounded by houses of the Ait Sidi Mulay household and those of their hived-off cousins, the Ait Sidi Moa (and also of the household of the disinherited brother of the same name). He would then pass under another gateway, built under a part of the Ait Sidi Mulay household, and emerge at the edge of the cemetery at a point where a diagonal path would take him straight to *the* shrine. The last gateway is referred to as *imi n'zawuyit* (mouth of the lodge). An imi n'zawuyit can sometimes be found at other lodges (e.g., at Tamgrut, the chief lodge of the Nasiri set of lodges), and it is a kind of generic concept. It is as it were the place where the head of the lodge receives incoming visitors. It is also the place round which most sacrifices are made at the Aid l'Kebir, and the place which, next to the wall of the Okdim house opposite the mosque, is most favoured as an informal meeting place for the villagers of Zawiya Ahansal. (But use of it tends vaguely to imply political affiliation to the Ait Sidi Mulay family, as it virtually forms their doorstep. It would be difficult to conceive members of the rival Ait Amhadar family unnecessarily passing the time of day there.)

To possess the area of the imi n'zawuyit, or perhaps to have the area one possesses considered to be such, is of course a significant thing in the struggle for leadership of a lodge and for the ascription of baraka.

The proximity of most of the big families to the shrine or to the natural path towards the shrine is of course not accidental. The only important exception is now the Ait Amhadar (family number two in importance), who no longer inhabit the gate-way house on the way to the shrine, though they still own it, but have an extensive, compact and highly fortified compound at the top of the village. There simply wasn't room for them to expand in the original and hagio-strategically better placed position. Expansion was necessary for them during their influence and affluence during French days (prior to their fall from grace and favour in 1952), and it is during this period that the development of the new compound, in the upper part of the village, took place.[1] In these later days the battle for power and holiness was no longer, in any case, fought out in terms of whose door would receive the pilgrims.

Something should be said of the mosque. It is perfectly easy for a visitor to pass through a Berber village without realising that it has a mosque at all. One's expectations are conditioned by European village churches or mosques and minarets of the Moroccan plain, and one simply doesn't notice the totally un-distinguished and indistinguishable buildings which serve as mosques in the villages of the Atlas. The houses of saints stand out: the village mosque never does. It looks like any other of the minor houses. If it is distinguished at all, it is by the fact of something having a kind of covered area for cover for waiting believers or use by passing visitors, who may use it if they fail to have a specific connection and host in the village. The *fquih* (village scribe and koranic teacher) is also liable to use a part of it as his sleeping place if he is unmarried or does not have his wife with him.

Finally, a terminological point. In Zawiya Ahansal, the castle-like houses of the better saints are referred to as *ighirmen* (sing. *igherm*), whilst ordinary houses are called *tigmi* or *zhgua*. Elsewhere, and more commonly, the term igherm is used to describe collective store-houses-forts (which do not exist in the lodge, though they do in neighbouring villages), which, architecturally, are most often very similar to the good saints' houses in the lodge. (For instance, in the nearby village of Amzrai, only the igherm – in the functional sense of collective storehouse – is also an igherm in the archi-tectural sense. No individual family presumes to have a dis-tinguished house.) Moreover, in neighbouring tribes, the term tigmi (house) can also denote a social group larger than the family. Meanings of these terms vary from place to place and context to

[1] By a fortunate accident, there is available a photograph of Zawiya Ahansal as it was before the major recent outburst of Amhadar architectural expansion, a photograph taken from fairly high up the opposite side of the valley. The rather melodramatic photograph 20 in René Euloge's *Les Derniers Fils de l'Ombre* (Editions de la Tighermt, Marrakesh, 1952, p. 81) shows Berber tribesmen in the foreground, and a village and cliffs in the background. Though not described as such, the photo is clearly composite, and made up from at least three separate photographs. The village itself is in fact Zawiya Ahansal, but without much of the present Amhadar compound. The rest of the background of the photograph and the foreground have been added by *montage*.

context, and shift between physical type of house, or group of contiguous houses, function of house, and the social group using the dwelling or dwellings.

The Location

Why is Zawiya Ahansal where it is? Or perhaps one should put the question the other way around: why is the village, located in this place, a zawiya of importance?

In terms of the inhabitants' beliefs, the location was determined by supernatural signs and agencies. When SSA had finished his saintly, scholarly and magical apprenticeship with Sidi Bu Mohamed Salah, he was sent off with an ass and a cat to find a home and found a lodge of his own. He was instructed by his master to make his home at the place where the cat jumped off the ass. There is still, near Zawiya Ahansal but nearer still to Amzrai, 'the house of the cat'. SSA is said to have wandered with his animal companions until the portents took place and the location was determined.

What mundane and natural reasons can also be invoked? It is worth noting that no special explanation is required why there should be a village in this position at all: Zawiya Ahansal is not one of those places (like Delphi, with which it otherwise has social and physical similarities) where religious faith and human ingenuity triumph over an adverse and unfavourable natural environment. On the contrary, the environment is favourable, indeed charming. SSA had chosen his place well, and it is in my view destined, when roads become adequate and the rise of national income in Morocco creates the demand, one of the favoured tourist centres in the Atlas. Quite apart from most outstanding natural beauty, splendid rock and much snow in winter, which may well have been a matter of indifference to SSA, there is ample and magnificent water in permanent supply, there is much forest and pasture, and there is some land suitable for irrigated farming.

What does require an explanation is why the village situated here should be well placed to become a centre of a quite outstanding concentration of baraka, of saintly influence. I believe the explanation to lie in the ecological possibilities of the surrounding area, in the fact that it is almost destined for large scale transhumancy, and this in turn requires some kind of machinery for the adjustment of relations between permanent inhabitants on the one hand, and on the other the annual 'invaders' who occupy the high pastures when the snow has receded. Given the institutional range open to the Berbers of the central High Atlas, the existence of a powerful lodge, respected and revered by both sides, would seem the most plausible – perhaps the only possible – solution of this problem.

The various services performed by saints described earlier were not specific to any particular Zawiya. There are of course great differences in the extent to which they are performed by various saints, even within the class of effective ones: some saints are more saintly than others. There are also minor details in the manner in which they are performed. But, by and large, the same type of service is performed by all effective saints.

But there is one particular service which is particularly characteristic of the main and founding Zawiya in the Ahansal constellation, and which must be singled out. This service is indeed only a modification of the normal role of mediation between important groups: it is, however, a very important modification, and one which is the clue both to the origin, and to the location of the centre of gravity, of this particular saintly system.

The Politics of Transhumancy

The Atlas Mountains near the main Sahara/Atlantic watershed in the Ahansal area, are in effect a high plateau cut by deep gorges. Much of the plateau is more or less uninhabitable in winter, but provides good pasture in summer. The area to the South of the main Atlas range, on the other hand, becomes extremely scorched every summer. This geographical background calls for transhumant pastoralism. The grass on the high pastures, after the snows have gone in about April, constitute a standing and virtually irresistible invitation from nature to the shepherds in the South, who by coming up provide their flocks with a far better chance of survival than if they remained in their own scorched homeland. The permanent inhabitants of the uplands, on the other hand, cannot themselves use up all the summer pasture.

Hence, there is a kind of annual and virtually inevitable invasion from the South. Each spring, the wave of tribesmen with their tents and flocks sweeps up, and it recedes again in the autumn.

This of course creates the problem of their relationship to the permanent inhabitants of the uplands (in the main, of the gorges, valleys and hollows in it). Indeed when the annual visitors from the south are on the plateau, they greatly outnumber the permanent inhabitants of the longest gorge which sticks out like a pointing finger towards the watershed. The inhabitants of this particular gorge, which thrusts deepest into the mountains, would in the normal course of events find themselves each summer in a hopelessly precarious position. Their fields and flocks would be a standing temptation to the numerically superior temporary occupants of the plateau.

And indeed, this inherently indefensible outpost of the northern barriers is not defended: this extremity is inherited by the saints, who only 'defend' it by their saintly prestige. It is at this very point that the saintly system of lodges, most plausibly, has its alleged place of origin and its recognised and most influential centre. This is the location of Zawiya Ahansal.

The arrangements existing between the permanent inhabitants of the uplands, (of north facing slopes and gorges), and the annual 'invaders' are complex and unstable. Boundaries are drawn not only spatially, but also temporally. In general, the pastoralists have 'closed pastures' which must not be entered by anyone before a certain date, on pain of heavy fines. The arrangements with the men from the South only reproduce this feature on a much larger scale. The incoming transhumants may go as far as a certain line by a certain date and then move on to another line to another date and so forth. There are furthermore boundaries between various segments of the incoming hordes.

These arrangements, even more than ordinary all-the-year-round tribal frontiers, need mediators and guarantors. From the viewpoint of the permanent northern inhabitants, the exposed promontory inhabited by the saints constitutes an effective general frontier mark, a kind of trip wire and a guarantee. But the same is also true for the men from the south. For them too, the arrangements made through the saints are a guarantee that they will not, one spring, find their way blocked as they try to move in on the high pastures.

The conflicts about and around these particular high pastures are endemic and still very much alive, year in year out.

The legends concerning the circumstances of the foundation of Zawiya Ahansal are in terms of co-operation between the general ancestor of the incoming transhumants, Dadda Atta, and the founding ancestor of the saints, Dadda Said. The one provided the temporal and the other the spiritual arm and between them they established the present status quo. (This was only ratified, however, by a deed or treaty between the previous inhabitants and the founding saint's great-grandson, Sidi Lahcen u Othman.)

The situation is complicated by the fact that three tribal groupings of the 'southerners', the Ait Atta, have by now permanently settled north of the watershed, and no longer retire annually to the south.

One of these groupings, the one actually nearest the watershed and on the edge of the crucial plateau, is itself in sharp opposition to its own 'brethren' who come in annually. The function of the saints is to provide mediation at two different and important levels: between the local and the migrating segments within the Ait Atta, and also between the Atta as a whole and the various old established locals. The violence of the former conflict internal to the Ait Atta did not mitigate the simultaneous vehemence of the larger conflict.

Indeed the first conflict has probably become sharper recently through the general pacification of the area. The Atta who are permanently settled north of the watershed (a) now need the support of their southern cousins less, if at all, and (b) are consequently very strongly tempted to turn some of their pastures into fields, an ambition which is furiously resisted by their 'cousins', who do not wish to see their summer pastures diminished.

Here as elsewhere in the central High Atlas, pacification can cause attempts at a kind of enclosure movement. Some of the best pastures on the plateau are situated in hollows, in which moisture stays longer and which provide grazing when the more exposed ground is already scorched, during the later part of summer. Such land however could also be turned into fields.

Pacification radically transforms, not merely the balance of power, but also the relative attractions of pastoralism in these conditions. In the days of siba, it was long-distance transhumancy which maintained clan cohesion: and in conditions of anarchy, the tribesman was glad to see his geographically distant cousins turn up periodically and claim and use their pasture rights, for their presence and shared interest in the territory provided him with security. But now, a modern state makes prolonged violent conflict between larger tribal groups – in other words, tribal war – impossible. Thus the military aid of the cousins is no longer either required or usable, and hence there is no motive for sustaining economic loss by recognising their rights in local land. Deeds are produced (whether these had lain dormant, as claims often do, or counterfeited ad hoc, may vary from case to case) to prove that the land really belongs to this or that group, and the pastoralists are trespassers.

At Talmest, conflict now arises – apart from the minor and endemic quarrels about flocks and shepherds who 'stray' across boundaries – between the members of the Ait Atta tribe who are permanently settled in the area, who would gladly enclose the best pasture and who also dislike their present fields being invaded by the flocks of their clan brethren, and their annually incoming cousins, anxious to maintain their pasture rights intact.

The methods and allies employed in the struggle have changed, in part. Small scale violence still occurs, and the government is from time to time forced to send up soldiers, and has on occasion even found it necessary to confiscate the old muzzle-loading guns, whose retention had been tolerated by the French. But the new political parties now also get involved in the conflict, or are willing to use it to recruit local support. By an irony of history, the left-wing party, well represented locally among the agents of the central administration, till they were compromised by the abortive little rising of 1960, was committed on the side of those who would practice enclosure if they could.

The Secular Arm

The relationship of the Ihansalen of the main lodge to the Ait Atta is, as indicated, a special one: the Ait Atta provided the secular arm in support of the spiritual authority of SSA, when the lodge was founded.

The Ait Atta are a very large and self-consciously Berber tribe: when asked they will stress that their founder and ancestor, 'Dadda Atta' was a *Berraber*. The Atta 'confederation' (as French historians describe it) is said to have been founded in the sixteenth century[1] and to have united the Berber tribes in or around the

[1]Date given in Capitaine George Spillman's *Les Ait Atta du Sahara et la Pacification du Haut Draa*, Editions Felix Moncho, Rabat, 1936, p. 32.

Jebel Saghro (still held to be the Atta 'homeland') in the struggle for the oases and pastures surrounding it, the oases being the strips of land along the rivers flowing Sahara-ward from the Atlas. The Ait Atta now occupy a great deal of the territory between the Tafilelt Oasis to the east (held by Filali *shurfa*, who produced the present Moroccan dynasty), the Atlas to the north, and the Draa oasis-valley to the west, (including a large part of this valley itself).

The crucial feature of the internal organisation of the Ait Atta is this: the clans of the topmost level of segmentation are highly discontinuous geographically. Each of the major clans tends to be represented both at the centre, the 'capital' in the Saghro (in the vicinity of Igherm Amezdar, where the Ait Atta held their 'national' court of appeal), and in each of the major areas of Atta settlement and on each of the Atta frontiers. The consequence and function of this territorial discontinuity of the major class was that not merely membership of the Ait Atta was as such, but equally membership of the constituent clans, could be and was a force enlisted in support of continued 'national' co-operation and loyalty. In fact, the Ait Atta do appear to have continued to operate as one unit, to support each other in war and have (inter-mittently) common leadership and legal institutions, right up to modern times.

The loyalty of the constituent clans despite their dispersion along the various frontiers was reinforced and sustained by the fact that such clan-membership carried and indeed carries pasture rights. The Ait Atta are transhumants and indeed move over very considerable distances in the course of their transhumance. The areas into which a man may drive his flocks within the general Atta territory depend on his clan. A man of clan A, settled (say) in the central territory in the Saghro, may in summer take his flocks to the land of the A clan on the northern frontier, where some of the A will also be settled permanently. (Some B will also be settled along the northern frontier, but at a different point, and the centrally-resident members of clan B will transhume to this point.)

Apart from pasture rights, marriages amongst the Atta seem to follow clan-affiliation rather than geographical proximity (as indeed is underwritten by tribal law and its priority rights), judging at any rate from the fact that members of clan A will claim to have close relatives amongst the *A* of another region. (Affiliations through a mother would of course not generate such a relationship, but they are indices of a belief in its existence: the term connoting 'father's brother' is used in a virtually classificatory fashion, and two families believing themselves to be in such cousinly relationship may continue to believe this over generations and exchange brides in the process.) Given the size of the Ait Atta and above all the size of their territory, the fact that they succeeded in continuing to some extent to operate as one unit is a considerable achievement for a segmentary society. They are themselves clearly aware of the difficulties inherent in this and significantly tell a story of a failure of one clan to repay the help previously provided in war by another. Their present distribution, as described, is such that clan loyalty is a lever aiding 'national' loyalty.

They possessed a double system of leadership: territorial chiefs, elected by rotation etc. from the geographical units, and a hierarchy of complementary-and-rotated chiefs based on the (non-geographical) clan system. This double system was activated by and concerned with quite different problems: the geographically-based one with local and internal issues, the other, in which the units eligible for voting and providing rotated candidates were 'kin' ones, for those occasions when the whole Ait Atta co-operated as one large unit. In the region of Ahansal it is firmly maintained that this non-territorial system did operate up to modern times and that the Ait Atta did have a 'national' (annual chief) and that tribesmen from the far South came to aid their local clansmen.

The Legend and the Land Deed

Concerning the legend of the early life of Sidi Said Ahansal, we know so far of his saintly (scholarly and magical) accomplishments, his urban training and affiliation to another prestigious saint, and his mission to found his own centre, whose location was to be identified, and was identified, by a supernatural sign. Now read on:

Having found the spot, SSA proceeded to call by telepathic means for Dadda Atta, the supposed ancestor of the Ait Atta, to aid him in establishing himself locally. He had to call for seven years, seven months and seven days before his call was answered. Dadda Atta came, and jointly the saint and the leader of the Berber warriors drove out the original inhabitants, who included the Ait Waster, in my view a mythical tribe, sometimes identified with the 'Portuguese'[1] and also the Ait Tegla, who still live between Azilal and Marrakesh.

No stories are told of what happened during the life of SSA's son and grandson. The story is resumed during the life of his great-grandson, Sidi Lahcen u Othman (buried at the village of Amzrai, and its patron saint, and himself, owing to lack of any kind of multi-lineal proliferation between SSA and himself, the general ancestor of all Ihansalen, with the exception of one much-disputed

[1] The belief that the proto-inhabitants of the area were cave-dwelling Portuguese (Portkiz, Portikze) is general not merely in this region, but throughout the Atlas and other Berber regions of Morocco. For instance, it is current amongst the Seksawa of the Western High Atlas (cf. Jacques Berque, *Les Structures Sociales du Haut-Atlas*), amongst the Glawa (reported by Oxford University Exploration Society expedition of 1955), the Anti-Atlas (reported by M. André Adam) and the Rif (reported by Mr David Hart).

My own view of the most probable explanation of this strange belief is that during the period of the Portuguese occupation of various places on the Moroccan coast, from the sixteenth till the eighteenth century, when they were in constant conflict with Moroccans and by far the most prominent of Europeans from a Moroccan viewpoint, the term 'Portuguese' came to be used interchangeably with 'Christian' (Nasrani). Thus the belief in 'Portuguese' proto-inhabitants is really a way of alluding to a non-Muslim or specifically Christian population prior to the coming or the conversion of the tribes presently in occupation.

This *may* indicate the existence of Christianity amongst the Atlas Berbers prior to Islam; but equally, the belief may originate from the need to attribute non-Islamic status to the previous and dispossessed inhabitants. During the period of Portuguese presence on the coast, the dispossession of Portuguese would be just the kind of thing which was not merely permissible, but laudable. Thus it would be to the advantage of a tribe to believe this of its predecessors. A *Muslim* predecessor might come back to claim his own, as men and groups in fact do within tribes.

Beliefs in partial (maternal) Christian ('Portuguese' or 'Rumi') ancestry exist concerning various tribes or their segments, (e.g., the Ait Bu Gmez or the Ait Isha). The 'Portuguese' are generally credited with ruins (real, or such as in reality are but cliffs) and the previous habitation of caves.

A confirmation of the above tentative theory can be found in the sixteenth-century Arab traveller Leo Africanus, who passed through the region (which he described as Dades, but plainly he meant the mountains as well as the present valley of that name) and was told of ruins left behind by Romans, without actually seeing them, a fact which puzzled him as there were no Roman records of a town built in this area. If he passed through the region today, he would still be told of such ruins, but their builders would be described, even more implausibly, as Portuguese. At some point between the sixteenth century and the present, the term 'Portuguese' appears to have replaced 'Roman' in this particular context (though Rumi is still the general way of describing Europeans). Cf. Leo Africanus, *The History and Description of Africa*, London, Hakluyt Society, 1896.

lineage.) Somehow or other the settlement made by Dadda Said and Dadda Atta could not have been wholly successful or definitive for we find the great-grandson, Sidi Lahcen u Othman, making it once again: but he took trouble to ratify it by a land-deed. He finally settled the Ait Tegla in their present distant habitat, compensating them and making the arrangement attractive for them by finding new springs and wells for them in the new area, by magical means. (This theme, of a saint making a territorial settlement and consoling those forced to migrate by magical water-divining, reappears in the lives of the later descendants of SSA, including some of recent generations.)

The legend says that the saint saw one of the women of the displaced persons-tribe crying, and on inquiring into the cause of her distress was told that she bewailed their forced migration into an arid land. He consoled her and in his kind way made arrangements for the prompt appearance of new sources of water. The important thing, however, is the land deed he drew up with the jema'as (assemblies, so described, and named one by one on the document) of the departing groups. This document, apart from naming the individuals representing the collectivity ceding the territory, also delimits it. The territory delimited is that at present inhabited by the Ihansalen of the main lodge and the three neighbouring Ahansal villages (Amzrai, Taria, and Tighanimin) and that occupied by the local segment of the Ait Atta, the Ait Bu Iknifen of Talmest.

This land deed is the crucial document concerning the local territorial claims and rights. In as far as the land is ceded to Sidi Lahcen u Othman, the territory delimited is rightly the property of his descendants, the Ihansalen. Nevertheless a very large part is occupied by the local Ait Atta. Their occupation is not disputed by the Ihansalen, for it is conceded that it was their help which enabled the original saints to impose their settlement in the first place. On the contrary, they are inclined to remind the Ait Atta that they were brought to Talmest as a kind of protecting army for the saint and his lodge. The deed, however, is invoked in opposing claims of the southern Atta who come to the pasture of Talmest and surrounding area as summer transhumants. In the annual and perpetual disputes with these groups, the documents invoked at present are (1) Sidi Lahcen u Othman's land-deed, (2) a settlement made by senior French officers during the years following the pacification, and (3) a settlement made by Moroccan officials in the years following Independence.

The land-deed is much-copied and numerous copies are about in the possession of various interested parties in the region. (The text is not in dispute locally.) Some of these copies are plainly recent, and some are old. I have come across two families (each moderately prominent but neither effective saints, though of Ahansal lineage) claiming to possess *the* original document, and there are probably others making the same claim. In view of the agreement of the various copies and the fact that the text is not disputed, the possession of the actual original copy is perhaps not a matter held to be of great importance.

Thus in terms of the early history of the main lodge, the Ait Atta and in particular its Bu Iknifen segment has a special relation to the Ahansal saints, being its appointed protector and being (locally) settled on land which 'legally' belongs to the saints themselves. From the viewpoint of the total Ait Atta tribe, the Bu Iknifen at Talmest are the guardians of the northern summer pastures (guardians who, since the Pax Gallica, perpetuated by the modern Moroccan state, would as indicated much prefer to plough up the pasture and be rid of their annually incoming 'cousins') and the Ihansalen are the spiritual guarantors of these northern marches, who are also used as igurramen when convenient. For use at their centre and in terms of legends of their origins, the Ait Atta are connected with another holy lineage, the Ait Abdallah ben Hussein.[1]

Since the early days, of course, the Ihansalen themselves are much dispersed and all except the four above-named villages, and the hamlet of the Ait Troilest, are settled outside the territory delimited in Sidi Lahcen u Othman's document. It is interesting to note that the legends of the main lodge's foundation which are found in other centres of sanctity, for instance in the Temga-Asker-Sidi Aziz group, tally with the stories retailed in and around the main lodge, except in that they omit the part allegedly played by the Ait Atta. These other lodges are on frontiers between tribes other than the Ait Atta, and have no need to perpetuate and 'remember' services performed by a tribe with whom they are not in constant relations.

Whilst the Ait Atta thus do, in terms of legend and deed, have a

[1]Cf. G. Spillman, *Les Ait Atta et la Pacification du Haut Draa*, p. 32.

special relationship to the main lodge, the main lodge nevertheless sees itself as quite neutral between them and their northern adversaries, notably the Ait Mhand and the Ait Isha, and negotiates as a neutral and saintly arbitrator between these opposed parties. The Ihansalen of the main lodge and adjoining villages are also quite clear that the Ait Isha protect them against the Ait Atta, if need be, as indeed the Ait Atta would protect them against the Ait Isha. The special relationship is not in contradiction with the usual agurram status and position.

CHAPTER SEVEN

INTERNAL STRUCTURE OF THE MAIN LODGE

Diagrams

Diagram 1

General Ancestry

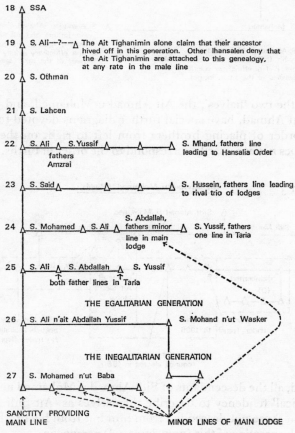

The numbering of generations is in terms of the number of steps,
in local belief, from the Prophet.

S. is an abbreviation for Sidi (My Lord)

Diagram 2   **Top Families**

(The main segmentation dividing them into two halves)

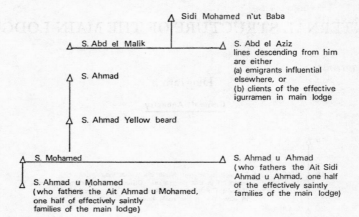

Each of the two 'halves', the Ait Ahmad u Mohamed, and the Ait Ahmad u Ahmad, have special further diagrams devoted to them.

The order of placing brothers from left to right on these diagrams does *not* necessarily correspond to the order of births.

Diagram 3   **Ait Ahmad u Mohamed ('Rivals')**

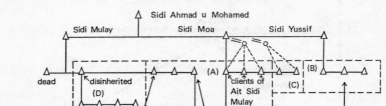

As stated, all the descendants of Sidi Ahmad u Mohamed now have an 'illogical' tendency to describe themselves as 'Ait Sidi Mulay' (i.e., even those not descended from him but from his brothers) in view of the prestige of this (now deceased) personage.

There are now four independent households in this segment, described in the text as

(A) The Last of the Marabouts. (Ait Sidi Mulay.)

(B) The Kulak Family.

(C) Comparatively Poor Cousins.

(D) The repudiated Brother.

On this and the next diagram, limits of existing households are indicated by dotted lines. Only living male saintly members are of course here indicated within dotted lines – i.e., the present saintly nucleus of the agurram households. The descriptive names used here for families (also on next diagram and in text) are the ones I came to use during fieldwork in my notes, and I retain them for identification. They are, of course, not used locally.

Diagram 4

Ait Ahmad u Ahmad
(Described in the text as 'More · Rivals')

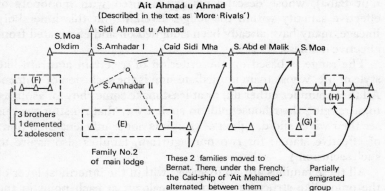

The following households remain in the main lodge (the names here given are those of their respective section-headings in the text):

(E) The People of the Upper Castle (Ait Amhadar – main rivals of Ait Sidi Mulay).

(F) Ait Okdim. Influential family, in temporary decline only, owing to lack of adult males.

(G) Into decline.

(H) Fragment of a partitially emigrated group. On this and the other diagrams, the ordering of names from left to right does *not* necessarily correspond to the order of births. The four diagrams can be fused into one: the points at which they link are obvious.

Top Families

There were at the time of the study, six or seven top agurram families. (At least one constitutes a borderline case – hence the ambiguity in the enumeration.) As indicated in the earlier analysis, the notion of an agurram, of an effective saint, is ambiguous: it is all a matter of degree and depends on the context, on the status of the observer, and on the number and above all proximity of rival claimants.

The range here given, which gives us six or seven families, is a little broader than 'those and only those naturally used by lay tribes for arbitration': some of the 'top seven' are not so used. And the range is narrower than the one defined by descent from the crucial special ancestor within the main lodge (Sidi Mohamad n'ut Baba), whose descendants are credited with monopoly of effective sanctity within the lodge. Even within this inner holy lineage, many have already been sloughed off and eliminated from effective holiness.

The range is based on the criterion of a certain agurram-like style of life, whose main immediate sign is the seclusion of women. All these families either do, or at least make some show of aspiring to, arranging their households in such a way that no stranger can see their wives and daughters.[1] (But it is not a sufficient condition: of effective status: for two non-agurram, families also aspire to such seclusion.)

All these families are, so to speak, within the innermost layer of the onion-like structure of holy genealogy: at each point in the genealogy when one segment can be stripped off as having become laicised or having emigrated or both, they remain in the 'inner' layer which is still in the running. Some no doubt are at present in the process of being stripped off, or would be if the whole system were not destined, as presumably it is, to share in a general secularisation. All of these families also have (with one exception, see

[1]This is the only form of seclusion practised by central High Atlas Berbers, and only rarely by them: the veil is never used, and is only seen, if at all, when worn by wives of government officials, or by prostitutes settled round large and de-culturated markets, so to speak, (such as at Azilal) where customs are now those of non-Berber Morocco rather than of the region. They wear veils as signs of urban sophistication. Thus, ironically, the veil can be inversely related to propriety, and directly related to modernity.

In this way as in some others, the heterodoxy of the tribe and the secularism

below p. 191) fine castle-like homes of the type locally described as an igherm.[1] No other family presumes to have such a house. No individual or family in any of the neighbouring Ahansal villages has one either, and it would clearly be very offensive, presumptious and provocative for a family which is out of the saintly running to erect one.

The Dynasts

Lineage diagram 2 (p. 180) illustrates the general relationship of the agurram families of Zawiya Ahansal. All of them are descended from Sidi Mohamed n'ut Baba, whose shrine has the uncompleted roof, its completion being spiritually prevented; and in fact, all of them are also descendants of his son, Sidi Abd el Malik, and hence, in strict logic, the top families should think of themselves as 'Ait Sidi Abd el Malik'. But they do not do this, and it is Abd el Malik's father Sidi Mohamed n'ut Baba, who provides the crucial diacritical mark of sanctity within the lodge. Why?

One possible structural reason is that the effective saints do not wish to offend and antagonise the offspring of Sidi Abd el Aziz, the other son of the man who at present does provide the dividing mark: these descendants refrain from acting as rivals, and make themselves useful as clients whose deference only underlines the sanctity of the effective line. On the other hand, these clients obtain some prestige and satisfaction from being within the holy line. In return for being included in it, which hinges on placing the agurram genealogical cut-off point just where it now is, they would always take the side of the igurramen in any intra-village tension

---

of modern society, come to resemble each other, standing as they do at opposite flanks of the Islamic city. For similar developments in Algeria, see Germaine Tillion, *Le Harem et les Cousins*, p. 194, and Pierre Bourdieu, *Le Déracinement*, 1964, p. 132.

[1]Elsewhere and more generally, this term designates a collective storehouse (of which there are none at the main lodge), but these storehouse-forts are indeed generally built in the same style as the top-family houses of lodge. For instance, the neighbouring Ahansal village of Amzrai has two, both built in this style, and no private citizen, so to speak, of Amzrai has presumed to elevate himself above his fellows by building a house in this style. Elsewhere still, igherm designates a whole cluster of such houses, a hamlet, and the social unit inhabiting it. (South of the Atlas generally – and in some regions north of it – this high type of house is very much more common and hence hardly provides a discriminatory status symbol. In Zawiya Ahansal, it does.)

between the effective saints and the rest. (Open class conflict on these lines is hard to conceive.)

It is of course possible that the reason is in part historical: perhaps Sidi Mohamed n'ut Baba really was a crucial figure, whose personality captured much of the available reverence, and perhaps his sons were less significant, even if genealogically, they represented a parting of the ways for effective baraka. If a personality and legends attach to the memory of Sidi Mohamed n'ut Baba, but not to his son or sons, it might not be so easy later to carry out a transfer and re-activate someone, who at present is a mere lifeless name in the family tree (i.e., Sidi Abd el Malik, son of Sidi Mohamed n'ut Baba) and re-endow him with significance.

This is possible; and certainly, no positive evidence is available to exclude this. Personally I doubt it, perhaps, in part, from a predilection for structural explanations, which invoke present structures, and treat the past as a slave of the present, rather than the other way round, as is done by 'genetic' explanations. But reasons can here be given in support of this predilection:

(1) Listening to stories about ancestors, it is striking that the story has a greater concreteness than its subject (i.e., its hero), and that the two are only shakily conjoined. Narrators will switch from a story about one ancestor and proceed with a later part of the narrative which, in terms of the inner logic of the story or its connection with other beliefs, applies to a *later* member of the genealogy, without mentioning the fact and without noticing it, as it were conflating diverse generations. If nudged (not generally or frequently by the anthropologist, who tries to be tactful) they will pull themselves up and say, 'Yes, this episode no longer belongs to the life of (say) SSA, but his great-grandson . . .'

It is as if the natural genealogical pattern for this kind of society were a minimal, Occamist one, such as is in fact found amongst the surrounding lay tribes, and as if the excessive genealogical wealth placed somewhat of a strain on the unlettered saints and tended to push them, in the endowment of character and life-story of ancestors, into conflation. Hence if it were necessary for reasons inherent in current village structure to stress Sidi Abd el Malik rather than his father, I do not think it would be difficult to shift the concrete picture to him.

(2) In fact, Sidi Mohamed n'ut Baba does provide a significant cut-off point: as an ancestor he defines, not the effective saints

alone, but roughly, the saints-plus-court-hangers-on, the sum of two distinct social categories, which sum however is also jointly distinct from the rest of the village. Roughly speaking, outside his progeny one finds those families of the main lodge which, whilst relying on some benefits of sanctity, some perks and above all physical protection of the sanctuary, concentrate economically on ordinary husbandry. Inside his progeny, one finds two kinds of more intimate relationship to sanctity: either effective sanctity, or conspicuous clientship to effective saints.

The Rivals

The branch of the dominant lineage which produces effective saints, descended from Sidi Mohamed n'ut Baba and his son Sidi Abd el Malik, does not split again until three generations later (see diagram 2), when it undergoes binary fission. The two sub-groups which separate at this point do not however define themselves in a neat and symmetrical manner, in as far as they take as their apical and defining ancestors not two brothers (as would be right and proper in a tidy segmentary system), but two men whose relationship to each other is that of uncle and nephew. Both groups spring from Sidi Ahmad Yellow-beard, the last shared ancestor: but one defines itself in terms of his son, Sidi Ahmad u Ahmad, and the other in terms of the son of his other son, Sidi Ahmad u Mohamed. I can think of no structural reason for this asymmetry, and suppose that it simply indicates an historic fact.

To what extent does each of these two sub-segments constitute an effective corporate group, acting in opposition to the other?

One of the two groups, the Ait Sidi Ahmad u Mohamed, is fairly cohesive and constitutes a kind of group, though there exists no ritual, nor any specific conflict, which would overtly manifest confirm or activate their cohesion.

The cohesion does however express itself in one very crucial form – the acceptance by all members in this segment (with one partial exception: see p. 93) of the pre-eminence of one of its own sub-branches, that springing from Sidi Mulay. In a sense, the collateral branches within this group have voluntarily opted out from amongst the front runners in the race, though not out of agurram status: they receive donations and reverence, (though not on the same scale as the Ait Sidi Mulay), they seclude their wives and claim effectively the prerogative of pacifism, but – and this is crucial – they do not compete with the Ait Sidi Mulay politically. The most striking expression of this acceptance, indeed of the eagerness to accept, the pre-eminence of the Ait Sidi Mulay, is in the way these minor segments specify their own names. A man in the Sidi Yussif family will describe his name as (say) Sidi Ahmad u Yussif n'ait Sidi Mulay, Sir Ahmad son of Yussif of the people of Sidi Mulay! This of course is contrary to all genealogical logic, which should constrain him to define his 'people' in terms of some apical ancestor higher up in his own line – the distance of the ancestor to be determined by the context, by the intended contrast. But, in fact, they chose to define their 'people' by a collateral ancestor, a father's brother, Sidi Mulay. Conspicuous deviation from logic, here as in other societies, underscores and expresses a social alignment: logic is shared by all humanity and thus defines no social group, but a defiance of it conveys a commitment.

These respectable, effective agurram families which nevertheless openly accept the pre-eminence and leadership of a collateral line, underscore another interesting feature of a saintly settlement: there are different styles or levels at which one can become a client to a more successful line. It can happen at a higher level or a lower one. These close cousins of the Ait Sidi Mulay (in the narrower and 'proper' sense), such as the Ait Sidi Yussif, do it at the higher level. They are in no way in economic need. Though they may be dependants politically, they are not such in any economic sense. Hence their reverence is not open to the suspicion of being a virtue of necessity. (If necessity there is, it is not economic.) This makes it, in one way, all the more valuable by way of testimony to the sanctity of the Sidi Mulay. In another way, such wealthy, near-equal clients are not sufficient: it would be inconceivable for one of the three Ait Sidi Yussif brothers to make and serve tea humbly, waiting to be beckoned on, whilst the dominant member of the Ait Sidi Mulay entertains an important visitor or pilgrim. For this type of service, which is also essential, the other type of 'fallen' cousin is employed, who serves in and from economic need. Very roughly speaking, one might say that the igurramen who have 'sloughed off' since Sidi Ahmad u Mohamed, i.e., are descended from him but no longer aspire to leadership (at least, not unless a radical change in the local situation provides the opportunity and stimulus) are clients at the higher level; whilst the remainder, those who have sloughed off since the more distant Sidi Mohamed n'ut Baba, are clients at the lower level. This is only an approximation. Some close cousins are also rather humble clients. The unsymmetrical relationships of the igurramen do not allow any simple, mechanical reading-off of status from kinship position.

Both expressions, for the half-lines or for the 'correct' name 'Ait Sidi Ahmad u Mohamed' and the 'incorrect' 'Ait Sidi Mulay' are used and understood. The latter and 'incorrect' one is of course ambiguous, as it can denote both the Ait Sidi Mulay proper, the family descended from him, or the wider group of families including those descended from his brothers but admitting the pre-eminence of the line springing from him directly.

An interesting trait of this group is that all of its members have chosen to stay at Zawiya Ahansal, that none of them have availed themselves of the opportunities for hiving-off which arose during the early period of the French advance (see below, p. 252). Their geographical compactness, contrasted with the dispersion of the other group, may be a consequence of earlier cohesion, and certainly is a pre-condition of continued cohesion. But this group cannot be seen as 'acting in opposition to' its genealogically balancing segment, the Ait Ahmad u Ahmad, precisely because of the dispersion and internal divisions of that other group. Whereas in the former group, one family now has, at least for the time being, the monopoly of political aspiration (with one ineffective exception, see p. 193), in the latter group a number of families retain all sanctity in the fullest sense, i.e., retain the whole range of agurram traits which includes striving for political eminence. This illustrates a pervasive theme of this study, namely, that in the case of the saints, alignments and oppositions, or even so to speak prima facie alignments and oppositions, the baselines of manœuvering, simply cannot be read off the genealogical map. That is only possible in the even, symmetrical, proper segmentary situation: the asymmetries of influence and of strategy among the igurramen, which in turn are inherent in their role, make this impossible.

The internal structure of this half of the top stratum, of the Ait Ahmad u Mohamed (properly speaking) is visible on diagram 3. Given that Sidi Ahmad u Mohamed had three sons, one might expect three households. In fact, there are four, given both fissions and fusions, (or rather, asymmetrical optings-out from fissions). There are two respectable non-competing high-level families,

(B) and (C). There is the family of effective leadership, (A), which has already absorbed some of its cousins at the lower level of dependence. Finally, there is the family of the disinherited brother, (D), impoverished, and certainly not 'respectably deferential', for he is neither respectable nor deferential: he would compete if he could, and make quite ineffective attempts in this direction. His status is somewhere between that of a low-level client (he cannot but be economically dependent, however reluctantly) and that of unsuccessful rival, whose very impotence, a kind of conspicuous display of sinful irreverence receiving its punishment, makes its own kind of contribution to the glory of the successful line, highlighting it by contrast.

The Social Register

(A) The last of the Marabouts

This family was the last of the main-lodge igurramen to hold power under the French system, which made igurramen into chiefs. (The traditional system had been one in effect, of indirect rule by igurramen, through direct elective lay chiefs; whilst French indirect rule turned igurramen into direct rulers, increasing their immediate power and decreasing their popularity.) Hence Independence in 1956 meant a grave if temporary blow to the ambitions, if not prestige, of the head of the family. The family has recovered from this, and even now its head is the most influential member of the main lodge; he can collect donations from a wider area, though he is nowadays sometimes obliged to go and fetch it. (He undertook one such journey, of considerable length, during the summer of 1959.) The family came out as clear victors in the first modern elections, the 'communal' elections of May 1960, in which the main lodge constituted one 'constituency', as it were, in electing the nine members of the newly designed rural council covering the four local Ahansal villages and the segments of the Ait Atta and Ait Abdi who 'depend' on the administrative outposts now located opposite Zawiya Ahansal. The effective head of the family, Sidi Mha, did not stand for election, in view of his record of office-holding under the French, but his youngest brother did, and came by far and away head of the poll.

The apical Sidi Mulay, who 'defines' the family, was one of the personalities involved in the crucial intrigues during the slow French advance in the twenties and early thirties. He and some others stayed behind at the main lodge whilst the main leader, Caid Sidi Mha (of the other 'half') with whom they covertly remained in touch, moved with some others to French occupied territory and set up the new centre of power there. After the military occupation of the main lodge during the summer of 1933 it was Sidi Mulay who mediated the surrender of the final resisters, the Abdi who were holding out in caves on the plateau (as some of them were to do again in 1960, against the Royal Moroccan army). As a reward from the French, he was appointed the Caid of the Ait Abdi, a post he held until his death, and the duties of which carried out *from* the main lodge. There was thus a somewhat curious position of a chief who was not merely not a member of the tribe, which of course happened on other occasions when the French turned igurramen into Caids, but not even resident in it.

That the saint should be resident outside the lay tribe is not odd, but that the chief administrator into whom he was now transformed, should live outside was perhaps slightly odder. In due course, when he was old enough, his son Sidi Mha, present head of the Ait Sidi Mulay, became his deputy in this post. The eldest of his sons did not live to succeed his father: he is reputed to have been a scoundrel and adept at black magic, rather like some women in the family. The next eldest, who is alive, must have been an outstanding scoundrel at any rate in his father's eyes, because he was formally repudiated by his father, an act which required a formal pronouncement three weeks running, and lives in great poverty with his children and is, as indicated, a kind of reluctant client of his younger brother. I do not know the full story of his repudiation, but the reasons given are that he prostituted his sisters to the soldiery quartered near the lodge during the French conquest, and that on one occasion he took a shot at his own father. Repudiation to the point of disinheriting is formally contradictory to the customary law as given by the elders to the chief of outpost, but it certainly took place in this case.

As of 1954, Sidi Mha's extended household contained thirty-nine people. These were distributed over a number of houses, the main being in the lodge, in the lodge's main centre of transhumancy at Tisselmit, and at a place within the tribal area of the Ait Mhand.

Of these, sixteen were kinsmen and their families, the kinsmen being of a fairly close kind. Within this group, there were three men whose position deserves special note: they remain parts of this household, to whose nucleus admittedly they are very close in kin terms, *despite the fact that another household exists to which they are closer still*. These three are brothers, and paternal first cousins to the nucleus; but their paternal half-brothers have established an independent household (*C*). They have chosen to remain under the wings of the top household (*A*) rather than either set up on their own, individually or jointly, *or* remain in division with their own half-brothers of household (*C*). Their status is consequently rather lower than that of their independent brethren. Three further members (a married couple and a young shepherd) were kinsfolk of a more distant kind. The remaining twenty-one were retainers of various kinds and their wives and children: two slaves, husband and wife, the husband's father having been bought by the family (these now technically emancipated by the French conquest but continuing to live with their masters); an old court hanger-on, whom we used to call Polonius, who had been a close friend of the deceased Sidi Mulay and whom the present head of the household kept on out of piety to his father's memory; employed workers, who generally have annual contracts and generally stay with the family for very long periods and virtually settle, drawn, apart from one family locally recruited, from various areas of Ahansal influence (Abdi, Usikis, Azilal). As described, some of the close kinsmen were in fact also clients or retainers: they had chosen to be small figures in a large household rather than independent ones in their own: humble security rather than risky and precarious freedom. They have thereby forfeited the possibility of effective sanctity, *and* evaded the dangers of failure or of lay life, for they share in some of the rewards of the effective sanctity of their master, in security, at least. It is they who come and serve tea and sit at a respectful distance, waiting to be beckoned on to join the party, when the effective saint is entertaining visitors. Their presence, their numerous presence, their willingness to serve the saint, all illustrate his affluence and influence, his baraka, and indeed, their own fall from baraka. This is one policy one may adopt if one is born near, but not right in, the stream of baraka.

The Ait Sidi Mulay household is the biggest in the village. Its size has no local rival in the four Ahansal villages, and I do not believe it has one in any of the surrounding lay villages. Anything much bigger is locally held to be well nigh unmanageable: the size it possessed prior to the (perfectly amicable) hiving-off of its close cousins in the last fission was held to be phenomenal and impracticable, a fact which (truthfully, I think) is given as the cause and reason of the separation.

(B) *The Kulak Family, Ait Sidi Yussif*

This family is at present centred on three brothers living in indivision. Of the three, the eldest exercises a dominant influence over the others. He looks rather like Charlie Chan, is fat whilst the other two brothers are lean and do the kind of work which involves going long distances, such as going to distant markets. Thus the relationship of the dominant brother to the others is not unlike that of Sidi Mha to the brothers with whom he lives in indivision, but in this case it is difficult to explain the phenomenon. There is great similarity in the two sets of relationships: for instance, in both cases the younger brothers are unwilling to smoke in the presence of the elder dominant one, or have him know that they do smoke.

As stated, the manner in which this family recognises the ascendancy of Sidi Mha's family comes out most clearly in their use of the name: in the third position in the deceased father's name, the place after the personal name and the father's name, the place reserved for the clan, affiliation, there figures the name of what was the deceased father's *brother*, namely Sidi Mulay.

At the time corresponding to the census of the preceding family, the household consisted of fourteen members. Five of these were non-kin retainers, all paid workers or wives of such. Two of the five were women, one of them simply the wife of a worker. One of the male workers was recruited from an area of Ahansal influence across the hills (Usikis). Of the four wives of the three brothers who are the nucleus of this household, two are from top agurram and close patrilateral families, one from a 'latent' saintly family of the lodge, and one is from an entirely lay client tribe of the Ihansalen, the Ait Haddidu.

This family is sometimes claimed to be the richest in the lodge. Such riches as it possesses do not spring from donations, from which it can only have a very small share, as handed over by its cousins who are more active practitioners of sanctity: but then, it does not have much of the saintly expenditures either. Its wealth lies in the careful husbandry of its flock, which is said to be about two hundred sheep and goats – a good number in Zawiya Ahansal. It seeks protection under the saintly prestige and renomé of its Sidi Mulay cousins. It thus enjoys few of the direct economic benefits of sanctity, but also few of the costs. The life strategy of its members is very clearly marked and conscious: no political ambition or activity, great caution in all matters, and concentration on wealth and careful husbandry. In the particular situation this family found itself – close to the mainstream of sanctity but not right in it, and under the general conditions of the modern pacification of the area – this strategy paid off. But it has not pleased God to send the family any male offspring: there are no boys in the youngest generation. The senior brother has however informally adopted the eldest son of the 'disinherited brother', household (D), whom God in his inscrutable way blessed with no fewer than four sons. No formal adoption has taken place (it would indeed be contrary to custom, which allows adults, in effect, to gain adoption from collectivities, but excludes formal adoption of children), but the young adolescent, as he was at the time of field work, was constantly and conspicuously in the presence of his elder kinsman, the senior brother of this household. There are, however, young girls in the Sidi Yussif household: it was difficult not to suppose that the son of the disinherited, as it were defrocked saint, would recover some grace through marriage with a daughter of the highly respectable but son-less Sidi Yussif family.[1]

(C) Comparatively Poor Cousins

Sidi Moa, brother of the deceased Sidi Mulay and Sidi Yussif, left five sons. Of these two have remained in indivision (and are sons of the same mother), and established a house which in its style of life implicitly lays claim to holy status. The one wife is carefully secluded. At the same time, this household is neither particularly rich nor influential and lives under the shadow and protection of the Sidi Mulay household.

[1]When I revisited the lodge at the end of 1967, I found that all three brothers had died very suddenly within a year of each other. A posthumous son, however, was born to one of them, so the household's wealth remains united, if the old rules apply.

The remaining three brothers have become unambiguously clients and dependents of the Sidi Mulay household and live within its general compound (see above, p. 190).

(D) *The Repudiated Brother*

This is a household of the repudiated brother. He is without wealth and without influence. He is also reputed to be lazy, a reputation no doubt justified in view of the fact that he seldom seems to be busy with agriculture or other work. His poverty is genuinely betrayed by a lean and hungry look. I know him to be in debt and when I have dined with him, the food consisted of nothing but thin spaghetti and very little grease (this kind of packed spaghetti being, with sardines, one of the few consumption foods that have reached the local market from the outside). When he has the opportunity he goes on donation collecting trips, but these are not very productive.

He is in fact economically a client of his younger brother, though his household is separate, but not an important one. His house is of a kind which would technically be compatible with agurram status, but this is alas not true of its style of upkeep. Architecturally, it is in fact more agurram-worthy than that of the Ait Sidi Yussif: yet it would impress no one, for its poverty is far too manifest. The difference between the two houses could be compared with that between an architecturally most elegant Georgian house, in such a state of dilapidation and manifest impoverishment as not to be worth locking, and an architecturally most undistinguished but extremely well-maintained and indeed well locked and guarded residence of a philistinical businessman. Given that, in this case, the 'businessman' has almost as good an ancestry as the indigent inhabitant of the good house – the former is first cousin, the latter is brother, of the main possessor of baraka – not even snobbery could mislead the pilgrim to the more elegant but less affluent house. In fact, the anonymous pilgrim would be unlikely to turn to either of these houses: poverty would prevent his being entertained in the one house, and unwillingness to compete in the saintly race, in the other.

We have here a family which seem definitely on the way out of the charmed circle of holiness. Poverty prevents the poor man from keeping up the marks of saintly status such as the seclusion of womenfolk, and he is even forced into the position of going counter to the ethos, not only of saints but even of lay tribesmen, by dishonourably accepting rent. The main possessor of baraka arranged for a house to be put at the disposal of the anthropologist during the first summer of field work. When payment was offered in the end, his instructions were that it be paid to the disinherited brother. Rent for housing is locally considered redundant. The arrangement thus could not have been better calculated to underscore the generosity of one brother, the fall from grace of the other. The fact that he has antagonised lay tribesmen makes him of little use as a mediator, and the fact that he is publicly recognised as having no influence within the Lodge also diminishes his usefulness as a patron to outsiders. Yet the poor man keeps trying. He flirts and intrigues with the Ait Amhadar (the more genuine and serious rivals of the Ait Sidi Mulay, drawn from the other half of the saintly line), though they hold him of little account; and after Independence, which brought temporary eclipse and even a brief period of imprisonment (by the semi-official 'Army of Liberation') to his baraka-possessed and effectively agurram-like brother, he not merely hoisted the flag of independent Morocco from his house (everyone of importance did that) but kept it flying much longer than patriotism, joy or caution required, and longer than anyone else – hoping that conspicuous adherence to the wind of change might help restore his fortunes. It did not.

As stated, it is a curious fact that this brother is more plentifully blessed with male offspring than any of his more saintly brethren or cousins. Locals do not comment on this paradox, but when it is pointed out, shrug it off with a reference to the inscrutability of the will of *Mulana* (Our Lord).

More Rivals

We now proceed to the other half, the Ait Ahmad u Ahmad. This apical ancestor had five sons. This generation died out in the 1940's, and their lives are reasonably well documented from French sources. Each of the five gave rise to a family of note.

Two of these families moved en bloc to what has in effect become a new lodge in the territory of the Ait Mhand tribe, this settlement taking place in the special conditions created by the French advance. These two families appeared under the French to be well on the way to providing a kind of rotating dynasty for the Ait

Mhand and some other tribes administratively joined to them by the French. This dynasty lasted from the early twenties till independence in 1956.

The relationship of these families is visible on diagram 4.

(E) The People of the Upper Castle, Ait Amhadar

This is the second most important household in the lodge, second only (and not always second) to the Ait Sidi Mulay. Within its own half of the holy lineage, it can hardly have a rival locally at present in view of the permanent departure of some, the decline in wealth and influence of others, and the absence now (i.e., during period of fieldwork) of healthy adult males amongst the Ait Okdim.

The present head of the household is a young man, Ahmad[1] (who is the grandson of one of the five brothers who included Caid Sidi Mha). The crucial personality of the household, however, was his father, known as Caid Amhadar (the younger – his father too was named Sidi Amhadar), who died in 1954 a few days after our first arrival at the lodge. He had been a person of great energy, ambition, ability and influence, though it is unlikely whether he understood the modern world in which he latterly had to operate, not without at least temporary success. He was involved in the Ahansal intrigues accompanying the slow French advance. He took active part in the military operations, on the French side during the latter stages, and according to the French outpost archives distinguished himself during the final capture of the capital of the Isha tribe in 1933, the most formidable if not the last opponents of the French in this region. Apparently on this occasion he displayed 'une très belle conduite sous feu' (so stated the archives of the French administrative outpost). He later became a Chevalier of the Legion of Honour, as did Caid Sidi Mha.

Under the protectorate he began as Caid Sidi Mha's deputy, and later on his decease became an independent Caid in charge of both the four Ahansal villages and the Ait Atta of Talmest.

[1]By the late 1960s, this man became the administrative chief of the four Ahansal villages. The first post-Independence occupant of this job had been from Tighanimin, this non-prestigious village having been selected by lot – an ironical fact much resented by the main lodge. But when the occupant was killed by an avalanche the post reverted to a prestigious line. The head of the rival Ait Sidi Mulay declined to compete, though his house continues to be the most influential, and the time of disqualification of pre-Independence office-holders has past.

He was ambitious and longed for greater powers, more tribes to rule, and a modern symbol of prestige in the form of a motor car. The latter he acquired though the family had to sell it again after his fall from power. His ambitions led him to intrigue not only against Sidi Mulay for the chieftaincy of the Ait Abdi, but also, and more dangerously, against the Glawi. His ambitions led to excessively extortionate behaviour towards his villagers, and the hostility aroused in high places by his intrigues finally coincided with popular discontent at home and he was made to resign, which he did two years before his death. During the two years of his life after his resignation he could hardly bear his humiliation to be witnessed by those over whom he had once ruled with an iron hand, and he was never seen outside the finely fortified household of his family.

The inherently most interesting episode in his career, however, was the five years in the late forties and early fifties when his rule coincided with the presence at the outposts of an interesting and also ambitious French officer. Caid Amhadar himself probably did not understand the modern world, as can perhaps be gauged from the fact that whilst coveting a car he did not provide a modern education for his son: but jointly with this officer, they provided a kind of composite tribal Ataturk.

The officer in question himself was a man who had risen from the ranks and though by that time in his thirties was merely a lieutenant. Jointly the Caid and lieutenant set in motion ambitious schemes for local development such as the building of a road to Tilluguit, the construction of new irrigation ditches and a new market place, and so forth. All this was obtained not with credits from above, which could not have been forthcoming, but by 'voluntary' labour, as is usual in forced economic development. Each of the two halves of this tribal Ataturk needed the other: the officer would not have had the power to conscript local labour for such schemes, but acting through the native chief the activity could be described as voluntary work, as tribal self-help. The native chief unsupported by the protecting authority could have come up against disastrous opposition. As it was, opposition manifested itself in emigration or in secretly performed magical rites against him, such as the naming of a stone after him which was then broken up by other stones into little bits.

At the time of my census, this household, the second in size in the village, had twenty-two members. Like that of the Ait Sidi

Mulay, it was dispersed over possessions in Zawiya Ahansal itself, at Tisselmit and places at, or on the way to, Ait Mhand. Its nucleus consists of the head of the household plus a man, his uncle (*ami*) for short, whose kinship position is very complex, which is itself a consequence of the situation in the lodge earlier in the century.

This man, also Sidi Ahmad, is the son of Caid Sidi Mha, by a wife who subsequently, after divorce, married Sidi Amhadar the Elder, and begat Sidi Amhadar the younger (who died in 1954, and was also the father of the present head of the house). It should be said that in the region, the levirate is known and held praiseworthy: it is honourable to take over and marry women left behind by deceased patrilateral kinsmen. In this case, the woman in question was 'left' not through death, but owing to the departure of Caid Sidi Mha for French-held territory in the early 'twenties. The offspring, the Sidi Ahmad under description, stayed with his mother and her second husband, thereby incidentally contradicting the rule of customary law to the effect that offspring of divorced parents should rejoin the father's family at the age of two.

He became a close friend and a kind of administrative adjutant of the politically active and important Sidi Amhadar the younger, to whom he was both patrilateral first cousin, and half-brother through his mother. His kin relationship to the present head of household is consequently of a complexity beyond words, though simple enough to grasp from diagram 3.

The main point he illustrates is perhaps the complexity of the division lines in a case when a lodge undergoes binary fission, as Zawiya Ahansal in effect did in the 1920s. He seems well satisfied with an influential and respected, as it were avuncular position in the household, in which his personal property is held in indivision. The interesting question of the standing of his line in succession to influence does not arise, as he has no children. The household had no male offspring during the field work period: a much celebrated son was born to the other saint, but the infant subsequently died.

The rest of the household consists of male retainers (seven at that time, of whom one is an ex-slave, bought by the family in his mother's womb prior to his birth as a speculative purchase, a fact commemorated in his nickname), the daughters of the head of household, and the various wives of the saints and retainers. The elder of the two saints has two wives, one from the Haddidu tribe, but this woman fled home following the prescribed ritual for wifely flight (requesting protection from a local in the village) in 1956. There were also two widows of the deceased Caid.[1]

(F) Ait Okdim

This household is under a temporary eclipse owing to lack of adult males. The father and apex of the household is deceased. He had been the youngest of the five brothers who included Caid Sidi Mha. When alive he was not very influential, though the family owns some fields amongst the Ait Mazigh tribe, who till it for them, and with whom this segment consequently has special connection and influence. This practice of ploughing fields for the saints was still alive very recently, though the saints themselves didn't know from year to year whether the fields would be sown with wheat or barley.

Of the three sons the only adult is mentally ill and totally ineffective.

At the time of my census, this household contained seventeen members. It thus comes in third place in size in the lodge, which indeed corresponds to its ranking in saintly prestige. The nucleus is the three brothers, of whom the eldest is incapacitated by mental illness. In addition there are two retainers, one an ex-slave, and assorted wives, widows and female children.

Despite the temporary eclipse of the household owing to the absence of sane male adults, there is no doubt about the remaining influence of the household, in terms of wealth, respect, the beauty and good maintenance of its dwelling and so forth. In the 1960s,

---

[1] One of the old women in the household was the mother of the Ahansal who had achieved fame as a Berber Robin Hood in the Tagzirt region around 1950, and who was later, though not at the time, claimed by the Nationalists as a precursor of violent resistance. With his fame he is now retrospectively referred to as Sidi Ahmad Ahansal, though coming of undistinguished Ahansal lineage from the undistinguished village of Taria, it is certain that in his lifetime he would have been known simply as Ahmad (no Sidi), and 'Ahansal' only in contexts when no others were close by. A street in Casablanca is now named after him. The name of Ahansal has left many marks on the map of traditional Morocco, which is, as much as anything, a map of saints and their shrines: but this is the only example known to me of the Ihansalen leaving their mark on the map of *modern* Morocco.

The story of this bandit fits the ideal type of the 'social bandit' as described in Eric Hobsbawm's *Primitive Rebels* (Manchester University Press, 1959, ch. II). This man's kinsman was also the only man from the four central Ahansal villages to lose his life during the transition to Independence of the winter of 1955–6. He prematurely looted the French outpost, was caught and shot while trying to escape. Witnesses confirm that he was shot while trying to escape and not 'while trying to escape'.

the two sane brothers are entering adult life, and an important group of pilgrims from the Ait Isha bringing donation to the main lodge paid their homage and were entertained by the *three* top households (Sidi Mulay, Amhadar and Okdim). During the summer of 1959, a crucial village assembly called ad hoc to deal with the case of the five corrupt headmen included the elder of the two sane brothers, though he was at the time only an adolescent.

(G and H) Into Decline

At the lower end of the village, near the river, there is a fine decorative igherm, belonging to the Ait Sidi Moa. The Sidi Moa in question (deceased) who defines the family, is one of the four brothers of the Caid Sidi Mha of Bernat, and himself left five sons, of whom three are alive. One of these, and the son of another, inhabit the house. They are *bdän*, i.e., they have separated their property, and the house is rearranged so as to have two entrances and constitute, as it were, two self-contained flats. The uncle only inhabits his part very rarely, being more frequently with his property at Ait Mhand, and can hardly be considered any more a part of the main lodge, except in the sense in which all recent migrants still possessing property or a reasonable possibility of inheritance keep a foot in. The nephew, on the other hand, lives there most of the time, though he does frequently go off on donation-collecting trips.

This family is really a fragment of one which has hived off, following the major move of top-saintly families, to Ait Mhand after 1920. What remains of the sanctity of those who have remained? A close genealogical proximity to the really effective saints; a highly decorative house with a good address, i.e., close to the shrine, but one now rebuilt in a manner hardly compatible with saintly prestige. (A real saint would not break up the unity of an igherm, he would build another.) There remains an aspiration to the saintly style of life and the enclosure of women – but one which poverty does not allow to be fulfilled.

The household consists of the young man (the nephew mentioned above), his two unmarried sisters (one young and one divorced), their mother, and one client girl. The daughters of the house present something of the aspect of distressed gentlefolk, or saintlyfolk: according to their mother they are all-suited for marriage into a lay family, being unused to hard work. For some reason which is not clear to me, they have not been claimed by a saintly family. The young man himself illustrates the fate of those near the mainstream of baraka who neither become effective saints, nor clients or such, nor firmly go lay. His life is in some ways one of mendicancy. He is, it so happens, extremely likeable. He has failed to get married – no doubt because his poverty makes him an unattractive groom.

But this household clearly is on the way out; little baraka is left, only the aftertaste of the baraka of recent generations. The present generation is paying the price of defeat.

The Population of the Main Lodge

The population of Zawiya Ahansal according to my census, 1954.

Saints			No. in saintly 'nucleus'
Ait Sidi Mulay (whole household)	1	39	3
Ait Amhadar	1	22	2
Ait Okdim	1	17	3
Ait Sidi Yussif	1	14	3
Repudiated brother	1	6	1
'On way out'	1	5	1
'Fairly poor cousins'	1	3	2
Total	7	106	15

Others	No. of families	No. of people
Families with 12 members	1	12
11		
10	1	10
9	1	9
8	2	16
7	3	21
6	2	12
5	7	35
4	7	28
3	7	21
2	15	30
1	9	9
Total (non-saintly households)	55	203
All	62	309

In the count of households, 'saintly' and 'lay' households can meaningfully be separated. For individuals, this cannot be done simply by adding the total personnel of saintly families, because of course not everyone in an effectively saintly household is an effective saint – far from it. Taking only the male 'nuclei' of the households, counted as saintly on the above table, we get 15 effective saints.[1] But this includes some impoverished ones, one feeble-minded, and two adolescents.

The criterion of being 'one household' is, in general, that the people so described are kin who are *män* (i.e., whose property remains undivided, who are not *bdän*, divided), and consequently work and enjoy it jointly. They may or may not have a recognised head and they will generally live in one dwelling.

In case of the larger units described as one household, the relevant criterion is that all the members take their orders, receive their rewards and nourishment, from a nucleus which is a single household by the previous criterion. The client members of these larger households may of course also own property in their own right, but they are members of the larger household in as far as the major part of their time and energy is devoted to work in connection with that larger household, from which they take their instructions. The degree of permanence and the status of such clients vary, from 'labourers' theoretically engaged for a season (though in Zawiya Ahansal, they tend to stay season after season), to kinsmen who become clients and bring their own small property into the pool from which they could withdraw it, and to slaves who in the pre-1933 situation were the property of the household. (Slaves could also be the property of the lodge as such, i.e., be at the service of the igurramen without being specifically the property of any one agurram family.)

Roughly, the general criterion for 'household' is a property-sharing, economically co-operating group under one direction. One must add that the clients have no rights in most of the property in whose administration they co-operate, but receive rewards in kind or money.

---

[1]But I have excluded from being 'nuclear' the four sons of the disinherited brother, though the eldest is older than the included youngest of the three Ait Okdim brethren. If 'nuclear' is to correspond to more or less recognised individual igurramen, this is correct.

Despite theoretical difficulties of definition, the limits of households are in practice fairly obvious. In most cases, co-habitation in the same dwelling is a fair criterion (though this does not apply to the larger 'households').

Nevertheless, there are ambiguities. The (to me) surprisingly large number of small or even solitary 'units' is in part explained by the fact that they are clients of larger units but that the dependence is not expressed in co-habitation or the inhabiting of a house owned by the larger unit. If these informal dependencies were included, the result would be a further increase in the size of the large saintly households and of some others. It would rather complicate matters in that some of these small units may receive charity and be dependent on more than one other group.

The inhabitants of Zawiya Ahansal, like all other surrounding villages and other Moroccan Berbers, practise a form of self-taxation: there is a self-imposed income-tax which is to claim one-tenth of both the harvest and the flocks. Of this one-tenth, theoretically one-third is to go to the poor, one third to relatives, and one-third 'to the mosque', i.e., to the scribe and for collective feasts. It is doubtful whether these 'thirds' are equal. (Lay tribes who tax themselves to supply donations to the saints, which may be as low as $1/144$ of the harvest, do this in addition to the 'internal' tax.) It is difficult to say how strictly this self-imposed taxation is carried out, but certainly a show is made of separating the tenth when the harvest is being brought in. Its relevance here is that it helps to account for the survival and status of the small (solitary and other) household units, who are near-clients, of larger, more viable and effective ones, in virtue of receiving this kind of systematic charity, without being properly incorporated in the larger households.

Another factor contributing to the existence of the small family units in Zawiya Ahansal is the frequent occurrence of childlessness. This may be attributable to venereal disease, presumably introduced at the time of the 'pacification', and perhaps particularly rampant among the saints. The troops were camped near the lodge for a considerable time. The theory of VD was held by the French administrator prior to 1955, whose wife, a trained nurse, did medical work in the villages. The phenomenon of frequent childlessness does not seem to be found in other villages, but has struck the main lodge, and its inhabitants themselves comment on it, as did the archives of the French administrative outpost after the war. Once the troops involved in the 'pacification' had departed, it is my impression that an infectious disease of this kind would not easily spread from village to village, intermarriage or cross-clan immorality being fairly rare, but would spread and maintain itself in any one village – marriages, divorces, re-marriages and amorous episodes inside a village being fairly frequent and with a high turnover.

A further factor in the childlessness might be a local contraceptive or abortion practices on the part of women preferring the enjoyment to the fruit of sex. Such practices exist. Just what demographic consequences these practices have I should not like to guess, nor how widespread or effective they are. Women normally profess a desire for offspring, and I have made no deeper investigation into the real truth of these matters.

Another noteworthy fact is that the large 'households' contain members not locally resident at all, in as far as the properties – houses, fields, and flocks – of the large households extend into quite distant areas. The top families own property – houses, fields – in other regions of Ahansal influence, in Usikis, Sremt (belonging to the Ait Bu Gmez tribe), amongst the Ait Mazigh, and amongst the Ait Mhand. These acquisitions are the results both of purchase and of simple gifts from the tribesmen in whose territory they are located. In the case of fields, these distant properties will be worked by the local tribesmen, thus performing a kind of voluntary *corvée* for their saintly patrons, who then deliver the produce during the annual visit to the shrine. As a result of the diminution of the wages of sanctity under the French, the saints, becoming poorer, found themselves selling some of these distant properties.[1]

Of these foreign investments, so to speak, by far the most important at present are those in the territory of the Ait Mhand. The reasons for the establishment and expansion of saintly property

---

[1]Those in Usikis, for instance, were sold to the then influential and rich amghar at Usikis, Sidi Said Ahansal, himself of the *contested* Ahansal lineage of Ait Tighanimin. Sidi Said Ahansal lost his chieftaincy in connection with the 'left-wing' revolt of the Ait Abdi in 1960, though not implicated sufficiently to go to prison. In the context of Usikis affairs, his name can be used without ambiguity, i.e., without any danger of confusion with *the* Sidi Said Ahansal, the ninth-century A H ancestor of all Ihansalen. Even the 'real' Ihansalen of Zawiya Ahansal refer to him by this name, though at the same time they deny real Ahansal status to the Ait Tighanimin and their offspring. See below, p. 236.

in this area are connected with the political condition of this tribe and its area in recent times, both before and during the French advance between the first World War and 1933. In pre-pacification days, this tribe was particularly dependent on the saints of Ahansal for diplomatic support.

The possessions in Ait Mhand are also the only ones which are actually inhabited and administered by members of Zawiya Ahansal households. The consequence of this is that included within the census of Zawiya Ahansal are some people, members of the big saintly households in the sense of identifying with them, recognising their authority and taking orders and wages from them, who in fact live elsewhere and may even seldom actually come to the lodge.

The reverse also holds: some actual inhabitants of Zawiya Ahansal may be members of households, family units, whose main centre of gravity, in terms of numbers of resident members and of property, is elsewhere. One such is the saintly family which owns half of the lovely igherm at the lower end of the village of which the other half is owned and inhabited by the people described above as 'on the way out'. This couple is not included in the census on the grounds that they spend more time in Ait Mhand than at the lodge though their position is marked on kinship diagram 4, as (H). (In fact, I have never seen the wife at the lodge, but then, as she is the enclosed wife of a more or less effective saint, I ought not to do so. But it is my impression that she was at the lodge even more rarely than her husband.)

All this is merely the consequence of Zawiya Ahansal being in the late stage of a recent schism or hiving-off: in the early 1920s, in consequence of the political situation arising from the French occupation of Ait Mhand and their failure to occupy the Ahansal heartlands, a number of top saintly families, led by Caid Sidi Mha, with their retainers, migrated to the land of the Ait Mhand, in effect setting up a new territorial centre of sanctity there (though one which, owing to the special circumstances of the time, never came to be called a zawiya, for Caid Sidi Mha's main source of authority henceforth was not that he was an agurram, but that he was a Caid).

The lines along which this fission took place illustrate a point made above (p. 56 et seq.), namely, that when ('episodic', event) real fissions, hivings-off take place, the line of such a fission is not identical with that of the segmentary, 'dispositional' division. It is not the case that one segment stays and another goes: within each group, some will go and some will stay. In this case, none of the igurramen of the one half of the saintly stratum went, but in the other half, the division between those who went and those who stayed not only cut across the segment as a whole, but also across some individual families within it.

A Note on Slave Population

The negro slave population – as it was till 1933 – is rather small. (They were technically liberated by the French advance.) There is one such family in each of the three top saintly households, no more. This is a little in conflict with the saints' image of themselves: it would be improper for an effective saint to work, and most proper to have slaves to do his work for him. In practice, the great agurram families appear to have just enough slaves – a family each – to establish the principle, whilst relying for their retinue and services of the 'court' on retainers and poor cousins.

Sometimes saints claim that in the old days they had far more slaves and really did live in a fitting manner. This no doubt is an exaggeration, boasting and the painting of a Golden Age, but there is an element of truth in the claim that there has been a diminution in the slave population of the top households. At least two negro ex-slave women live in a semi-client status vis-à-vis the top families, not incorporated but performing services and dependent on their good will. One of these is married, the other not. Another is incorporated in a laicised household. Furthermore, some negro ex-slave families are settled on land owned by the igurramen in the neighbouring village of Amzrai and in Ait Mhand. These slaves were liberated and given this land to till. There is not enough of it and they are poor: in French days they added to their income by working as labourers at the administrative outpost, and they were badly hit by the decline in quantity of public works after independence.

I am not fully clear about the terms on which they were given the use of this non-local, saint-owned land nor of the motives for this. The saints claim that goodness of heart, and the desire to do what is pleasing in the eyes of God, were the motives. The operation is a little surprising in that one might have expected saints to be anxious to retain the services of Negroes, whether their slave status was underwritten by the administration or not, for prestige reasons. One may suspect the following: with the decline of the income from donations to saints after the French conquest, a decline due to the emergence of new authorities and political boundaries, poor cousins came to have first claim on the client positions in a saintly household. Secondly, the lands given to ex-slaves were those located in lay or laicised villages or tribes, and not very large or valuable: to hand them over, even on terms, to free lay locals involved the risk that in due course the local in question would claim them for his own. This is precisely what did happen in the course of some lands temporarily ceded to lay local tribesmen in Ait Mhand: they became a subject for protracted litigation between saint and occupier. (A saint's prestige is ephemeral, and certainly not effective in helping him get his own way once the prestige is no longer underwritten by the general pattern of reverence, so to speak, i.e., once he can no longer speak with the authority of the respect of numerous religious clients. After pacification, lay tribesmen litigated against their own ertswhile saintly leaders concerning land, in the case of saints who had been on the losing side i.e., had led the determined resistance; after the 'breaking' of Caid Amhadar, and particularly after Independence, the villagers of Tighanimin litigated against the Ait Amhadar and the whole of the main lodge concerning land at Tisselmit.) By giving the use of it to people whose colour made their non-belonging to the local tribe manifest, people also more dependent perhaps on the good will of the saints, the generous saint retained more hope of keeping some control over it and disposal of it later if he wished; the generous act, by leading as it were to a conspicuous new pattern in settlement, also stood out more noticeably and permanently.

If the semi-independent and the resettled slaves are allowed for, the slave population in the top families of the main lodge becomes more than double what it now is. This gives a more accurate picture, I think, of the size of the black slave population in the lodge in the traditional situation.

Tisselmit

Most of the inhabitants of the region are, in one way or another, transhumants. The form which transhumance takes varies a good deal: for instance, there is the use of tents to migrate very large distances from their permanent villages, by the Ait Atta; or the combined use of tent, cave and tree (a stone wall round a tree and the tent canvas fixed between the branches and the stones) to migrate frequently but over very small distances, by the Ait Abdi; or the physical reduplication of the socially identical village at a number of places, by the Ait Tighanimin.

This transhumancy is of course a consequence of the mountainous nature of the terrain, the extremity of seasonal variations, and the fact that even within small areas places differ a very great deal climatically and in the kind of use for which they are suitable. One major factor making for this transhumancy is, of course, that various pastures are usable, suitable or unusable at various times of the year. Fairly complicated social arrangements exist governing the use of pasture, and their closure (*agudal*). Complex movements are necessary to ensure the survival and prosperity of the various flocks. Local land can be divided into irrigated fields (*dawamen*), non-irrigable fields (*lbur*), forest and pasture. A distinction is also drawn between ordinary pasture and good meadow (*almu*), which generally becomes *agudal,* i.e., with regulated entry, with severe penalties for anyone attempting to use it prior to the agreed date. Pastures are owned by collectivities, fields by families, though with restrictions on sale outside the group, fellow-members of group having the option of first refusal, (as for brides), at a price determined by local elders. Forest is or was owned collectively amongst the Ihansalen (though now owned by the state) who have plenty of it and are fairly rich in other resources: amongst the Ait Abdi, very poor in other resources, trees are owned individually.

One common pattern is for a village to be physically reduplicated in the following way: each family owns a house at the village proper, whilst each family also has another dwelling in the forest or near the pasture, used mainly as a base for surveying the flocks. Thus one village will be rather concentrated and have the appearance of a village, whilst the other will be highly dispersed. Of the four Ahansal villages in the area of Sidi Said Ahansal's shrine, this pattern applies strikingly to two, Zawiya Ahansal (Ait Aggudim) itself, and Amzrai, rather less to Taria and less still, in a different way, to Tighanimin.

The dispersed second habitation is of course generally (and with the local Ahansal villages always) much higher than the concentrated proper village, and the pattern of movement of a family between its two habitations is roughly one of being up in summer and down in winter. (But it is not always as simple as that: trees, crucial in feeding the animals in winter and under snow, are sometimes more plentiful higher up, and this may on occasion reverse the pattern.)

This habit of frequent movement, on the part of families often too small to keep some representative at each of their two homes, helps to explain the survival and vitality of collective storehouses (*igherm, ighirmen*, is one sense of that word) in which each family has a locked cubicle for its stores, with a permanent warden surveying the whole. (Amzrai and Tighanimin have such ighirmen, the main lodge and Taria do not.)

If one thinks of a Berber household as a 'farm', it is of course quite unlike a (territorially) reasonably continuous farm in a European plain. A characteristic Berber household will own: some discontinuous irrigated fields (which commits it to contributing towards the collective labour, particularly in spring, on the irrigation ditches), and which it owns in virtue of inheritance or possibly purchase; some non-irrigable fields which, though they too can be inherited and purchased, it owns essentially in virtue of working them, for more such territory is available, and rights arise and lapse through use and non-use, though of course only members of the group owning the general territory may acquire fields in it in this manner. Further, the household will have rights in communally owned forest, except where it is very close to the fields of others; and rights in communally owned pasture, which may be seasonal both for the tribe as a whole (by agreement with other tribes), and internally, by agreement to restrict use of better pastures to certain periods. The general principle on the plateau is: first use up the higher slopes which are only kept green by the melting snows, and reserve the hollows, which retain moisture and green grass till much later, for the latter part of the season.

The area in which the homes of the households of Zawiya Ahansal are reduplicated is named Tisselmit. Tisselmit is a valley, tributary to the main Ahansal valley, but running parallel rather than at right angles to it. The homes owned there by most households are very dispersed and less well built than those at the zawiya itself, though naturally they often have a good capacity for giving shelter to animals. Two top families – Ait Sidi Mulay and

Ait Okdim – have decorative ighirmen there (in the architectural sense of the word), but most dwellings there are not built for display. There are a few irrigated fields near the ighirmen. 'Tisselmit' is a place name: it makes no sense to refer to 'people of Tisselmit' (Ait Tisselmit) as some kind of social unit, for none such exists. Up to four or five families only, to my knowledge, may live at Tisselmit. They were not included in the census. This error I noticed too late to remedy. The total number of people in those families is unlikely to exceed twenty and probably amounted to far less.

Zawiya Ahansal itself is, as a cluster of buildings, amongst the most compact kind of Berber villages of the region, and unusually compact for a village of its size. It is, for instance, much more compact than its neighbour, the laicised people of Amzrai, and also more compact than most of the ecologically similar villages of the adjoining areas north of the watershed. One must go to the more agriculturally oriented villages situated on the edge of more extensive irrigable fields, in the alluvial bases of valleys such as Bu Gmez and Imdghas, to find similar compactness. It is as if everyone here were pushing to live as close to the shrine of Sidi Said Ahansal as possible, and indeed in a sense this is so: the competing saints require this proximity in order to compete successfully, and the minor client families stay close to their patrons.

At Tisselmit, on the other hand, one sees the saints as they are when, so to speak, they are not saints. This is perhaps a good point to stress that every saintly household and every lodge is, apart from being a centre of sanctity, also a Berber household or village like any other: sanctity is an extra, which only rarely (and then only in the case of individuals, not of households) becomes a wholly absorbing speciality. Berber society is on the whole unspecialised and undifferentiated, and this in the end is true even of the most differentiated feature of it, agurramhood. At Tisselmit, one sees the life of igurramen as it is when least affected by their also being igurramen: at Zawiya Ahansal, as it is at its most differentiated. Tisselmit possesses no special shrines connected with the cult of Sidi Said Ahansal and his descendants, despite the fact that it is owned by his most celebrated offspring.

As the income from sanctity has declined and continues to decline, the importance of Tisselmit in the life of the villagers of Zawiya Ahansal, already considerable, continues to go up. The main valley, in which the lodge is located, is in effect a gorge, even if one less fierce in the vicinity of the lodge than it is both upstream and down, and it contains little more than space for some irrigated fields in the bottom of the valley, and relatively poor slopes covered with shrubs. Its main asset is plentiful and permanent water in the river-bed. (It is conceivable that a determined effort could extend the irrigable areas.) Tisselmit, on the other hand, is a much broader and gentler valley, and much richer in trees. Cultivable land in it can still be expanded.

Small Families

The count of numbers of lay households on the table (p. 200) for Zawiya Ahansal gives the figure 55. This figure is perhaps misleading. It does indicate that, after the seven top saintly families, one can locate no less than fifty-five doorways in the village leading to interiors (*zhgua*, also used in the sense of 'house') whose inhabitants are as it were autonomous units,[1] entitled to take their economic decisions without convoking any conseil de famille larger than the inhabitants of that 'interior'. Nevertheless, a very large part of these households are very small, consisting of two people or less: 24 out of the total of 55. If households of three people or less are counted, we get more than half of the total of non-saintly families: 31.[2]

But it is doubtful how many of these smaller households – not to mention the nine solitary individuals – are autonomous to any very real extent.

My belief about the situation is as follows: more wealth flows in the form of charity in an effective zawiya than does in an ordinary Berber village. It is obvious that more charity (religious donations)

[1] There is of course a far larger total number of doorways, for the larger households consist of whole complexes of buildings.

[2] It is important to remember the shiftiness and ambiguities of the notion of saint, agurram. I am using 'non-saintly' here simply in the sense of 'those other than the seven top families'. There are some families in the lodge included in this non-saintly count who are as close genealogically to the top saints as they are to each other, and who would in some contexts be classed as igurramen, though they fail by the criterion of wealth and style of life; there are others, who come to approximate to some features of the style of life, but are genealogically further; and, in wider contexts, *all* inhabitants of Zawiya Ahansal (or all claiming descent from Sidi Said Ahansal, i.e., the great majority) are referred to as igurramen.

flows *into* it, for that is virtually the definition of a zawiya. But more also flows inside it. This is partly a consequence of the need on the part of the effective saints to allow some of the incoming donations to spill over to the non-effective ones. (In the days of the French, this was meant to be formally regulated, the rule being that half of the donations should go to the non-saintly part of the village. It is more than doubtful whether this was enforced or enforceable.) The saints need clients and support, locally as well as in the distance among the lay tribes. What reaches them as a donation partly goes further as patronage. Furthermore there are consequences of stratification and of the concentration of wealth and power which is characteristic of a zawiya as opposed to ordinary villages. This means that work, wage-labour, is available. (This was customary in the traditional situation prior to the French, though labourers were engaged by the season or the year and generally paid in kind.) This in turn means that families relying in large part on such employment will, as wage-earners, have little incentive to remain together as larger groups (except when taken under the wing of a large saintly family as a whole). Similarly, security may be found relatively more often in being a client of a top family than in being a member of an ordinary one.

Thus a good proportion of the smaller 'households' are, in one way or another, dependents of the larger ones. As stated, the local belief is that it is a duty to impose a ten per cent tax on one's income, both from fields and flocks, and a show is made after the harvest of fulfilling this and measuring of this tenth. There is however no harm in combining this fulfilment of duty with extending or confirming one's influence, and distributing it with this end in view.

The various minor families – minor in size and in wealth – are thus dependents of the major ones in a variety of ways: sometimes as labourers, sometimes as part-time labourers, sometimes through one member of the household working for the major family whilst the others work on their own fields, and in old age as recipients of straight charity. (They may then also have such fields as they possess tilled by others on a share-cropping basis. Similar arrangements exist concerning flocks.)

Owing to the complexity, frequent informality, and the exaggerations and boasts of charity involved, I am unfortunately quite incapable of giving an accurate quantitative assessment of the operations involved, and must content myself with simply sketching the general situation in this way.[1]

The inner structure of a zawiya is distinguished from a lay or laicised village as follows: there is the obvious feature that it is stratified; there is the almost as obvious feature that the household units in the top stratum grow to a size larger than those in the lower stratum and those of unstratified, lay villages; and finally, there is the least obvious fact that the lower stratum in a holy village is probably more fragmented, possesses more really small units, than do the populations of lay villages. This, one may suppose, is due to the fact that material aid in a zawiya flows relatively more along the channels of patronage and charity, and relatively less along the line of kinship, than it does in an ordinary village.

This in turn illustrates a general point of some interest. A zawiya, like any other Berber social unit, possesses a 'segmentary' genealogical structure: but the actual economic life follows its lines rather less than in a lay village. Concerning political life there can be no doubt that this is also true, and this indeed follows from the general account of agurramhood.

Ait Aggudim

It is, of course, necessary in describing a zawiya to describe the small, fragmented and semi-independent households living in the shadow of the great agurram families. But it would be quite wrong to think of the whole village as nothing but a court of hangers-on, buzzing around the competing agurram monarchs and giving their support to the most rewarding patron. There is an element of truth in such a picture, but on the other hand Zawiya Ahansal also contains a sturdy yeoman population, as it were, no different from the mixed farmers of ordinary villages, except in as far as they

[1]The proper study of the economics of a Berber village in general and of Berber sanctity in particular remains to be done. Some material of this may be in the possession of the administration, in connection with taxation. A study of the economics of sanctity in particular would of course be specifically hampered by two facts: (a) This aspect of sanctity has been more severely affected by modern developments than most other features of the saints' lives; and (b) the ideology of sanctity is in conflict with the willingness to provide accurate information. Both saintly receipts and saintly charity are liable to be exaggerated, and a saint should, according to his own ideal, have a 'consider the lilies' attitude.

receive some overspill of the wages of sanctity and are involved in a political life different from the simpler one prevailing in ordinary villages. But it would be quite unfair to assimilate these families to court hangers-on. The Bel Lahcens, the Sidi Husseins, the LeKadis, the Sidi Lahcens, the Troilests, Moha u Hamo, U Ben Ali, are names that roll off the tongue and ring with solid respect and sterling worth. They may give their support to one or another of the agurram families – or, sometimes, not – and be discreetly respectful to all: but they are not economically dependent on them.

The point is, really, that a zawiya is two things at once: a centre of competing sanctity, and a Berber village like any other. The two images are superimposed on each other, ideologically not quite consistent with each other, and in conduct either may emerge and manifest itself according to occasion. The competing-sanctity, zawiya-proper aspect is visible in its symbols of stratification in housing of the living and of the dead, the existence of conspicuous shrines of Sidi Said Ahansal and other crucial ancestors side by side with the more normal nameless graves of the cemetery: the ordinary village aspect is manifest in its mosque and its *fquih*, its prayers (in which igurramen have no specialised ritual role) and informal assemblies, its ordinary economic life – notably at Tisselmit – and its regular internal festivities, both those tied to the Muslim calendar and those tied to agricultural life and its no special role: it is also manifest in the use for these festivals and the autumn harvest festival) in which, again, igurramen play no special role: it is also manifest in the use for these festivals (and other purposes, including oaths) of non-Ahansal shrines, in which the area is as rich as any lay territory, if not richer. There is even a duality of name. Normally one does refer to the main lodge as Zawiya (in Berber: zawuyit) Ahansal, which of course carries the connotation of special status. But it is equally possible to refer to the people of the main lodge as Ait Aggudim, which is as it were their clan name, of obscure origin. When I discussed this duality of name with the main possessor of baraka of the period, he repudiated the term 'Ait Aggudim' with irritation: he wanted the people of the lodge referred to as the people of the zawiya. And well he might: the notion of 'the people of the zawiya' carries hierarchical implications, for it would be absurd for the minor personages of the lodge to describe themselves as such without admitting their dependence on the saints, whilst the other term is parallel to expressions such as Ait Taria or Ait Amzrai, the people of Taria or of Amzrai, and by implying a symmetrical relationship with them, also implies symmetry internally.

If one is to believe the theory that ritual expresses, reinforces and advertises the social status and position of the various recipients, then it is most revealing that a zawiya takes part in two kinds of ritual, those in which igurramen do have a special position and those in which they do not. The former are centred on the shrines of the ancestors of the igurramen and of course mainly on that of Sidi Said Ahansal, and are connected with the relationship between the lodge and other tribes, whilst the latter rituals are those drawn from the common pool of Islamic and 'Islamic' practices of the region, and are connected mainly with the internal life of the village. (There are borderline cases between the two types, such as the annual pilgrimage to Azurki, which are intertribal, but not specifically agurram-tied, but in which agurram families strive to be conspicuously represented.)

There is of course no explicit terminology for distinguishing the two types of ritual, and in the nature of things there cannot be: for it is of the essence of effective Ahansal saintliness to believe that reverence for it *is* Islamic, is indeed the culmination and core of Muslim reverence.

The Village of Taria

The structure of households in this village is according to my census carried out in 1956 as follows:

		No. of people
Households with 9 members	1	9
8	2	16
7	2	14
6	1	6
5	3	15
4	2	8
3	5	15
2	3	6
1	2	2
Total number of households	21	Total 91

214

There are two reasons for giving this specific account of the village of Taria: it is, in one sense, 'part of' Zawiya Ahansal (which also justifies its inclusion in this chapter, devoted to the main lodge), and secondly, it is my belief that in size and internal structure it is a fairly typical Berber village or hamlet of this region, so that this comparatively detailed account of it helps to illustrate the contrast which can be expected between a successful saintly lodge, described in the previous sections, and an ordinary village.

Taria is not 'part of' Zawiya Ahansal in any physical or geographical sense: it is as far from the lodge as Tighanimin, (much further than the closest of the numerous physical habitats of that most multiple village), and a good deal further than Amzrai. It is however part of the main lodge in being män and not bdän with it, i.e., never having divided its property from it but on the contrary remaining in indivision. The inhabitants of Taria do have individually owned irrigated and non-irrigable fields, but there is no delimitation of the general territory and of pasture between the people of Taria and those of Aggudim. In fact, the people of Taria do take their flocks to Tisselmit: I have not come across any case of Aggudim (main lodge) flocks near Taria, but there is nothing to stop a person from the main lodge from making use of the pasture and forest around Taria. This unity with Zawiya Ahansal, in terms of land tenure sense of identification, did not prevent the people of Taria from possessing the de facto features of village autonomy, namely their own mosque, fquih and annual village headman.

In what sense are the inhabitants of Taria igurramen? As indicated, they do not possess the saintly attribute of pacifism, and indeed are credited with unsaintly ferocity. (As described, they produced the Berber Robin Hood figure, and his kinsman, who perished at Independence.) They do not aspire to play the characteristically saintly political game. They possess no shrine nor even an apical ancestor[1] to enshrine in it, in terms of which they could attempt to play it. Their hagiological position, so to speak, is as follows: they emphatically claim that their chief patron is Sidi

---

[1]Though this would not necessarily be an absolute obstacle. The effectively saintly Ait Temga only possess an apical ancestor whose shrine is geographically distant and whom they share with other lodges, and locally have a cluster of shrines none of which has achieved pre-eminence, thus mirroring the competing local top families unlike the main lodge, where the situation is *one* clearly pre-eminent shrine, but a *number* of families struggling for pre-eminent connection with it.

Said Ahansal, whom they share with the main lodge and, in a sense, with all Ihansalen; locally they have the shrine of the non-Ahansal saint known as Sidi l'Hajj, one of the Seven Saints,[1] none of whom have left any descendants, and whom they can also use; and also – though this is a matter of some shame and ambivalence – they are liable to make sacrifices at and to the superb source of the Ahansal river, which gushes out of the rock in a large number of close places, like the wounds of a saint, a matter of a few minutes' walk above the village.

But there is one respect in which they are and do claim agurram status: they are 'pacific' in the sense that they do not feud and fight with the surrounding lay tribes. These, as far as the Ait Taria are concerned, are mainly the Ait Atta, notably of the Ilemshan clan, who every summer occupy the plateau in which the village's gorge is embedded. Of course, there is no question of their being able to do so: when the Ilemshan are on the plateau, the Ait Taria are vastly outnumbered, encircled and cut off. They are quite clear that it is the Ait Isha who protect them from the Ait Atta. From the viewpoint of the Ait Isha, the saints or semi-saints of Taria are a kind of first but important frontier trip-wire: Atta aggression against Taria would be the first sign of a new Atta move against the North, and an overt attempt by the Atta to upset the existing and accepted territorial settlement.

[1]See below, p. 282.

CHAPTER EIGHT

OTHER AHANSAL CENTRES

The Lay Option (*Amzrai*)

Of all other Ahansal settlements, the village of Amzrai is the one geographically closest to Zawiya Ahansal. It is less than half an hour's walk downstream from it, and, unlike it, on the true left bank of Asif (river) Ahansal. The uppermost part of its territory is within sight of the lodge. Whereas the main territory and pasture of the lodge (Tisselmit) stretches to the right of the river, the upper pastures and forest of the Ait Amzrai stretch upwards from the left bank of the river towards the Ait Atta of Talmest. The fact that the Ait Amzrai are separated from the Ait Abdi by the belt of saintly territory does not prevent them feuding with the Ait Abdi, who are their bitterest enemies. The fact that the Ait Amzrai are allies (*leff*) of the Ait Atta does not prevent them having pasture-border disputes with them either, and occasionally fatal disputes. My local assistant was a native of Amzrai, and his late father, for instance, whom I knew, had killed the father of the post-1956 chief of the Ait Talmest, Zuza, and had for years been in straitened circumstances owing to the blood-money required, Zuza's father turning out to be somewhat expensive.

The addiction of the Ait Amzrai to external feuds already indicates their most striking feature, namely, that they are almost wholly laicised. Yet in their case, as in the case of the Ait Taria, there is no doubt whatever concerning their descent from Sidi Said Ahansal. (I mean, of course, that there is no doubt in the mind of any of the parties concerned that the Ait Amzrai are the progeny of Sidi Said Ahansal.) The Ait Taria are 'one' with the lodge. The Ait Amzrai, rather emphatically, are *not* 'one' with the people of the lodge, but nevertheless their genealogical standing is as good, and in a way even better, than that of the other two villages mentioned: for it is generally admitted that Amzrai is the first place of settlement of Sidi Said Ahansal and the Ihansalen.

It is from Amzrai that the Ihansalen separated out in their dispersion, or so they believe. It is near Amzrai that there is 'the house of the cat', the place where the cat jumped off the back of the donkey, thus giving the magical sign pre-arranged by the Founder's Teacher, Sidi Bu Mohamed Salah, to indicate to Sidi Said Ahansal that he had reached the place at which he and his offspring were to fulfil their mission. Moreover (and in local eyes this is perhaps the most important of the indices that Amzrai is the original place of settlement): though the shrine of Sidi Said Ahansal is at the lodge, the shrines of his son, and so on for a number of generations, including the crucial Sidi Lahcen u Othman, are at Amzrai.

No explanation is given concerning how it came to be that whilst the father's shrine is in one place, those of the son, grandson and great-grandson should be in another, nor are there any legends explaining how and why the present saints should have hived-off and moved upstream. It would be a little difficult in terms of the logic of local beliefs to make up such a legend, for the rules are that the original place of settlement is the holiest and those who stay near the home and graves of the ancestors are the most meritorious; these, at any rate, are arguments used by the saints of the main lodge against their rival-cousins of Temga and elsewhere. This argument could be used by the Ait Amzrai against the Ait Aggudim, if the Ait Amzrai aspired to effective sanctity, which they do not. The only reply would be that the shrine of Sidi Said Ahansal himself is at Ait Aggudim, though this in turn leaves the mystery of how it comes to be there or, alternatively, how that of his son and offsprings come to be at Amzrai. This question is not raised any more than the question of how there comes to be another shrine of Sidi Said Ahansal at Marrakesh.

A further relevant piece of evidence of Amzrai being the original place of settlement is that it contains the shrine-tomb of the general ancestor of the Ait Tighanimin, a man claimed by his offspring to be a son of Sidi Said Ahansal, whilst all others consider him to have been merely one of Sidi Said Ahansal's servants, who was at best given a daughter of Sidi Said Ahansal in marriage.

In a sense, the absence of a legend explaining the differentiation between Aggudim and Amzrai only highlights the total mutual acceptance of this de facto situation, and any retailing of stories and justifications explaining it would only indicate that this relationship is precarious, which it is not, and could only give the Ait Amzrai ideas and encourage them to resent a situation which in fact they accept and in which they actually take pride. Legends explaining intra-Ahansal differentiations seem to be found mainly to justify relationships which, in reality, are fluid and not quite accepted.

To say that the Ait Amzrai accept unquestioningly their own non-agurram status, and have no choice about the matter, is not to say that their relationship with the Ait Aggudim is good. It is not. But it takes the form, not of resenting that they, the Ait Amzrai, are not igurramen, but on the contrary of resenting that the Ait Aggudim fail to live up to the standards of lay tribesmen. The Ait Amzrai see the pacificism of the igurramen not as a necessary concomitant of baraka, but as simple cowardice, and resent the fact that the Ait Aggudim are useless to them as neighbour-allies for defence, thus forcing them to turn to the Ait Atta for help. Admittedly, they also resent that the saints cannot or do not use their saintly influence sufficiently to protect them, the Ait Amzrai, thus forcing them to display the martial virtues of which they are also proud, and whose alleged or real absence among the saints they treat with scorn.

The hostility between the two villages does not reach overt violence, but it did go as far as mock demonstrations. On one occasion, it is remembered, some Ait Amzrai disturbed a festival of the Ait Aggudim, and in order to add insult to injury then proceeded to hold one of their own right 'under the walls' of the lodge, i.e., facing the noble house of the Ait Okdim, which limits the lodge on its downstream side, scornfully daring the saints to come out and interfere. The craven saints did not do so.

All the same, despite these occasional outbursts, the Ait Amzrai took part in the general system of saintly adjudication based on the main lodge, as the following story illustrates. Some Abdi passing through Taria territory forced the Ait Taria to give them hospitality. The Ait Amzrai heard of this and set out to capture the Abdi, who, they maintained, had stolen some of their sheep. They successfully caught them and informed the Ait Abdi that, unless ransom and compensation were paid, the captured Abdi would be killed. No compensation came, and one of the Abdi was killed by being thrown off the igherm, the high collective fort of Amzrai. Another, however, succeeded in fleeing, and was only caught after he had reached the territory of the lodge, which is sanctuary. He was nevertheless killed by his pursuers, who, however, thereby made themselves liable for the blood money, not under the circumstance, to the killed man's family, but to the saints. The saints, it is claimed, arranged the affair by secretly giving the appropriate sum to the killers, who then publicly paid it as a fine to the saints. It is said that the Ait Abdi still do not know what really happened. In this way, all parties were, more or less, satisfied: the Ait Amzrai had done a killing in sanctuary on the cheap, the Ait Abdi at least saw the violators of sanctuary properly penalised, and the saints saw their prestige augmented in both directions, in the eyes of the Abdi, by demonstrating their own authority over Amzrai, and in the eyes of the Amzrai by showing goodwill, skill, and even partiality to their fellow Ihansalen. I have come across other stories concerning disputes in which settlement involved a fine to the saints, or a fine to the wronged party, and in which either the saints themselves provided the fine with which they were paid, or even provided the means to pay the third, wronged party. These stories are not to the saints' discredit locally, for they illustrate both generosity and skill in mediation, and it is not impossible that some of them are put about or encouraged by the saints themselves.

Amzrai now approaches the size of Zawiya Ahansal though in the past it seems it was significantly smaller.[1] In internal structure, it is markedly different from it. It possesses no large, differentiated families, but is rather like the lodge without its top saints, but also without the hangers-on of saints. There are, of course, individuals who are influential, but it is a matter of individual personality rather than family. No one in Amzrai has presumed to build himself an igherm-like dwelling, and all houses are equally undistinguished. They are not closely clustered.

Whilst no individual family presumes to have a high igherm-like dwellings, there are two proper ighirmen in Amzrai: these fine buildings are such in both senses of the word, being both collective

[1] G. Drague, in *Esquisse d'Histoire Religieuse du Maroc*, Paris, 1951, gives the following figures for number of households in the main lodge, Amzrai, Taria and Tighanimin: 85, 43, 25, 63. This is probably based on an estimate made not long after the pacification of the region.

storehouse-forts and possessing the architectural features which qualify for this name in the lodge and elsewhere. These buildings, or rather the ordinary houses immediately attached to them, are permanently inhabited by wardens, who possess the key to the building as a whole, whilst the individual families hold the keys to their respective cubicles inside. This institution is as vigorous as ever it was. Though one factor, general insecurity, which provided it with its function, is now absent, another source of its usefulness is as operative as ever: given frequent and seasonal movement between the homes in the village and the second dwelling in the forest and high pasture, and given fairly small household units which cannot always be represented at both ends at the same time, it is preferable to have stores jointly guarded. The only effect of security brought by the Pax Gallica is that the warden is now sometimes a woman. The work is paid for in kind by all users. The task was an onerous one in the old days, as is suggested by the rule which forced the first man to touch the igherm's keys, if the warden resigned, to take on the job. As indicated, the height of the buildings makes them useful as places of execution of Abdi hostages if necessary. The structures are elegant but not adorned with decorative mud patterns like those of the lodge.

A priori, one should expect these buildings to have some ritual significance: they are striking, and the wealth and security of the village is concentrated in their walls. They are the place where visitors who do not have individual hosts are liable to be entertained; they are the place of refuge; they are also the places left guarded if, owing to failure of the harvest, the village or a large part of it is forced to migrate temporarily. (This appears to have happened to the Ait Amzrai in the past, and being allies of the Atta they moved for a time to the Southern Atta across the watershed.) But though one should, for all these reasons, expect some recognition of the fact that the soul of the village is within the walls of the collective igherm, in fact there is no ritual connected with it at all.[1] The village has two ighirmen but one mosque, and if its soul

---

[1] I was pleased to have my a priori reaction to the ighirmen confirmed to this extent, that they do have ritual significance in other parts of the Berber world, notably in the Aures. Cf. Pierre Bourdieu, *Sociologie de l'Algérie*, PUF, 1958, p. 38. In the Aures they are called *guelaa*, and in Southern Morocco *agadir*. Incidentally, it is wrong to say that throughout the High Atlas the term *agadir* is used this way. In the central High Atlas it simply means 'wall', and, as indicated, *igherm* designates collective storehouse, or the type of building.

is anywhere it is in its assembly at the mosque or at the shrine of Sidi Lahcen u Othman. The two ighirmen are some distance from each other, and most of the dwellings in the village are grouped around one or the other, which gives rise to a distinction between 'upper' and 'lower' Amzrai. But these quarters do not appear to have any political significance,[1] nor do they correlate with the internal segmentation of the village.

Internally, the Ait Amzrai are segmented into three sub-clans, who rotate the chieftaincy, or did until the French came, along the normal rotation-and-complementarity rules customary among the lay tribes. The genealogical beliefs associated with the segments are again of the 'Occamist' pattern usual among lay tribes, that is to say there are not many more ancestors than required to express the relationship of nested groups. There are one or two units which in terms of genealogical belief do not fit into the three major groups (e.g., one family believed to be of Ait Aggudim origin) and these, as usual, are for purposes of the rotation and so forth incorporated in the major groups.

In its external politics, Amzrai fits into two systems: its own chieftaincy rotation is not part of any wider system in which Amzrai would itself in turn be a rotating segment, but on the contrary, in case of a dispute getting beyond the powers of the local chief, there would be appeal to the effective saints of the lodge. On the other hand, in case of major inter-tribal conflict Ait Amzrai would activate their alliance with the Ait Atta, though they do not share a chief or a rotating-election with them.

The internal segments also find some ritual expression. For instance, during the spring and autumn festivals, the occasion is terminated by a prayer during which participants form a complete circle. Ill people desiring cure and women desiring pregnancy congregate in the middle, and are touched by three men each representing one of the clans, whilst the other participants request divine assistance.

The actual central shrine of the Ait Amzrai, the alleged tomb of Sidi Lahcen u Othman, is as suggestive as any of the theory that the 'personal saint' cult now prevalent covers an earlier nature cult: for the shrine does not even look like a tomb. It consists of a

---

[1] At any rate, they do not now. One would suppose that at any time the ighirmen were used for defence they would have to have some significance, in as far as those sharing an igherm would also share in its defence.

space separated off by four low walls, which is overhung by an immediately adjoining holy tree. The numerous branches overhanging the 'tomb' are covered with bits of cloth left behind by women who had come to request favours of the saint. This is not the only holy tree in Amzrai: the other, less important, has not been personified. (There is also a holy tree in the vicinity of the more plausibly tomb-like shrine of Sidi Said Ahansal, a tree particularly noted for its power to assist pregnancy.)

The worship and sacrifice at Sidi Lahcen u Othman is more Durkheimian than most, in as far as giving something 'to the saint' is giving it to the community, and the saint is identified with the community as the ancestor of all its members. Such a fairly neat situation is exceptional, and can only arise among laicised saints: fully lay tribes worship saints who are not their own ancestors, whilst effective saints make use of their ancestors for encouraging worship and donations from others, and in fact, as indicated, have a tendency to perform their 'internal' rituals at other shrines. It is only a laicised saintly village which can both have an ancestor of its own to worship, and is not likely to share his worship very much[1] with anyone else: and thus can practice a kind of social narcissism.

The Pangs of Ambiguity (Tighanimin)

This is the fourth of the four Ahansal settlements at the upper end of the Ahansal river. Going upstream, the Asif Ahansal divides into two branches about an hour and a half's walk before the highest springs, thus forming a Y. Zawiya Ahansal is on the lower part of the Y, below the point where the two branches meet, and so is Amzrai, further down still. Taria and Tighanimin are on one each of the separate upper branches, Taria being on the right one (looking up valley) which is a gorge cut into the plateau, whilst Tighanimin is on the left one, in a curving valley located between the Atlas watershed and the lower and gentler ridge separating

[1] In strict logic, they could be asked to 'share' him with the other Ihansalen (bar Ait Tighanimin, even on their own account of their ancestry), for they share Sidi Lahcen u Othman as an ancestor: Ahansal segmentation only begins with his son (except for the contested hiving-off of Tighanimin). In fact, no such request is ever made. The other Ihansalen use SSA, 'higher up' in the genealogy than Sidi Lahcen u Othman thus in a way conveying the seniority of status of the igurramen intimately connected with the shrine of SSA.

the main valley of Ahansal from Tisselmit. The territory of the Ait Tighanimin is constituted by this upper left branch of the valley plus some additional land in upper Tisselmit and some across the ridge on the plateau of the Ait Abdi.

In some respects, the Ait Tighanimin are the most interesting phenomenon amongst the Ihansalen. In the eyes of all other Ihansalen, they are pseudo-Ihansalen: they are descended, not from Sidi Said Ahansal, but from the clients/servants of Sidi Said Ahansal. According to their own firm conviction, they *are* descended from Sidi Said Ahansal – and indeed they feel they are, by certain criteria, his most worthy descendants: they have the purest Ahansal blood, for there is no one, male or female, in the village of Tighanimin who was not born there and of Tighanimin stock. Unlike the fickle top saints of the lodge, the Ait Tighanimin do not, they proudly point out, import brides. This virtue is somewhat of a virtue of necessity, but this does not prevent the Ait Tighanimin proudly stressing it. They have on their side a local belief, that sherifians should not mix their blood with the laity.[1] This is a belief not lived up to by mountain igurramen (nor, incidentally, by the Moroccan Royal house), and particularly not by the successful saints. They compromise by allowing import but not export of brides, and by claiming that even the import is restricted to certain tribes from whom it is traditionally allowed. (The Ait Tighanimin comment with particular disfavour on the marriage of Sidi Mha n'ait Sidi Mulay to a woman of the Ait Abdi, an alliance unhallowed by any such tradition, though in fact it made excellent sense as a dynastic alliance in terms of local politics under the French.) There are emigrants from Tighanimin, both individual and collective, but there are no immigrants into Tighanimin.

The collective status-ambiguity of the Ait Tighanimin is something which thoroughly pervades their life and relations with surrounding communities. The surrounding communities, and particularly the Ihansalen and among these particularly the Ait Aggudim, consider the term and notion of Tighanimin to be something between an insult and a joke. This does not, of course, preclude individuals or even the community as a whole being treated courteously if the context demands it. It is for some reason held to be a particular defect of the Ait Tighanimin that they are

---

[1] G. H. Bousquet comments on this belief and the failure to observe it by the small (non-Ahansal) Zawiya among the Ait Haddidu.

Ait Sus, people from the Sus (an important region in Southern Morocco). There is no very good logic about this, as otherwise being a Susi is not a bad thing, and in any case Sidi Said Ahansal himself came from Asfi, which is not far from the Sus and almost as distant from the present home of the Ihansalen. But, in the case of the Ait Tighanimin, Susi origin becomes a vice.

In size and internal organisation the Ait Tighanimin are similar to the Ait Amzrai. The internal division is into three clans, who annually rotate the chieftaincy amongst themselves (or did until modern superimposed administrations led to permanent village headmen). Genealogically, there is in fact a fourth clan, but as it is too small to operate in the rotation system it is for this and other purposes affiliated to one of the three large ones. In case of internal dispute getting out of hand, the next court of appeal for the Ait Tighanimin, as for the Ait Amzrai, is the top saints of the neighbouring lodge (and the 'Kadi' dispensing judgment with their authority); but unlike the Ait Amzrai, the Ait Tighanimin not merely do not form part of any wider system of rotating chieftaincy, but also have no lay or other allies. They are diplomatically quite isolated, a feature connected with the severe ambiguity of their agurram status. For, with far less of a recognised genealogical claim to this status than the Ait Amzrai, the Ait Tighanimin are in fact far more anxious to claim it. Claiming it, they also stress their agurram-like pacificism, which they practise unless provoked too hard.[1] But these protestations make them unsuitable allies, assuming some were available,[2] and in any case to seek lay alliances would from their own viewpoint be incompatible with their saintly pretensions. There is a certain circle here: their isolation drives them to seek such safety as there is in agurram-like pacifism, which in turn further reinforces their isolation. In practice, they confessedly have to seek protection, notably against the Ait Abdi, from the more effective saints of Aggudim and of Temga.

---

[1]There is memory of the Ait Tighanimin avenging the murder of one of their own number. Also, this is one of the villages in which a murder occurred in French days. This was a somewhat political affair, as it is claimed that the murder was instigated by the then headman at the higher instigation of the then Caid Amhadar, in order to get rid of a man who was undermining his authority.

[2]In fact, the Ait Tighanimin are on good terms with the Ait Atta and on bad terms with the Ait Abdi, in this respect like the Ait Amzrai. But they claim that their relationship to the Ait Atta is that of saints to clients. This claim is treated with derision in the main lodge.

The concomitants or consequences of the position of the Ait Tighanimin include the fact that they have a most marked and distinctive accent. In general, most local Berbers can do a Professor Higgins and locate a man by his speech, but this is quite outstandingly easy with the Ait Tighanimin. Their manner of speaking is very high-pitched and sing-song, so much so that when first encountering it with an individual one supposes one has come across a personal idiosyncrasy – until one finds this trait very common among them. For what psychological significance it may have, it is worth reporting that the Ait Tighanimin are of all locals the most addicted to smoking, except perhaps for some of the top saints of the lodge. (This matter of smoking is easy to assess impressionistically: a European is considered to be a source of cigarettes, and of course an anthropologist anxious to encourage contacts and information quite particularly so.)

The stereotype possessed of the Ait Tighanimin by the others includes both the complaint that they are too poor (look at their miserable hovels) and that they are too rich (they do very well), that they are comic (consider their accent, and they come from the Sus, too), they deprive the real Ihansalen of their due by going on donation-collecting missions on false pretences, they have the impertinence to litigate with the Ait Aggudim over a piece of land when *all* the territory belongs to the descendants of Sidi Lahcen u Othman, of whose number they are not, instead of being grateful for being allowed to settle locally at all; they make grotesque claims of being descended from Sidi Said Ahansal when everyone knows they are descended from Sidi Said Ahansal's servants, and so forth. It is very tempting to see an analogy between the attitude to, and of, the Ait Tighanimin, and what one finds among collectively status-ambiguous groups elsewhere.

In fact some parts of the stereotype do hold or have come to hold. The homes of the Ait Tighanimin are generally poor and badly built, conspicuously so, as though they were inhabited by people wishing to avoid attracting envy or aggression by conspicuous poverty. They are anxious to claim agurram status and receive donations. (The Ait Amzrai do not, and no theory exists why they should not: the Ait Tighanimin do try, and a theory, concerning their origin, does exist why they should *not*.) The flocks of the richer ones among them seem to do at least as well as those of the top saints; they do also remember extreme poverty in the days of siba, poverty which on occasion reached the point of starvation, whilst the saints remember the old days as days of affluence and plentiful donations; they do appear to practise more internal mutual help than the others, and to be more cohesive[1] and inward-turned.

A striking feature of their ecology is that, within the small territory they possess, the village as a physical place is multiplied more frequently than is usual. (The usual thing, as with Aggudim and Amzrai, is for the village to be double, for every household to have one home down and one up, as it were.) Tighanimin is multiplied almost six times. In their main valley there are four villages, in the physical sense of clusters of habitations, two on the (true) right bank, each low by the river near irrigated fields, one higher upstream and one lower, and two on the higher slopes under Timghazin, near pastures. Moreover, some families have homes in the Tighanimin's part of Tisselmit, and some near Tafraut of the Ait Abdi, where they also own territory, though they were only assured of its possession under the French.[2] If one counts their representation at Tisselmit and near Tafraut, the village has six physical locations; otherwise, it is still multiplied four times.

It is worth noting that the miserable quality of their housing (not merely not comparable with the conspicuous display of the saintly ighirmen, but equally not with the bourgeois solidity of lay houses elsewhere) obtains where they are together. Their houses at Tisselmit, by contrast, are about the same standard as the ordinary, non-igherm houses of the Aggudim at Tisselmit. Their villages by the fields are ordinary houses of bad quality, their pasture villages consist of what are no more than rough walls of stones plus some branches. This, one should say, is no worse than

[1]When in 1959 the four headmen and one top-headman were arraigned for corruption in connection with collecting contributions to the present for the then King, who was visiting the provincial capital at Beni Mellal, the Ait Tighanimin were the only village who did not join in the movement to get the headmen punished and to make them pay compensation. The top-headman was of their own number – owing to the drawing of a lot in 1956 which had decided this – and they stuck to him loyally. I very much doubt whether members of the other villages would have been so loyal even if the top-headman had been one of their own number. They were not inclined to spare their own local 'little' headmen.

[2]My belief concerning the disputed territory of Tisselmit is that during siba neither Aggudim nor Tighanimin could use this land much, owing to its dangerous and extreme proximity to the boundary of the Ait Abdi.

the pasture habitations of the Ait Abdi, but they too, after all, are looked down on as barbarians by surrounding tribes. I think it would be a mistake to attribute the poor quality of their dwellings to some consideration such as that if a family has its dwelling multiplied fourfold or more, it cannot afford to make any one of them decent. (In fact, between seasons, there is time to build.) The need for a protective colouring of poverty is a much more convincing explanation.

Insecurity is also the clue to the unusual degree of village reduplication. The more normal pattern found in Aggudim and Amzrai – compact *down* villages, dispersed *up* habitation – does have the consequence that the upper pasture dwellings are relatively isolated. The territory of the Ait Tighanimin is not so great (on the contrary), nor are local Berbers averse to walking, as to make it difficult for them to make do with only one upper dwelling and one lower for each household. But the arrangements they usually adopt have the consequence that they always remain grouped together. For a politically isolated group such as they are, this must have been a significant consideration.

The Ait Tighanimin do have and use ighirmen, in the sense of collective store-houses. In fact they have two buildings serving this purpose, close to each other, so that one warden is sufficient for both. Even in these collective buildings the Ait Tighanimin have avoided all ostentation. The buildings are solid, well-built (incomparably more so than their individual dwellings), and have two storeys; but they have none of the elegance or the height of the three-storeyed ighirmen usual elsewhere. They are located in none of their villages, though fairly near the lowest, at a point as far away as possible from the Ait Abdi and fairly close to the main lodge, both features relevant to its security. In parts of them grain and other supplies are stored not in locked cubicles, as is customary elsewhere, but in large jars, so that apart from the locking of the building as a whole, there are no physical precautions of one family against another – a curiously striking testimony of the internal cohesion of the Ait Tighanimin. Of the two buildings, one is owned by and was built at the expense of Sidi Yussif of Zawiya Tidrit (see below, p. 230), who however places it at the disposal of his kinsmen of Tighanimin proper.

The story of the Ait Tighanimin is not one of unredeemed gloom, however, quite apart from the fact that their flocks seem to have prospered, at any rate since the French peace. Some have hived-off and settled elsewhere: individuals live as workers at the main lodge, some women have married out, and I know of one Tighanimin naturalised family among the Ait Isha and another among the Ait Atta. But of all emigrants from their village, two at any rate are conspicuous success stories: one is the settlement at Tidrit, and the other the family settled at Usikis. Both will be described separately.

For ritual purposes, the Ait Tighanimin lack a shrine of a common ancestor. Their own specific *and* general ancestor (i.e., ancestor of all of them and of no one but them) is buried at Amzrai, and his shrine does not appear to be used for festivals, or possibly at all. On their own territory they have the shrine of one of the non-Ahansali 'Seven Saints',[1] whom they do use; and they also use the shrine of Sidi Said Ahansal and another of the Seven Saints, Sidi Bushaq, who is also close to the main lodge. (The two can be used simultaneously. At one harvest festival which I attended, the men spent most of the time at Sidi Bushaq, whilst the women were in the shrine of Sidi Said Ahansal or dancing outside it. The men prepared the meat, the women prepared the *sksu*, the North African dish more generally known to Europeans as couscous.) The existence of rival views about the true nature of their relationship to Sidi Said Ahansal does not cause the guardians of the tomb, the saints of the lodge, to object to the Ait Tighanimin using it.

The lack of a shrine of their own ancestor on their own territory is of course a hindrance in wishing to set up as igurramen (or an index of the failure to do so), as Ait Aggudim (the people of the main lodge) are only too willing to point out to them. The Ait Tighanimin claim to receive a regular donation from the Ait Atta, who pass through their territory on the way to pay homage to Sidi Said Ahansal. The Ait Aggudim deny the truth of this, maintaining that all donations from pilgrims to Sidi Said Ahansal are due to *them*. (I have never been present at the time the Ait Atta passed through to be able to verify this. It is probably true that some Atta segments do pay a minor homage, en route, to the Ait Tighanimin.)

To sum up, the Ait Tighanimin, like the Ait Amzrai, are prevented from being effective igurramen by their proximity to the effective main lodge; but they do explicitly strive to be recognised

[1]See below, p. 282.

as such and display some agurram-like qualities (e.g., pretensions to pacifism and abstention from intermarriage with the laity, though both are somewhat virtues of necessity). They are, however, the only Ihansalen, if such they may be called, some of whose number have successfully hived-off across the Atlas watershed. All other Ahansal settlements are as it were downstream – or at least not against the stream – of what historians say is the direction of the Berber 'push towards the Atlantic plain' from the area between the mountain and the desert. The Tighanimin settlements at Tidrit and in Usikis are 'upstream' of this pattern of migration.

With Tighanimin, we complete the description of the four villages which, since the French conquest, have formed the administrative unit 'Ihansalen'.

A Case of Reactivation (Tidrit)

Zawiya Tidrit is on a small tributary of the Dades (pronounced Dads) river, near the Dades river itself. The Dades is one of the most important valleys on the Sahara side of the Atlas.

The place at which Zawiya Tidrit is situated is on a frontier between the Ait Atta and the Ait Seddrat. This is a 'new' frontier, believed to be owing to a peace settlement some four generations back. The inhabitants of Zawiya Tidrit place the origin of their own lodge, founded by emigrants from Tighanimin, in the same period as the establishment of the present Atta/Seddrat frontier. Whether either dating is correct I know not: the Ait Tidrit support their theory about the age of their own lodge by an appropriate 'genealogical memory', but then it is not difficult to have one of four generations. (Lay tribesmen can do as well as that.)

Whatever the truth about the age of either this lodge or the local frontiers, the tie-up of the two is obviously significant. The Ait Tidrit receive donations and respect, and if necessary arbitrate, for both their lay neighbours; their position is a kind of living document certifying and giving religious authority to a status quo. The scale on which they operate is of course much smaller than that of the main lodge: they deal with two tribes, or rather two segments of much larger tribes, who happen to have a 'live' frontier here. They are used for festivals by these tribes, and even by tribes further up the valley (Ait Merghad).

Apart from being known by its place name (Tidrit), its people are also sometimes referred to by the name of their alleged ancestress, as the sons of Lalla (Lady) Aisha, who was a *tagurramt* (feminisation of *agurram*), and also by the name of the present head of the zawiya, Sidi Yussif. The use of the female name is explained by the alleged fact that the male founder was born after the decease of his father, so he used his mother's name. The shrine at the lodge, however, is said to house him, not the tagurramt. I have found no legends connected with the founding of this lodge.[1] The fact that the lodge is often referred to by the name of its present and not its deceased head testifies to his influence. We may well here be in the presence of a genuinely young lodge and centre of sanctity, where legends are being made rather than inherited.

The lodge is sharply stratified and indeed has a most pointed pyramidal structure. Leadership is concentrated unambiguously in the hands of one man, Sidi Yussif. There does not seem at the moment to be any saintly rat-race, for his position is not challenged. (A circle is operative: as he is known far and wide, it is not to the interest of the locals, fellow-members of the lodge, to challenge him; and being recognised as leader inside it, he will be recognised as such by visitors coming to use the lodge as a holy centre.) There isn't a wide range of people who could challenge him, for the top saintly stratum here hasn't multiplied to being more than one 'family'. The effective saints remain in 'indivision', and partly thanks to the extinction of some collateral lines do not seem to be further removed from each other than ego to father's brother's son.

Apart from this one family centred on an undisputed leader, there are about ten plainly lay families (lay but for the fact of their Tighanimin origin) who are said to have followed the original saintly settlement at various times, having been granted permission or even been invited to come and settle.

The difference in style of life between this lower stratum of the lodge and the top undivided family is extremely striking. The top family has an extensive and truly elegant and well-kept dwelling, a compound of high buildings forming a fully enclosed easily defensible unit, not far from the shrine and above the area of

[1]When I stayed in this lodge, the head of it was absent and the young men – son and nephew – may well have been shy of giving away unauthorised information, as often happens. I did meet the much-respected head of this lodge on other occasions, when he was travelling about, but he was reserved and uncommunicative. There may be more to be found out.

irrigated fields. The *petit peuple* live in a line of hovels dug into the hillside between two strata at a steep place, so that they are half-houses, half-caves. This humble style is all the more striking if one considers that Zawiya Tidrit is in the southern region where high mud buildings are common and do not express an aspiration to leadership, as they do in the region immediately around Zawiya Ahansal. (In the Dades valley, where so many of the clients of Zawiya Tidrit dwell, *simply everyone* has them.)

It should be stressed that the 'clients' of Zawiya Tidrit are not such in anything like the complete sense in which some of the clients of the main lodge are its clients. They use it only on some occasions for some purposes. They do not hold their elections there. Indeed the upstream clients of Zawiya Tidrit are, in the first instance, clients of Zawiya Ahansal itself, where they *did* hold their elections (and had their elections supervised by its igurramen), and for whom they regularly taxed themselves.

In fact, the people of the surrounding region had a number of alternative saints to use in different contexts: the main lodge above all, but also a local shrine called Sidi Said (but not Ahansal) who has left no one claiming to be his descendants and hence no Zawiya, and also, among the Ait Merghad, one clan recognised as igurramen but not claiming to be sherifian.[1] They can use others

---

[1]This is the only instance of *non-sherifian igurramen* I have come across in the region. Elsewhere this may be more common. This does, however, support the idea that such a conjunction is not contradictory – though immediately around Ahansal it almost appears so – and also gives some support to the plausible view that the 'shurfa' among the Berbers, performing agurram roles, are a continuation of a pre-Islamic institution given a Muslim cloak by the attribution of sherifian origin to its holders.

The small clan in question, which I shall not describe in detail as it is not part of the Ahansal system of sanctity, does, and does not, live up to agurram qualities in various ways. It apparently feuds and otherwise lives like any others. All it does in a specialised kind of way is to collect donations and then transmit – presumably a part of them – to another saint, its saints, who are an influential group near Tazzarin, in the heart of Ait Atta country

The function of this is fairly obvious. The Ait Merghad are enemies of the Ait Atta, indeed form a major part of the Ait Yafelman group who 'balance out' the Ait Atta in the politics of the Sahara-ward valleys. Here we have a clan of the Ait Merghad religiously affiliated to the national saints, as it were, of the Ait Atta, with annual access to them. This is a way of permanently keeping a channel of information and even of pressure and persuasion open, under an impeccable religious cover.

The legend justifying the practice is: a virgin founder of this clan was the only person in the region to take in and succour a man of the holy lineage at Tazzarin when he was wandering about the country. In gratitude he revealed his saintly

still, in the other areas of Ait Yaffelman settlement. There are almost always alternatives in sanctity.

The most interesting light thrown by Zawiya Tidrit on the possible form centres of sanctity can take is this: Zawiya Tidrit unambiguously has one and only one leader. Baraka flows pure and deep in one central channel. This is interesting for the following reason: in other lodges (especially in the Temga group) one is told that in the past leadership was clearly concentrated, the possession of baraka was so manifest that no rules of succession were required. (This is not the situation there at present, any more than it is in the main lodge.) But for the existence of the situation found so clearly at Tidrit, one might well suspect – and it might well still be true – that this past unity and unanimous recognition exists only in retrospect. Tidrit demonstrates that this is, on the contrary, one possible situation in a zawiya.[1] But it is reasonable to suppose that this possibility is connected with the smallness of a lodge. If it prospered in influence and grew, attracting residents as well as donating clients, could its top stratum fail to grow – if only through the supply of brides to it.[2] (There may be truth in the main lodge belief that the various sub-clans sprang from co-wives.) And if the top effective-saintly layer grows in size, could it fail to undergo fission? Giving the equal rights of brothers to inheritance, Berber family units, even saintly ones, seem to have a fairly low upper ceiling of size. There isn't enough concentration of power in any

---

powers and transferred some of them to her and her progeny. (She later ceased to be a virgin, evidently. There is no suggestion that the wandering saint fathered her offspring.) This is a variant on a theme common in the Atlas, the anonymous poor-seeming saintly stranger who rewards the hospitable host, a theme well-calculated to underwrite the obligation of hospitality. The founding lady of this special clan is remembered as Tafqirt – a Berber feminisation of the Arabic 'f'qir' – and she has left the name to the clan she has mothered.

[1] In the main lodge, there is not much emphatic claim made for past unity. In recent generations, it is perfectly manifest that there was inter-agurram rivalry such as one finds at present. For the preceding semi-legendary generations, the legends claim not unanimity, but the resolution of implicitly admitted competition by a wise father. (See above, p. 153.) Unity is only implicit in the very early generations when, as far as the beliefs go, there was, in the time of Sidi Said Ahansal and for several generations subsequently, only one agurram, no one else being mentioned. (The early fissions which follow are only such as explain hivings-off. After that, there comes the generation-in-conflict, with multiple offspring all bearing the names referring to rival wives of one father, in whom baraka was still uniquely concentrated.)

one person in lay families to prevent fission. Even holy ones, among whom the *concentration* of baraka mitigates the segmentary *diffusion* of authority, the same principle in the end operates – or so it seems, in other lodges which have grown.[1]

Another outstandingly interesting feature of Tidrit is its relation to its 'village of origin', the status-ambiguous Tighanimin. Tidrit itself has, of course, lost this feeling: baraka is known by its fruits, and having prospered, even moderately, the taint appears to be removed from the source. (In any case, the local prestige enjoyed by Tidrit is somehow connected with the prestige of the present head of the house, rather than with the contested descent from Sidi Said Ahansal.)

This relationship has two aspects, one being what I shall call the Inverse Pilgrimage, and the other a kind of village-scale Marshall Aid, or rather, in this case, Sidi Yussif Aid.

Inverse Pilgrimage: in all logic (given the local concepts) people should visit the tombs and shrines of their ancestors. (It is a corollary of this belief that those who stay put at the shrine of the ancestor are the ones who receive the pilgrims and thus have higher status, other things being equal: fidelity is better than migration.) But, in fact, it is the Ait Tighanimin who annually visit Tidrit and have a feast there in the autumn, whilst the Ait Tidrit do not in general visit the larger and older Tighanimin village[2] (though their leader does). So ancestors visit descendants rather than vice versa. Of course, in a sense everyone now alive and available to go visiting or receive visitors is roughly equidistant from the common ancestor, so that one might say that equal is visiting equal. But the common ancestor defining *all* Ait Tighanimin, (Ait Tighanimin 'at home' plus Ait Tidrit), is much further back than the common ancestor of the Ait Tidrit alone, and the latter is a descendant of the former. Thus genealogically Ait Tighanimin trump Ait Tidrit.

In terms of the logic of local concepts, no explanation can be offered of this strange behaviour. In social terms, on the other hand, there is no difficulty: the Ait Tidrit, or rather the nuclear agurram group within Tidrit, have successfully reactivated their

[1]The past of Zawiya Temga, for which there is interesting evidence in the form of physical ruins, appears to have been similar to the present of Zawiya Tidrit. But by now, Temga has grown and its baraka diffused.

[2]Actually they also claimed to do so when I visited them, but it was quite plain from what they knew and did not know about Tighanimin that they had not in fact done so for some time.

sanctity, mainly by moving away to a propitious place out of the stifling shadow of the main lodge into which the 'old' Ait Tighanimin were driven by need for protection. They thus provide a suitable focus of prestige and influence. It may be contrary to all reason for 'ancestors' to visit 'descendants' and bring gifts, but there is nevertheless much point in it if the influential hosts' goodwill is well worth having, and if they possess the material and spiritual facilities of a good centre of pilgrimage – a shrine (whereas the common ancestor of the Ait Tighanimin is not on their own land but on unfriendly Amzrai territory), a fine house, centralised authority (i.e., someone who can make arrangements for the minor graces of prolonged entertaining: the visitors bring the beasts for slaughter, but the locals see to all the details).

And so it is. The arrangements between Tighanimin and Tidrit are of course advantageous to both sides. The difference of climate between the two places makes them suitable for seasonal commuting of flocks, though in this respect it is Ait Tidrit who profit most, for the Ait Tighanimin with their forest have a better chance of keeping flocks alive even in winter, than their southern cousins have during a scorched summer. Given the hostility of the people of the main lodge to Tighanimin, I often wondered how the precariously placed Ait Tighanimin survived in the days of siba, in the days of maximum Aggudim influence and power. Tidrit provides the most plausible explanation: it was impossible for the main lodge to commit or initiate some real major act of aggression against Tighanimin without at the same time offending Tidrit, who being more distant were a bit out of range, and who would certainly spread the news with a Tighanimin angle to the story, and thereby risk alienating a large part of the population of the Dades valley. The leapfrog pattern of lodges, exemplified both by Tidrit and Ait Tafkirt, provides a political check on saints, just as their own location on the frontier provides a check on lay tribes.

Sidi Yussif Aid: Sidi Yussif, head of the lodge at Tidrit, at his own expense constructed one of the two adjoining ighirmen of the Ait Tighanimin, which he continues to own but which is used by other Ait Tighanimin (and not even only those from the subclan from which the Sidi Yussif has sprung: lay emigrants to Tidrit are only from this clan, though).

This is, in my Berber experience, a most unusual act of benevolence on the part of an individual or family towards a community –

and one from which they have hived-off, at that. It is hard to conceive of such an unsymmetrical act among either the segmentary lay tribes or the competing effective saints of Zawiya Ahansal itself. This unusual relationship confirms one's impression that the Ait Tighanimin are an unusually isolated and at the same time status-ambiguous group, and make up for it by greater cohesion: the fact that a successful son of such a group is exceptionally active in helping the poorer brethren left behind, reminds one of similar phenomena among the Jewish minority in Morocco.

The construction of this adjoining second igherm of the Ait Tighanimin, used by locals but owned by Tidrit, implies a strengthening of the Ait Tighanimin's safety on their downstream border: any act against their igherm is ipso facto one against its owners, the igurramen of Tidrit – and an act hostile to them is also in some measure a hostile act against their lay clients. Thus the igherm is not just a piece of physical capital, but also, politically, a trip wire connected *through* Tidrit with people more weighty as a deterrent force, than the Ait Tighanimin themselves. So, through the success and loyalty of their offshoot, the Ait Tighanimin escape some of their isolation.

Private Enterprise: 'Sidi Said Ahansal' and Some Other Atomic Emigrants

Sidi Said Ahansal of Usikis is of Tighanimin lineage, i.e., of a segment whose genuine descent from the like-named original saint, Sidi Said Ahansal, is generally denied. Thus this man's very name is a kind of defiance of those who would deny the Ait Tighanimin the right to class themselves as Ihansalen. The fact that he is generally known by this name, is an index of his success.

Sidi Said Ahansal is one of three brothers, who remain in indivision. The family has in the last generation acquired some property in Usikis, i.e., among the highly sedentarised Ait Atta in this part of the Dades valley. In this generation, this undivided family straddles the Atlas watershed, possessing property both at Tighanimin and at Usikis.

From the viewpoint of classification of Ahansal settlement, Sidi Said Ahansal provides an example of one particular species, the solitary family which acquires land by donation, by purchase, or by privileged purchase in a lay village. Such solitary family settlements are not called zawiyas, and they are not centred on a shrine. They may or may not be influential. If not, they tend simply to become like their lay neighbours, with nothing but the preserved memory of Ahansal origin distinguishing them.

At least two such settlers, however, are influential in the communities in which they have settled. One is the Sidi Said Ahansal described here (who is also somewhat special in that the links with the village of origin are kept alive, an ambiguity of rights which would hardly be tolerated from a wholly lay person); the other is a solitary Ahansal family settled among the Ait Habibi near Tagzirt, on the edge of the Tadla plain (part of the Atlantic plain of Morocco). This family claims to have moved away from the effective saintly lineage of Zawiya Ahansal (the Ait Mohamed n'ut Baba) some four generations ago, and to have acquired land locally by purchase. It still claims land in the main lodge, and it is interesting that its claim and associated genealogical position are recognised. During the summer of 1956, a close affine of this family visited the region by accident, and overtures were made through him for the purchase of the land. (The land had in the meantime been held in trust and used by others, without payment.) I also visited this solitary Ahansal family in its settlement near Tagzirt: it retained a 'memory' of certain aspects of the legends and ideology of the main lodge, notably those connected with the self-image of insouciant wealth and generosity. For instance, allusions were made to the reputedly magical bowl possessed by one of the top lodge families (now with the Ait Okdim, the 'Senior People', temporarily eclipsed through lack of sane adult males), a bowl used for giving *sksu* to visitors and pilgrims and magical in that it is inexhaustible, and remains full however much is eaten from it. It is also interesting that this isolated Ahansal had a lively image of the main lodge which he supposed to be applicable to the present, but which was in fact based on the lodge as it was two generations ago (i.e., that there were three main clans, two saintly and the rest: indeed, a few generations ago there were the Ait Ahmad u Ahmad, the Ait Ahmed u Mehamed, and the Rest).

This section has specifically commented on two cases of Ahansal families settling in lay villages and achieving influence. There are also more numerous examples of such individual family settlements which do not attain much local prominence. For instance, from among the Ait Tighanimin, I have come across one family settled among the 'Southern' Ait Atta, and another among the Ait Isha. From the Ihansalen proper, there are such families among the Ait Haddidu of Imilchil administrative district, among the Ait Bu Gmez, and no doubt in many other places. In the nature of the case, when they fail to achieve prominence and are small in number, one does not discover them unless one happens to hit upon them by accident, or has one's attention drawn to them by kinsmen who 'remember' them over generations. They tend however to be personalities of note at least within the villages in which they are settled.

Ihansalen of effective or near-effective lineage are 'born to lead': somehow their upbringing or situation are more likely to produce anticipation or striving for prominence. I once interviewed a French official who in his youth had taken part in the pacification of Ahansal-land and its subsequent administration, and he commented on the difficulty of finding, among the lay tribes, suitable candidates for the permanent chieftaincies which, under the French, replaced the elective imgharen. As he put it, 'no one rose above the general level of the water'. In fact, ambitious men do arise among the lay tribes – such as Haddu u Mha, who managed to be chief of the Abdi of Koucer both under the French and under Independence, only to fall as leader of the abortive rising of 1960, and who sprang from the Ait Tus family whose position was based not on baraka but on priority of possession of a modern rifle; but ambition is rarer among the lay than among the igurramen.

Igurramen are led to have greater expectations, and they pay the price or status ambiguity. Citizens of more complex societies sometimes suppose that this ailment is their exclusive privilege, the price of 'openness' and mobility, and that it does not occur in traditional societies, or only in consequence of some breakdown. This tribal society generates it not as a consequence of breakdown or even friction, but as an essential part of its normal working. It produces its potential leaders a little to excess, and places them in a situation in which they can only compete slowly: they cannot seize the instruments of power, partly because they do not exist, partly because the norms of their role preclude it. They are thus doomed to be teased by a shadow of ambiguity, from which only defeat and its acceptance can entirely free them.

A Case of Identification

The Ait Troilest form a small hamlet in the territory of the Ait
Atta of Talmest. They have hived-off a not very large number of
generations ago directly from the main lodge,[1] sufficiently near to
spring from the 'better' half of it, i.e., the half from which the really
effective saints spring, but far enough back to be related less closely
to the top families than to some other semi-igurramen. One family
of the Ait Troilest has moved back to Zawiya Ahansal and is prosperous and influential there, though only in intra-village affairs and
not at an agurram level.

The Ait Troilest are settled in the territory of the Ait Atta of
Talmest but then, the whole territory of the Ait Atta of Talmest
'belongs' to the Ihansalen in virtue of the land-deed left behind by
Sidi Lahcen u Othman. Thus in a sense they have been allowed to
settle what is theirs anyway: they are like a man who is a lodger in a
flat which is itself rented from the lodger's father. The Ait
Troilest are keen advocates of the validity and respectworthiness
of this document, but not at all out of hostility to their hosts, the
Ait Talmest, but from a hostility shared with these Ait Talmest and
directed at the annually commuting transhumants from the South,
their 'brothers' the Ait Atta from the South.

Though the sheer fact of their descent from Sidi Said Ahansal
and Sidi Lahcen u Othman should provide them with sufficient
justification for being able to settle where they are they also possess
a legend explaining the settlement of their own segment in particular on their own territory in particular. Indeed their name reminds
all of the legend, being derived from the Berber word for panther.
The legend is, in substance, that the immediate area of the present
hamlet of the Ait Troilest was made uninhabitable by a ferocious
panther with whom the lay tribesmen could not cope. The first of
the Ait Troilest peacefully disposed of the panther family, including its cubs, by carrying it elsewhere. Handled by the agurram and
sensitive to his baraka, the panthers allowed themselves to be
dispossessed and resettled. (In fact, there still are panthers in the
region as a whole and from time to time one is shot.)

The hamlet is small (well under ten households), but never
referred to as a zawiya and not really very saintly in the agurram
sense: for one thing, it possesses no shrine around which a pilgrim

[1] Cf. above, p. 213.

239

cult could be centred. It does possess a very prominent family, but its prominence seems a consequence of its accomplishments and achievements in this generation and in the fairly recent past: it does not reflect any deep, saintly social stratification in the hamlet. The Ait Troilest do claim when interrogated to have been recipients of donations from a wide area in the days of siba, but it seems likely that they are exaggerating the size and importance of this.

The Ait Troilest are not saintly in the sense of acting as arbitrators and being the centre of a cult, but they are influential and prestigious with the Ait Atta of Talmest, in whose territory they are. But it does not seem that they are invoked by them so much for internal disputes; for instance, these Ait Atta use other internal (descendant-less) shrines or mosques for internal oaths, and as a court of appeal or for major issues still go to the main lodge itself. The Ait Troilest are used by them as leaders and spokesmen in their literally perennial conflict with the southern Atta who arrive each spring.

If one contemplates the geographical location of the Ait Troilest and considers a kind of pure theory of saintly geopolitics, one might suppose them well placed to prosper as mediators between the Ait Atta of Talmest and the transhumant Ait Atta from the South: for they are placed on the southern border of the Talmest Atta, facing the crucial holy mountain of Azurki which constitutes the boundary for the transhumants up to a certain date. But, whatever one might suppose a priori, in fact the Ait Troilest in all the endless disputes about pasture boundaries and the extent to which the southern Atta are entitled to use local land, have identified with the permanent inhabitants and made themselves their spokesmen. (One of their arguments is that as descendants of Sidi Lahcen u Othman, they are in any case entitled to arbitrate and decide the use of the land secured and delimited by him.)

Why has this happened? One can think of two sets of reasons. Firstly, they are not so genuinely 'on a frontier' as a merely static view of the boundary lines might suggest. In winter, when Azurki and the surrounding high ground are covered in snow, the southern Atta have not merely departed, but departed behind the high, snow-bound and rugged ground which separates this area from the southern slopes of the Atlas. Then, the Ait Troilest would be in no position to balance the wholly absent and distant southerners against the local Ait Atta, who then become their only close and numerically overwhelming neighbours. These neighbours do not need the igurramen (or semi-igurramen) of the Ait Troilest lineage to unite, for they form a political unit with an annual chief and a shared group of storehouses and, at that level of segmentation, use the 'bigger' igurramen of the main lodge for their elections and arbitration. So the Ait Troilest are ill-placed not to identify with them in winter, assuming they wished not to do so. On the other hand, in full summer when the southerners pass beyond the high pasture and are allowed to graze on and around Talmest, the Ait Troilest are fellow sufferers from the incursions of their flocks, and so again ill-suited to be mediators in this issue. They are too small and ecologically non-delimited to be a frontier post, and in any case, that function has been pre-empted by the main lodge.

Pastures and Frontiers (Sidi Ali u Hussein)

This saint, a descendant of Sidi Said Ahansal and Sidi Lahcen u Othman, is the apical and revered ancestor of the igurramen of the Temga-Asker-Sidi Aziz group of lodges, their inhabitants include the most important live saints who rival those of the main lodge: and indeed, the shrine of Sidi Ali u Hussein is second in importance only to that of Sidi Said Ahansal. The supposed progeny of Sidi Ali u Hussein defines the most important hiving-off in the regional dispersion of the Ihansalen, and the most important opposition within the specifically saintly segmentary system.

It is worth noting that the genealogical system is not so neat as to oppose him by a correspondingly prominent general ancestor of the specifically stay-at-home igurramen: they define themselves either by reference to an ancestor further back who is *his* ancestor too, or put. The stay-at-home effective saints do not appear to need genea-by locally differentiating ancestors 'lower-down', i.e., later in time, who help to distinguish them from lineages which have also stayed logical aid or stress to conceptualise their distinctness from and opposition to the rival and emigrant group. Having the old and shared ancestors and staying so close to their shrines is enough. (For the genealogical pattern, see below, p. 261 et seq.) On the contrary: the stay-at-home igurramen refrain from having or stressing an ancestor who would define them vis-à-vis the progeny of Sidi Ali u Hussein: indeed, by defining themselves by an ancestor who is *his* ancestor too, they trump his progeny.

But the effectively saintly descendants of Sidi Ali u Hussein do not live around his shrine in the zawiya bearing his name. They live elsewhere. The explanation is simple and obvious. Like the saints of the main lodge, the igurramen of this lineage fulfil (among others) two important roles: the supervision of transhumancy arrangements on a really important summer pasture, and the guarding of frontiers (with the associated mediation and protection of travellers).

But the local tribal geopolitics are such that these two main jobs cannot conveniently be done from the same spot. The big pasture and the septic frontiers are not close enough to each other. So the shrine of the crucial ancestor is in one place (convenient from the viewpoint of the transhumancy problem), whilst the permanent settlements, zawiyas of his effectively saintly descendants (three such settlements, in fact) are elsewhere, located on three septic frontiers. These three settlements are described below (p. 246 et seq.). This section is concerned only with the minor and less significant settlement around the very significant shrine itself.

It follows that this shrine does not belong to the people settled around it – mere wardens, in effect – but to the effectively saintly lineages living elsewhere, whose genealogies connecting them with this ancestor are complete and recognised, and who have the respect, prestige and saintly know-how to be influential igurramen. The donations to the shrine are concentrated into certain festivals, and at these times and others, if convenient or necessary, the effective descendants come back to collect their due and to perform their duties. The division of the saintly spoils of Sidi Ali u Hussein is, in principle, one-third each to the saints of Temga, Asker and Sidi Aziz, with a minor informal reward to the resident guardians of the shrine.[1]

---

[1]The picture given by these local guardians of the proper division is quite other: one-third to them, one-third to the saints of the main lodge, and one-third to those of the Temga-Asker-Sidi Aziz group. There can be little doubt but that this merely corresponds to their own desires and not to the real past or even present practice. Their (to my knowledge quite unsolicited) willingness to grant one third of what in fact they do not control, to the saints of the main lodge, indicates an interesting attempt to play off these against the Temga group. It is the view of the effective saints, descended from the saint-of-the-shrine which corresponds to reality: their effectiveness enabled them to impose their view, and indeed their effectiveness is a reflection of the fact that they did impose it. Their view of the role of the saints from the main lodge in this connection is that they are merely entitled to respect and proper entertainment if they choose

The inhabitants of the little lodge around this shrine amount to ten families. Of these, in the past only two were recognised to be proper Ihansalen, actual descendants of Sidi Said Ahansal, etc., whilst the others were held to be descendants of clients settled locally to assist in the guarding of the shrine. (This situation was recorded in the archives of the French administrative outpost, and the report based on inquiries which must have been made in the late thirties or early forties.) Latterly, however, (though still in French days) the eight excluded families claimed to be full citizens of the lodge and took their case to court (i.e., the local customary law tribunals operating in French days). The full story of this intriguing court case has eluded me, but the party claiming full and equal citizenship appears to have won, whether formally in court or informally, in as far as now there is a reluctance to talk to strangers (at any rate to me) about the internal genealogical differentiation of the lodge, and an – admittedly unenthusiastic – tendency even on the part of the two special families to admit that all are equal and Ihansalen. The victory of the egalitarian party, whether formal or informal, was clearly aided by the fact that even the two families whose Ahansal descent was not in dispute, and who originally wished to maintain their local pre-eminence, are fairly thoroughly

---

to turn up, but that is all. This is confirmed at the main lodge, if not in such almost disrespectful terms, in as far as no one there claims to collect or to have collected any donations from the shrine of Sidi Ali u Hussein.

It is however worth noting that the difficulties one encounters in trying to discover the rules governing the division of the spoils of sanctity are inherent in the situation. There is no unique and correct answer. The ambiguities of this division correspond to the ambiguities of the rules of saintly succession. Indeed it is the flow of donations which determines the flow of baraka and of the succession, and each interested party strives to direct these flows to itself: possibilities and opportunities for influencing the flow may continue to arise over a long period of time. In order to affect it, one must first have or display a firm conviction that one is entitled to the flow (although no doubt one would not display it in the presence of those who both disagree and are influential enough to penalise the presumption). Thus, there is only the de facto division, which one can guess at, more or less reliably according to circumstances, and a multiplicity of competing views concerning the de jure division.

During the years following Independence, this shrine, like some others (though not Sidi Said Ahansal's), was enlarged, and was structurally (I mean the building, not the social structure) and decoratively improved. This was not due to a religious revival, but the fact that the weight of the administration, which in French days was friendly or at least not hostile to saints, was now not on the side of diverting donations from what seemed either an archaic cult or corruption, and when consulted on distribution of income advised that donations should be turned towards the improvement of the shrine which had earned them.

laicised, and are not very distinguishable in influence or in style of life or habitation from their genealogically ambiguous neighbours. They are incapable of tracing their genealogy accurately to their illustrious saint. It is true that they did not take part in the feuding and alliances of their lay neighbours, but then, neither did their genealogically ambiguous neighbours. (Next to the Ait Tighani-min, this is the most prominent recent case of contested Ahansal descent.) They too, well born though they may be, were little more than guardians of the shrine, whose blessing had flown in other directions.

The position of the shrine in connection with local transhumancy patterns is as follows. The main lodge is well placed to regulate dis-putes arising from the transhumancy of the Ait Atta from south of the Atlas, and also for the provision of an attractive place down in the valley at which they can celebrate and ratify their coming and going: the shrine of Sidi Ali u Hussein is similarly placed with regard to the transhumancy of one half of the big and important tribe of the Ait Daud u Ali. This tribe is, like the Ait Abdi, a seg-ment of the large Ait Sochman. It is itself bifurcated in the following way: each of its various segments is represented in each of the two main territories of the Daud u Ali, the two territories corresponding to the modern administrative areas of Anergui and Taguelft.

The tribe has, like the Ait Atta, both a territorial and a clan organisation and the two cut across each other. The tribe believes, plausibly enough, to have 'begun' at Anergui and to have expanded to Taguelft, each of the clans dividing in such a way that some 'stayed at home' and some went to the new location. This direction fits in with the general directions of the drift or *Drang* of Berber tribes reported by historians. But Taguelft is 'lower down' in the direction of the Atlantic plain, and the members of the tribe who settled there come back annually in summer to the high pastures which are closer to Anergui and where they share rights with their 'brethren' who stayed behind at Anergui. The shrine of Sidi Ali u Hussein itself is also in Anergui. Just as the Ait Atta come down to the shrine of Sidi Said Ahansal from the high plateau above the main lodge, so the incoming transhumants among the Ait Daud u Ali come, both at the beginning and at the end of transhumance, but especially at the end, down to the shrine of Sidi Ali u Hussein for a celebration which, in effect, ratifies their pasture rights. Sidi Ali u Hussein's effective descendants, who do not live at the shrine, are at the same time the guardians of the same tribe's frontiers, where they have their homes. They also come to the shrine, of course, to receive the donations brought and by their presence to ratify the pasture using arrangements, and if necessary arbitrate disputes arising from it. Fustel de Coulanges' ancient city may have required both hearth and shrine: in the life of the Atlas saints, the geopolitics of sanctity may sometimes make it necessary to have the two at separate places, as both shrine and home perform functions for other tribes – that is why they are saints – and these functions, given the lie of the land, have to be divergently located.

Ait Mhand u Yussif

This is a very small lodge consisting of four families, which performs for one of the segments, Ait Bulman, of the Ait Daud u Ali, what the shrine of Ali u Hussein (cf. previous section) does for that tribe as a whole. This segment, like the tribe as a whole, is territorially divided into two parts, one located at Taguelft and the other at Anergui. This little lodge is located within the Ait Bulman permanently resident at Anergui, and provides a kind of focus for the festivities, occurring mainly towards the end of the summer transhumancy period, when the opposite numbers of the segment come down to their 'cousins' before returning to Taguelft.

It was claimed to me in 1959 that this little lodge does not receive donations but merely provides locale for the festivities for which of course both the visitors and the locals provide the sustenance. The lodge is situated well within the segment, adjoining a cemetery which is not a specialised cemetery of these little saints but of the adjoining villages as well. The cemetery contains the bodies of two local men who had lost their lives in the tribal battles against the French in the early thirties, and after independence their tombs received some decorations – a stick with a white cloth attached to it, in belated recognition, as a kind of reinterpretation of what had been a tribal struggle as a national one.

The members of the lodge claim in virtue of their sanctity to be endogamous, but in fact are not: they not merely receive wives but give away daughters to the surrounding tribes. I have met a man whose mother came from the lodge and whose father was a lay tribesman.

Local beliefs about the founder of the lodge are very similar to those to be found at Temga, and concern annual flights by the founder direct to Mecca and the failure of a lay companion, owing to worldly interests in immediate pleasure, to join him on this pious and remarkably swift trip. This trip is held to be continued by the spirit of the founding saint each year. The members of the lodge however are not capable of tracing their precise genealogy in relation to the main saintly lineages nor even to that of the important shrine of Sidi Ali u Hussein, which is merely an hour or two downstream from it. They also have no views, or profess none, about the priority or otherwise of their settlement to that shrine.

The Puritan Rivals (Temga)

The igurramen of the lodges of Temga, Asker and Sidi Aziz form a group which on the whole co-operates (which of course does not exclude internal conflict), which shares descent from Sidi Ali u Hussein in the privileged lines and a special relation to the Ait Sochman. Each of these groups guards a Sochman frontier: Temga is situated between the Ait Abdi (a Sochman tribe) and the Ait Isha (Messat), Asker between the Ait Daud u Ali and the Ait Isha, and Sidi Aziz between the Ait Daud u Ali and the Ait Said u Ali (both Sochman tribes).

In as far as they are genealogically, and in terms of the periodic festival, centred on the shrine of Sidi Ali u Hussein of Anergui, which is well inside Sochman territory and as described ministers to internal transhumance problems, these igurramen can be seen as national Sochman saints; but in as far as they themselves live on the frontier, they exemplify the main Ahansal tendency to be a form of the sacred which symbolises not a group, but a boundary between groups.[1]

These three lodges are not as yet fully separated off from each other, in the sense that the top saintly strata in each still have close kin links with each other which cut across residential proximity: a

[1]In general, as indicated, there is a one-many relationship both ways: one saintly centre has many clients, but each lay tribe is client to more than one saintly centre. There are few lay tribes who can be said to be uniquely orientated towards one zawiya. The Ait Mhand come close to this in their relationship to the main lodge, which they visited twice a year. The important Ait Isha tribe also come close to being exclusively Ahansal-oriented, but they nevertheless divide their reverence between both the main lodge and Temga, visiting both, in that order, in the autumn. The elections are held at the main lodge, to whom they bring grain, and they then also visit Temga, to whom they bring beasts.

man from one may be a closer agnatic kinsman of a man from another lodge than he is of some fellow-inhabitants of his own lodge. Similarly, families are liable to own land in more than one of the three lodges. This is quite unlike their relationship to the main lodge, from which their separation is complete: There are no cross-cutting agnatic or indeed other kin links with it (other than, of course, the one which can be found by going back to the common ancestor), and they do not even claim to have retained land in the main lodge, still less actually to control any. This trio of lodges is, in fact, the main rival of Zawiya Ahansal itself.

In internal structure, these lodges in some ways resemble and in some ways differ from the main lodge. They are, each of them, severally somewhat smaller than the main lodge, though larger than villages such as Taria or Tidrit. They display their 'youth' by the fact that the lay families incorporated in the village unit, notably at Temga, possess non-Ahansal genealogies: they are plainly seen as 'people of the sacrifice', who have been allowed to settle as refugees from feuds or other troubles elsewhere. Non-incorporated genealogically, they are non-incorporated legally: they do not share in all the rights (e.g., pasture rights) of the igurramen's village. Whereas almost all the members of the main lodge who are not effective saints have a similar standing genealogically (in their own eyes and those of others), qua lineages eliminated in the saintly rat-race – and no doubt a good many of them are just that – most of the lay part of these lodges are lay rather than laicised, resident outsiders whose exclusion from sanctity is due to their external origin rather than elimination from inside. Presumably with the passage of time, as on the one hand branches of the prospering saints are eliminated and laicised, and the client lineages slowly slip in under the cover of shared prestigious origin, these lodges would come to look, socially and genealogically, more like the main lodge.

In the past there was the fascinating conflict between Temga and the main lodge.

Berber tribes have no war dance. But they can boast, or at least the saints of the central Atlas can, a *war of the dance*.

At about the turn of the century, or shortly before, an oecumenical council, so to speak, of the igurramen both of the main lodge and of the northern trio of lodges agreed that dancing is immoral and un-Islamic and not to be indulged in by igurramen. Dancing (notably the *haidus* dance) is widely indulged in in the central High Atlas, includes women (though on the whole not married women) and some forms of it even involve men and women dancing shoulder-to-shoulder (!). The whole issue of dancing possesses an emotive charge similar to that which the theatre, and later drink, held for noncomformist puritanism in England. It is a pastime particularly favoured at festivals, including religious ones, or during the nights of Ramadan. That the practice is immoral is widely conceded, though on the whole this does not affect its popularity.

Thus the saints imposed a self-denying ordinance upon themselves. Some kept it. (For instance, up to very recent times, if not even now, the villagers of the Sidi Aziz lodge impose a fine on anyone indulging in dancing.) But not the igurramen of the main lodge, who, then as now, secure in their saintly origin and proximity to the most revered of shrines, and surrounded by tribes concerned much more with their real local functions than with their technical orthodoxy or propriety, were easy to tempt, and seldom inclined to resist temptation. A male infant was born in one family in the main lodge, and the overjoyed father, unmindful of either propriety or of covenant, organised a feast which included dancing. The chips were down. The casus belli was there. The Ait Temga, secure in their faith, and incensed by this affront both to respect for inter-village agreements and to propriety and Islam, took up arms.

Or so they say. The War of the Dance is somewhere on the borderline between memory and legend. On one occasion I was assured that it lasted seven years, and on another that there were seven casualties on one side: the figure is suspect. On the other hand, the event is firmly correlated with the 'reign' of plausible recent figures in the main lodge, and I was assured that the man whose birth occasioned the fateful birth-party is still alive, and he was once pointed out to me.

There can be no doubt about the moral laxity of the saints of the main lodge, nor about the careful puritanism of the saints of Temga. For instance, whereas nowadays very many among the males of the main lodge smoke, no one in Temga does so, and so forth. Nor is it very difficult to give an explanation of this divergence of moral development.

The clients of the main lodge are tribes in the heart of the mountains, and from the lands between the Atlas and Sahara. They have no conceivable motive for concern with whether or not the saints they revere live up to the standards of Islamic propriety held valid in the cities of the plain, with whom they have little if any contact· On the contrary, they clearly prefer it if their joint visits to the shrine, a break in the monotony of pastoral life, are joyous ones. But the clients of the Ait Temga and the related lodges are, some of them, on the very edge of the plain. They are in direct contact with the plain, both economic and in the past military. The Ait Temga could not be insensitive to the change that they were immoral mountain heathens. They compete for clients who are under some urban influence. Moreover, as saints they were on the make, whereas the position and functions of the old igurramen of Sidi Said Ahansal's shrine were not in doubt.

The extent to which that which is expressed by collective memories or legends is also manifestly present to the minds of the people involved no doubt varies a good deal. In this case, however, it is plain to everyone concerned that the issue of dancing was only a pretext, or at best a last straw. Nevertheless, accounts of the dancing war invariably begin by telling of this formal issue. There is also another, extremely involved episode, which I have neither fully unravelled nor properly understood, which involves the failure of the main lodge to punish a slanderer: in outline, two men, one from each side, jointly slandered the saints, and a joint council of both parties agreed that each should be responsible for penalising their own man. The lax saints of the main lodge took no action, however. (This story is not an alternative but complements the dancing matter.)

Everyone concerned, however, is clear that the real issue was the saintly rivalry between the main lodge and the northern saints and cousins. An amusing aspect of the affair is its man-bites-dog dénouement: the scandal of pacific saint fighting pacific saint was terminated by peaceful persuasion, by the surrounding lay, feud-addicted tribes. Even quite distant clients came in on the pacification of their saintly patrons.

Neither side scored a victory, and both divine grace and mundane donations continued to flow into each of the channels. Each had its own clients, and one most important source of revenue, the powerful Ait Isha tribe, was a client of both: so were the Ait Abdi of the Koucer plateau.

The manner in which the Dancing War is remembered is interesting. Anthropologists sometimes speak of 'structural amnesia', by which what is inconvenient or irrelevant to the social organisation of the group is forgotten; the corollary of this notion is of course that what *is* remembered is so in virtue of a 'structural memory', i.e., it is recalled because circumstances systematically arise which give someone a motive for recalling and/or repeating it. On the face of it, the remembering of the Dancing War is not to anyone's interest: such conduct goes dead against the image of a pacific agurram. Strange peaceful Elect of God who have to demonstrate their election by striving to eliminate rivals by force!

All the same, the episode *is* remembered and retailed, and not specifically (as is the case with certain other stories) by the enemies of the igurramen. It is told with an air of amused ambivalent shame: 'It wasn't a proper thing to do, but that is how we are.' Almost as if to say – igurramen will be igurramen. To ask about the Dancing War is a sure way of provoking amusement (as it is to ask an Abdi about feuding and the story of Ohmish and of Tuda Lahcen, his wife, concerning a murderous snowball of feuds, the telling of which is both forbidden and utterly familiar among them). On this point, the igurramen have a kind of joking relationship with their own past or their own self-image. It is noteworthy that the pretensions of igurramen are not something to be taken always or wholly seriously,[1] not even by themselves.

But the paths of the two centres of sanctity diverged again sharply with the appearance of the French danger. As described, the Ait Temga and associated lodges became the leaders of the genuine and determined resistance: as neutrals between tribes they became their leaders, unneutrally fighting the infidel. The saints of the main lodge, on the other hand, persisted in their saintly habits and strategies, and acted as skilful mediators not merely between tribes, but equally between them and the French. Their success in dealing with the French as one further tribe, and the necessary modification of their strategies in doing so, are described below (p. 252 et seq.).

The final victory of the French left the saints of the northern (Temga) group without political power. However, some individuals of the group have made attempts to recover it since Independence.

[1]The same appears true elsewhere, e.g., in the Middle Atlas. 'Les Ait Oumalou [people of the shadow, i.e., of the North slopes of the Atlas] . . . ont en outre beaucoup d'égards pour les marabouts . . . mais, frondeurs et malicieux, ils ne se gênent guère pour les ridiculiser dès qu'ils ont le dos tourné . . .' S. Guennoun, *La Montagne Berbère*, Paris 1929, p. 57.

Zawiya Sidi Aziz

This lodge is one of the Temga group. It shows a common ancestry with it and looks towards its genealogical apex at the shrine of Sidi Ali u Hussein at Anergui, where, like Temga, it has a claim to one-third of the main bulk of the donations.

It is a smallish village located on a slope whose summit, not very far distant, is the frontier between the Ait Said u Ali and the Ait Daud u Ali, both major segments of the Ait Sochman: this lodge, like other important lodges, is a frontier guard. Its direct donations came from these two tribes on either side of it. The members of this lodge are very clear about their intimate relation to Temga, and describe it as a part of their function to provide a local service for those people or circumstances when the litigants, or seekers after mediation with the deity, cannot be bothered to go as far as Temga.

The local version of the story and legends of the founding saint of the main lodge tally with the stories told around the main lodge, except for one interesting divergence: it is denied that the initial general founding saint received any help from anyone – in other words he did not receive any help from the Ait Atta. The 'remembering' of this 'fact' would of course be pointless locally; the Ait Atta are far away and of no local relevance.

After Independence, I saw the local shrine decorated with some illustrated political material, including photographs both of the Algerian FLN leadership and the Saudi Arabian royal house. The saints of Sidi Aziz probably were not aware of the anti-saint-worship traditions of both the Wahabi royal house and of Algerian socialist leaders.

Zawiya Asker

This lodge was settled after that of Sidi Aziz, although its apical ancestor was an uncle of the apical ancestor of Sidi Aziz (and thus one generation earlier). This founding ancestor was the great-grandson of the famous saint enshrined at Anergui, the apex of the whole trio of lodges, in whose donations he had a one third stake. From him, four further generations lead to the great Hussein, who was the leader of the resistance to the French in the 1920s and early 1930s. This man had ascendancy over all three of the related lodges (apart of course from the surrounding lay tribes), and the French literature of the 'pacification' wrongly describes him as being 'of Temga'. He moved a good deal but his main court is said to have been at Anergui, in other words at none of the three permanently settled lodges.

Like the Ait Sidi Aziz, the families of this lodge also have lands at Temga. This lodge guards the frontier between the Daud u Ali and the Ait Messat. There are about thirty households, of which fourteen are Ahansal and the rest are either refugee clients or black slaves.

A story told locally and not encountered elsewhere concerns the semi-legendary dancing war. It is about Sidi Ahmad u Moha, a leading figure of the lodge and possessor of baraka at the time of the dancing war: SSA, father of all the Ihansalen, rose from his tomb and appeared to him, tied up his horse's legs and warned him that if the northern lodges continued to make war on the founding lodge, all Ihansalen would be as cinders; he assured him that they who had left the homeland of the founding saints were not as good as those who had stayed behind, even if the latter did dance. Moved by this intervention, the man in question voted for peace.

This story is not known to the members of the founding lodge who are the beneficiaries of the supernatural intervention described in it.

Adaptation to a new-style Frontier (Bernat)

The Ahansal settlement at Bernat is not a typical zawiya at all: and, in fact, it is never referred to as a zawiya. Nevertheless it deserves to be classed as such, albeit as an exceptional case. Bernat is the product of the adaptation of the Ihansalen to early twentieth-century conditions which, in Morocco, meant to the expansion of French power. This being so, the general facts concerning its establishment are on record in writing.

Herewith the French account of the conduct of Sidi Mha, then a leading saint of the main lodge:

En 1916, il tente de s'opposer à la marche de la colonne du général de Lamothe sur Azilal mais sa harka est battue . . .

Notre installation à Azilal . . . pose avec acuité pour Sidi Mha le problème des relations avec le nouveau Maghzen.

Il comprend qu'il ne faut pas adopter une attitude systématiquement hostile. Il cherche à gagner du temps . . . Soucieuse de ménager l'avenir, sa politique consiste à empêcher toute manifestation susceptible d'attirer trop vivement notre attention sur les tribus de son fief. Il conclut avec nous des trêves et veille à leur respect.

En 1918, la colonne de Bou Yahgn [i.e., in the territory of the Ait Mhand] ne décide pas Sidi Mha à la soumission . . .

En septembre 1922, les troupes du colonel Naugès et la harka du pacha de Marrakesh, forte de huit mille hommes, menacent directement son fief. Avec huit cents guerriers seulement, le marabout fait face au pacha et arrête sa progression en pays Ait Bou Guemmez.

Puis il se tourne contre la colonne Naugès, arrivée à Bou Yahia, au coeur des Ait Mhammed [Ait Mhand]. Là, un sanglant combat le convainc . . . Une trêve est à nouveau conclue et Sidi Mha promet sa soumission à la première occasion.

Au cours del'hiver 1922–1923, Sidi Mha a plusieurs entrevues avec le . . . chef du cercle d'Azilal [i.e., French commander] . . .

Le 27 juin (1923), Sidi Mha, fidèle à ses promesses, se soumet avec les Ait Mhammed [Ait Mhand] et les Air Hakim des Ait Bou Guemmez . . .

Sidi Mha, bien que marabout, est alors investi du commandement des Ait Mhammed et des Ait Hakim. On l'appelle désormais le caid. Cette volte-face est d'autant plus audacieuse que *le Maghzen n'occupe qu'une partie de son fief* . . . [Italics mine. This is the crucial fact.]

Officiellement, il rompt avec la dissidence, mais, comme il ne veut pas que sa zaouia tombe avec ses serviteurs sous l'influence de . . . Temga, il laisse à la maison mère [main lodge] ses frères . . . et son cousin . . . qui lui sont dévoués.

Les parents demeurés en dissidence critiquent ouvertement sa trahison et gardent ainsi la confiance des tribus. Ils restent toutefois en relations suivies avec Sidi Mha, le renseignent et le servent. La fissure n'est qu'apparente.[1]

The above-quoted passage to my mind calls for only one critical caution: it seems to me doubtful whether Sidi Mha really feared that, if he disavowed dissidence completely and caused his agnates and fellow-saints to join him in French-occupied territory, Temga would take over the main lodge. There is in the main lodge no sign

[1]Georges Drague, *Esquisse d'Histoire Religieuse du Maroc. Confrèries et Zaouias*, J.Peyronnet & Cie, Paris, 1951 (?), pp. 176–8. The author's name is a pen-name: in fact he is General (as he now is) G.Spillman, who as a young man took part for many years in the conquest and administration of this and adjoining regions, and who is the author of a study of the Ait Atta (G.Spillman, *Les Ait Atta et la Pacification du Haut Draa*, Rabat, 1936).

that there was at any time a fear of a Temga take-over of the main lodge itself, and indeed it doesn't make very good sense. For another thing, whilst *primus inter pares* among the igurramen of the main lodge, it is doubtful whether his influence over the others was so complete as to be able to force them to follow him, even if he wished to do so; and finally, there is no reason to suppose that he and his cousins and brothers wished them all to do so, for it would have been contrary to their interests. More than half their clients and sources of donations were still in dissidence, and to go over completely would have cut them off from these resources. What they did do was perfectly rational: they divided themselves in such a fashion that each of the bifurcated parts should 'catch' half the available donations, one part in French-occupied, one in dissident territory. Moreover, here there was one further septic frontier, this time between the French and the dissident tribes, and this frontier too needed its mediators! Thus there is no need to postulate a fear of actual Temga occupation to explain their conduct: they merely did, on a new frontier, what they had always done on the old ones. A good septic frontier is an important resource for a saint and ought not to be wasted. If the French created a new frontier of this kind, then arrangements for well rewarded mediation should be made along it. But it is quite plausible that a fear of a Temga take-over was the reason Caid Sidi Mha saw fit to give to the French.

What the passage does in fact admirably describe is that the igurramen succeeded, once again, in placing themselves along a troublesome frontier and deriving influence from mediation on it. At this time, the main lodge and the settlement at Bernat were, spiritually and socially, *one* lodge. In the main lodge, it is remembered that this strategy was decided by a top saints' reunion to discuss policy, and that the apparent traitor to Berber dissidence, Sidi Mha, used to visit Zawiya Ahansal, arriving and departing at night. The way in which this bifurcated lodge differed from traditional ones was, of course, that physically it had to be situated in two places: it was impossible, given the requirements of administration in the French-occupied zone on the one hand, and the hostility of dissident tribesmen to the French on the other, to set up a shrine on the frontier and have annual festivals for both, helping to elect their chiefs in the process. For one thing, the French appeared to have their own non-annual methods of nominating their own and tribal chiefs, and for another, the French had new ways of subsidising igurramen, presenting them not with sheep but with a proportion of the newly imposed taxes. Of course, it was necessary to tell different things to clients on each side of the frontier, but there was nothing very new in this. Even the physical bifurcation was not a radical innovation: other circumstances had forced the progeny of Sidi Ali u Hussein to do something similar.[1]

This doubly incarnated centre of baraka, resembling traditional lodges in this matter, played an important part in facilitating trade across the bridged boundary. The laicised Ihansalen cohabiting with the saints in the main lodge and in the adjoining Ahansal villages were perfectly well in on the secret, as perhaps were others, and profited from the arrangement by carrying on trade between the dissident and the occupied territory. With their help, the impact of cheaper consumption goods – notably that great popular passion of modern Morocco, tea – hit the mountain Berbers even before the actual pacification of the area.[2]

Another aspect of the cited account which may be queried is the assumption that the final resolution of the situation, when conquest was completed, can be seen, in as far as it was aided by the saints, as a fulfilment of a promise on their parts. They did make the promise, and it did come to be fulfilled, but I find it hard to believe that they intended, initially, to see it fulfilled. Qua igurramen, their future lay in the perpetuation of the frontier, not in its termination. The slowness of the fulfilment of the promise supports this view. It took the French army, much of whose élite appears to have been concentrated on this frontier (one of the few violent ones at that time), ten years from the submission of Sidi Mha, to cover a distance which a Berber can walk in a day. If the igurramen were anxious to fulfil the promise, they were not in any undue hurry.

It so happens that there exists an English description of this septic frontier. In 1925, Rear-Admiral Hubert Lynes, CB, CMG,[3] visited the region in order to study its birds. The record

---

[1]Cf. p. 242.

[2]The French tolerated the trade across the frontier with dissidence. They distinguished dissident tribes into two classes: and one, those who refrained from attacking French-occupied territory, were allowed free access to its markets.

[3]Also, one should add, Commander of the Legion of Honour, the membership of which he thus shares, though at higher rank, with at least two igurramen.

of his trip[1] unfortunately tells us fairly little about its human inhabitants other than French ones, but it does give a very good picture of the impingement of dissidence on submission:

The Cercle d'Azilal . . . was one of the politico-military districts . . . towards the east and south it was 'dissident' with an indefinite boundary controlled by a series of small military outposts . . .

At Marrakesh I had been told that not until I got to Azilal . . . would I be able to know exactly where and where it would not be safe . . . to go, since that would depend on conditions local and somewhat transitory. To my dismay I now found that practically all the high ground was actively 'dissident' and that it would be impossible . . . to get anywhere near . . . the high ground up at the junction of the Great and Middle Atlas ranges . . .

. . . the whole workable part of the Cercle – that part of it limited eastward and southward by the ring of outposts . . . except for the southern part, which was only workable under heavy chaperonage.[2]

In 1925 I gathered that the state of dissidence in the Cercle d'Azilal did not necessarily imply active hostility to the Government, but that a great deal of it represented mere brigandage and robbery, as, for instance, the ambushing of a few soldiers in order to get their rifles and cartridges for the purpose of better raiding a neighbouring tribe.[3]

This boundary, unfavourable though it was to ornithological research, suited the doubly-based saints well enough, and they enjoyed it for ten years.

Ironically, but not surprisingly, it was the unification of the territory by French conquest in 1933 which led to the real fission and hiving-off of the Bernat settlement. As long as the frontier of dissidence existed, the two halves of what structurally, if not geographically, was *one* zawiya, needed each other: structurally, they were on that frontier. Once deprived of the frontier which sustained it, they split, and indeed also in part ceased to be igurramen in any real sense, becoming Caids or would-be Caids instead.

Others

Other Ahansal settlements exist. For instance, there are various medium-sized villages of recognised Ahansal descent and varying

[1]Rear-Admiral H. Lynes, 'Ornithologie du Cercle d'Azilal', *Mémoires de la Société des Sciences naturelles du Maroc*, No. XXXVI, 31 mai 1933, Rabat, Paris, London (Janson & Sons).
[2]Ibid., pp. 10 and 11.
[3]Ibid., p. 63.

degrees of complete laicisation: Tassamert, Aganan, Akka n'Ahansal, Tamderrut, Igli, U'Tarra, Tabarocht. I have visited each of these, and a brief sketch will help towards completing the typology of saintly settlement.

Tassamert: is wholly laicised. They believe themselves, plausibly, to be descended from emigrants from Amzrai, and they consequently do make pious pilgrimages there from time to time, to the shrine of Amzrai's Sidi Lahcen u Othman, where their cousinly status is recognised. (It is understood that they left Amzrai after its laicisation, unlike the lineages of the main lodge, and hence that they automatically share the laicised status of the present Ait Amzrai.) Their beliefs concerning the proto-population they displaced in their present habitat, in the general area of the Ait Mhand, are similar to the legends concerning the displacement of the original inhabitants of Zawiya Ahansal itself: the arrangements were made under the aegis of an effective saint (though not one of their own number), who found new springs by magical means for the displaced population.

They do feud, emphatically, and early in the century drove out their neighbours, the Ait Wamluk (a segment of the Ait Mhand: and the story is confirmed from both sides) who then settled in poorer land near Azilal. Later, Caid Sidi Mha gave judgement in favour of Ait Wamluk and enabled them to re-occupy their original lands: an interesting case showing that influential saints are not necessarily swayed in their judgement by kin links. (There are good reasons for believing this to be so anyway. It is interesting that *living* saints should be unlike enshrined ones: parties in a dispute culminating in collective oath would not allow the testifying group to swear at the shrine of a kinsman, on the assumption that he would be partial to them even if they swore falsely.) Thus Tassamert is almost completely laicised. The same is true of *Tamderrut*.

Tabarocht: this settlement is also completely laicised. It is deep in the heart of the Ait Isha tribe, and it is said to have been founded at the same time and by the same prominent saints as the northern trio of lodges, and at that time, it is said, was referred to as a zawiya. This is not the case now. It does not possess a shrine, though the Ait Isha do use a nearby non-Ahansal shrine for internal oaths. It is of some interest that it is near one of the traditional markets of the Ait Isha (though one which has lost importance in modern times in virtue of the new pattern of communications, unlike markets situated near modern administrative centres). The explanation of the decline of Tabarocht seems obvious: it is not near any important frontier.

Akka n'Ahansal: this is at the edge (or almost beyond it) of the area of Ahansal influence. This is a gorge (*Akka* means gully or water-course) emptying into the Tadla plain (part of the general Atlantic plain of central Morocco) in the vicinity of Tagzirt. The geopolitical position is actually quite favourable, as beyond the gorge there are the plainward frontiers of the Ait Sochman, whilst downhill there are non-Sochman Berber tribes on the edge of the plain. Nevertheless, this is not an effective centre of sanctity: no shrine, no inner stratification. The explanation seems to be that whereas the Ait Sochman group of tribes used Ihansalen as mediators on their mountainward frontiers, on their plainward side there were other, well established centres of sanctity which did not allow themselves to be easily displaced. Again, these local Ihansalen may simply have lacked saintly know-how and, above all, a continuous tradition of effectiveness: re-activation is not easy, for it is difficult for the son of a laicised saint to decide one day that he will be effective. How are clients to be notified of this re-emergence? Other Ihansalen believe this group to be descended from Amzrai emigrants, which would support the supposition of long-standing extinction of sanctity.

But whilst thoroughly laicised in fact, they do (unlike for instance the people of Amzrai or Tassamert) have a desire to re-assert their saintly position, a desire springing presumably from the exiguity of their actual resources. I visited them in the summer of 1956, just after Independence, and they were wondering whether to improve their position by vigorous political activity or by re-asserting their Ahansal status. (My visit coincided with an intra-village feast at which these possibilities were discussed.) They over-estimated, I am sorry to say, the effectiveness of either alternative. They were hampered in the second strategy by having no clear idea of just how they were descended from the Ahansal tree, though they were clear that they were descended from it, and this is denied neither by their local lay neighbours nor by their distant Ahansal cousins. Their only close Ahansal neighbour is the influential single top-descended family among the Ait Habibi on the edge of the plain (see above, p. 237) and its members do not deny it either. They requested me to aid them in their genealogical research, but I have unravelled only that, in the Ahansal heartlands, they are held to be descended from Ait Amzrai.

Aganan is also a fairly fully laicised village at the westerly end of the land of the Ait Mhand. It does have a shrine – that of a brother of Sidi Said Ahansal, Sidi Ahmad u Amr, who left no progeny. They themselves are descended, like all Ihansalen, from Sidi Said Ahansal himself. They are fully laicised except in as far as they claim not to feud and take no part in the system of alliances of surrounding lay groups. But they receive no donations, and are not stratified.

Igli is a smaller settlement between the main lodge and Ait Mhand, in which there are possessions of top families and emigrants both from the main lodge and from Taria and Amzrai.

U'Tarra is a similar settlement, mainly with possessions of the top main lodge and Bernat families, and with clients originating from other nearby Ahansal centres.

Finally, within my range of knowledge but not personal acquaintance, there is an influential small settlement of Ihansalen at Demnate: an influential shrine near Ouaouizaght, enshrining a legend-adorned founder of the Hansalia fraternity of the plain and Algeria, who is also said to be the ancestor of the Demnate group; and there is a minor laicised settlement in the land of the Ait Isha, other than those already mentioned, whose members I only encountered when in 1959 they made a pious pilgrimage to their ancestor, Sidi Said Ahansal, and in particular to his present effective stay-put descendants, the Ait Sidi Mulay.

The shrine of the fraternity-founder does enter into the life of the Ahansal mountain-system in as far as the saints of the northern group do claim to make pilgrimages there and do have legends concerning him. His descendants at Demnate are too far to interact with the main body of Ihansalen in the mountains, at any rate at present. I have visited neither them nor their ancestral shrine, and cannot say whether this shrine is surrounded by a settlement of claimants to Ahansal origin. If so, they are neither numerous nor prominent.

I do not believe my study of Ahansal settlements to be complete. The lacunae which still exist fall into two classes: local gaps and non-local ones.

With the area of the Ahansal mountain-agurram system, I am

confident that I have not missed out any settlement of importance. But it is quite likely that I have missed out small and unimportant ones. I suppose this simply because some of those which I did find I only stumbled on by accident in the course of cross-country wanderings. The region is badly mapped and the map does not indicate the tribal affiliations of smaller groups (nor of larger ones reliably). Apart from a thorough and complete survey of the whole area, which is extensive, very rugged and ill-mapped, the only way of discovering settlements is to be led to their existence by kinsmen or by lay tribes. But not all the settlements claiming Ahansal origin are related to the others in any clear way: in fact, the less important they are, the less likely are they to be able to place themselves with any accuracy on the Ahansal tree. Similarly, the smaller and less important they are, the less likely is one to have one's attention drawn to them by lay tribesmen. So unnoticed small and un-important Ahansal settlements may well exist. This naturally does not affect my picture of effective and semi-effective sanctity. It does however indicate that the central High Atlas tribal map may be even more pock-marked with Ahansal settlements than one would suppose from my listing of those which I do know.

Ahansal centres outside the region are a different matter. There is in fact an Ahansal diaspora not merely of the kind described, in the frontier interstices of central High Atlas tribes, but all over Morocco, and indeed the Maghrib at large. These are partly mountain kin groups analogous to those described here,[1] and partly lodges, zawiyas in quite a different and 'proper' sense, i.e., urban shrines – religious clubs, deriving from the fraternity founded by an Ahansal agurram around 1700. Neither the distant mountain villages which also claim Ahansal origin, nor the quite different phenomena of urban shrines or religious clubs, affect the system found in the central High Atlas. They do not interact now. The question of the 'fraternity' sharing the name, and part of the history, of the mountain saints should be treated quite separately. They are not now in any sense one unit.

---

[1]For instance, one of them turns up in the only really intensive published study of the social structure of a Berber tribe, Jacques Berque's *Structures Sociales du Haut-Atlas*, an account of the Seksawa in the Western High Atlas; see p. 66 of that work.

CHAPTER NINE

THE AHANSAL GENEALOGY

The Status of the Genealogy

The previous chapter surveyed the Ihansalen as they are now to be found on the ground. In depth, over time, we can only see them in terms of their genealogical beliefs and connections.

The two approaches are of course neither strictly comparable nor separable: the spatial survey was based on actual observation and fact, whilst the backward sweep of their genealogy is based on their own assertion and belief, and requires interpretation, and doubly so – both for the light it throws on their current organisation, and for such tentative conclusions as one may actually draw from it concerning the real historic past. Again, the spatial survey of the present Ahansal settlements had already to invoke genealogical considerations in their description, whilst an account of their genealogical beliefs would make no sense without specifying the various contexts in which those beliefs are invoked.

What is the status of the information contained in the total Ahansal genealogy? Who, and on what occasions, believes and invokes the genealogical connections recorded on it?

Members of effective saintly families can rattle off the list of ancestors between themselves and Sidna Ali, the Prophet's son-in-law, without difficulty and with assurance. Both the matter of being descended from Sidna Ali, which they share with more laicised Ihansalen, and the ability to tell at a moment's notice just how they are descended from him, which distinguishes them from the laicised ones, are sources of pride and prestige. One might suppose that a lay Ahansal, for whom the information concerning his ancestry requires some thought, research, consultation and/or invention, might some time take the necessary trouble and there-after be as proficient as his effectively saintly cousins. But in fact they are not. A skill requires practice for its maintenance, and practice requires occasion and motivation. Who was going to ask a lay tribesman (or a laicised saint for that matter?) to go over his distant ancestry? He often has occasion to be aware of those ancestors who define his group membership, his pasture rights, and, closer by, his co-juring group with marital priority rights; but to know about others would be a case either of pure scholarship, or a demonstrative display of ambition to achieve saintly effectiveness. The first is pointless, the second, presumptious.

Thus the 'memories' of effective saints are the main source for the long lines of names along the genealogies. The saints in question generally know only the line leading from Sidna Ali to themselves, plus the ramifications relevant to their own 'cousins', where both rivalries and shared rights keep the relationships relevant and remembered. Thus saints of the main lodge know their exact relationships to each other, and those of the Temga group are equally familiar with the pattern of the saintly proliferation within that group. Concerning other groups their knowledge is naturally more hazy and schematic; those of Temga know about the general segmentation pattern of the main lodge and are familiar with the chief families and personalities, and can give a kind of minimal account of their kin alignments, and vice versa, but in each case the knowledge of the *other* group will be of an Occamist kind, invoking no more, or not much more, ancestry than is required to explain the present situation. Similarly, their knowledge of the lay groups will go no further than a belief which locates the alleged hiving-off point of that group (and sometimes even this knowledge is lacking); whilst the lay groups' own beliefs include no more than this, plus of course the necessary minimal Occamist beliefs required for the internal segmentation of the villages concerned.

Some of the effective saints aid or insure their 'memories' by possessing written lists of ancestors. Such copies of these lists as I have seen were, as evident from the paper, recently recorded documents (unlike the crucial land-deed of Sidi Lahcen u Othman's, the alleged original of which looked like a genuinely old parchment). These lists are just lists, i.e., they specify one line, the one leading to the possessor of the list, and do not bother about the collateral lines. The only family which possesses a schematic tree which actually records on paper the relationship of the various branches of the Ahansal lineage are the Ait Amhadar of the main lodge, and I believe that this schema was worked out by them in co-operation with a district officer interested in genealogy after the Second World War.

Skill in recounting genealogies is markedly in decline. The skill can be found in its most marked form among the saints of the Temga group who, having been out of power since the French conquest, are least corrupted by the modern world; it is found in a lesser form among the saints of the main lodge, where most of the old siba generation of effective saints died by the early fifties and where the younger generation is far less sure-footed, if still fairly well oriented, among the names of their ancestors. The skill is totally lacking among the young men of the top saintly families in Bernat, who have been operating in a modern context since the 1920s: genealogical inquiries among them soon showed that the anthropologist was much better informed than they are. Among the lay and laicised, the loss has of course been much smaller, if indeed there has been a loss at all: there, genealogical knowledge never went much beyond what was necessary for accounting for the existing social groups, and as these have in no way disintegrated in the Atlas but are still as clearly delineated on the ground as probably they ever were, the genealogical lore associated with them has not declined. Even among lay tribes, there are of course differences in skill. Any chance encounter will produce a man capable of producing a schematic, but socially adequate, genealogical map of the local group. But if one's inquiries become searching, a neighbour or cousin renowned for his skill is produced, who will produce an enriched version of the ramifications of the local tree. The relation of the schematic version to the ramified one is reflected in daily life by the near-classificatory use of the expression *yus n'ami*, son-of-paternal-uncle, by means of which the villager refers to his patrilateral kinsmen on whom he relies, unless he formally re-aligns himself, in case of oath or conflict. The ramified version will show that many a yus n'ami is, in fact, not a 'first' cousin at all.

In speaking of genealogical skill, it is of course necessary to distinguish two things which are essentially rather different: the skill of giving an account of the interrelationships of existing groups, and a skill in giving an account of – and, indeed, possessing – a really impressive long list of ancestors terminating in a prestigious origin.

A crucial matter in interpreting the total genealogy, constructed out of partial pictures, is of course the lacunae, and, above all, the contradictions between those partial pictures. The contradictions found fall into two classes: first, there are some minor ones 'higher up' (i.e., further back in time) in the genealogy. I don't believe these have any particular significance, other than that some people remember better than others, or that when invention took place there was a failure of full co-ordination, whichever of the two may apply. Some people rattle off a slightly shorter list than others, omitting a couple of ancestors here and there, even in their own line, and of course more often in a collateral one.

Secondly there are the 'structural' contradictions in the genealogy, corresponding to or perhaps even really causing the ambiguous and contested status of certain groups. This has been discussed in connection with the Ait Tighanimin and the guardians of the shrine of Sidi Ali u Hussein.

The lacunae, as indicated, occur mainly at the 'joins' of the less distinguished groups, corresponding to vagueness concerning the precise point of their hiving-off.

Distant Ancestors

The 'feel' of the Ahansal genealogy can perhaps best be conveyed by following the line from the Prophet Mohamed to a male child, born to one of the top families in the late 1950s. If, as is the local custom, we begin with Sidna (Our Lord) Ali, the Prophet's son-in-law, thirty-five steps will bring us to the child. Needless to say, locals do not number generations: for clarity of exposition, I do so.

Seven steps take us from Ali to Dris Achater (Idris the Elder: the Berber 'achater', big, old, is equivalent to the Arabic 'kebir'). This would if true mean that the Ihansalen are descended from the founder of the early Muslim dynasty of Morocco, and are part of the 'Idrisid Shurfa' of Morocco. This notion is not in use, or socially relevant, in the region.

It is in generation 18 that we come to Sidi Said Ahansal, descent from whom defines the Ihansalen. The names of the first eighteen generations run as follows: Ali, Ben Ali, Lahcen, Lahcen, Abdallah, Abdallah, Dris, Dris, Mohamed, Abd el Krim, Ahmad, Yussif, Brahim, Majuz, Juz, Amr, Amr, SSA. In each of the cases when there is a father and son of the same name who succeed each other, locals will attach 'achater' or 'kebir' to the name of the elder. This list differs somewhat from the one given to Spillman, which runs: Ali, Hassan Sibt, Hassan el Muthena, Abdallah el Kamel, Dris, Dris, Mohamed, Sliman, Mohamed, Abd el Krim, Yussif, Brahim, Majuz, Juz, Amr, Amr.[1] 'Amr' is the local pronunciation of the name more commonly known as Omar: the customary French transcription is Ameur. The list is interesting for its curious inclusion of Juz and Majuz – Gog and Magog? – who also occur elsewhere in North African genealogies.

But not one of the personages or names figuring on the list plays any part in local life, through shrines, specific lineages, or in any other way. Not surprisingly, the list offered is liable to vary in details. Its significance is simply the display of genealogical wealth and knowledge, and the crucial kin attachment to the Prophet.

SSA is known to have had three brothers, possibly more. In the region, none of them are credited with descendants.[2] Only one has his shrine locally, in the vicinity of the Ahansal settlement of Aganan. Its inhabitants, whose sanctity is extinct, do not claim to be his descendants.

SSA is locally believed to have arrived in the region in 800 AH (1397–8 AD). Three further steps – Ali, Othman, and Lahcen, lead to the crucial Sidi Lahcen u Othman, whose land-deed is the basis of the local territorial settlement.[3] No segmentation takes place

[1] G. Drague, *Esquisse d'une Histoire Religieuse du Maroc*, p. 166.

[2] Drague and Spillman, *op. cit.*, p. 166, reports that one of them, Sidi l'Hajj, is credited with descendants in the Todra region, where he has his shrine. (He is not to be confused with the Sidi l'Hajj who has a shrine in the vicinity of the main lodge.)

[3] *Kitab Aayane al-Maghrib 'l-Akca, Livre des Grands du Maroc,* by Marthe et Edmond Gouvion, (Paul Guethner, Paris, 1939), gives (p. 745) two steps only, Othman and Lahcen as does Spillman. This is certainly a mistake, in the sense of misrecording the local view, rather than recording a variant of the belief. The names prior to SSA are a little shadowy and do not enter daily conversation, and hence may well vary; but the three steps between SSA and Sidi Lahcen u Othman are something very familiar to everyone in Ahansal-land.

The Gouvions' book is somewhat of an oddity. It is a kind of semi-official *Who's Who* of Morocco, research on which was begun in 1923 with the recorded blessing of Lyautey. Its account of the Ihansalen contains various mistakes, but claims to have been written at Asif (river) Ahansal in 1931, two years prior to the conquest of the region. No explanation is offered.

What is interesting is that the book reports as true the Idrisid origins of the Ihansalen, but at the same time does not include them in the preceding section (p. 719) on the Idrisid Shurfa. This seems an elegant solution of a diplomatic problem. In Europe, compilers of *Who's Who* are not obliged to double up as the College of Heralds.

Spillman, who had his variant of the genealogy conformed by Caid Sidi Mha on 12 March 1938, is less polite: '... cette chaine ... n'est evidenment pas serieuse et les lettres qui l'establirent se sont moques de naifs Berbères d'Ahansal'.

between SSA and Sidi Lahcen u Othman, unless we count the hiving-off of the Ait Tighanimin immediately after SSA, the validity of which is denied by all the other Ihansalen. If Sidi Lahcen u Othman's crucial land deed is genuine, then Sidi Lahcen u Othman was alive towards the end of the sixteenth century.

The Middle Belt

From SSA, allegedly arriving in the region of 800 AH, to Sidi Lahcen u Othman, signing his deed in 1006 AH, there are but four generations. Moreover, these early igurramen, if this account were accurate, not merely produced their offspring very late in life, but produced only one surviving son in each generation. In other words, but for the highly contested Ait Tighanimin, this part of the genealogy is still decorative rather than functional, raising the status of the descendants, but not ratifying any group relationships.

Thereafter, on the other hand, the igurramen become prolific. Generations 21 to 25 could be called the middle belt: it charters, in the main, inter-village relationships, and in each generation there is a fair number of brothers. Following the main line, the names are as follows: Lahcen u Othman (21), Ali (22), Said (23), Mohamed (24), and again Ali (25).

Ali (22), was one of five brothers. Not all of them left offspring, though those who did not are, oddly enough, 'remembered'. Two brothers who did leave offspring, however, both raise questions of interest. One was Yussif, who fathered the Ait Amzrai; the other was Mhand who fathered the line which was to found the Hansalia religious order, which survived in Algeria until our time. (Cf. below, p. 275.)

The interesting question raised by Yussif is this: why is he not the symbol of the unity of the village of Amzrai? He is, more or less, the ancestor of the whole village, and of no one else (i.e., of everyone but a few later immigrants, and of no one else except subsequent emigrants from Amzrai, who think of themselves as ex-Amzrai in the general Ahansal context). So, in all segmentary logic (which would be obeyed by the Occamist lay tribes), Yussif should be the symbol of Amzrai. In fact, the immediate, obvious and striking fact about Amzrai is that its centre and symbol is Yussif's father, Sidi Lahcen u Othman. Yussif himself is just a name.

The answer seems to be that this fixation on Sidi Lahcen u Othman (whose name, incidentally, is never abbreviated, unlike the Founder's to whom one may refer to simply as Sidi Said or Dadda Sad), is the one residual trait of sanctity in this otherwise emphatically and proudly laicised village. By stressing their special connection with Sidi Lahcen u Othman – after all, *they* live around his shrine – the Ait Amzrai keep a kind of genealogical hold on all other Ihansalen, who are, all without exception (but for the Ait Tighanimin, who seem particularly disliked in Amzrai) also descended from him: for although Ihansalen are defined by descent from SSA, no multiplication took place before Sidi Lahcen u Othman.

The social implications of the situation are considerable. The Ait Amzrai are physically very close to the main lodge, and not on strikingly good terms with it. They are not physically afraid of its inhabitants, whose alleged cowardice they despise, even assuming that the igurramen would be willing to sin blatantly against their pacifist status: but one cannot but wonder what protected Ait Amzrai against the wrath of lay tribes whom the igurramen could muster at the height of their influence. Sidi Lahcen u Othman's shrine must be part of the answer. An Aggudim-inspired attack on Ait Amzrai would be an attack on an ancestor of the Ait Aggudim themselves: the success of the attack would display, to all those having the wish to interpret it thus, the impotence of an ancestor of the igurramen as a protector, and hence a spiritual failure of the whole line.

Thus whilst the Ait Tighanimin protect themselves from the main lodge by a storehouse on the border, owned by a fairly influential saint located some distance away, whose clients could be activated if this trip-wire were violated, the Ait Amzrai are protected from their more saintly cousins by holding them in check genealogically. They do not control the most crucial ancestor of all, SSA: but they do hold the shrine of locally the second most important one, who is as pivotal genealogically, and thus have a kind of spiritual strangle-hold on the main lodge.

Thus one can see how the criss-crossing of saintly ties and allegiances, clientships and kin-links, complemented the ordinary functioning of the segmentary balance in keeping some peace at least in an ungoverned area. The lay tribes guard each other and obtain arbitration from the saints. Who guards, not the guardians, for there are none, but the arbitrators? In part, the lay tribes themselves (as illustrated by the Dancing War); in part, they themselves somehow weave cross-bonds and trip-wires which ensure that potential aggressors will think twice, by ensuring that the consequences of aggression are likely to have repercussions which cannot be circumscribed, which may be greater than the aggressor can contemplate with equanimity.

It is perhaps significant that the only Aggudim-inspired aggression against a close Ahansal village, which is locally remembered, was directed against some men of Taria, notwithstanding the fact that Taria is 'one' with Aggudim. Taria is not protected against Aggudim by either of the devices available to the other two villages in the group.

The other line going off in generation 22 raises problems of quite a different order, less relevant to the local situation: these will be discussed separately (see p. 275).

In generation 23, Said had four brothers. One of them, Hussein, is credited with having fathered the saints of the Temga/Asker/Sidi Aziz group, the main rivals to the main lodge.

Mohamed, of generation 24, was one of four brothers. One of them fathered a minor lineage still extant in Taria.

Ali, of generation 25, is the first of the ancestors since SSA to be buried at the main lodge: the intervening generations are interred at Amzrai. This again is suggestive: for with his two sons, the internal segmentation of the main lodge begins in earnest. (It is in terms of his two sons that the internal headman-ship of the lodge is rotated.) He also had two brothers: each of them fathered a lineage in Taria.

With this generation, what I have called the genealogical Middle Belt comes to an end. Generations in the middle belt are fairly prolific. They charter in the main inter-village relationships, and also anchor the mountain igurramen to a religious order of the outer world (or the other way around).

Though the middle belt does provide an account of inter-village relations, within the Ahansal system, it has a certain complexity which ensures that on the whole, villages do not possess, genealogically, neat and unique 'apex' figures. On the contrary, the lines of ancestry and village groups intertwine somewhat, in a plait-like pattern. The lineages of Taria hive off at three points and in two distinct generations. The first intra-main-lodge segmentation occurs already in generation 24, though the main bifurcation, in terms of which the inner politics are organised, only occurs at generation 26. An exception to this untidiness are the Ait Amzrai, and they, as stressed, conspicuously refrain from ritual use of their neat apex.

Lineage and Stratification

Generations 26 and 27 are the crucial ones for the internal segmentation of the main lodge. Generation 26 may be called the egalitarian generation: in it, there are two brothers only, Ali and Mhand, who generate the two moieties of the main lodge, between whom the internal headman-ship is rotated symmetrically. In the next generation, 27, there are seven men – the five sons of Ali and the two sons of Mhand. The five include Sidi Mohammed n'ut Baba, who outshone his brothers and cousins and who defines, within the lodge, the line of effective sanctity. This could be called inegalitarian generation.

These two generations chart the internal relationships of the lodge. The first charts the initial steps of the ordinary, non-agurram organisation of the village, as it would be if sanctity became extinct; the second charts the uneven and stratified aspects of lodge life, arising from the concentration of sanctity.

The names of the members of these two generations are fairly alive in the minds of the inhabitants of the lodge; they are essential to its internal workings, and need to be invoked if one man wishes to work out his relationship to another. No Ahansal in the lodge is free-floating genealogically: they all can, at worst with a bit of head-scratching and consultation, work out their relationship. If two men are distant from each other, they need in order to do so work their way back to this stratum of ancestors. In other words, these ancestors differ markedly in their function from the earlier ones, whose role is connected either with glory or, from the village viewpoint, with foreign affairs.

Yet it is in these two generations that one comes, more often than anywhere else, across contradictions or obscurities. It is here that unexplained names intrude. Thus one of the two brothers of generation 26 is known as Sidi Ali n'ait Abdallah Yussif. Who were the Ait Abdallah Yussif? I found no answer to this question. In generation 27, feminine names (Sfia, Nzhma) intrude, credited to co-wives of the previous generation, and help to identify members of this one.

From Sidi Mohamed n'ut Baba, at generation 27, it is of course possible to reach the present generation of top saints along the lines given in earlier diagrams (see pp. 179–181).

In generation 28, there is some further sloughing off of emigrants and laicised lines. At 31, the top family bifurcates. Following the slightly longer of the two lines, we find at generation 33, men who took part as leaders in the political intrigues accompanying the arrival of the French at the main lodge, and at 34, those who did the same at their departure and subsequently. Generation 35 contains the present youngest generation.

Schema

Schema of line running from the Prophet's son-in-law to the present family No. 1 in Zawiya Ahansal. (The locals do not, of course, number generations in this way.)

1 Sidna Ali. Descent from his union with the Prophet's daughter Fatima defines *shurfa*.

7 Dris Achater (i.e., Idris the Elder). Descent from him defines 'Idrisid Shurfa' – but this concept is not in use in the region.

18 Sidi Said Ahansal. Descent from him defines Ihansalen. Is believed to have arrived in the region in 800 AH (1397–8 AD). Had three brothers who are not credited with offspring, but who do have shrines. Only one of these in the region (at Aganan).

19 First segmentation of Ihansalen but only of the Ait Tighanimin, whose descent from Sidi Said Ahansal is denied by other Ihansalen.

21 Sidi Lahcen u Othman. Patron saint of Amzrai, where his shrine is located. Left behind important land deed dated Shawal 1006 AH (May/June 1598).

22 Five brothers – first generally recognised segmentation of Ihansalen – hiving-off of main part of Amzrai. Also of line leading to founder of Hansalia fraternity in the plain and throughout North Africa.

23 Five brothers again. Here hives-off line leading to principal rival group outside main lodge, the Temga-Asker-Sidi Aziz set of lodges.

24 Four brothers. Hiving-off: part of Taria, and first segmentation within main lodge.

25 First in main line to be buried in main lodge, apart from Sidi Said Ahansal himself. (Intermediate generations buried at Amzrai.) Three brothers here – the two 'off' main line provide two of the three ancestors of Taria.

26 Two brothers. Real beginning of intra-main-lodge segmentation. This is the segmentation in terms of which internal main lodge headmanship is 'rotated'. (This is a post of only internal-administrative and not of religious or other great significance.)

27 Two brothers plus five brothers, totalling seven cousins. Sometimes referred to as seven brothers. The differentiation of effective holy lineages from the rest is located in this generation, by a legend about a test imposed by father, a test selecting for uncalculating generosity. Ancestor of effective igurramen – Sidi Mohamed n'ut Baba (though some of his descendants too have since become laicised – and others have emigrated).

28 Two brothers, sons of Sidi Mohamed n'ut Baba. One 'sloughs off', providing ancestor for people who have either become laicised clients of effective saints, or emigrated.

29 A personage without brothers, i.e., no segmentation in this generation. Sometimes he drops out from accounts (a concession even in saintly practice to Occamist principles of genealogy).

30 Ahmad Yellow-beard – on the horizon of living memory.

31 Two brothers. Both leading figures. Time of 'Dancing War', with Temga. One of the brothers, Ahmad u Ahmad, fathered branch which provides saintly migrants to Bernat, and also family No. 2 of main lodge (Ait Amhadar) and No. 3 (Ait Okdim). Ahmad u Ahmad was the most influential figure in the main lodge in 1883 and 1884, when Father de Foucauld twice passed through the region of Ahansal influence without, however, coming close to its centre. The other brother, Mohamed u Ahmad, had one sone son, namely

32 Ahmad u Mohamed, whose three sons included

33 Sidi Mulay, prominent both before and after French conquest in 1933, much revered, died in 1952. He

34 had five sons, one dead without offspring, one (eldest surviving) disinherited and impoverished, and three living together in a joint household. Of these, eldest was chief during the last years of the French, and remains informally the most influential. The youngest became secretary of the rural council elected in 1960. Of all these sons, only the youngest and the disinherited one have offspring:

35 the former has one son, Sidi Mulay; the latter has four sons.

Interpretation of the Genealogy, and Social Change

The manner in which the genealogy serves the current arrangements of its society and the current purposes of its members are obvious, though it is interesting to note the points at which the genealogy curiously fails to ratify or even goes counter to current arrangements. For instance, there is nothing in it to explain the difference in status and function between the main lodge and its neighbouring village, Amzrai.

But apart from the light it throws and the services it performs in current relationships, it also illuminates the past. It would of course be absurd to argue from the genealogy and legends to past conditions directly. But it is not absurd, and indeed it is necessary, to do so indirectly.

The genealogy and the history contained in it tell a story of growth, expansion, dispersal, the survival of power and blessedness in some lines and the elimination of others. This story I believe to be correct in substance, if not necessarily in detail and genealogical reckoning.

What would be the simplest alternative? To suppose that the situation is in principle stable. One could suppose the lodges were always distributed in more or less the way they are now, and that the story of expansion and diffusion and elimination is just a convenient way of expressing their present relationships.

But such an assumption of stability seems to me as strong, and less plausible, than the assumption of change. If we do not know what kind of change could have taken place, the assumption of stability *seems*, or is sometimes taken by anthropologists to be, the least exposed guess. But is it? And when independent evidence exists, the situation is different.

The independent evidence does exist if we compare the various type of lodges and consider the internal situation in each. Here we have a basis of a kind of small scale evolutionary theory – not indeed of societies in general, but of a particular kind of institution in a reasonably stable environment, this last point being an essential pre-condition of any such evolutionary interpretations. Without it, assumptions about the direction of past change are extremely tricky. But if we are granted it, we have ipso facto some knowledge of the factors making for change.

The lodges carry within themselves the seeds of change, unlike the lay tribes where endeavour, disturbance or accident can only produce, as in the child's pattern-producing toy, a new version of the same basic pattern. The lodges are different. Here endeavour and the minor changes do have a cumulative effect which leads to relatively more fundamental changes in pattern.

Lodges must grow. The influx of refugees, the natural growth consequent upon prosperity, the use of clients to buttress saintly prestige, desire to move in under the protective umbrella of the holy descent – all these are to be expected a priori, and all these are also to be found in fact.

Within the lodges, destined to grow if successful as effective centres of sanctity, we can also see the spectrum which we should expect: the dominant and secure holy families; the secure but not dominant; those on the way out and those virtually pushed out of effective status, though their fathers and grandfathers had it; those out, but waiting for an opportunity to re-activate the status; those out and resigned to staying out, or proud of it.

Outside the lodges, there are the segmented tribes. Segmentary tribes are almost infinitely rich in frontiers. There is always a further line of division in any group, until individual males are reached. So, there is a vast number of frontiers, on which holy men about to be pushed out of holiness or desiring to re-activate it could settle. Of course, most of these frontiers, being so to speak a great number of decimal places down, between very small groups, are not very lucrative. A profitable frontier is an as it were non-decimal one, between very large groups. The main lodge is not merely at a crucial frontier, indeed near a number of frontiers – it is at a place destined by ecology to be a frontier, and in a gorge which, if not protected charismatically, would be indefensible. Opportunities for settlement along such frontiers are very likely to arise: the land there is unsafe for settlement for either of the two sides. Holy men are sooner or later invited to settle along it, the place being not much use to anyone else. A frontier guarantor, who is at the same time a kind of bridge for trade, is welcome. Thus saints are pushed both into proliferation and dispersal.

A Segmentary System

The genealogy of the Ihansalen is and is not an example of a segmentary system: it is necessary to separate the respects in which it is, and the respects which are rather special modifications of its own.

It possesses the characteristic tree-like structure, which puts everyone in his place (with some ambiguities, contradictions and lacunae) and accounts for most of the existing relationships.

But the tree-like structure is unsymmetrical. Those branches on which holiness grows are longer.

As in the case of lay tribes, the tree cannot account for those relationships which spring from geographical, territorial considerations, although it is connected with the territorial distribution in interesting ways. Saintliness makes for dispersal. These are diacritical saints. The long branches with saintly fruits tend not to be close to each other. Branches only grow to great genealogical length and produce saintly fruits if no other such branch is near.

Territorial and genealogical distance do not correlate. Ahansal settlements leapfrog lay tribes to reach important frontiers, and the dispersion is not such that further settlements would also be those which hived-off further back, longer ago.

There are two really important ways in which the structure of Ihansalen is not like that of a 'proper' segmentary society:

(a) One cannot simply 'read off' the structural oppositions and alliances of the groups concerned by considering their genealogical relationships, one cannot simply say that those which are closer genealogically are opposed on the local plane, but unite in opposition to a balanced segment at a higher level, and so forth. And the reasons why one cannot do this are more profound ones than merely the co-existence of voluntary or territorially based alignments cutting across kinship. The reasons are that the crucial oppositions are those arising from the conflicts for the wages of sanctity: thus genealogically close effective saints are much more opposed to each other, in a kind of very slow and non-violent 'war of succession', than they are jointly opposed to local laicised groups, who are complementary rather than opposed to them. These lay groups (e.g., the laicised families in the main lodge) again are aligned more as clients of effective saints than in terms of their respective genealogical position. Again, the effective ones together, and the lay ones together, cannot generally oppose each other – this would be an admission of the inefficacy of the saintliness of the would-be effective saints.

Thus the crucial conflicts do not spring from the segmentary position as such and cannot be explained from it, though they leave their mark on it. One can tell that there will be conflict among the fellow-members of the long branches, and between various long branches (as between Temga and the main lodge), and this latter kind of conflict ignores the short intermediate branches.

(b) The Ihansalen as a whole cannot unite and fuse in opposition to non-Ihansalen. They cannot, for a variety of obvious reasons:

their territorial dispersion and discontinuity; the fact that, facing any group of comparable genealogical 'abstractness', they would be hopelessly outnumbered; and their self-image and custom, which preclude violence anyway and which have habituated them to being complementary to the lay tribes rather than ordinarily opposed to them. In brief, it is inconceivable, for all these quite decisive reasons, that all the descendants of Sidi Said Ahansal should unite against all those of Dadda Atta, say, or those of Sochman. (But local clusters of laicised Ihansalen can and do unite against lay tribes of comparable size. But faced with larger ones, they must either strike up alliances with other lay tribes or retire, at that level of segmentary conflict, into agurram-like pacifism.)

Thus the Ihansalen are a group with a segmentary genealogy, whose crucial political alignments, however, are not to be interpreted in its terms, but in terms of the role they play among lay tribes, and in terms of the geographical dispersion which is its consequence; and in terms of the conflict for the fruits of that role, which has its own non-segmentary principles.

A Branchline to History

As stated earlier, generation 22 in the Ahansal genealogy 'leads' to a religious Order, the Hansalia. One of its members fathered a line whose offspring, a few generations later, founded this Order. The existence of this order in Algeria is well documented from French works which antedate considerably any exploration of the Moroccan Atlas.[1] Messrs. Depont and Coppolani, in their book published towards the end of the last century, give remarkably detailed statistics concerning the Order in the departments of Constantine and Oran: the total membership, it appears, was 4,253. (The exact date of this census is not given.)

The holy lineages of the central Atlas, and the lodges of a religious order, based on Eastern Algeria, are in no sense parts of 'one' organisation. The mountaineers of the Atlas do not even know about their Algerian spiritual cousins. The adherents of the Order in Algeria do know that their Founder came from Dades. (Ahansal-land has no name. The upper Dades valley is certainly a part of it. This is another case of the use of the *part* of the territory

[1]Octave Depont and Xavier Coppolani, *Les Confréries Religieuses Musulmanes,* Alger 1897, p. 492. Louis Rinn, *Marabouts et Khouan,* Alger, 1884, p. 386.

to describe the whole, given the fact that the 'whole' is nameless.) Note that the relationship is indeed spiritual and not genetic. The Order believes that its founder was an Ahansal. But after the murder or disappearance of his son, representative of the founding holy lineage, (apparently at the instigation of the then Moroccan ruler and/or the shurfa close to the court), the leadership, care and dissemination of baraka passed into the hands of spiritual, but not physical, descendants.[1]

Nevertheless, there is a significant overlap in legends concerning Said u Yussif, as related in the region on the other hand, and on the other those concerning Said ben Yussif el Hansali, founder of the Order, as recorded among his Algerian followers in the nineteenth century. The distance, separation and lack of contact between the two groups makes the overlap all the more significant. For instance, the Order treasured a mystical poem called Damiati.[2] This work and its magical powers are still referred to at the main lodge, though no one has been able, or willing, to show me a copy. It was claimed to me during my fieldwork that the work had been lent to the people of Zawiya Tidrit, and never returned. This is a plausible Aggudim comment on the resented saintly success of the parvenu Ait Tighanimin of that lodge. In any culture, you ought not to lend books.

Sidi Said u Yussif, the founder of the Order, is in local belief placed, in our count, in generation 26. From Sidi Lahcen u Othman, the author of the land-deed, the line of this saint hives off and has following members: Mhand, Moha, Yussif, Said. A locally retailed legend about his son and successor is given below (p. 291). Drague[3] was evidently given a longer list of ancestors, namely: Mhammed, Said, Mohamed, Mohamed, Yussif, Said.

As stated, the two organisations – an Order in Algeria, a system of lineages in the Moroccan Atlas – are either unaware of or indifferent to each other's existence. They are different in social type: the Algerian organisation was a mystical brotherhood,

[1]Depont and Coppolani, *op. cit.,* p. 493.

Rinn, *op. cit.,* p. 391: 'Un jour, on manda Sidi Youssef [son of the deceased founder of the Order] à la cour . . . sous prétexte de lui rendre honneur; on s'empara de sa personne, et il fut mis à mort . . .' His movement was becoming too influential. It sounds as if this might have been the Ben Barka affaire of its time.

[2]A poem which is claimed to be a version of it is given in M. & Mme. Gouvion's book, p. 749.

[3]*Op cit.,* table VII.

specialising in flagellation. This is conspicuously not true of the people of the main lodge. Nevertheless, there can be no doubt that the Sidi Said u Yussif, of the Atlas lineage branch line, and the Said ben Yussif el Hansali, founder of the Order, are the same person. If he is legendary, then what is at issue is the same legend. The legends of the Order point to a geographical origin which is indeed the area where the Ahansal igurramen flourish, and where stories of the saint of this name abound.

This has both sociological and historical implications. Sociologically, it shows that members of mountain lineages can become founders of genuine religious orders. Even if the story is legendary, it shows that a genuine Order can think of its point of origin in this way. In other words, saints of North Africa originate, or are conceived as originating, not merely from learned men who go out to the tribes as missionaries, but also as tribal holy men who come to gain converts outside their home ground and in quite a different milieu. This double movement is inherently plausible anyway: the Ahansal situation confirms it. The Founder of the line, SSA, was according to his legend a missionary proper; his descendant Said u Yussif exemplified an inverse spiritual brain-drain.

Historically, the beliefs collected and recorded quite independently in Eastern Algeria in the nineteenth century provides us with some evidence about the real historic depth of the Ahansal lineage. The crucial part of this legend is the dating of Sidi Said u Yussif's death as 1114 AH (1702 AD). The legends go on to allude to the participation by his son in the dynastic succession troubles in Morocco at the times of the death of the Sultan Mulay Smail (1727 AD), and allude to the elimination and presumed murder of the representative of this holy line, at the instigation of the central power. M. & Mme. Gouvion[1] give an exceptionally precise date of the death of the father (21 November 1702) but, diplomatic as ever, do not allude to the suspected political murder of the son, by an ancestor of the present ruling house.

The various North African chroniclers and French authors who relate these events and date them so precisely do not, of course, constitute witnesses who are necessarily independent of each other. Nevertheless, it is important that external legends, collected partly in areas long-separated from what is now Ahansal-land, refer to important Ahansal holy lineages in the region, and presuppose that

[1] *Op cit.*, p. 748.

they are active and well-established by the end of the seventeenth century. If the legends were invented later, it is hard to see why their heroes should be credited with a geographical location which, in fact, corresponds to local belief independently preserved. The region of Constantine in Eastern Algeria is too far from central Morocco to make it plausible that anyone in Constantine should try to raise his prestige by attachment to a lineage drawn from the Central Moroccan Atlas. If on the other hand the legends were invented early, they prove virtually as much as if they were shown to be true: namely, that the central Atlas was credited, already at an early date, with influential *Ahansal* holy lineages. The dating of these external legends tallies well with the date on the crucial land-deed. If we accept both, tentatively, and ignore the earlier Ahansal stories in view of their lack of corroboration, we shall conclude that Ahansal saints were well established at any rate in the seventeenth century. Their record of stability thus compares favourably with most European dynasties.

So we possess at least some, admittedly less than fully conclusive, external corroboration for what is suggested by an 'internal' study of the saintly system: namely, that it was remarkably stable. This cannot be firmly established, given the lack of records. But everything about the saintly system suggests that, in general principle, it had functioned for a long time roughly in the same way it did when the modern world first revealed and then disrupted it. Individual lodges grow, expand, undergo fission or extinction of sanctity, but the system of lodges as a whole is fairly stable. No other crystallisation of power seem to have occurred in the central Atlas; had it occurred, it would surely have left some mark. The saints themselves, though credited with great authority, evidently did not attempt to establish more that their saintly quasi-state. The saint/tribe balance seems to have survived for three centuries at least.

CHAPTER TEN

OTHER FORMS OF THE SACRED

Classification

Even within their immediate region, the igurramen do not exhaust the forms of the sacred. They are merely the most important form of it.

There is a variety of other forms, classifiable as follows:

   (a) The meta-saints, the progeny of the Founder's Teacher.
   (b) Shrines of non-Ahansal saints who have left no progeny.
   (c) Un-personified holy places (cliffs, trees, springs, caves).
   (d) Mosques and *foquaha* (the Uses of Literacy).

The Meta-Saints

Sidi Bu Mohamed Salah was the teacher of the Founder in holy learning, sanctity and magic. It was he who sent Sidi Said Ahansal to found his own lodge. This is a fact stressed by local legends. It is a way of making concrete the original 'missionary' aspect of the role of the lodges.

The local tribes give donations to the saints in virtue of, ideally, their ancestry and the powers. But the ancestor of the saints had learnt his trade from Sidi Bu Mohamed Salah,[1] whose ancestry is also distinguished. If the lay tribes are morally indebted to the saints, by the same token are not the saints indebted to the teacher of their ancestor? And if the teacher has left any progeny, should they not, by the same token, present donations to them?

Such progeny (or rather, men who hold themselves to be such) does exist, and the saints do give them donations. In fact there are

---

[1] A historical figure, who lived 1150–1234. These dates are given in Drague's book. Local legends cite no date for him.

a few families living in various places in the plain, including at present Beni Mellal (the nearest market town at the edge of the plain), who claim such ancestry, have the claim recognised and derive some profit from it. Annually, individuals come up and are entertained and are given presents by the saints, including those of the main lodge, in virtue of their descent from the Founder's Teacher.

These men are of no visible political or other significance, either in their homes, or in the places which they visit. The donations received by the local saints themselves can be explained structurally: but this is not so for these second-order donations by the saints to their saint in turn.

In 1955 the annual visit of a descendant of the meta-saint did not take place, owing to the general restriction on movement in and out of the region due to the political crisis and 'terrorism' culminating in the great massacres – both ways – of Oued Zem. Subsequently there were violent floods around the main lodge which at the time caused great damage. People in the main lodge, including the chief saint of the chief family, attributed this disaster to the failure to give the appropriate donations to the meta-saint, although the failure was not their fault, but was due to his failing to arrive. The damage caused by the floods was the destruction of bridges, carrying away of cattle and the destruction of fields adjoining the river. Later on however the harvest turned out to be extremely good, compensating for what was lost in the fields adjoining the river. Moreover it was agreed that the mud brought down by the floods was good for the fields. What had seemed to be a divine sanction turned out to be a blessing. The failure to make donations to the descendant of the meta-saint was then forgotten.

The general principle underlying the giving of donations might be schematically summed up as follows: donations are not on the whole called for amongst kin, where aid in assistance can be taken for granted. (There are important exceptions: emigrant saints for instance sometimes bring donations to those who remained at the 'home shrine'.) Where an obligation and/or affiliation exists between people of groups who are not kin, donations are called for by the inferior to the superior (although of course the superior is also liable to exhibit superiority by generous entertainment). Thus the lay tribes give donations to the saints, and the saints to their saint, the meta-saint. Similarly, a person joining a new group gives the donation to them, thereby putting them under an obligation to accept him (though this kind of donation, unlike that to saints, is once-and-for-all, and is not repeated annually).

In this way, a kind of chain is created: A reveres and brings donations to B, and likewise, B to C. The chain here described has only three links, but there is no reason why it should not have more, and one could find more if one tried. (Some among the religious clients of the Ihansalen themselves receive reverence and donations, and doubtless the progeny of Sidi Bu Mohamed Salah themselves occasionally make a pious pilgrimage to some meta-meta-saint.) But this is not politically significant, for reverence is not transitive: A's reverence for B, and B's for C, does not necessarily commit A to any reverence for C. There is no pyramid of power or dependence built up in this manner. The fragmented worship of saints is indeed a specimen of the 'catholic' syndrome of religious life: but although the various cults are linked to each other in this way, they do not come to fuse into one grand unified system. They remain, each of them, marginal.

It is also said by Drague[1] that the Ahansal saints were affiliated to the Derkawa religious fraternity. In fact, there are many cairns dedicated to Mulay Abdel Kader. These cairns are places where it is claimed that he sat down on his travels. His name is invoked in expletives. Locals who have rosaries, the specific emblem of fraternities, will generally say it is a *Kadiri* rosary. On other occasions the rosary has been attributed to Sidi Said Ahansal or to Sidi Bu Mohamed Salah. (In Morocco, rosaries, *werd*, are emblems of religious fraternities.)

As described, an offshoot of the Ihansalen did found a fraternity of his own, the Hansaliya. This would have to be studied separately. My own efforts in this direction, undertaken unpropitiously in the middle of the Algerian war, proved, not surprisingly, abortive. It is of interest for the comparative study of maghrebin religious life, but of no importance for the social and religious life of the Ahansal heartland, where its existence is hardly suspected and makes no impact, although legends about the *founder* of the fraternity and his son are told.

Some saints of the Temga group do claim to be agents, or to have been agents, of the Kadiri fraternity and to have collected donations for it. This would be a not unusual relationship of rural popu-

[1] *Op. cit.*, p. 175.

lations to these diffused fraternities. But whereas I have come across wandering descendants of the meta-saint, I have never come across wandering agents of the fraternity. This does not exclude their having wandered locally in the past. During the last years of French rule there were few people coming up wandering from the plain, of any kind, and the period after Independence was one unfavourable to fraternities, so that it is unlikely that anyone should have gone out of his way to proclaim himself such. Moreover, claims of affiliations to it were made more convincingly in the area of the Temga set of lodges rather than around the main lodge, and they are far more likely to have been true in that group, with its closer proximity to the plain, than in the area of the founding lodge.

It is not wholly clear what political function, if any, affiliations to either meta-saints or fraternities[1] based on the plains could have in the old pre-pacification set-up. It is true that in the modern post-Independence period local persons of influence need and have patrons in the plain (obtained mainly through and for either a political party or trade) – but then, the situation is different now; the region is incorporated in the wider society and the local dignitary, saint or not, needs a friend at court. In the days of siba this was not so. One can surmise that it was in part a way of obtaining information and contacts (possibly for mediating trade), and in part of augmenting local standing by possession of such distant and prestigious links. It is hardly sufficient to suppose that the institution was simply called into being because it was a logical corollary of a local legend and a logical extension of a local custom.

The Seven Saints

In the heartland of the Ihansalen, in the region of the four villages, there are seven saints who are grouped together, generally mentioned together and indeed connected by the legend of their origin. One holy place, in the vicinity of Amzrai, is also simply referred to as *sbaat-urizhel*, seven-men. The others have proper names of their own. The legend is that they jointly flew from the summit of Timghazin, the mountain which finally closes the Ahansal valley in the direction of the watershed, and each landed on his appointed place lower down. No motive is ascribed to the flight.

[1]Spillman suggests that this was important. Cf. Drague, *Esquisse d'Histoire Religieuse du Maroc*, p. 175.

Of the seven, one is near Taria – Sidi l'Hajj, the pilgrim; Sidi Bu Yaacub and Sidi Bu Tumlalen at Amzrai; Sidi Bushaq and Sidi Maruin near the main lodge; and Sidi Abd el Aadim and Sidi u'Basus at Tighanimin.

These personified saints can be used for prayers and requests, for village festivals, and for collective oaths. They are, in fact, used extensively in this way by the four villages. Spring and autumn festivals are held more frequently at these shrines than at ancestral ones. The point is, that ancestral ones are more generally used for relations with outside tribes. (The Ait Amzrai do more frequently use their own favoured ancestor's shrine, that of Sidi Lahcen u Othman.) Just as, ecologically, the Ahansal villages are simply ordinary villages with flocks and fields in addition to being groups of actual or potential saints, so hagiologically, they also possess all the shrines which they would possess if they weren't saintly centres. Underneath the successful bid for sanctity, there is an ordinary Berber village hoping it need not emerge.

No particular legends attach to the seven saints, but it is said that they antedate the local settlement of Sidi Said Ahansal. It is my impression that they do indeed antedate the effective development of Ahansal settlement, but in any case the belief reflects this, that they represent a more basic, widespread form of worship, the undifferentiated form of village religious life which these villagers share with others and to which they can revert if their grace dries out and special claims are abandoned.

The preference for using them for internal purposes, festivals and such, springs naturally from the fact that in the face of these shrines all members of the village are equal. Even though the overwhelming majority of the inhabitants of the main lodge could claim to be equal at the shrine of Sidi Said Ahansal, as his descendants, yet somehow Sidi Said Ahansal is specially linked with the effective igurramen, if only because his shrine now also includes some recent saints who of course are the ancestors only of a small part of the main lodge. This is not so with the non-Ahansal saints.

The Ait Tighanimin sometimes use Sidi Bushaq for their festival despite the fact that they have two of the seven saints near home, whilst they have to come and hold their feast right by the main lodge by choosing him. By doing so however they can combine it with a use of Sidi Said Ahansal's shrine itself: whilst the men play games and roast meat by Sidi Bushaq, the women prepare sksu and dance by Sidi Said Ahansal, having previously spent some time inside the shrine, requesting good health and pregnancies.

The Impersonal Saints

The seven personal saints – plus the one named 'seven men' (which is held to refer to the others) – are, as was described, barely personal. No clear image or stories attach to them. They have buildings, varying from shacks to small houses, attached to their name but they are never distinguished dwellings. In their anonymity they differ clearly from the Ahansal shrines, whose inmates, as it were, are connected with the world both by a fairly rich store of legend, and of course, by their living descendants.

There is a kind of spectrum,[1] or perhaps a number of spectra, starting at one end from the fully personal and ancestral saints such as Sidi Said Ahansal. One spectrum connects the distinguished and the undistinguished dead: both share a cemetery, but the one has a building and retains a name, whilst the other has a grave which does not rise much above the level of the surrounding soil and cannot but lapse into total anonymity after some time. Another and more important spectrum however ranges not so much along the level of distinction as along the degree of personification.

The spectrum begins with fully personified saints such as Sidi Said Ahansal, endowed with both name and character, and ends with what is almost undisguised nature worship, of holy springs or trees, whose worship is justified – if at all – by beliefs about the presence of unnamed spirits in it or near it. At intermediate positions along it one finds named but characterless saints (such as the Seven) or places held holy in virtue of a tenuous connection with a person.

The purer forms of Islam are opposed to the worship of saints. The Berbers of the Atlas are not closely acquainted with such high standards as the rejection of graven images or intermediaries between God and man: they are, however, aware of another, less rigorous standard, one which condemns unpersonified saints and sees proper Islam in the worship of personages connected with it, preferably shurfa. (Both Sidi Said Ahansal and Sidi Bu Mohamed Salah are such, and hence, by what one might call genealogical

---

[1]Cf. Jacques Berque, *Les Structures Sociales du Haut-Atlas*, p. 256.

induction, so are all their offspring – who between them amount virtually to the totality of live saints locally worshipped or revered.) Thus there is a tendency to use the impersonal shrines less, or with some shame, if other things fail: a given spring held to be well-connected with rain may not be used for a ritual sacrifice if rain is plentiful, but will still be used if there is a drought and proper appeals have failed.

Berque, in the work cited, gives a statistical break-up of per-sonified and other saints and holy places among the Seksawa.[1] I am somewhat reluctant to do the same in as far as at one end of the spectrum, among the impersonal holy places, it is almost impos-sible to feel that one has covered the total of available local holiness. The more impersonal and undistinguished the type of holy place, the less likely one is to have one's attention drawn to it, unless one happens to pass in the vicinity. But the general picture would be similar to Berque's: a few fully personalised saints, more semi-personal ones, and still more wholly impersonal ones.

An interesting kind of holy place, very common, is one connected with a personage who is not really supposed to be enshrined in it. In the area around Ahansal, there are numerous ones of Mulay Abd el Kader. This distinguished saint is not supposed to be interred in these places – generally a simple cairn – and in any case his body could hardly be found in *all* of them: if an explanation is sought, it is said, without insistence or any elaboration by way of legend, that he is presumed to have passed through the region and to have sat and rested and thus hallowed the place now named after him. These places too are eligible for the making of prayer-requests, oaths, and so forth.

There are (at least) three holy mountains in the area close to (within a day's walk) of the main lodge: Azurki, Aruden, and one in the land of the Ait Abdi. The most interesting justification of holiness is that in the case of Azurki (to be discussed below, p. 289). The holy place on Aruden is personified only by a vague and plural name, Aitrudent, the people of Aruden. (Spirits congregate.) Holy springs, trees, caves, passes abound. In 1955, a holy tree among the Abdi, which its devotees had made quite shiny with the butter they rubbed into its trunk, was burnt down by a brother of the chief – secretly – in order to demonstrate its impotence. This

---

[1]Jacques Berque, *Les Structures Sociales du Haut-Atlas*, p. 260.

was a progressive act by people secretly inscribed and active in the Independence party. The tacit premise was the connection between purer Islam and nationalism. In fact, after Independence the new authorities did not bother to combat local cults.

Berbers are liable to class their mosques with the saints in as far as they believe the Archangel Gabriel (Sidna Jibril) to be resident in them.

Mosques and foquaha. The Uses of Literacy

Mosques are said to be the home of the Archangel Gabriel; but otherwise they are also, sometimes, more literally, the home of the *fquih* (pl. *foquaha*), the village scribe. (If he does not have a family, or does not have it with him, he may sleep in the mosque.)

The term fquih (or talb, teacher) generally designates the village scribe/Koranic teacher, but it can be used to designate simply a man who is literate (in the traditional and Arabic-Koranic sense, of course); and some foquaha earn their living not as scribes to villages but as secretaries to men of note.

Mosques, or the area just outside them, often with a shelter, are also the centres of the male social life of a village, and though not used for festivals they do resemble shrines in being usuable for oaths. They and the scribe who runs a rudimentary Koranic school in it – the syllabus of which goes no further than the teaching of some of the set Muslim prayers and some Koranic sayings – are, however, the one piece of local religious life which does more genuinely derive from Islam proper.

The scribe is an employee of the village. He is very seldom local. In the area around Ahansal, foquaha are almost invariably men from south of the watershed, generally the Dades and Draa valleys. The fquih is on an annual contract and is paid by arrangement by a levy on households. His perks are invitations to weddings, collective festivals, or pious parties sometimes given by individual families.

If the igurramen are a religious institution which seems to emanate from the local social structure, then foquaha are one which does not, and which is the tribal concession to real Islam. Foquaha are non-local in origin, generally have no local kin affiliation and are in a very weak position. They often quarrel with their parishioners and are often sacked. It is not much of a commendation for them to be too learned or ambitious. Turnover is fairly rapid. In my years of visits to Ahansal-land, I have often come across the same scribes on successive visits, but not in the same village. (In the main lodge, there is a scribe who is, for once, well dug in, and has the sister of the head of the Ait Sidi Mulay family in marriage. I was told that, contrary to local custom but correctly by Muslim law, she claimed her inheritance and obtained it. This fquih was secretary to his brother-in-law during his days of power under the French: subsequently, after Independence, the brother-in-law lost his position and did not need such a secretary and the village scribe was sacked in order to vacate the post for him. Later still, when this well-connected fquih managed to find a post with the administration, a new scribe was found once again for the village.)

Apart from teaching in the Koranic school, the foquaha write and read letters, and deeds. Unlike the Western High Atlas and Southern Morocco proper (the Sus region), the use of writing for family records, or *kanun* (codes) was not very extensive or absent altogether. But writing is in sufficiently general use to enable the foquaha to make some additional income by producing false land deeds, and during the French period, convictions of foquaha for this did occur.

The foquaha are also technologists of magic; knowing how to write, it is widely held that they can effect cures, invoke the devil (by, for example, reciting Koranic passages whilst retreating, or writing them backwards), and some do make extra income by these means.

Summary

It is natural to view 'the Sacred' in Ahansal-land as composed of a number of layers: the sanctity concentrated in live and dead igurramen and their connecting lineages and their very specific social role; the lineage-less and anonymous, but named and personal saints, with their different social role, one which is rather standard in kind from village to village (unlike the saintly lineages, whose role is connected with more long-distance relationships and is thus unsymmetrical as between holy, laicised and lay villages); the mosques, tied partly to village assemblies, partly to the universalistic religion of Islam and the wide Muslim world, and partly to the individual's identification with it in addition to his local niche; the shrines which are not tombs, such as those dedicated to Mulay abd el Kader, tied to something more-than-regional; the impersonal holy places, sometimes endowed with a Muslim rationale and often not, playing a part both in village and inter-village, tribal and inter-tribal relationships.

The temptation to speculate about the disparate historic origin of these strata is reinforced by the fact that they are not welded into a fully coherent whole: their 'joins' do show up. No explanation is given why the saints, the Prophet's flesh and blood, should need foquaha to teach them the Prophet's Koran. Not all the local holy places or named but progeny-less shrines are connected with the cult of the igurramen; and this is not merely a consequence of a failure to think up a suitable synthesising rationalisation, but is also functional. These holy places serve the ordinary village hidden, as it were, inside the saintly one.

CHAPTER ELEVEN

THE RELIGIOUS ROLE

I *Some Legends*

(a) *The Cloak of Islam*

As stated one of the holy places in the area of Ahansal is the mountain of Azurki. Specifically, a large hole near the summit, and a cave much lower down, are holy and the focus of a pilgrimage on the eve of Aid el Kebir (in other words a festival tied to the Muslim and not to the agricultural calendar). As at other holy places, women leave bits of cloth there in the hope of obtaining their requests. On the appropriate night, spirits congregate here in a kind of *Brockennacht*.

The really significant thing about Azurki is, however, the legend explaining its holiness.

Azurki was, it appears, destined to be the burial place of the Prophet Mohamed. The cave near the summit was to be his grave. The camel carrying the body already arrived, but was thoroughly frightened off by the noise habitually made by the inhabitants of Bu Gmez valley (at the foot of one side of Azurki) in order to frighten birds off their fields. So the camel returned to the Hejaz, and thus, unfortunately, the Muslim pilgrimage has to be made to Mecca:[1] otherwise, it would have been to Azurki, much to the convenience of those living around it.

The pilgrimage to Azurki, which involves spending a night on the mountain, is much favoured, and the pilgrims go either to the summit or to a very striking cave lower down, and come from a wide range of surrounding tribes. When I went, the party included a representative of the top main lodge family (who,

[1] The locals suppose that the pilgrimage is based on the location of the tomb of the Prophet, as local pilgrimages are to the shrines of the saints.

impiously, spent the night on the bare mountain smoking *kif*),
women desiring pregnancy, and brothers of such who come on
their behalf.

(b) *Saintly Learning, the Mission and Territorial Settlement*

SSA was originally called Ahsal. Two different folk etymologies
exist for this name. One relates it to learning (he learnt the Koran
by heart very quickly), the other to saving (he saved half his ration
of food for the morrow). These two meanings of course immediately
suggest two themes prominent in the image of SSA and his
progeny: legitimation by saintly learning, and by prosperity.

SSA was a pupil apprentice with Sidi Bu Mohamed Salah,
patron saint of Safi on the Atlantic coast, who died in AD 1234.[1]
One feast day (Aid l'Kebir), the Teacher announces, that he will
make a sacrifice of all his seven students. In fact, he has seven
sheep ready, as well as seven students. He calls his pupils into his
chamber one by one, but then cuts the throat of a sheep: the
remaining students outside, seeing the blood flowing, suppose that
their fellows had been sacrificed, and that a similar fate awaits
them. SSA is the third in line, but he enters the Teacher's chamber
unhesitatingly when called – though his successors flee in terror.
The Teacher sacrifices the sheep, and proceeds to have it roasted
in preparation for the feast.

The Teacher then orders SSA to enter the oven. SSA does so,
with his learning tablet. He is then seen in the flames, studying!

After the feast, the Teacher tells him – 'Plainly, you have
enough baraka now, you must go and found your own centre'. He
gives him a donkey, a cat, and a sickle, and instructs him to found
his lodge at the point at which the cat jumps off the donkey.

SSA sets off on his travels, passes through Marrakesh, and
finally reaches a place near Amzrai, now known as igherm n'mosh,
house of the cat, where the cat jumps off the donkey's back. SSA
settles here. He is at first treated with scorn by the proto-inhabitants, but he impresses them with magical signs, such as the
appearance of a flame in a cave to which they had ironically
referred him for hospitality, and with his ability to rise instan-
taneously with his donkey to the summit of their building, when at
last they invite him to a meal.

[1] This date is cited in Drague, *Esquisse d'Histoire Religieuse du Maroc,* p. 164,
but no corresponding date is given locally as part of the legend.

So he settles among them, but there is friction between them and the saint, notably when their animals spoil his gardens and fields. He is obliged to call in a lion who kills many of their beasts, and it is only then that they beg his forgiveness.

The friction over land leads him to call Dadda Atta, ancestor of the Ait Atta, by telepathic means. He needs to call 7 years 7 months 7 days and 7 hours. When at last Ait Atta and his retinue arrive, the river is in spate, and the Ait Atta are obliged to wait three weeks. Then SSA with a wand causes the river to open, and the Ait Atta cross it, with dry feet!

When they complain of having had to wait, he points out to them how long he had had to wait for them. But he makes it up to them. Jointly they drive out the proto-inhabitants (Ait Uzru and Ait Waster), and he assures the Ait Atta that they may bring their flocks to his land – but they are entitled to the grass only, for the land is not theirs.

(c) *Problems of Leaders of Dissidence*

This is a story told of Sidi Yussif u Said, son of founder of the Hansalia fraternity of the plain. The story is more relevant to the northern (Temga) group of lodges, who make an annual pilgrimage to the shrine of this saint, but it is also known in the main lodge.

His father (Sidi Said u Yussif) and predecessor in sanctity had warned him: if anyone comes to your lodge and places his foot on a certain rock (which he pointed out), refuse his request, whatever it be!

After the father had died and Sidi Yussif u Said was running the zawiya, one day a man called Ahrmud turned up. Ahrmud was a tribal leader of the Ait Attab tribe on the edge of the plain, and was at the time having trouble with the Sultan. Ahrmud requested the agurram to raise the tribes in his support, to organise a *harkt* (military following) – and as he asks this, he places his foot on *the* rock!

Naturally, Sidi Yussif u Said refuses. So Ahrmud places a shame compulsion on him by making a sacrifice to him. This would normally be conclusive, but under the circumstances, much as it may go against the grain to refuse a man now, Sidi Yussif is firm.

So Ahrmud threatens to sacrifice his own son unless the agurram complies with his pleading. So Sidi Yussif gives in.

He supplies Ahrmud with seven horsemen. A mere seven!

exclaims Ahrmud. This plainly is insufficient. Sidi Yussif reassures him and urges him to have faith. When you get near Fez, look to the heavens! – and continue. But, the saint adds, there is one condition: when you conquer Fez there must be *no* massacre!

Ahrmud sets off to Fez with his own supporters plus the seven supplied by the saint. Approaching Fez, he looks to the heavens as instructed, and lo! further horsemen come down like snowflakes, and as numerous. They conquer Fez, but, alas, contrary to the instruction, they *do* massacre.

The saint also turns up at Fez. He comes to discuss with a local learned and saintly man who, in order to save Fez from the savage tribes brought in by the agurram, deprives the saint of his magic sword. This Fassi learned man manages this by possessing even more baraka than the agurram.

In the meantime, the victors have quarrelled: the saint and the tribal leader are at loggerheads. They turn on each other, and the saint, being now without his magic sword, is defeated. He has to flee and is pursued by Ahrmud's men, who burn down his zawiya. All the utensils in his lodge had been of gold, but happily the saint had time to bury them before his enemies arrived. After their departure the saint emerged from hiding and went to settle at Krud near Demnate[1] where his descendants still live.

About 1900 three foquaha tried to find the gold buried by Sidi Yussif u Said. But the treasure is protected by spirits, and the three foquaha were blown into the air by them. Two were never seen again, and the one who lived to tell the tale was found on a distant pass, badly mauled and, for some reason, with a woman's kerchief. (This he sold for a very good price.) He was interrogated by the informant's father about the adventure.

I was told this story a number of times, but the most detailed and confident version came from a prominent member of Zawiya Asker, since deceased. This informant himself claimed to have visited the emplacement of Sidi Yussif u Said's original lodge and to have seen imprints of money on rock in red and yellow. These have, it appears, disappeared since.

The son of the saint (of Sidi Yussif u Said) named Abd el Aziz, also had trouble with the Sultan, who attacked his new lodge at Krud. He went to hide in a cave. The sultan had a cannon fired at

[1]A little outside the present area of the main body of Ahansal settlement.

him. The saint caught the projectile, which did not explode, and kneaded it in his hands as though it were dough. It is still kept as a souvenir at Krud. (So the people in the northern lodges say: only recently someone who had visited Krud had seen it and told them). The Sultan, seeing this and impressed by such potent baraka, took the hint and left them alone.

(d) *The King-Maker Story*

This story is popular in the region of the main lodge. Its hero is Sidi Mohamed n'ut Baba, the ancestor of the effective-saint lineage within the lodge.

The Sultan sent a messenger to the Ahansal agurram of that generation (namely, Sidi Mohamed n'ut Baba) wishing for more information concerning how he managed to have quite so much baraka. The agurram amazed the messenger by a special display of saintly powers, by making a mule give birth to a young mule. (An implausible parturition reinforces the faith of the faithful.) But in return he requested the Sultan, Mulay Rashid, to liberate some Ait Atta whom he had imprisoned. The Sultan refused. The incensed agurram decided to 'break' the monarchy by magical means: he hammered a magical *tagust* into the ground. A tagust is a metal peg used for attaching mules and other animals.[1] This not merely led to the end of Mulay Rashid, but caused an anarchic interregnum in the governed part of Morocco, in Fez.

Mulay Ismail, the next Sultan-to-be, failing to overcome the troubles and frondes, came to the agurram for advice. (There were many other claimants, and he could not overcome them.)

He stayed at the main lodge a few days, presenting his case. In the end, the agurram told him: you must go to Amzrai, and must ask the first person you encounter for food.

Mulay Ismail followed the irrigation ditch in Amzrai and encountered a woman of the Ait Amzrai surveying a cow. The woman says 'welcome!'

After a while she asks – may a person owning one cow, one chicken and one measure of wheat entertain a King? She proceeds to use eggs, butter, and one half of her store of flour. Whilst she

---

[1] The *tagust* is extremely phallic in appearance and function, and the term also means 'penis'. The Freudian suggestiveness of the whole of this legend is striking. It is as neat an example of a 'Waste Land' story, of national well-being depending on regal virility, as any.

mills down the flour, she unwittingly uses more than the half she intended but her original store remains undiminished!

She gives Mulay Ismail to eat and prepares a place for him to sleep. A child comes to tell her, 'I have slept better than a King!' (in a manner of speaking). The woman chides him – 'Think not of becoming King!' (i.e., excessive ambition is harmful). The King embraces her in recognition and gratitude. She proceeds to grind more flour, singing 'Mulay Rashid is dead, Mulay Ismail survives and will be King, if God wills'. Whereupon the would-be and incognito King embraces her gratefully again.

Thereupon she instructs him: 'You must take three steps without looking.' He does so: the first takes him to Ouaouizaght, the second to Tizi (pass) n'ait Aissa, the third to Tizi n'ait Amir. On the third step he finds himself placing his foot in the middle of a cairn. He removes the stones and finds a tagust underneath (as pre-arranged by Sidi Mohamed n'ut Baba). He liberates it by pulling it out, and with it makes the fourth step – to find himself in Fez and acclaimed by the populace as King!

(e) *The Enemies' Tale*

This story is never told by the Ihansalen themselves. It was told me by an enemy of theirs, a certain fquih. This scribe had been in the employment of a number of them, as a secretary. Able and intelligent, he was not, like other foquaha, content with his position, and attempted to intrigue against the igurramen – quite unsuccessfully. He now makes a fairly good living as a free-lance scribe – largely as a technologist of magic – among the Ait Isha.

He claims to have been told this story by the Ait Tegla, who could be expected to be enemies of the Ihansalen, being the recognised original inhabitants of the Ahansal valley (or rather, the only ones of the original inhabitants who do not seem mythical). They are somewhat outside the general area of the Ahansal lodges now and I have never visited them, and hence cannot say whether this story is current among them and whether they still harbour a resentment, and whether there exists some kind of Tegla revisionist movement for the return to Ahansal-land.

The story: a man of the Ait Tegla went to the main lodge. He was nine-times-a-Hajj, i.e., had performed the pilgrimage to Mecca nine times. (The point is: a man of such piety must be wholly trustworthy in his report.)

He saw the then top agurram, Sidi Ahmad u Ahmad, saintly, prosperous, well-attired, and felt due reverence. He did not dare approach anyone in the lodge in which such saintliness was evident, so he modestly went to the mosque to take shelter.

He was unnoticed: the igurramen who had failed to notice a humble and modest pilgrim thereby did themselves harm, for they were not aware of his presence in their mosque.

At night, the top agurram went to the mosque. Now he was *ill*-dressed, in torn clothes. He pissed three times into the water prepared for the ablutions of the faithful – thus invoking the devil. The devil turned up, and Sidi Ahmad u Ahmad paid his homage to him – thus disclosing his true nature, unaware of the presence of the witness!

Interpretation

I have selected these legends for the significance of their implicit comment; but all of them except the last are prominent in local minds, and would be the first to require mention even if one were selecting purely by popularity as stories, rather than for revealing the nature of their content.

The legend of Azurki, with its associated annual ritual, eloquently testifies to the fusion of local particularism and Islam. We are Muslim and Prophet-oriented, yet properly Islam should have been centred on our local mountain. The story of Sidi Said Ahansal's scholarly prowess, and the whole story of the origin of the main lodge in Muslim missionary work, testifies to one aspect of the role of the Ihansalen, as aids to Muslim identification (whilst also functioning as parts of a highly local structure).

The legends of the raid on Fez deals with the issues likely to arise for an influential agurram whose clients are on the borders of the land of government: coping with requests to organise raids into the plain, or rather, activate a following for them (and the legend contains a caution against conceding such requests, and a precedent and reason for refusing); the probability that petitioners will be disappointed by the meagre number of supporters (a mere seven in the story) which an agurram can call up rapidly – *and* the legend contains an answer to this, that when an agurram-led movement gets going, the following of the igurramen snowballs and becomes plentiful – which is no doubt true. It alludes to the danger of allowing the tribesmen united under their aegis to massacre when victorious (thereby provoking reprisals); the persisting threat to saints both from lay chiefs who acquire prestige, like the evil and ungrateful Ahrmud after his victory, and from the central power with, latterly, its cannons. Also, the recurring theme that effective igurramen are not merely potent magicians but also conspicuously rich.

The King-maker story illustrates both the real and the desired relationship of the saints in the recesses of the Atlas vis-à-vis the central monarchy: it begins with the plausible episode of the central power imprisoning some members of the saints' client tribes, and to the existence of anarchic and violent interregna in the plain: it fuses this with episodes bringing out the superior baraka of the saints (the fecund mule, the power to make kings and to terminate chaos; I shall not insist on the 'Waste Land' interpretation which would give the igurramen control over national prosperity through the virility of the monarch). It also contains a virtue-of-necessity commendation of abstention from political ambition – in fact, these igurramen had no opportunity of replacing the dynasty, but it is made to appear that modesty, a condemnation of excessive ambition, stopped them from trying; and it also contains two themes frequently encountered, namely the need to be hospitable to wandering strangers who turn out to be people of distinction in disguise (in this case, a Sultan), and the theme commending insouciant generosity when entertaining them, a generosity rewarded by a supernatural replenishment of supplies.

The Enemies' Tale inverts all, as enemies would. The igurramen, seemingly wealthy, pious and well-clad, are in fact humble and torn servants of the devil, before whom they appear in their true abasement – and it is only with his aid that they cut a fine figure in the daytime. (But something analogous is often told among the Ahansal igurramen themselves and within the main lodge. Some members of the top agurram families are credited by others with black magical powers and intercourse with the devil.) The story confirms all the values, but only redistributes their application.

In fact, it is remarkable how very economical and functional these tales are. Needless to say, the locals who retail these stories do not offer such explanations of them. Yet under a superficial appearance of logical inconsequentiality, and even extravagance, there is very little in these tales which does not have close relevance to the real life of igurramen, to the problems, opportunities, fears and hopes of saint-arbitrators of illiterate tribes in dissidence on the margin of a centralised, town-and-literacy-based Muslim monarchic state.

Spiritual Lords of the Marches

The main role of the saints has already been described. They provide services for the lay tribes who revere them, and their own organisation complements that of their lay clients. This part of their role is reflected in the more recent part of their genealogy, that which starts with Sidi Said Ahansal and then 'fans out' after Sidi Lahcen u Othman.

But the part of the genealogy 'above' Sidi Said Ahansal, between him and the Prophet, seems to have no specific local role. Why had anyone bothered to invent it?

There is one other service performed by the saints: and that is to aid the inhabitants of the region as a whole in their Islamic self-identification. This is a subtle and elusive matter, but very important. Not to mention it would be to leave out something essential. On the other hand, it is very difficult to document or substantiate this properly. We are here in the realms either of psychology, or of social relationships which are very diffuse indeed.

The earlier services of the saints could be substantiated in a comparatively specific way, and their 'functions' indicated by describing the consequences that would follow the non-fulfilment of those services. This matter, however, can only be made concrete by appealing either to a kind of intellectual atmosphere which the individual Berber would not know how to verbalise, or to rather general consequences.

Morocco, like other Muslim countries, is, or was, *enthusiastically* Muslim. Being 'Muslim' and being 'good' are very intimately linked. One is *for* Islam just as one is against sin. Partly, the adherence to Islam is formal: substantive moral allegiances will be conceived as Islamic terms whatever they happen to be. One concrete consequence of inadequate Islamic identification would of course be territorial dispossession. In this sense, one can document the 'need' for identification in hard, concrete terms: non-Muslims could not own land, and a tribe which could not make manifest its Muslim status would provide a splendid excuse for its neighbours to combine and take its land. The case is hypothetical, for the very idea of a non-Muslim tribe seems far-fetched in Morocco: nevertheless, or all the more, one can be sure that this would be a consequence of a failure of Islamic identification. (After all, present possession of land is in part justified by attributing a non-Muslim status to the proto-population.)

To put the matter in another way: it would have been an unthinkable scandal for a major region of Morocco not to be Muslim. Islam is a religion of the Book. Berbers, on the other hand, are illiterate. Islam in Morocco has its acknowledged centre in urban centres of learning, notably in Fez. But the citizens of Fez despise and disapprove of the barbarian illiterate brutal mountain tribes. Tribesmen are not unaware of this. Again, official and good Islam is rather puritanical: it disapproves of feminine freedom, and of dancing. But Berber morals in these matters are not above reproach. Berbers, again, are aware of their own deficiencies in these respects. They are aware of them and keen on Islamic identification – and nevertheless very attached to their own very enjoyable moral defects. Like another, earlier and famous North African, St Augustine, they may wish to be pure – but not yet.

Some of the (technical) needs of participating in a Muslim civilisation by illiterate mountain tribes are made up by the foquaha. But as indicated, the fquih's political position is weak. His appointment is annual and often terminated. Foquaha have no local clan alignment and they do not, like priests in other societies, have any organisation whatever behind them. They are that rare thing among Berbers, a professional. (The few other professionals, blacksmiths or cobblers, are drawn from people who are outsiders by pigmentation or by religion, haratin or Jews.) They are professionals in a society organised in terms of kinship and without bureaucracy: as individuals, they have no kin support, and there is no bureaucracy to sustain them either. At the mercy of their parishioners, politically isolated and weak, the foquaha do not have a great deal of prestige or power.

Hence it is in revering the saints, believed to be the descendants of the Prophet, that the Berber manifests his identification with Islam. He is aware somehow of the fact that his own law and custom are not quite orthodox. (His is a self-ironising culture.) He can, however, reassure himself by revering the saint, and by accepting his verdict in disputes (which in fact will be based on the same principles as his own custom) and believing that in so doing he is submitting to Koranic doctrine. Even without using the saint as arbitrator or adjudicator, he will give him donations and obtain his approval and blessing. After all, the region as a whole was in dissidence against a central dynasty, which was also identified with Islam and believed to be descended from the Prophet. It was re-assuring to have one's own, local Sherifs. Through venerating them one could defy the central power, and yet show as much respect for descendants of the Prophet as anyone. One had one's own local supply.

The legends which are locally believed about the origin of the saintly dynasty illustrate both aspects of the saintly role. They describe the founder Sidi Said as a kind of missionary endowed with magical powers and trained by a recognised and famous saint in the plain, who had come to found his own Zawiya in the mountains, and who was endowed with special holiness. They also describe him as the author of the local territorial intertribal settlement. If one may lapse into speculative history, one is tempted to say (a) there must have been Muslim missionaries responsible for the Islamisation of the remote areas, and (b) that pre-Muslim Berber tribes must have had special lineages performing services similar to those carried out by the saints under Islam. Indeed, the existence of an unambiguously non-Arab word, *agurram*, suggests this. The two things have fused: and the present role of the saints seems to be some kind of testimony to its own pre-Islamic existence.

Thus we have two possible theories of the origin of the saints: they may have started as missionaries, who subsequently acquired all the local characteristics and a local role, or alternatively, they may have started as non-Islamic holy lineages who assumed a Muslim garb with the coming of Islam. The legends assert the former, but contain ample suggestions of the latter.

There is, of course, in the total absence of real records, no way of deciding which of these theories is historically true. In a sociological sense, both are true. One may look at the saints as necessary 'artificial foreigners': many societies, consisting of balanced and mutually jealous parts, need foreigners either to rule them or to arbitrate between them (after all, most dynasties are of foreign origin). But if foreigners are lacking, they must needs be invented. The culture of the saints is as Berber as that of all the surrounding tribes: and presumably they are as much or as little Berber in a 'genetic' sense as anyone is. But, by being ascribed an outside origin, they are the region's artificial foreigners. Its isolation, poverty, the physical and human ferocity might have made it difficult to persuade real foreigners to come there, and, if they had come, they might have proved unsatisfactory.[1] Better to make one's own foreigners than to import real ones. Equally, however, one may look at the saints as missionaries who have betrayed their trust, albeit unwittingly. No Berber tribe has either the desire or the ability to opt out of Islam: nor, on the other hand, has it either the ability or the desire to behave like the bourgeoisie of Fez, the recognised paradigm in Morocco of Islamic behaviour. The Berber does not even wish to give up his music and dancing and other practices which are held to be heterodox. Under the circumstances, could anything be better than to receive and recognise permanently installed missionaries, who will preach and practise what is locally desired and understood, but at the very same time provide one with a means of identification with Islam? Who is there to know any better? The fquih? His own learning is only rudimentary and he is unlikely to know much better. And if he does, he will know better than to criticise the local powers that be. (The whole situation is slightly different as one gets nearer the plain. It is not that the foquaha are any more powerful: but awareness of the standards and prejudices of the plain do impose some pressure on the saints. There ancestry is not enough: dancing must also be given up.

Historically, we shall never know whether Sidi Said was a missionary who adapted his teaching to local needs, or whether he was a member of a local lineage who reinterpreted its position in Islamic terms, if indeed he ever lived at all. In as far as there are many saints in the Atlas, the historical truth may vary from case to case. But in a sense both theories are true: the activities of the saints can only be understood through the needs of the local social

---

[1] At least one local legend, concerning the Ait Abdi and their invitation of a man they supposed was a learned foreign fquih, suggests this. He mocked them by reciting local place names to them and abusing them as 'ass-head' (*ichfaun-ighiel*), pretending that these utterances were Koranic passages. In their ignorance, they did not spot this at once, though they killed him when they discovered the truth, by throwing him off the cliff which also forms their boundary. (By a final piece of trickery, he took two of them with him.) They themselves tell this tale, though its moral is their own ignorance!

structure, and the needs arising from its marginality, its dissidence from a wider culture whose authority it recognises, albeit ambivalently.

From the viewpoint of the local tribes, the saints are frontier posts they are not so much tribal saints as frontier or diacritical saints. It is common in anthropology to try and see in the sacred an expression of the social group: the saints 'express', in this sense, not groups but the boundaries of groups. They are also spiritual Lords of the Marches in quite another sense: from the viewpoint of Muslim culture in general. But the personality-centred and hierarchical form of religion they represent could not grow into some universal church. This kind of reformation-in-reverse, so to speak, was doomed to remain fragmentary. They were spiritual tribes, rather than a spiritual state.

The secular and transient Lords of the Marches of southern Morocco proper[1] were men who stood somewhere between pacifying a mountain region for the central government, and protecting its inhabitants from it. In the central High Atlas – thanks mainly to the efficacy of the saintly and chieftaincy-rotating system – no such secular Lords emerged: but the old-established spiritual ones, the igurramen of Ahansal, similarly played, in the main unwittingly, a kind of double-faced role – but on a spiritual plane. The separation of powers in which the pacific and judical-appellate authority of the saints complemented that of the elective, feud-involved secular chiefs, saved the region from political tyranny. Like the legend of Azurki, which invokes the Prophet to perpetuate the worship of a local mountain, the saints confer an appearance of Islam for local practices and cults, or, to put it the other way around, express and facilitate reverence for Islam by giving it a local and personal anchorage, a concreteness, and a role.

[1]Cf. Robert Montagne, *Les Berbères et le Makhzen au Sud du Maroc*, 1930.

NOTES ON METHOD

The field work on which this study is based was carried out during the following periods:

1. Summer vacation, 1954
2. Easter till summer vacation inclusive, 1955
3. Summer vacation, 1956
4. Christmas vacation, 1957–8
5. Summer vacation, 1959
6. Easter vacation, 1961

I also visited the central High Atlas during Christmas vacations 1953–4 and 1967–8.

In the study, the present tense refers to the period 1954–61, though of course more precise indications are given where necessary. Census data were collected on the first three field trips.

No special or paid informants were employed. During periods (1) and (2), my wife and I occupied a house in Zawiya Ahansal and in effect constituted one of its households. During period (3), the new Moroccan administration provided me with a house, of the type normally used by government soldiers, at the administrative outpost, which I used as a base; but I continued to spend most of my time at Zawiya Ahansal. During the periods (4), (5) and (6), I did not set up a base at any point, but travelled extensively throughout the area.

Thus my knowledge of the main lodge is based on prolonged residence and frequent and prolonged visits subsequently. Amzrai, Taria and Tighanimin are all within two hour's walking distance of the main lodge: I know them both from frequent visits and from staying in them. I also stayed repeatedly in the following settlements: Temga, Bernat, Troilest. I stayed once each at Asker, Sidi Aziz, Tidrit, Sidi Said Ahansal of Usikis, the settlement among the Ait Habibi near Tagzirt, Ait Mhand u Yussif, and Akka n'Ahansal. I visited more than once, without staying, Aganan and Sidi Ali u

303

Hussein. I visited once, without staying, Tassamert, Tamderrut, Igli, u'Tarra and Tabarocht. The description of saintly settlements is thus based on direct observation and not on reports, though the thoroughness of the observation varies from settlement to settlement.

NOTE ON TRANSLITERATION

The principles observed in transcribing local names and words are
(1) that the reader who wishes to do so should be able to identify
the objects of those names or words, be they places, groups,
people, or institutions, and (2) that the reader should get some
impression of the actual sound of those names and words.

It is not always possible to satisfy both these principles at once,
and I have given the first principle priority, partly because I am
ill-equipped to satisfy the second, possessing a bad ear and no
linguistic training. The reasons why it is impossible to satisfy both
principles at once, or to attain consistency, are the following: even
in independent Morocco, the French language has an official
standing. Moroccans normally transliterate local names in the
French manner and continue to use the resulting spelling, whichever European language they may be using. To disregard this
completely might make some names unrecognisable. For instance:
the plateau on which the Ait Abdi are located could be spelt Kusr,
and the Victorians, I imagine, would have spelt it Cooser. But
the mapmakers were French, and anyone who looks for it on the
map will have to look for *Koucer*.

Thus I respect ordinary French transliterations, which have, as
it were, become the official names of people and places, but only
within reason. I use the customary English *zawiya* rather than the
French *zaouia*, for anyone who looks for Zawiya Ahansal on the
map will easily recognise Zaouia Ahansal as the equivalent. Or
again, I write the title and name Mulay rather than Moulay, for the
same reason. In particular, I write the patronymic connective *u*, as
in Moha u Said (Moha son of Said) rather than *ou*. The French
style of using 'ou' for the sounds which can be rendered as 'u' or
'w' in English leads to particularly bad mispronunciations on the
part of English-speaking readers. During the Algerian crisis, BBC
announcers referred to the Algiers district of Bab el Oued as Bab el
Oo-add, which would not have happened had it been spelt Bab
el Wad.

There is also the relationship to previous literature to be considered. When referring to holiness, I write *baraka,* so as to tie up the discussion with previous sociological writings on the topic, notwithstanding the fact that Berbers assimilate the Arabic particle to this loan word and speak of *lbaraka.* (At the same time, they use the term *baraka,* without the particle, in the significantly related sense of *enough.*)

It is not only French which has a privileged position in the transcription of Moroccan Berber words. In the eyes of both Muslims and many Orientalists, Arabic has a privileged position. But the historical accident, so to speak, of a shared life and religion, implies nothing, one way or the other, about the phonetic affinity of Berber sounds and Arabic letters, and I have not attempted to use this method.

With respect to words heard locally and not occurring significantly in previous records, I have preferred to rely on my untrained and insensitive ear, rather than to allow myself to be persuaded retrospectively that I *must* have heard something other than what I remember having heard or recorded in my notes. Thus, for instance, there is a local name which, with the respectful form of address which accompanies it, I write as 'Sidi Moa'. Some linguistically trained scholars assure me that 'Moa' is a phonetic impossibility. I am partly re-assured by the fact that some French administrators also, and of course independently, transcribed the name in the same way, though others write it 'Sidi Moh'. Anyway, phonetically impossible or not, Sidi Moa is what I hear.

I take responsibility for the social and semantic information contained in this study. In view of my incompetence in this field, the *phonetic* information has in any case been reduced to the minimum compatible with leaving places, institutions, etc., identifiable, both in the real world and in other writings on the subject. But anyone who wished to use this residual phonetic information for serious scholarly purposes would, I fear, be misguided.

BIBLIOGRAPHY

Bibliography (of the central High Atlas and adjoining areas, of the Ihansalen and of the religious order derived from them).

Adam, André, *La Maison et le Village dans quelques Tribus de l'Anti-Atlas,* Paris, 1951

André, General P.J., *Confréries Religieuses Musulmanes,* Alger, 1956, esp. pp. 232–5

Alpinisme (Revue du Groupe de Haute Montagne), Christmas 1953, no. 106

R.Aspinion, *Contribution á l'Etude du Droit Coutumier Berbère Marocain,* 2nd ed., A.Moynier, Casablanca & Fes, 1946

Berque, Jacques, *Structures Sociales du Haut-Atlas,* PUF, Paris, 1955, pp. 66 and 312 et seq.

Bousquet, G.-H., Le droit coutumier des Ait Haddidou des Assif Melloul et Isselaten, *Annales de l'Institut d'Etudes Orientales,* Tome XIV, Alger, 1956
Les Berbères, PUF, Paris, 1957

G.Couvreur, 'La vie pastorale dans le Haut Atlas Central', *Revue de Geographie du Maroc,* no. 13, 1968, pp. 3–54

Depont, O. and Coppolani, X., *Les Confréries Religieuses Musulmanes,* Alger, 1897, chapter X

Drague, Georges, *Esquisse d'Histoire Religieuse du Maroc,* J. Peyronnet & Cie., Paris, 1951(?), notably Part II, chapter III

Dresch, Jean, 'Migrations pastorales dans le Haut Atlas calcaire', Institut de Geographie, IV: *Melanges geographiques offerts a Ph. Arbos,* Paris, 1953
'Dans le Grand Atlas calcaire. Notes de géographie physique et humaine', *Bulletin de l'Association de Geographes français,* Mars–Avril 1949, p. 56

Euloge, René, *Les Derniers Fils de l'Ombre,* (fiction), Marrakesh, 1952

Foucauld, Vicomte Ch. de, *Reconnaissance au Maroc 1883–84,* Paris, 1888, notably pp. 264 and 265

Gouvion, Marthe et Edmond, *Kitab Aayane al-Maghrib 'l-Aksa, Livre des Grands du Maroc,* Paul Guethner, Paris, 1939

Guennoun, Capitaine Said, *La Montagne Berbère,* Editions du Comité de l'Afrique française, Paris, 1929

Guillaume, General A., *Les Berbères marocains et la Pacification de l'Atlas central (1912–1933),* R.Julliard, Paris, 1946

Hart, David Montgomory, 'Segmentary Systems and the Role of "Five Fifths" in Tribal Morocco', *Revue de l'Occident musulman et de la Méditerranée,* no. 3, 1er Semestre, 1967

Jongmans, D.G. and Jager Gerlings, J.H., *Les Ait Atta, leur sédentarisation,* Institut Royal des Tropiques, Amsterdam, no. CXV, 1956

Leo Africanus, *Description of Africa,* second part, French edition, Adrien-Maisonneuve, Paris, 1956. English edition by Hakluyt Society

Lynes, Rear-Admiral Hubert, CB, CMG, L'Ornithologie du Cercle Azilal (Maroc central), *Memoires de la Société des Sciences Naturelles du Maroc,* Rabat (Janson & Sons), Paris, London, 1933

E.Masqueray, *Formation des Cités chez les Populations Sédentaires de l'Algerie.* Paris, 1886. (Notably p. 41)

G. Maxwell, *Lords of the Atlas,* London, Longmans, 1966; presents, in English, an account of the type of tyranny which the tribes of the central High Atlas avoided, thanks to the saintly system.

Michaux-Bellaire, M.E., *Conférences,* Archives Marocaines, Paris, 1927, chapter IV

Montagne, R., *La Vie sociale et la Vie politique des Berbères,* Paris, 1931

Les Berbères et la Makhzen au Sud du Maroc, Paris, 1930

Montagnes Marocaines (Journal of the Casablanca Section of the Club Alpin Français), May 1954, No. 3

Monteil, Vincent, *Les Officiers,* Editions du Seuil, 1958, pp. 121–42

Rinn, Louis, *Marabouts et Khouan,* Alger, 1884, chapter XXVI

Schnell, P., *L'Atlas Marocain,* Paris, 1898, pp. 147 and 148

Segonzac, Marquis René de, *Au Coeur de l'Atlas,* Paris, 1910

Spillman, Capitaine Georges, *Les Ait Atta et la pacification du Haut Draa,* Rabat, F.Moncho, 1936. (See also Drague, G., Spillman's pen name)

Terrasse, H., *Histoire du Maroc,* Casablanca, Editions Atlantides, 1950

Tharaud, Jerome and Jean, *Marrakesh ou les Seigneurs de l'Atlas,* Paris, 1920 (semi-fiction), esp. chapter XIII

Westermarck, E., *Ritual and Belief in Morocco,* London, 1926

Zartman, William, *Morocco : Problems of New Power,* Atherton Press, New York, 1964

Unpublished Sources

First intelligence reports made to French authorities concerning Ahansal-land seemed to have been made by an officer-interpreter named Coliac. I have never seen these reports, but I believe that their content is probably the basis of the account of the Ihansalen found in Michaux-Bellaire, who is cited in the bibliography.

During the period of French administration, it was customary for each district officer to compile a 'fiche de tribu' concerning the tribes of his district. These varied greatly in quality. The one compiled for the Ihansalen and surrounding tribes was quite out-standingly good, thanks largely to the pains taken by its author, Captain J.-A. Ithier. I do not possess a copy of it, but I was at one time in a position to read it. I have used no facts in it without independent checking, and I am not in agreement with all its interpretations. (As the work is not published, I refrain from discussing these issues.) But it is a most remarkable piece of work, invaluable for any further researcher. It is to be hoped that copies in possession of Moroccan and French authorities will remain preserved for scholarship. I believe that Captain Ithier now teaches geography at the University of Rennes.

Since Moroccan independence, various college and school exploration societies have sent expeditions to the Atlas. Two such expeditions went to Ahansal-land, one from Wye College, Ashford, Kent, and one from Bedales School, Steep, Hampshire. Their reports are presumably available at the colleges or schools concerned.

To my knowledge, there are no indigenous family records, *kanun* (codes), etc., in the central High Atlas, other than occasional land deeds. For the modern period, important documentation may be in the possession of Moroccan and French administrations and of Moroccan political parties.

INDEX

The name of a person or of a place can automatically be made into the name of a social group by prefixing Ait: for instance, the Ait Sidi Hussein are the progeny, in the male line, of Sidi Hussein, and the Ait Talmest are the inhabitants of Talmest. Names are generally listed in the index in one of the two possible forms, with or without the Ait, but not both.

311